THE GHOST AND THE DARKNESS

BOOK 2 OF THE FALLOCAUST SERIES

VOLUME 2

QUIL CARTER

© 2014 Quil Carter
All Rights Reserved

All Rights Reserved. No part of this publication may be reproduced, stored in a retrieval system, or transmitted, in any form or in any means – by electronic, mechanical, photocopying, recording or otherwise – without prior written permission.

www.quilcarter.com

Cover by Quil Carter

First Edition

1533071144
978-1533071149

The second half of this book is dedicated to Jon and Ashkan. You both have been there from the very beginning, since before Fallocaust was even an idea in my head. Not once did you two ever waver in your love and support and it is because of your constant encouragement that I am seeing my dream come true.

Thank you.

CHAPTER 35

Reno

I LEANED MY BACK AGAINST THE DOOR, MY FACE buried in my hands. I wiped my hands down and looked at the large picture windows, seeing nothing but grey rocky mountains in front of us.

Another secret base of Elish Dekker. Though as he carried my dead best friend through the grey carpet halls and into the freezer down the stairs, he reminded me that this was the same one he'd originally brought us to.

I hadn't remembered, blood loss did that to a man. But I was glad for this small oasis in the grey desert. Where my friend could heal, recover, and rise up from the ashes.

My mind had been in a thousand different places over the last several days, but in the end they all focused to one point in time, one single event that I'd had the horror of witnessing.

When I had barged into that storage room and saw Nero raping Reaver.

I had frozen, my feet glued to the spot. All I could do was stare, my mouth open in a soundless scream. Caligula and Nico had charged ahead, shot Nero, and tried to retrieve Reaver…

All I could do was stare.

My best friend. I held a respect for him that I held for no one else. I loved that man, more than any person in the entire world, and seeing him like that, with his eyes black, staring pits as he snarled at Clig and Nico. He had a madness in him I knew would not disappear with his death.

And his hand. Fuck, his hand.

Reaver had chewed his own hand off to escape Nero. And it wasn't only that… the cigarette and cigar burns, the blood draining out of his backside, so many bruises, cuts, and welts.

How many times had Nero killed him? How many times had he raped him?

I glanced up as a mug edged into my vision.

Elish was looking down at me. Tall, crystally, god-like Elish. I took the tea with thanks and swirled it around in the cup.

"Do they make opiate tea?" I asked him as I smelled it. It smelled like chocolate cinnamon.

Elish took a sip and shook his head. "No, this is chai. It is soothing and will relax you."

Ice Man turned from me and took out the remote he was always glancing at. He looked down at it, then sighed and placed it back into his robes.

"Looks like you need to relax too," I commented. I got up and sat on one of the couches. Elish sat down on an opposite couch. It was just the two of us here. Caligula and Nico had left a couple days ago so the Falconer wouldn't be missed. They were returning as soon as Reaver woke up.

"I am fine," Elish said back.

They would be returning as soon as possible because… because, well… we didn't know where Tinky and Biter were.

As soon as we'd gotten Reaver into the freezer, the two of us immediately flew to Kreig. After flying above the city and the surrounding towns we still hadn't found anything. Until Clig left, Elish and I had been taking the plane over the towns but… we hadn't picked up Jade's tracker.

It was kind of sad… and in a way it scared me a bit. When we failed to get a signal Elish was adamant that the batteries must be dying in his tracker. He flew all the way back to the greyrift apartment for new batteries then we returned. When we still didn't get a signal, he kept telling me that surely there must be something wrong with the device. He commented that it had gotten wet at one point, and then told me that perhaps it had shorted out while he was using his lightning touch. So we went to the outskirt towns that surrounded Kreig and looked on foot, but there was still nothing.

It really was heartbreaking to watch. Elish kept bringing the device out of his pocket to check it, again and again.

But no signal, the tracker was silent. All of its little icons showing N/A and NULL. No beeps, no chimes… nothing. Jade was out of range, and that thing had like a twenty mile range on it.

The day Clig and Nico left, I think Elish realized… the boys were gone.

They had left the outskirts of Kreig where Elish had told them to stay.

We didn't know where they were. Killian, Perish, and Jade were out in the greywastes, alone and without Reaver to protect them. And we couldn't get an idea as to where they were until Reaver woke up.

Elish took another sip of his tea, before he rose again and went to the window. He stared at it for exactly nine seconds before he walked over to the bedroom we had moved Reaver into.

Poor guy, he'd rip my face off with his bare hands if I brought attention to it... but I knew Elish was scared right now. He hated to admit it, but that dude really loved his little husband.

I turned on the television and started sorting through his DVDs to see if I could find something good. I looked over my shoulder when I heard his soft footsteps.

"Any change?" I asked.

"He's still breathing comfortably, it will be any time now," Elish replied. "I wish I would have thought to ask Reaver before I dispatched him from his pain. It's unlike Jade to stray far..."

I shrugged. "You made Reaver his temporary master though. So if Reaver wanted to go somewhere he'd have to follow."

"Yes, I was hoping Reaver would be intelligent enough to stay put... he's unfamiliar with the area. Lycos says he never ventured farther than Gosselin, yes?"

I nodded.

Elish carried on, "So I see no reason why they would travel far. That tracker has twenty miles of range, which means–"

Elish's lower lip tightened, I finished his sentence for him.

" –it means they're not only far away. They're *really* far away."

"For all I know they've been on the road for over a month. For all I know Kessler already has them, knows everything, and Silas is stalking my heels at this very moment."

This made me do a double take. I stared at him as he, very tensely, brought his tea back to his lips.

"You... you really fucking think that?"

"No, I have no reason to, but what Silas pulled in Aras, disguising himself as a greywaster, that alone should shed light on just who we are dealing with," Elish said. He made himself sit back down and I popped in a DVD I deemed adequate. "He's a mastermind."

"Well, so are you at least, and not as batshit crazy." I started dishing out my little drug supply, doing a hell of a lot more of them than I used to, but I justified it. After I laid out my lines of Dilaudids and snorted them up my nose I offered the sniffer to Elish.

He stared at me like I had just offered him a stick with a dead rat on the end and shook his head. "I do not indulge myself with such things."

I rolled my eyes. "You can be all hardass all you want but it's just the two of us. I don't give a shit, and you know I don't give a shit. That's why we get along." I stood up. "I need to take a piss anyway. If you wanna do them while I'm gone I won't say anything when I come back."

After I took a leak I ducked into Reaver's bedroom to check on him.

My best friend was laying where we had put him. On a comfortable bed with his head resting on a pillow. I had been able to wipe the blood off of his face but the rest of his body was rather bloodstained.

It was fascinating to see that his hand had knitted back to his arm. With just some twine and a hook they'd been able to put it back on, and with that, it just… fused back with his body. Apparently you had about half a day to stitch their limbs or whatever back to their bodies before they started to rot.

Because he wasn't awake to rip my hand off, I stroked his warm cheek and just appreciated that I was back with him. That at least when he woke up he could be with someone he tolerated.

I belonged with Reaver… that was my place in the world, near him or helping him…

It had been three days since I had left Garrett. It had also been three days since Garrett had called Elish hysterical, and three days since Elish had told him, for me, that I was going to be gone until Reaver recovered.

I had left the room when he took the call and when I had returned Elish had said nothing to me. That was the easiest way to go about it. I knew Ice Man understood and if Garrett didn't that was his problem. My now ex-fiancé had held me in his apartment against his will when Chally had told me where Reaver was. He had tried to prevent me from rescuing my friend and… Reaver came first.

Before anyone.

Feeling brave, I leaned down and kissed my friend on the cheek and ventured back into the living room area.

Just as I thought… the lines of yellow powder that I had left behind were all gone.

I passed out on the couch; I always had a knack for being able to sleep anywhere I wanted. When I woke up the lights had been turned off and the television too. Elish was also nowhere to be found so I assumed he went downstairs where his own suite was. It looked like it was early morning; even though the blinds were drawn on the big windows I could see the first hints of daylight through the cracks.

I got up and started towards my bedroom when I froze.

Reaver's bathroom light was on.

A wave of anxiety washed through me which I banished immediately. I felt angry at myself for being wary, I walked into Reaver's bedroom and looked around before slowly walking to the bathroom. I could hear water lapping; I think he was taking a bath. Couldn't blame him... I remember when Bridley –

I gasped when I saw him.

Reaver was kneeling in almost a foot of red bath water covered in pink bubbles. He was savagely scrubbing his skin with what looked like steel wool. Almost his whole body was bright pink with angry red scratches all over it. His inner thigh and his backside were the worst, with puffy, crimson lesions that dripped blood into the rosy water below.

"Fuck! Reaver, NO!" I screamed. I ran over and ripped the steel wool from Reaver's hand. Though as quickly as I did, he snatched it back, and started roughly digging the scrubber into his skin. His chest rapidly rising and falling as his breath bordered on hyperventilating.

I took it from him again and when he tried to snatch it back I held it above him.

"GIVE IT TO ME!" Reaver suddenly screamed. His tone was manic, uncontrolled... not the tone I was used to. It immediately made tears sting my eyes. He was deep into it... I had been too... there wasn't a word for the crazy state you fell into after getting tortured and raped but I knew that's where he was.

"You're okay... it's okay... I know..." I took in a deep breath and held out my hands to try and calm him down. I thought back to the painful time after Bridley raped me and remembered my almost obsessive need to clean every inch of my body. "I know you want to get clean and we have a lot of soap. But, baby, you can't scrape your skin off..."

Reaver turned away from me; he grabbed a normal bathtub scrubber beside him and started desperately washing his already angry, swollen skin. My heart shattered as I saw the pain in my best friend's eyes. They were wide and depthless, fixed in an almost permanent state of shock.

Then he stopped and I saw the scrubber fall from his fingers into the pink water below him. He stared down at his hands, scratches and lesions all up his arms, down his stomach… in some places so concentrated his skin looked like red sandpaper.

I looked down and groaned. Through the water I could see patches where he had scrubbed his groin raw, chunks of his pubic hair gone and replaced by red.

Then I made the mistake of looking behind him. His backside was even worse and I didn't even want to see what state it was inside. I… fuck, I should have at least washed the cum out of him but I… I didn't want to violate him any more than he had been.

"Baby…" I whispered after he'd been quiet and still for more than a minute, staring in shell-shock at the faucet of the tub. I had never seen his black eyes more wide, more staring.

Then he turned to me and I froze like a block of ice. His eyes moved back and forth as if analyzing my face.

"Reno," he whispered, like he had just realized who I was.

I nodded, my eyes burning as he made eye contact with me. "Yeah, I'm here, baby."

He stared at me. "We need to have sex, right now. I need you to fuck me. Now. Now…"

I stared back at him; my mind blanking over his strange words and the odd… desperate tone he said them.

Reaver got up, the bloody water dripping off of his naked body. He stepped out and grabbed a towel. "Now, Reno. Now. You have to do it, now."

My mouth opened, like my brain was commanding me to respond but all I did was stutter. "W-wha… no, baby…"

Reaver whirled around, his eyes desperate. "I need you to do this for me, Reno."

"Baby… no. I can't. That's… that's – that can't happen," I whispered to him. I put my hands on his shoulders and led him out of the bathroom. He let me, which surprised the fuck out of me, and I directed him towards his bed.

Then Elish was there. He looked at Reaver with his usual cold and emotionless gaze, taking in my friend's bloodied, raw body before his purple eyes found Reaver's face. "Well, you're in a much different state than the last time you resurrected in here. Perhaps–"

Reaver clutched his towel to him and walked up to Elish. To my shock, he grabbed the forearm of Elish's robe and started trying to pull him to the door.

"Where… are we going?" Elish blinked.

"We're having sex."

This was serious, dear god, I knew this was serious. I knew my friend was in mental agony, and I knew he had been through hell…

But the perplexed and confounded look Elish gave Reaver almost made me burst out laughing. I hated myself for feeling that way, I really did but… it was what it was.

Ice Man put his hand on Reaver's and gave it an awkward pat. "That will not be necessary. It looks like you have already cleaned yourself… to excess. Now you can sit down with some food. I have questions you must answer."

Reaver looked down at Elish's hand, then back up at him, then over to me.

And he started laughing… hard.

Tears sprung to my eyes. I made a move to comfort him but Elish raised a hand to stop me. "Reno… leave the room."

"What?!" I exclaimed. I stared at Elish in shock. "I'm not leaving… what are you… why?"

Reaver was still laughing, clutching the towel that was wrapped around him even tighter. His shoulders hunched and his head turned down.

"Do not go near him. Do not make eye contact with him. Slowly leave this room and get the leather briefcase resting beside the coffee table." Elish's voice was steady and calm, but it held a stern tone to it that rubbed me the wrong way.

"I've known him since he was two, he's not–" Just as I was outstretching my hand to pull Reaver away from Elish, my best friend snapped.

Elish grabbed Reaver as my friend lunged at me, his arms outstretched like he was going to gouge out my eyes. Reaver thrashed and tried to claw his way out of Elish's arms, his legs rising off of the ground as he kicked and screamed.

"Briefcase, NOW!" Elish snapped at me. Even with his chimera strength he was having trouble holding Reaver. I immediately bolted and ran into the living room, hearing them scuffle as I grabbed the suitcase.

When I returned Reaver's arms were being held behind his back, crushed against Elish's chest as he held him in a death grip. Even though Reaver wasn't thrashing anymore, he was breathing heavily, his dark, glassy eyes wide and staring. I could hear a growl in his throat, and the corner of his eye twitching.

"What do you want me to get?" I asked anxiously. I cracked the briefcase open and started rooting through things.

"Amber liquid… hurry, he's about to go into his psychosis again," Elish commanded. He tightened his hold on Reaver and, sure enough, Reaver suddenly let out a bellowing yell before kicking his legs and desperately clawing Elish's arms.

I got the needle full of amber liquid. "Does it need a vein?"

"No, put it into his neck."

I inhaled a deep breath and positioned the needle. Elish grabbed Reaver's head and yanked it back. I sunk the syringe into his neck and pushed down on the plunger.

"Shhh…" I shushed him. As Elish held Reaver's teeth far away from my hand I stroked his neck. I knew I was probably stressing him out even more, but I think I needed it more than he didn't.

In a matter of seconds, Reaver's muscles started to relax. Elish loosened his grip until Reaver's breath started to slow to a normal level.

"Are you back?" Elish asked calmly.

"Yeah," Reaver said breathlessly. I could see faint hints of Reaver start to come back to his face.

Then he made eye contact with me and nodded his head. "I'm… I'm okay, I think."

Elish let him go and Reaver, now naked with his towel forgotten on the floor, sat down on the bed. He stared at his arms before once again looking at me. "Where am I?"

"The greyrifts apartment again. You're safe and have been here for several days. Nero will not find you here," Elish said. I noticed Reaver tensing when Nero's name was mentioned.

My friend pushed past the reminder though and rose. "I want drugs… heroin. I'll be okay, I just need something."

Ice Man seemed to believe him. He picked up his briefcase and handed him a small white baggy. "Caligula was able to retrieve your pants, they are on the dresser. Your shirt was destroyed in the gunfire but Jade has many shirts you can wear. Do the drugs you need and join me in the living room as soon as possible."

"I need to talk to Killian," Reaver replied as he started to put on his cargo pants.

An awkward silence crept into the room. Or at least it was awkward for me. I watched Elish and saw his jaw lock.

"Come… join me in the living room." Elish walked past Reaver and left the bedroom without another word.

Reaver belted up his pants and ran a hand along his skin; though he didn't comment on the swollen, red chafe marks that I knew must be hurting him. Then, without a word, he dumped a pile of the china white onto the top of his fist and snorted all of it in two inhales.

After dressing himself, Reaver joined us in the living room. He looked around and I knew he was looking for Killian, wondering why his boyfriend wasn't with us.

I knew my friend's mind was shot. I knew the gears weren't working properly because he was still looking around for Killian when Elish handed him a cup of tea. The Reaver who had his mind entirely there would have clued in just from the way we were acting.

My poor Reaver. I didn't want to know the details of what went on when he was with Nero, but I knew it had done damage to him. He was just… he felt like an open wound, for lack of a better word, a wire frayed at the edges, still holding an electric current. Reaver had never gone through anything like that. He had never been dominated in that way.

I didn't know how someone like him, so full of pride and control, would handle it.

With me and Killian… we had both been raped but we were the more… submissive types. We were Reaver's best friends, so we were used to being the sidekicks, the subs, or well… the bottoms.

But him…

He was made out of marble, and Killian and I more like rubber. He was stronger than us but we could bend and adjust… Reaver was strong but when he cracked…

… he cracked.

Fuck. My eyes closed and I took a deep breath. Anyone but him. Not Reaver.

Reaver isn't strong enough to handle this; he's strong in so many ways but he isn't strong when it comes to him being controlled.

Because no one dominates him. How could he build up a defence against something he never fathomed would happen? Someone taking that from him, taking that control, it goes against the very fabric of his nature. I was almost surprised the world hadn't imploded all around us. That another Fallocaust hadn't started just from the vile and heinous act that had happened in that mansion. I knew Reaver's personality, and I knew the opened wound he was now, was soon going to start to rot.

I watched Reaver, staring into the tea mug, and for the first time in our friendship...

I feared for him.

Elish seemed to understand him and I suppose someone like Elish had been around chimeras similar to Reaver. He must have dealt with this thing before with his brothers.

I watched Elish take a sip of his tea before lightly clasping the mug with both hands.

"Reaver... where were you four heading? Why did you leave the outskirts of Krieg?" Elish asked calmly.

Then... it dawned on him. Reaver's eyes widened and he looked at Elish. "You... you don't have Killian?"

Elish slowly shook his head. "I do not know where you were heading, or why. We rescued you from the mansion several miles from Cardinalhall. That is all we know. No one else was with you."

Reaver stared at him for a moment. "We were... Jade was able to see something in Perish, unlocked something inside of his brain, I think. Falkland was its name. The Legion were swarming and we had to get out of there. A slaver offered us merc work to help them pass the mountains. We took it thinking it would make us blend in. They should be... they're near the town by now. I think–"

Elish held up a hand, but I saw a hardness come to his eyes. "Jade was able to infiltrate Perish's brain? Falkland is where the O.L.S is located?"

Reaver nodded. "We left after you told Jade that Jack was coming."

Reaver paused and tried to think. "In an abandoned town we met a slaver named Hopper. He said he was heading to a town close to Falkland, or Falkvalley as it is called now. I saw it as a good opportunity to not only get far away from the Legion, but blend in with the greywastes."

"Falkvalley?" Elish repeated. "I know that town. The slavers were heading to Melchai I am to assume?"

Reaver nodded. "He was bringing slaves there to sell."

Elish took this in, his brain seeming to mull the information over. I assumed to figure out how safe his pet and husband was at that moment.

"How long after you fled from Jack and the Legion did you join up with this slaver?"

"Pretty much right away. A day after, maybe?" Reaver replied.

"So, the boys have been... on this road and with those slaves for over a month and a half?"

Reaver nodded again. "Hopper seemed alright though. The boys will hate us for quite a while but... they're fine. When are we going to get them?"

"As soon as I can get my plane." Elish rose and reached into his pocket. He brought the remote phone up to his ear and left the room.

When he was gone I reached over and poked my friend in the face. "You okay, baby?"

Reaver batted my hand away and nodded, still staring into his tea mug. "Yeah, why wouldn't I be? I'm... good."

Why wouldn't you be? Well, I guess this was normal for him, a normal reaction anyway. He would never let me under his armour now, he wouldn't let anyone. Now he was going to steel himself up, erect his barriers and bandage the wound so it could rot out of sight.

I had done the same thing... and it hadn't worked out too well for me.

My tooth found my lower lip but I pushed down the tendrils of fear that were weaving their way up my throat. I wonder if he knew that I had seen first-hand what Nero had been doing to him.

But he knew I knew... though perhaps that was as far as it would ever go.

"I love you, man," I said quietly. "I missed you."

Reaver's face didn't change; he just stared into his tea mug. I wonder if he was looking at his own reflection. I know I couldn't stand to look at myself in the mirror for months.

My friend nodded and proceeded to do more drugs. Nothing else was said until Elish came into the room. After a quick mention that the plane was on its way, we all got ready to leave.

"Are... are you sure you're okay, buddy? You kinda..." I began as we walked down the hall towards the plane.

Reaver tensed a bit, a duffle bag full of food and supplies now on his back. "I'm fine," he replied in a dangerous tone. I decided to leave it at that, though I knew he wasn't. How could he be?

But I let it go, because I knew as sure as I knew the breath in my lungs that pushing him would do no good. I guess we all had our own bad memories we wanted to shove down. My memories of the Crimstones and Trig had been barred off and welded shut.

I smiled at Nico and Caligula as they jumped off the plane, but it quickly faded when I saw Caligula's eyes shoot to Reaver.

Immediately a dark mood pressed down on us. Reaver's eyes, fixed on Caligula, watched the soldier chimera shift his gaze away and start loading in our supplies.

"I killed Tim."

Those words brought such an ice to the hanger that it seemed time stood still. I stared at Reaver in shock, wondering if I was going to have to unhinge his jaw from Caligula's neck or vice versa.

I looked to Elish to interject, but he only watched as Caligula slowly turned around.

"Yeah, and it was me who ambushed Lycos. If you want to spend the rest of our eternal lives ripping each other to shreds over it, fine. But I would rather forget the past and move on fresh. There are more important things at stake," Caligula replied coldly. "We would make better allies than we would enemies, brother."

Reaver seemed to be taken off-guard by this; even I was a little bit. I'd assumed from what I had seen from Caligula that he was going to be a little demon shit just like the other chimeras around our age. But he seemed oddly… controlled.

My friend regained his composure pretty quickly though. His eyes found Elish's. "You trust him?"

Elish nodded.

Reaver nodded back, but I knew he didn't like it. "Alright." And that was it on the matter. "The more people to help us find the boys, the better."

We all jumped onto the plane, Nico disappeared into the cockpit and I sat down on one of the metal benches. Soon we were flying over the greywastes, the streaks of greys and blacks passing quickly below us.

I glanced over and saw Reaver and Elish both standing side by side, looking out the cargo window of the plane.

Elish was holding the remote in his hand, glancing down at it every few minutes. His lips were a thin line and his face firm and without emotion. But what was seen on the outside of Ice Man and what was going on underneath the surface were two different things. My stone-faced, dark chimera staring out the window with him only solidified that.

They watched the greywastes below us without a word, neither of them moving from their spots. Not an emotion crossed their faces as they watched for any sign, remote control or visual... of their partners.

And my partner? I sighed, but like my friends, I tried not to show it on my face. My partner was in Skyfall... without me.

But well... Garrett had made his decision and as he was making that decision he had showed me that, deep down, he really was a chimera.

He chained me to the bed, and not in a good way, so I couldn't help rescue my best friend. I know Garrett was scared and I know, to him, maybe it was even justified. But I was a greywaster, I wasn't a cicaro, and no one would keep me from helping Reaver.

What did that mean for me and Garrett after we found the boys? I didn't know. I still loved Garrett deeply but...

Fuck, I had told him Reaver and Killian would always come first. I had told him that from the beginning. Hell, in the beginning I had only been there to get that Kreig keycard.

I had really dug myself into a hole. I loved Garrett but my home was in the greywastes with my boys. So maybe I didn't know what my future would hold.

I was still homesick...

Several hours later we were in the mountains, a single stretch of highway below us. I couldn't see much though, just small brown spots that had once been cars, and many dirt roads and small shacks miles away from the main road. No sign of the boys, but I could barely see a thing.

"Elish?" Nico called from the cockpit. "Do you want us continue with an aerial search of the highway all the way until Falkvalley, or touch down?"

Elish was quiet for a moment, both him and Reaver silent statues. "We can't fly low enough to search properly. Touch down. I want to find some sort of sign of them before we continue on this highway."

Reaver's head shot to him. "Why would you say that? Shouldn't Jade's chip be alerting you if he's near?"

Elish nodded slowly. "Yes, but I cannot rule out that it hasn't been tampered with. I will not put my faith in technology when it comes to my... pet."

Then his face tightened. "I do not know why you thought it was a wise decision to trust my cicaro with slavers. I expected more from you."

Reaver continued to stare at him. I saw a flicker of apprehension, almost bordering on shame. "Hopper was fine," he replied flatly. "They got...

along well."

Elish looked back at him, the two alpha males locked eyes. "Then, tell me, Reaver. How did Nero find you?"

I took a step back, my brow starting to sweat. I saw a mixture of emotions pass through Reaver's face before he broke his locked gaze from Elish.

"That… was my fault. I took the blocker off of the remote phone; I didn't know what it was."

Shit…

Elish's purple eyes became hard. "Indeed? So if these slavers decide to enslave my pet, your boyfriend, and our only tie to finding the knowledge we need to kill King Silas, it will be because you were stupid enough to broadcast your location to my maniac of a brother? Bravo, Reaver. I suppose it was my fault for expecting more from you." Elish's spoke slowly but swiftly, I could see Reaver's shoulders dropping with each serrated word.

I couldn't read the expression on Reaver's face, but I knew that he was in emotional agony right now. He was harder on himself than anyone, and I knew he was going to hate himself for a long time over this error.

But Elish wasn't done. True to form, he continued his verbal beat down. "If you think greywaster slavers will not think of an excuse to imprison those three, since most likely it was *you* that they feared, you're not only ignorant, you're naive as well. I should have raised you in Skyfall. Obviously it wasn't only your social skills that suffered under Lycos's parenting."

"Lay off!" I snapped, glaring at Elish. Enough was enough. Reaver didn't need this shit right now, especially since we had no proof that that was the case.

I walked up to Reaver and put a supportive hand on his shoulder. "It's okay, baby… we don't even know—"

All at once, Reaver whirled around, and like the lightning fast switch that had turned on back in the apartment, he put his hands out and lunged at me.

Elish, once again, grabbed Reaver as Reaver started to shout and yell at me, calling me every derogatory name he could think of.

Though as my feral friend thrashed and screamed at me, for the first time… I saw real fear in his eyes.

CHAPTER 36

Jade

SNOWFLAKES WERE FALLING, DANCING AROUND MY head, falling onto pale skin but they didn't melt. They stayed and more gathered, sticking together to create the thinnest of film. A separate membrane that was mostly white… but I could see the red underneath.

Icy red, cold, and freezing solid. Polka dot snowflakes on dead flesh, but not melting; no, not melting. There was no warmth coming from the skin, no blood, hot and coursing through.

I opened my mouth and took another bite, the snowflakes stinging the inside of my mouth.

My teeth pinched together and I ripped out the piece of meat. I looked around to make sure the dog wasn't going to sneak a bite of my kill, and shredded it with my pointed canines.

The dog had his own arm; my arm was mine and I wasn't sharing. I was hungry. I had woke up ravenous, thirsty, and in a haze. Now I was able to satiate at least one of those problems.

I swallowed the flesh. It was cold in my mouth, but as my body heat warmed it, I felt blood trickle down my throat. I savoured its sweet taste and leaned down for more.

When my stomach was full of fresh meat, I rose. And though the dizziness took me it had lessened since the first time I had stood up. I rubbed my gloved hands together and looked around for the dog.

The dog was jerking his head back, trying to pull a finger from the frozen arm he had been chewing on. I looked down at the arm I had been eating and picked it up.

I waved it back and forth and chuckled to myself.

It had been beautiful when I first woke up. The snowflakes falling thick around me, so mesmerizing because I was on my back staring up at the sky. I had called to someone to lie down beside me and look... look up... look up, snowflake.

My eyes travelled back down to the severed arm and I waved it again. The dog saw this as an invitation for fetch and bounded over, blood and snow covering his muzzle.

I was in front of a structure, surrounded by carnage, surrounded by mutilated bodies, missing faces and strips of skin and flesh. The snow around me had been reduced to slushy crimson pools that were only now just starting to get covered by the fresh flakes.

I walked over to the body of a man whose face had been chewed off. I had already harvested all of their warm clothes and the blankets inside. They were bundled over me and in a knapsack I had taken from their cart; a useless cart now. The bosen had been killed and now lay, uneaten, and soon to be lost in both time and snow.

Something bad had happened here, I could feel it in the colours so tangible to my mind. They swirled around this place like misplaced spirits, leaving shadows wherever they flew past. It was dark here, even with the bright mixtures of red and white this place was just black in my mind.

And what was I? My colours were silver and black, with the faintest ribbons of purple, but in those colours I had remembered my own name

My name was Jade, I knew at least that.

It was early evening when I reached the highway. An expanse of mountains around me covered in snow, now a silvery hue from the twilight darkening the sky. Though no new snow was falling, I could only see the thick clouds above me and the miles upon miles of rolling snow-capped mountains. The cold night was now clear of fresh flakes, but with the clouds how they were I held no faith that it would stay that way.

I walked along the abandoned road, my knapsack stuffed with freezing meat, blankets, gloves, and even a spare pair of army boots I had gotten from a man who had been chewed in half.

The dog panted ahead of me, his nose up in the air and puffs of steam shooting from his nostrils. I had woken to him licking my face, his breath putrid and hot. He nuzzled and nipped me until I managed a sitting position.

As I walked along the road, I put a hand on the back of my head, feeling the gash open and exposed. I had been putting snow on it, but now, now I just covered it with a wool hat. That was the extent of my medical knowledge.

I slept that night in a blue van, huddled in all the blankets I had managed to carry and with the dog beside me as extra body heat. He had growled several times during the night, and at one point bounded off into the darkness, but when I woke up in the morning he was there.

I ate a meal of arm meat, my teeth chewing around the bone now. I took off a finger to chew as I walked and carried on down the road.

Where was I going? I wasn't sure but I wanted to get off of this highway as soon as I could. I knew I was in the greywastes, even a hard blow to the head couldn't kick that fact out… but besides that it was just a barrier of static, one that filled me with distortion every time I tried to push past it.

I knew I was someone, I knew I was with friends… but it looked like they were all dead. Torn to shreds at the hands of ravers, so disfigured I couldn't tell who was a raver and who was an arian. I had seen footsteps in the snow on my way up the winding road though, boot prints and raver prints alike. But where they were going, I didn't know.

My mind told me to not go up hill, but I was close to the summit so I decided to climb to the top and then enjoy the road slowly sloping down.

Sometime late in the afternoon I took a rest. I leaned against a rusted out car and I whistled for the dog. He bounded over, happy as can be. I pet his head and started to pay a bit more attention to the jacket he had on.

It was a dirty thing and damp too, but he had supplies in it. I unzipped some zippers and rooted through it, happily finding a pack of cigarettes and a bottle of rum. Also in a far pocket covered in plastic: two lighters, some money, a bag of gummy worms, and a note.

I read the note.

This is Deek, he is a deacon crossed with a dog. If you have found him please tell him to go home or go to town. He is very smart and will know where to go. Thank You. K

Did I write that? Nah, my name is Jade, and that didn't start with K. I looked at the dog.

"Deek?"

He tilted his head to the side.

"Bring me to town." I knew enough to know we weren't anywhere near where his home used to be, but if the dog could find me a town I could get warm in…

The dog ran ahead, and to my dismay, he disappeared out of sight. I assumed he would come back once he found any signs of civilization, but for all I knew he was finding a town just for him and I was screwed.

Oh well, I could always talk to myself. I was high in the mountains now with only my boots and the chafing of my pants making–

Wow… wait…

I stumbled forward and managed to brace myself against a vehicle when a sickening wave of heat swept over me. I closed my eyes and sunk down to my knees, feeling my teeth start to press together.

My throat went dry and my pulse suddenly started to get erratic. I took in a deep inhale of frozen breath and groaned, feeling a pressure start to gather behind my eyes.

Then pain, a pain that made my body clamp down and seize on itself, a screaming, clustered ache behind my eyes that spilled me onto the snowy road.

It was bad… this was bad. I bit my lip to stifle the groan clawing up my throat, but as the rapid, pulsing pain started to explode from my head I found not just a groan but a scream rip through my lips.

The next several minutes of my life were pure agony. I spent it writhing and twisting in the snow, grabbing and clutching my face and my head to try and lessen the extreme pressure boiling inside of my head. My brain felt like a canker, swelling and expanding behind my eyes to the point where I thought I was going to die.

When it passed, I stayed laying for quite a long time, staying as still as I could for fear that the migraine would come back.

I whimpered and put my hand on my head. I rubbed it and flinched as my fingers brushed over the gash in the back of my head. My blood had dried and the gash was now fused with my wool hat. I'd never take that hat off now; I was probably going to die with it.

Eventually I carried on, my head hung low and my hopes of finding civilization starting to fade with the winter sun. Not even the dog was around to keep me company; he had taken off to go find a town… or a new owner. Whatever one came first, I guess.

That night I was a bit more comfortable, and proud at how far I had managed to walk even with my migraine attacks. I found shelter in the back of a semi and was even treated to a couple of wooden pallets which I broke up for firewood.

Slowly I stripped off my clothes and warmed them by the fire. When I had nothing on me but a blanket, I took a chunk of thigh I had been storing in the knapsack and roasted it over the flames until it was dripping grease. Enjoying my comfortable night, I sang a few songs to myself, but that was more from loneliness than just wanting to express my contentment.

Well, buddy, you know your name is Jade; you have that going for you... I knew I would remember the rest of it eventually; it seemed to be tickling the very tips of my brain. But I had gotten bashed on the head rather hard, so I understood if my brain was taking its time getting the gears running again.

I hope the asshole who bashed my head was dead. One of those faceless, limbless corpses I had harvested for meat and warm clothes.

That night I was hit with another migraine, one that once again had me clenching and hitting myself on the head to try and kick it. It was an intense, blinding pressure that seemed to be centered behind my eyes, like a rabid beast running rampant inside of my brain, bashing itself against my skull like it was a battering ram. It was such a horrendous pain I felt like gouging my own eyes out, just so I could relieve some of the pressure.

That morning the dog still hadn't returned. I gathered up my stuff, all alone, and carried on down the snowy, lonesome road; only my whistling breaking up the sedated silence around me.

I coughed and felt a scratching behind my throat. I rubbed my chest and pulled up a hoody that was on one of the jackets I was wearing. I drew the draw strings up tight enough so I was now breathing through the cloth.

Because... my lungs were shit. My brow furrowed as I remembered this small nugget of information about myself. *Yeah, my lungs were shit... I used to get pneumonia every winter; last winter was especially bad.*

Last winter... I was here last winter, in the greywastes. I remember being on a four-wheeler and being so cold I thought I was going to die. My clothes were soaked and I was shivering.

Perhaps every winter I get dropped off here and that's why I'm sick.

I coughed again and trudged through the snow, a layer of crispy ice coating the top of the snow like a shell. My boots crunched every time I stepped down, like I was breaking through a crust of bread.

At least it hadn't snowed more.

As evening approached I hit my biggest jackpot yet. An abandoned shack! I didn't have the energy or the drive to do it but deep down inside I was jumping up and down with excitement. I wasn't sure what kind of shack it was; there were only mountains and the occasional old logging road. I think it might've been a ranger station or something. Well, whatever it was for I didn't really care. The peaked roof was still up and there was an intact window, that was good enough for me.

Just as I was getting the boards off of the shack, I felt the first drops of rain. I kicked the door open and immediately my nostrils flooded with the smell of musty wood.

I brought out my assault rifle and looked around cautiously. The shack had been stripped down to the insulation and the studs, and most of the wooden paneling had already been burned for firewood. There was a small little stove in the corner and a musty, sour-smelling mattress. It was all only three rooms; the other room off to the side looked like a kitchenette, and the one to the right, a bathroom.

My boots crunched against the floor, plaster from the ceiling coming off in large chunks, spilling the electrical wiring from the holes like it had been disembowelled. I sized it up and deemed it heaven, so I started settling in for the night.

That night I tried to clean some of the small wounds on me, though I left the one on my head alone. I didn't have any antiseptic or anything like that, so I boiled snow and some pieces of cloth.

I winced and sucked in a breath, but I steeled myself and pressed the hot cloth against a cut on my face. It was where I had been punched, I assumed. I doused and dressed every injured part of my body before refilling an old rusted out pot with snow.

Then, with a mug of hot water, I drew my blanket tighter around me, the rain pattering on the tin roof and dripping down the dirty glass in hypnotic drips. Tomorrow I might just stay here; I didn't think it would be smart to walk in the rain. I was already coughing more and more, and my headaches were a constant fear on my mind. I was warm enough here so… perhaps a day to gather my strength. I had been on the road almost four days now.

I treated myself to a cigarette after I had dried out all my clothes, and ate the last meat on the arm. Then I broke up the arm bone into sizable bits with a hatchet I found and started boiling myself up some soup. I left that to simmer on the stove and tried to get some sleep.

I was woken up with a start that night. My heart gave a convulsive hammer as I heard something snarling and snapping outside.

My eyes widened. I shot up from my nest of blankets and grabbed a knife. With my hands trembling from adrenaline, I made sure I had a firm grip in place, and pressed myself up against the wall. As the noise continued outside, I braced myself and listened.

Then a screech from a different animal. I clenched my teeth, wondering just what the fuck was fighting outside, and who was going to win.

Then, as the growling and snapping got louder, my chest started to vibrate. I felt a brief feeling of recall as I remembered that deacons and deacdogs could shake your ribcage with the low, bass-like growls they could make.

Going against my fear, I rose and looked out the window.

It was Deek... the deacon dog was staring out into the darkness, the grey fur around his hackles raised and bristling. I looked ahead to try and see what he was growling at, but the firelight behind me made it impossible for my night vision to kick in. I wasn't sure how long he had been out there for, he could have barked or something, I would've let him in.

"Deek? Come inside, boy," the stranger living in my voice croaked. The door creaked with rusted hinges and my head warily poked through.

I heard a huff and the shifting of snow. I took a slow step out onto the front porch and scanned the darkness. Just rocks and slushy snow. I couldn't see anything moving.

Then the dog darted off out of sight, barking and snapping like a lunatic. With that act, the hairs on the back of my neck prickled, but my isolation during the last several days had given me a small vein of bravery. I had survived so far, I had been on this road for a while – I should take charge. I should show I was strong enough to survive here.

So I took another step outside and continued to try and find the source, my knife ready to kill myself some game.

Then several things happened in that moment, none of which I was prepared for. I heard a shifting of snow, and as soon as I heard it my reflexes took my gaze in that direction, but it wasn't what I thought.

A pair of burning eyes, the size of tennis balls, burrowed into me, but, before my hand could raise the knife, they rose into the air. The next thing I knew I was on the ground with a startled scream, jaws clamping on my arm with a vice-like bite.

My head cracked against the side of the porch, breaking open the scab and filling me with an incomprehensible surge of pain. I felt my limbs go rigid and my breath get ripped from my lungs.

"Deek!" I choked. I wrenched my arm further into the animal's jaw to try and unlock its grip, as my other one fumbled for the combat knife at my side.

Then, with a jerk of my head, I managed to get a good look at it.

A large cat, the size of a mountain lion, stared at me as it snapped my arm forward. A cat which I knew had six legs, long, gut-ripping claws, and a thick scaled tail. It was a carracat, a mutated animal from Skyfall.

The creature bit down harder and tried with jerking thrusts to tear my arm from its socket. I gritted my teeth and struggled to raise myself but four of its legs were pinning me down.

Thick fur pressed against me as it pulled me under it, warm and strong from ropey muscles that I could feel flex against my body. It smelled like sour and dander from its fur-covered skin.

"DEEK!" I tried to scream. I choked as two of its paws climbed higher up my chest, digging its serrated claws into my neck in its struggle to snap my arm. I pulled my free hand down, and with a shaky but focused thought, I managed to grab the combat knife.

I dove the blade inbetween its protruding ribs, and in a flash, it released my arm.

I struggled to get to my feet, but as I rose it pounced on my back, taking the hood of my jacket into its teeth. I felt a hot snort as it pulled, its weight throwing me off balance and bringing me to my knees.

I dropped the knife, but with a burst of adrenaline, I jumped back to my feet, the creature still on top of me tearing apart my hood.

My mind suddenly flashed to a time long ago when I had jumped on someone's back. They had run backwards until I was slammed against a wall. Well, I might not have a wall, but I had the ground.

I flung myself backwards, and with a hope and a wish, I landed on top of the creature hard, snapping its jaws from my clothing and temporarily leaving it stunned.

I rolled off of it and ran towards the door, smelling rain and blood in my nose as I tried to climb the steps. I reached my arm out to the handle but my legs were shaking my entire body. My hand grazed the door knob and I fell forward; half in the safety of the house, half in the rain, the darkness, and the awaiting predator.

My chest rose and fell, my mind seemed to race in all directions, but at the same time, it stood frozen and still. Unable to command my body to rise, I took to crawling through the door frame.

An overwhelming weight slammed my body down, knocking the wind out of me. I gasped and waited for the jaws to wrap around my throat.

Then, with nothing but a breeze against my neck and body, the weight was gone, only to be replaced by the intense and bone-chilling sound of a vicious fight. A violent and emotionally-jarring racket of two beasts tearing each other apart.

I crawled into the door frame and collapsed onto the wooden floor, my chest frozen and clenched in a terrorized stupor. I couldn't breathe, and with every desperate gasp, my body only turned to thicker ice; the snarling and snapping of a fight to the death happening only feet away from me.

I collapsed beside the stove and grabbed a combat knife with a shaking hand. I leaned up against warm stove and held the knife.

Then the next blow to my mind, I heard a rattling behind me. I turned and saw a medium-sized carracat with my salvaged meat in its jaws. We looked at each other in shock for a split second before it shot past me and ran out the door into the darkness.

I wanted to crawl into the kitchen to see if there were any others, but my brain forced me to stay stationary with the knife.

"Deek!" I cried, knowing the deacdog would never hear me in his frenzied mind. The once silent mountain pass was filled with such deafening noise I thought the fabric of reality had burst around me. My ears hurt, my senses hurt, and my mind felt like it was edging inch by inch to a breakdown I had only been holding off from sheer will.

Without telling them to, my hands cupped my ears and I stared at the shadowed silhouettes of my boots. The sounds of the fighting awakening every primal instinct in me. I put my hands to my ears and pressed, not because I was a coward, unable to deal with the reality, but because I feared at any moment my mind would break unless I got away from that horrible noise.

But pressing my hands into my ears wasn't enough; I could still hear the vicious fighting going on around me. I found myself starting to sing, loudly, with my eyes staring unblinking. I sung the first song that came to my head and tried to drown out the shaking anxieties in my chest, bloodletting each shudder of fear as the words rolled off my tongue.

I moved my lips to the music in my head, one hand on the cold gun and another on the combat knife. I would focus on the words and nothing else.

Then the pressure behind my eyes. I closed them hard and sung louder, feeling the pounding migraine start to gather itself for its orchestra of pain. It hit me with its full strength and soon my singing turned to screams.

That morning I stumbled to my feet, only several seconds passing between the haze of sleep and the closing jaws of reality. In a robotic movement, I walked to the door and opened it with a bloodstained hand.

There was the body of a carracat, its stomach ripped open with pink and red innards strewn around, half-eaten and covered in dirt and red snow. A skinny, chipped mutated cat with a thick coat of brown fur, a black-scaled tail, and six legs.

Beside it, Deek was wagging his tail at my sudden emergence, the snow flattened all around the animal. I guess he had decided to sleep beside his kill.

I mumbled him praise before sinking to my knees. I looked down and saw my arm. It had two lacerations starting at the elbow and ending several inches from my wrist. Deep gouges that split right through the yellow layer of fat, opening up my muscle like a filleted fish.

I squeezed my eyes tight as my head gave an angry throb. I groaned and swore, hating where I was and hating that I didn't know how much farther I could go.

My name was Jade, that was all I knew. Where I had come from I didn't know, and where I was going also a mystery to me. But as the days went by one thing came clear–

–I was probably going to die in these mountains.

I looked up at the sky, though as soon as I did, I felt a wave of vertigo, of dizziness that filled my head with cotton balls. So I didn't look up, I stared forward, watching the road stretch out in front of me, wrapping around the snow-dusted mountain as we slowly found our way to level ground.

With my last remaining strength I had done the unthinkable, something so clever, so intelligent it probably had saved my life.

I had made it half a mile, a full day after the carracat had attacked me until I had found it – Well, there were a lot of them, but it was a half-mile until I found a trunk hood I could pull off. Then I had taken the sheet of metal and had looped a piece of rope around the key hole. I tied the rope to the dog's harness jacket and there it was…

I had made myself a dog sled.

See… I could be a mountain man if I tried hard enough.

Though, in all respects, it was the fact that the dog was pulling me that was saving my life right now. My energy was gone and my will to carry on was quickly leaving me too. Not only had the carracat destroyed my arm and freshly bruised my body, my headaches were becoming uncontrollable.

I coughed and watched a spray of spittle fly out of my mouth and onto the frozen ground. The rain we'd had a couple days ago had frozen under the cold, and though it made the sled skate effortlessly along the ice, it had also fucked my lungs even worse.

All in all… Jade wasn't doing too hot.

But to my credit, the dog seemed to know where to go. Deek hadn't minded at all being hooked up to my trunk hood sled. I don't know if he had been trained to pull things or what but he happily trotted along the highway. The deacon dog seemingly in his element, he even walked like he had somewhere to be.

When he eventually stopped after darkness took the two of us again, I unhooked him from his sled and let him be free. I didn't move out of my blankets, I only chewed on snow and a few more remaining gummy worms. I wasn't that hungry anymore and I was out of flesh anyway. The carracat that had broken into the ranger shed had taken my last big chunks of meat and the soup I had made was gone.

Light snow fell around me, but my energy had dissipated to where I couldn't even shift myself under a vehicle or one of the trees on the side of the road. To shield my body from the elements, I threw the blankets over my head and breathed in my own breath inside my stuffy cave.

Whoever I was, I was alone now. Any friends I may have had were dead, days and days back in that resort town. Perhaps I should have stayed there, there had been enough dead bodies to last me months. But there were ravers around, and though up here it was cold and frozen… the mad subhumans seemed to be long gone.

The next morning I was woken by the sensation of being yanked again and again, and on top of that, and odd pinging noise. I opened my eyes but found they were covered in sticky goop. I managed to pull them off of my eyelashes to see what was going on.

Deek was in front of me, his teeth clipping and nipping the corner of the trunk hood. He was trying to pull it with just his mouth.

"Sorry, Deek," I rasped. Then, as my lungs filled with the icy winter air, I coughed and rubbed my fluid-crusted face. He looked at me and wagged his tail, his tongue hanging out in happiness that I had woken up.

With shaking, weak hands I clipped the leads back onto his jacket, and showing off the advanced intelligence I was only beginning to realize he had, he started to pull me once again.

A while later, I was jarred out of my half-conscious state by the metal underneath me bumping and scraping along. I pulled the blankets off of my face and saw the highway behind me with thick trees on either side. The trunk cover left a unique imprint as it bumped and slid over the unbroken ground.

I poked my head underneath the dog's legs to get a view of where he was taking me, but all that filled my vision was the same as what was behind: huge black trees with many spindly branches, rough brush, and the highway. All of this framed by the slight dusting of snow that fell lightly around us.

I sighed at this and resigned myself to my fate. It wasn't like I could tell the dog where to take me; I didn't know where to go…

The world around me was too far away for me to care; I didn't even feel the cold anymore. My entire body was a single entity of throbbing pain, most of it centered around my head and the large gash that seemed to be the root of all of my problems. There was no use being upset, or trying to remedy the error in the dog's thinking – I was at his mercy, and where he was bringing me would be where I ended up.

And where I died perhaps.

I wondered if I would be missed, or if all of my friends had died in that resort. Maybe it was stupid not to have died with them. Though I knew it wasn't in my nature to quit, if that had been the person I was before – I wouldn't have made it this far.

Absentmindedly I wiped my nose and flicked the string of red and snot onto the white ground. I squinted hard as white dots appeared in my vision and closed my eyes as the vertigo took me again. Feeling a jolt of nausea start to swell in my gut, I groaned, the sled scraping against the snow background music to my slow drowning. Though as the hours went on, the sounds of the world around me faded, and all I heard was the blood roaring through my ears.

Time dissolved around me into a muddled pool, the sights and sounds mixing and stirring into one another becoming nothing more than background noise. I don't know how long or even how many days I stayed in that trunk sled, I just knew sometimes the dog stopped and sometimes he didn't. Oddly, I was aware of times when I was in the trunk lid and he wasn't there, I think I unhitched him sometimes or maybe he could do it himself now. The rope I had recovered had once been a hitch on the caravan back in the resort, it was just a thin rope with a metal hook on each end.

It was during one of those half-aware times when I was dying and alone that I heard a noise I knew all too well. A noise that came to my ears only; the dog had been unhitched, to hunt perhaps since I could no longer feed him.

It was the familiar sounds of humans screaming, high pitch, manic screeching that ripped its way into your ears and clawed at your mind's membrane, shredding and ripping your bravery, leaving you nothing but a cowering shell.

And I was no different. My crusted eyes opened, the bright snow searing my eyeballs so used to being in darkness. I squinted and shifted myself. It looked like I'd been placed near several stacks of car tires. I was out in the open, exposed to the elements and to what horrors the greywastes delivered.

And I knew one of those deliveries were at my door.

Sure enough, my weak heart swelled with anxiety. I looked up from my trunk lid eyrie and saw five ravers skidding down a rough embankment. All of them were dressed in soiled clothes, missing chunks of skin and fingers, and some were wearing headdresses of scalps or wearing severed hands and feet on their leather belts. They had their yellowed clouded eyes fixed on me and their broken teeth bared and snapping as if anticipating my flesh.

Immediately I struggled to raise myself, only to fall back onto my ass from not only weakness, but my badly injured arm. I swore loudly and scrambled backwards until I hit the stack of tires. I desperately looked around for a knife.

Another manic scream, the one leading jumped onto a median and crouched down as if anticipating pouncing on me. But to my surprise, he stayed crouched, the other four rallying behind him, their teeth snapping and clicking. I think he was their leader.

My heart was racing. I looked around with my teeth grinding around, wondering where that fucking dog was. I gave the ravers one last glance before I tried to get to my feet.

But I fell again. I ground my teeth and did the only thing I could think of.

I pursed my lips and tried to make the unique sound, the sound I knew in the back of my mind would summon the dog.

Then a shock ripped through me, and all I could do was stand there, paralyzed. Because the moment I made that whistle… the ravers screamed.

I jerked my head back towards them and my mouth dropped open.

The raver… the leader, his hands were raised in an… in an almost pleading way. His yellowed eyes were wide and his head slowly shaking back and forth.

I stopped whistling and stared at him, backing away like a wounded animal as he stepped towards me, letting his heavily scarred hands drop to his sides.

Then the leader looked behind him, then back to me.

And dropped down to one knee.

CHAPTER 37

Reaver

ONCE WHEN I WAS YOUNGER, I WALKED IN ON Greyson hunched over himself, sitting on the couch. I was only five but I remember it as clear as day. I had found my left sneaker which I'd once again lost, and I had ran inside to tell him he didn't have to be cross with me anymore.

I remember stopping like I had just hit a concrete barrier and just watching in shock. I felt my insides turn to ice as I witnessed this hard-as-iron man with his face red and his eyes shedding tears, staring down at the kerchief he was holding, crumpled in his hand.

It had jarred me. I felt uncomfortable, almost shy in a way, feeling like I was watching something I shouldn't. I wanted to run because I felt so awkward being in the same room as him.

Greyson had been my hardass dad; the mayor of Aras and someone who took everything standing tall. He was like the soldiers in the old army magazines they would read me.

I'd point to them and say, "Grey?"

"Yeah," Leo would chuckle. "It does kind of look like him, huh? Always the bad boy."

Greyson had seen me in the doorway and immediately he tried to hide his face. He turned away and wiped his nose. "What is it, Reaver?"

I looked at my bare feet, black from dirt. I pivoted one and twisted it around the ground.

"Why…" I stopped. I shouldn't ask that of him, even back then I shied away from any conversation that might lead to uncomfortable emotions. Instead, I put the shoe down that I had found and ran back outside, so I didn't have to see such an uncomfortable sight, from a man I held so much respect for.

Even mayors… even big badass dads have emotions…

Elish wasn't Greyson, but without realizing it, I'd started to see him as a figure of strength, endurance, and stoicism. He put it forth without effort and I had gravitated to it. I trusted him, without realizing it or knowing when it had happened, I trusted him with my life and that of my boyfriend.

So when I walked up behind him and we stood side by side, I got the same coy feeling that I had gotten when I was a child. The feeling that I was witnessing this man, seemingly carved from the ice flows of Hell, show the small hints of vulnerability.

A state that would only ever be brought forth by the fear that his pet, his young husband, was in mortal danger.

Danger I had put him in, Killian too.

Elish's eyes scanned the black trees and grey rocks below and around us. His jaw was tight and his movements stiff, and his tall frame dressed in greywaster attire complete with an assault rifle on his back. I hadn't seen him like this in years, and now that I knew who 'James' really was, I looked at this chimera in a whole different light.

I glanced behind him, and when I saw Caligula, Nico, and Reno out of earshot, I turned to Elish.

"I'll find him, I promise. I'll fix it, alright?"

Elish didn't move, nor did he speak, but I did see his jaw tighten. I knew he wouldn't, and in truth, just saying those words had made my ears go hot. I was feeling… not just guilty for possibly putting the boys in danger, I was feeling like I failed the most important task, at least in Elish's eyes, that he had given me.

I lost the damn cicaro.

This filled me with frustration and rage. I had never been the self-loathing type, or at least I never saw myself as that. But this heavy burden of emotion on my shoulders was crippling me. I was the Scourge of the

Greywastes, the Raven, and the Reaper. Now I just felt like a fucking dirty piece of shit, not just a failure who couldn't even keep Killian and Jade safe, but a beaten down victim of Nero Dekker. Some fucking idiot who let all of this happen because he didn't think.

I didn't fucking think.

I killed Timothy because I didn't think of the repercussions.

I fucking travelled with slavers because I was desperate to protect Killian from the Legion closing in on us.

I even left Jade with Perish and the slavers because I was more concerned with getting away from those bickering idiots. I could've and should've brought Jade with us to charge the Ieon and I knew it.

With a swallow I tried to push it down, though like I was swallowing a bone my own self-hatred stuck in my throat. Though there was nothing more I could do but mentally beat myself up, and I wasn't that kind of guy. Loathing got you nowhere; it made you hate yourself and made others hate you. I had to stop being a fucking pussy about it and pull up my fucking bootstraps.

I was the Reaper. And though I will still make mistakes – I will fix them.

I – will – fix – them.

There was a crunching of snow, Nico came running up to us. "I got bad news…"

Both Elish and I turned around at the same time.

"What is it?" Elish said sharply, his eyes hard.

Caligula had been on the phone with Kessler for several minutes now. The call coming in while we were landing the Falconer, a few miles from where Killian, Chally, and I had branched off towards Mariano.

"Kess is assuming that Reaver is hiding in the Death Canyons near Cardinalhall. Which is good for us; it will take them weeks and weeks to comb it to the Legion's satisfaction but…" Caligula's mouth twitched to the side. "Uncle Elish… he's ordered… *demanded*, we return with the plane. Now."

"Fuck, seriously?" I snapped. I growled and kicked a nearby median, feeling the dark rage I had been suppressing start to raise to the surface, but Elish was calm beside me.

"What explanation did you give him as to why you have the plane?" Elish asked.

"We just told him we were visiting Nico's father. Kessler isn't talking to Zhou right now after what happened with the ransom so it'll fit." Caligula looked behind him and shook his head. "What are your orders?"

Elish didn't miss a beat. He walked past Caligula and towards the plane. "You and Nico will be returning to Cardinalhall… Reaver and I will continue on foot."

"And Reno?"

"You will be taking him back to Aras."

At the same time, both my and Reno's heads jerked towards Elish.

"What?" we both said.

Elish stepped onto the plane and started packing supplies. "Mr. Nevada is still nursing a bullet wound and internal bleeding. I can be cruel and draw attention to the fact that he will slow us down, or I can be kind and tell him he needs more time to rest before he permanently joins us. You may choose which one."

Reno looked crushed, but I couldn't come to his defence. My friend had showed me his war wounds on the way to the mountains and he was still in rough shape.

"The residents sold us out…" I said confused. "He isn't safe there."

Elish, who was still packing bags, reached into his pocket. There was a jingle as he threw a set of keys to Reno. "Take out the key with the blue cap. That is for the bunker and in that bunker is a quad you can use to stay in Tintown if needed be, money too. Nico will drop you off and you will not leave that bunker until I personally retrieve you. If you must stay in Tintown, or want to make the journey to Anvil, write a note."

"Why can't you take him to Garrett?" I asked. Though oddly at the mention of his suppose 'fiancé', Reno's bottom lip disappeared into his mouth. I knew then that there was a reason and probably a story too.

"Because right now, to Silas at least, Reno begging a ride back home to Aras from Caligula and Nico is extremely plausible. Unless Reno is preparing to stay in Skyfall forever, it is unsafe for him, and our end goal, to have him bounce back and forth."

I blinked as Reno gave him a single crushing look before his face tightened. I put a hand on his shoulder and patted it. Elish though, didn't have time to comfort him.

"You three need to go, now. If Reaver and I start right now we can make twice the speed their caravan would be going... and if needed be, we have the advantage of silence and stealth the plane would not offer." He put on a knapsack and I put on my own. "Let's go."

Arms were thrown around me; I almost lost my balance as Reno hugged me hard. "I'm sorry, baby."

"Ah... you'd just slow us down; you always had clumsy, Bigfoot feet." I tried to be supportive, Killian's influence heavy on me. "I'll come and get you soon, I promise."

"You'll come and get me?" Reno's voice suddenly went all high and squeaky.

I smiled, even though he couldn't see me. "Of course, we'll always come for each other. You're my bud. If you're good I might bring you a slave boy too."

Reno sniffed. "Just watch yourself..."

I stiffened. I didn't like that he knew my thoughts so well; he knew the battle that had been going on inside of my head. On top of that he had seen the state I had found myself slipping into.

The one that required the injection into my neck.

"I will," I whispered back. And with that, the three of them went into the Falconer and were soon out of sight. At least I knew my best friend would be safe, even if he did venture into Aras he would be alright. He didn't know I had killed Redmond and Hollis, and Carson had died during the attack. Nico would make sure his father, the legion general currently in charge of Aras, would treat Reno like royalty.

Elish and I started walking down the snow-covered highway, snow clinging to the spindly branches of the black trees. Elish had his blond hair hidden under a panama hat, and a grey duster over his Skyfall clothing. He was James right now, James the greywaster seeking out his travelling partner.

We walked in silence, our strides long but slow enough that we could sentry the area. We didn't exchange any words, both of us listening and paying attention to the world around us. Elish keeping an eye on the belt of trees to our right, and I was watching the white and grey rocks below us, where the road dropped off into the valley.

There were no signs though, and I wished then that we had at least some caravan tracks to follow, but the snow had fallen long after the bosen had walked this highway. Elish and I had nothing to go on, just a long and lonely strip of road.

The silence between us was consensual and fitted the quiet personalities I knew we both had. Though with the silence went my imagination, and there were several things that kept creeping into my mind that had to be banished back down to the void.

I entertained myself with how I was going to kill Hopper if he did hurt the boys in any way. But without wanting it to… Hopper kept turning into Nero.

A dark feeling gathered in my gut, a cancer that seemed to be growing its own blood supply.

I reached into my cargo pants pocket for a reprieve. I took out my last baggy of powder and took a generous amount in each nostril. Killian had our heroin; I was looking forward to indulging on that when I found him.

I could feel Elish's eyes on me as I sniffed the opiate powder up my nose. I tilted my head back to catch the drip and tried to hide the sigh on my lips.

"Do you want some?" I looked over at him.

Elish shook his head. "Your friend Reno offered me some as well. I suppose it is a communal thing amongst greywasters?"

I shrugged. "It keeps the edge off of… life. Keeps my mind from going to places I would rather it not go."

Elish nodded but kept walking. I swallowed down the weight of my own thoughts but Nero was starting to become an ember in my brain. The more I was quiet the more his face came into my head. Even though I knew I shouldn't, I felt like I had to make my plans known.

"When we figure out how to kill Silas… I'm going to kill Nero."

He didn't even flinch. Not a single waver, not a twitch out of place. When we spoke about Jade I could see the small signs, but not with anyone else did I see that frozen resolve thaw.

"You will not need too. King Silas will permanently condemn Nero for taking what was his to take."

My... I didn't even want to use that stupid word. It made me cringe just thinking about it like that. I wiped the expression of disgust from my face but the barbs were already on my tongue. "Silas wouldn't have taken it either."

"Yes, he would have." Elish's face darkened. "Usually the day after his chimeras turn fifteen. You would be one of the rare ones to have to wait. I do not envy what consequences my brother will face for what he did to you. Rest assured, he will be punished, severely."

"I want to be the one to punish him, and kill him," I said, the emotion draining from my voice. I could feel the dark cancer in my gut grow even larger. "I will rape him, torture him… I will keep him alive for years until I decide it is time for him to die." My hands clenched into a fist, and without warning my breath started to become short.

Nero… my hatred for him, I realized in that moment, was starting to become as strong as my hatred for Silas. What he had done to me…? That festering pocket of rot in my brain, it put such a blind anger inside of me I didn't think I could contain it in my head. How was I going to explain this to Killian? I couldn't… ever tell him.

Elish's cold voice cut the thoughts boiling inside of me. "You are an immortal and so is Nero. You will have your revenge on him. Let that cool down your mind. I need you present and listening, aware and in this reality. I caution–"

His voice faded until it was nothing but a low-toned hum in the back of my head, a world away from where my mind was going. In its place, I felt a roaring start to rush through my brain, lighting my dark thoughts on fire like they had been coated in oil.

I felt Nero's touch, I felt him licking my lips, biting and nipping my neck. Then his thick cock being mercilessly shoved inside of me as his cicaro watched. The pain, fuck, it was painful. The first time it broke inside of me, the burning pressure, the assault of pain as my tense body constricted around him. Back and forth. Back and forth.

One twist. Two twist.

A scream broke through my clenched teeth. I started to run not knowing where I was going, when I felt hands grab me. I tried to yank myself away but they held me firmly in their grasp.

I struggled to get away but he crushed me tight against his chest. I howled and screamed feeling like an animal caught in a trap.

"Scream louder," Elish's frozen voice pierced the destruction going on in my head.

I gritted my teeth and tried to twist my body away from him but he only said it again.

'Scream louder."

"No!" I snarled at him.

"Do it. Scream, bite, kill… do what you must, just do not internalize it," Elish commanded me. "I have dealt with chimera youth. I have trained Jade and I have counselled many others. You need to drain the infection, and to a chimera that is through blood, destruction, and revenge. I have no revenge for you, so scream."

I pushed him away and this time he let me go. I pursed my lips trying to force down what I was about to say but, betraying my pride and dominance, I said it anyway. "I'm not weak, I'm not some… fucking wimp who gets torn up over… over some physical act!" I yelled. "I'm stronger than that. I'm… better than that!"

I put my hands on my head; I despised myself for my trembling hands. Why was I saying this to Elish? I was the toughest, I was the most emotionless.

I was…

I WAS THE REAPER!

"You have never had competition before," Elish responded calmly.

I stopped, my hands dropping from my head. Elish sensed the temporary pause in my madness and continued.

"Yes, you are quite the emotionless sociopath… in Aras. In Aras you were king. A king next to a soft, innocent little blond boy and a happy-go-lucky greywaster with cripplingly low self-esteem. Bravo." Elish rose and dusted the snow from his knees. "But you are no longer in Aras. In your new world… you have chimeras that have refined and perfected the art of cruelty. Ones who have been honing their craft for almost a century. Yes, Aras has certainly given you a big head; I saw that every time I visited. But unfortunately, Reaver… you're playing with the grownups now. Not half-starved arians."

I stared at him, every word pinning me down.

"There is no way to steel yourself other than endurance and experience. Use what Nero did to you as strength, because, Reaver, it-will-happen-again. If not with Nero than with Silas, or many of my other brothers who see you as a prize to claim and dominate. You are amongst brothers who are smarter than you, stronger than you and—"

"I am King Silas's clone. I'm better than all of them," I snapped, before I started to stalk back down the road.

Elish's cold laugh sounded behind me. "Yes, and Jade is a genetically engineered chimera with strands from our most successful, superior brothers. Caligula as well. All three chimeras in your generation have been selectively bred. You? You are the genetic copy of someone so full of madness he has driven his own hyper-intelligent mind into insanity. You may have chimera enhancements but you are not better than us… quite the contrary. You are prone to insanity, susceptible to addiction, obsessive-compulsion, violent outbursts, and self-hatred. Do not forget that."

I was listening to every word he said, and I was remembering them but still my prideful mind could only spit back, "You're the first born… you are pretty much a clone too, aren't you? All the first generation? You're no better than me."

I saw Elish in the corner of my vision, catching up to me with only a few long strides. "Yes, but I am ninety-one years old. I have learned how to deal with what ways my engineering wishes to sabotage me. If you wish, I can teach you to deal with your own, but you must listen."

He was quiet for a moment, though the silence between us was deafening. "Lycos and Greyson tried to teach you how to be the best person you could, the best arian. Now it's my turn to teach you how to be the best chimera."

My head turned towards him. "They failed though."

"Which is why I had to take over."

It almost felt like I was being dominated again, though this assault grated against me mentally, not physically.

Still though, like Leo and Greyson I held a respect for Elish. Looking back on my childhood, all the times he was there without me even knowing it. If there was one thing I was lacking right now it was men I could trust.

I didn't trust anyone outside my core group, but since the incident in Aras, that group had been whittled down to two: my boyfriend and my best friend.

Elish was the last man in charge; the only one remaining who knew what had to be done to kill Silas. So far I'd had no choice but to trust him. Now he was almost approaching me with the prospect of training me.

That made a bitterness flood my mouth. "I am not your pet."

"I'm not seeking a pet."

"Then what?"

"An ally eventually, but for now... my student," Elish responded. "We will be spending an eternity with each other running Skyfall and the greywastes. We may as well start getting used to each other." Then he gave me a cold look. "I have been making an effort to get along with you, Mr. Merrik. I have been more than patient with your inexperience and youth. Especially considering my pet is missing because of your errors. I urge against making my attempts be in vain. Seeking counsel and help from someone who holds more experience is not a shortcoming. It does not say anything against your pride or dominance. You would be a fool to convince yourself to already know everything, and a bigger fool to convince yourself you know more than me."

I had known everything, back when my world was centered in Aras.

More bitterness in my throat. I didn't like that he was making sense. I had been the king in Aras... I had been in control of everyone and everything.

But here? And in Skyfall? Or amongst my chimera brothers? I was more inexperienced than Jade, and that stung.

I felt like I was letting go of control, which, especially at this moment... I didn't think I could do. I wanted to hold onto every bit of control I could, because I felt like I was twisting in the breeze right now.

In Aras... I controlled the residents and made them fear me. I controlled the legionary by killing and sniping them. Hell, I even controlled my boyfriend and my best friend. I was the dominant alpha male and those who didn't bow to me wound up dead.

Then I learned I was a chimera... and in quick succession, all of the control got taken away from me. Men, engineered from the same DNA, the same strands as me... had come. They had dominated my life, killed my dads, stolen my best friend, destroyed my home, and... had tried to enslave me.

I was a fool right now for thinking I could get that control back in the state I was in. I had to submit myself to someone who knew more than me so I could rise from the ashes and be the immortal-killer I was.

"Okay," I said simply. I nodded my head and took in a long, drawn-out breath. "You got me. I... hate it, but I'll trust you."

No expression came to Elish's face as I said those words. No relief, no acceptance, nothing but his usual frozen gaze which continued to scan the area around us.

"Good," he said. "The first thing you will do... is tell me everything that happened with Nero."

I looked at my hand and wiggled my fingers, then glanced at my wrist. The wrist that, not even a week ago, had been severed with my teeth. Now it had fused nicely back to my skin, only the still aching steel wool marks remained. My entire body was still hurting from those rub burns.

"You learned something valuable in that bedroom." Elish broke the heavy silence that had fallen over us. It was night time, the evening of day three on this highway, and we were taking a break. Since we were both immortal we decided there would be no need for us to take watch. We were sleeping underneath a black tree; all of the vehicles we had come across were too rusted out and dirty to make adequate beds. Being the chimeras we were, both of us would wake up if so much as a scorpion coughed. So if we had anyone passing us by on the highway we would know.

"Oh?" I ran my fingers along my wrist before flexing my thumb until I saw the tendon move under my skin.

Elish was leaning against the tree; I still couldn't get over how different he looked. I bet it would have been even more of an adjustment if I had seen him in Skyfall.

"Your body is a weapon, and because you are immortal your physical body is a weapon. What you figured out is something no human would ever think of doing. Because you can mutilate yourself if needed be. Your ulna and radius…" When I stared he gave me a pained look but dumbed it down for the greywaster. "Your… *arm bones* can be snapped and carved to be a weapon. Your hands can be chewed off to avoid cuffs; even your intestines can be used to strangle someone if needed be. Sanguine was always fond of that method. If you can stand the pain, which you can, and you can do it in a way that minimizes blood loss… you can get out of situations in a way that will kill you, but will kill you after you're free."

He was right about that. There were a lot of fringe benefits to being able to regenerate yourself after you died. My chewed-on arm bone had done a good job on Nero's face.

After we took three hours to rest we were back on the road again. We were in the dead of night now; it was so quiet out boot steps seemed to echo in the valley below us. It was dark too, but the snow absorbed the moonlight so, for the greywastes anyway, it was rather bright.

Then the sun started to rise, coating the world around us in a silver blue until it began to peek over the mountains. As the grey sun burned away the night and our quick walking started to affect our energy, the conversations between the two of us trickled down to nothing but short exchanges.

Though it wasn't just the fatigue that had halted our conversation. We had both been walking at a quickened speed, much faster than the caravan would have gone. And though the boys were probably a few days ahead of us, the closer we got to the summit the more tense the air seemed to get.

It was a weight that was on both of our shoulders, and the more distance we covered the more we knew we would start to see signs of the slave caravan. Both of us had no idea how long it had been since the snow had fallen, for all we knew we might start seeing tracks soon, or at least some bosen shit.

Elish had taken the left side of the highway which stretched off into miles of bush and bare rock, and I had taken the right near the tree belt. We were high above sea level now, though the sharp drop offs and sheer cliffs we had started out on had risen up to naked valleys and flat rolling hills. Everything was flatter the more north we got and Elish said it would carry on as such until we hit Melchai.

I glanced down a single-lane road which curved off into the black trees. "The trees might be bare here, but it's still a pain with them being so close together," I commented.

Elish was quiet; his sharp eyes were continuing to sweep the area.

"Do you think–" I shut my mouth when Elish raised a hand. I started to listen but I couldn't hear anything.

"Nose. Smell… don't use your ears," Elish instructed. "There are ravers near here."

For a brief moment I stared at Elish in shock, before, not missing a beat I started to walk around the area, trying to pick out tracks, blood, any sign that something had happened to the boys.

Though as I looked and picked apart every tipped over median, every old highway sign, Elish's eyes were fixed on a sloping ridge a few yards from the highway. I followed him as he glided towards it, my hands starting to itch from wanting to grab my gun.

But there was nothing but the faint aroma on the air and even that smelled stale. I jumped up onto one of the medians as Elish walked along the ridge.

"If it's ravers… they're gone," I spoke my thoughts out loud. "It hasn't been snowing enough over the past two days for it to cover fresh tracks…"

Elish turned from the ridge, his face showing me no window into his emotions but a tightness in his lips. "Yes… let us continue."

Then, despite all of my self-control, I felt a strong surge of anxiety shoot through me as I spotted something.

"Elish…" He immediately turned at the tone of my voice.

I jogged over to the winding road and kneeled down. I brushed my hand over a spot of red.

My heart dropped as I dug under the fresh layer of snow… there was blood.

I brushed more snow aside… more blood. I rose to my feet and scanned the winding road.

Elish bent down and picked up a mound of the bloody snow. He put it to his lips and tasted it.

"It's not chimera…"

I tried to hide the relief on my face. Elish looked behind me and started to walk down the road. I got out my gun and so did he, the tension inside of my body now reaching a boiling point. I wish I could hide the heart hammering in my chest, or at least calm it down like Elish seemed to be able to do.

The road had trees on either side of it, large, twisted trunks with raised roots that contorted into each other. It carried on as we walked down the incline, twisting through many turns but continuously leading us downhill.

Then more signs, footsteps mixed in with the smears and sprinkles of blood. The bare feet of ravers, dozens of them. All of them moving around each other like they were in a frenzy. I knew ravers and this wasn't typical behaviour for them. They didn't hunt like this, they pursue their prey in a straight line, never wavering until they either died or they couldn't find you anymore. Not this sporadic, miss-matched pattern. And why only one direction? There were no prints pointing back up to the highway.

"What came down… never came back up," Elish spoke my own realization out loud as we examined the prints. "All of them… are going downhill…"

"To where?" I almost didn't want to ask. Alarm bells were ringing in my mind, flooding me with the urge to run down the hill to see what I would find at the bottom. What were the ravers running towards? It couldn't be the caravan, why would they veer off the road?

"There was a sign a half kilometre back. A resort. They were heading towards the resort, where this road will lead us," Elish replied placidly.

"Why?"

Elish continued to stare down at the road, analyzing the tracks. "I think perhaps the caravan got caught in the first snowfall. They may have sought the resort for shelter."

Elish looked up from the tracks and down the road; an odd expression crossed his face. "It is time we run the rest of the way."

Elish started to jog down the hill, I followed behind. "But… Jade can't be down there… your tracker hasn't gone off."

I kept pace with him, our boots landing heavy on the ground. We weren't even trying to keep our movements silent now. The calm atmosphere that had followed us since the Falconer had taken off had disappeared the moment we saw the blood.

"There are many things that could happen to his tracker. Anything from a strong electrical charge, a heavy blow to his head, or a gunshot wound," Elish responded in a tone that told me he wouldn't appreciate any more questions.

I was fine with that. Though I remained calm, inside I was screaming, tearing out my hair, and shooting everyone at the faint prospect that Killian was in that resort. Killian hated ravers; he would have been scared shitless.

Calm down... they had guns, big guns. They could all shoot the ravers... use them for food... Killian is down there right now and he's going to cry and sob knowing that you're alright. Perish was experienced, so was Jade and, fuck, so was Killian – they would be just fine.

Let that be my reality.

But as we rounded the last bend, and several buildings came into view, the real reality hit me.

Both Elish and I stopped in our tracks, for a fraction of a second we both stared, stunned.

A massacre... deep red stains of blood on the old snow, pounded down with dozens of footsteps, clustered around a single-storey building with a large overhang. The blood framing dozens of corpses, most already eaten, with severed body parts holding thin layers of frost, strewn across this kill zone.

My eyes flickered to the corner of the building, where I could see two caravan carts. The bosen, dusted with snow, dead and frozen where they were left.

"KILLIAN!" I screamed, a desperate shriek that cracked my voice. I ran down the road, as fast as I could, hearing Elish's quickened breathing behind me.

Then I slipped and fell. I looked down and saw a slick of blood, frozen onto the ice, leading to the decapitated head of Hopper.

No... no...

"Killian?" I screamed again. Elish was ahead of me now, standing in the middle of the worst carnage. His face more cold than the winter air around us, but I heard his heart – Oh god, I heard his heart. He couldn't hide that from me.

So many body parts, both ravers, slavers, and slaves alike. I pushed past the weakness in my legs and the nausea clawing up my throat. They had been eaten by ravers, chunks were missing from their frozen bodies, now with ice clinging to their exposed skin and bones.

Silence. All there was around us was silence. Invisible winter air that held on it such a thickness my shoulders buckled.

I sank to my knees. In front of me I saw Chomper, with his face half-missing, chewed off to ribbons, a single intact eye staring at me from its socket.

"You must get up and check the bodies." Elish's voice stung me, the indifferent tone poisoning my heart.

I turned to him, and when I looked into his eyes I felt the darkness creep the corners of my vision.

"If they are amongst them, we must know. Push past it and–"

I lunged at him, my hand throwing down my assault rifle and instead going for the knife at my hip. I let out a scream of rage as I swung it at him.

In that moment I hated him. I hated that he was calm. I hated that he could still stand, still function.

But most of all, I hated that he was immortal. I hated that when I killed him, he would come back, I would come back.

But Killian wouldn't.

Killian wouldn't.

Elish dodged me. The bodies were strewn in their mangled shapes, surrounding us like an audience in a ring of compacted, bloodied snow, and watching with frozen eyeballs and teeth-chewed smiles. I bet they were drinking this in.

"Reaver, get a hold of yourself!" Elish snapped. The first emotion I had seen on his face. But I couldn't hear him, I couldn't hear his words. They bounced off of my own agony and stark disbelief for what we had just discovered.

My eyes burned, my teeth clenched and I didn't realize I had been biting down on my tongue until I could taste copper. I was too inside of my own turmoil to manage a response for him. All that was within my abilities at that moment was to glare him down. Surprised, in my madness, that the snow hadn't thawed just from my own burning gaze.

"We don't know they were amongst them. Save your descent into delirium for when we know for sure. I need you present." Elish's words pierced my madness like a lance.

He was right... or was he trying to convince himself as much as he was me?

I dropped the knife and stared at the crimson snow; my boots resting beside a chunk of brown-haired scalp.

There were no legionary soldiers to revenge kill. No factory to bomb. Everyone around me was dead. Just like Perish had told me would happen. He had told me stop putting Killian in danger. He had warned me.

Why didn't I listen?

At the sight of the madness leaving my body, Elish reached into his duster. I looked up and saw he was holding a remote in his hand.

He saw me staring at it. "This is a remote for my laptop, a simple remote to turn it on. Jade... would never leave that briefcase. The range is bad but..." Elish pressed on the button and held up his hand for silence. I watched the chimera walk towards the caravan, resting beside the door; his gloved finger continuing to press the ON button.

We both listened.

A half a minute later we heard the faint chime of Windows XP loading, coming from inside the lobby.

"Jade?" he whispered.

My heart sank. I closed my eyes as I heard it... something I never wanted to hear.

I heard fear in Elish's voice.

Elish and I both ran into the lobby, a dark, debris-covered wreck of a house with boot prints leading in and out of all of the doors. Immediately we both turned to the left, where the Windows chime had come from.

Elish was ahead of me, what internal precautions he had taken to hide his heartbeat from me now forgotten. His pulse, his body language, and his face showed the emotions that were ravaging his insides. No amount of chimera training and discipline could hide the fear that had claimed both of us.

We got to the backroom and both of us paused.

The boys had been here.

I wanted to examine the bedrolls, and the clothing and trash that had been left behind, but I couldn't take my eyes off of Elish. The cold chimera, the oldest disciple of King Silas, was staring at a closed closet door. Unmoving. Like his own overwhelming emotions had frozen him in place.

The laptop was in there.

It took me a moment to realize what I was witnessing, but I soon understood. I understood that there was a strong possibility that Jade's body was in that closet. That Elish's cicaro and husband had fled from the ravers and died inside that cold, wooden tomb.

Elish reached out a hand, but once again he paused. As he lowered it, I saw his jaw tighten and his chin rise just slightly. I wondered what would happen if he found his dead body inside of there.

I wonder what would happen to me if Killian was in there too.

Then, as if he had never paused at all, Elish opened the closet door.

His eyes closed for a moment, his chest rising and falling like he was saying a prayer to a faceless god that had died years ago. Though whether he was thanking it or cursing it wasn't clear to me, until he reached in and pulled out the suitcase.

Elish left the door open and turned. I peeked in the closet to make sure it was void of bodies and it was. Nothing was in that closet but dusty shelves and loose silverware.

"Reaver, I need you to check the bodies and confirm Jade and Killian are not with them. You must also check their temperatures, especially any mangled heads. If Perish is amongst them he would be in the middle of resurrecting." Elish looked around at the bedrolls. "The blankets I gave you four are all gone…" He brought out the laptop and opened it. "I want to check and make sure this wasn't left with a message on it for me. I will join you momentarily."

There was nothing more for me to do, and no words I could say. The prospect that I was now going to be sifting through mangled remains to make sure they weren't our partners was both terrifying and sobering.

I walked over to where Hopper's head was and slid what I assumed was the rest of his body into a pile. Then I started kicking over other corpses, trying to recognized clothing and footwear.

Every time I found a severed body part my heart would give a shudder, but then as I examined it more relief would wash over me. Surprising even myself, I felt relief when I could confirm it wasn't Jade either. That brat annoyed the fuck out of me sometimes, but he was still my brother, and had slowly been growing on me.

I reached down and grabbed a torso with a jacket on it. I yanked it up off of the frozen ground, a peeling, scraping sound filling the quiet ambiance. When I had ripped it from the snow it had stuck to, I shook the jacket off and checked it out.

It wasn't Jade's; even though he tried to muck up his leather clothes you could still tell Skyfall clothing from scavenged greywaster clothing.

I bunched up the jacket and threw it into the pile. That was all the bodies... I had found all the slavers except Jimmy and all of the slaves but three. But there was one last place I could check.

I backed out from the overhang I had been standing under before I grabbed the ridge and hoisted myself up. I stood up on the roof and the first thing my eyes were drawn to was my M16. I picked it up with cautious relief and examined it. This was my confirmation that Killian had made it back to Hopper's caravan from Mariano. Though right now I didn't know if that was a good confirmation or not.

Then I made the mistake of looking around. A string of curse words flowed from my mouth.

"Elish?" I called.

I looked around and felt a rock get dropped into my stomach. Immediately I took a step back, realizing I was standing in a pool of frozen blood.

I leaned down as I saw something out of place. I picked up the metal fireplace poker, and as I examined it, my grimness grew.

It had several bloodied black hairs stuck to the top.

Elish was there in a second. I saw a hardness in his eyes, like he had already prepared himself for the thousand different reasons I was calling him.

"Come up here." There was nothing else for me to say.

Elish grabbed onto the carport like I had and flawlessly lifted himself up. He then walked over in silence, his eyes widening when he saw the large pool of blood.

Then his eyes looked over to the iron poker. He took it from me, seeing the hairs right away.

"They are Jade's," he replied. He knelt down and put his hand over the pool of blood.

A flicker of steam erupted from his palm. Then a moment later, the frozen pool started to thaw. When his hand had been coated in blood, he brought a finger to his lips.

The expression on his face said more than his words ever could.

It was Jade's blood.

"His body isn't here though…" I said slowly, but something else was confusing me. "And… ravers don't use weapons."

What the hell had happened here? Ravers, plus they were attacked by greywasters? It wasn't the slavers that was for sure, it looked like they all died from the initial raver assault.

"The dog is also gone," Elish said as he rose to his feet. "A deacon dog would never leave who he has deemed his master. He would have lain with him until he got hungry; there is too much uneaten food for the dog to have left." Elish looked around the structure we were standing on top of.

"I think someone took them."

My heart suddenly clenched. "Silas?"

But Elish shook his head. "No. Though I'm unsure of many things, I know for sure this was not Silas's work." He jumped off of the roof, poker still in hand and landed onto the icy snow. To my surprise, he reached into his pocket and pulled out his remote phone.

"What are you doing?" I asked, jumping down right behind him.

"I'm calling Reno. He will be at the Aras bunker by now. I suspect Lycos has been hiding things from me."

CHAPTER 38

Killian

"DRINK…" I WHISPERED, KNEELING BELOW HIM WITH A cup of water in my hands.

The slave, who I learned was named Danny, took it from me and gave me a smile.

"Thank you," he whispered. Like the other two, we always kept our voices down. Perish's moods came and went like the tides, and I didn't want to make him mad.

Mr. Fallon was several paces ahead of us, his assault rifle slung over his back and Reaver's M16 at the resort behind us. I had nothing on me now, no weapons or anything I could use against him. We were in the middle of the greywastes, veering off the highway days ago, and only he would be able to defend us from ravers or radanimals.

Perish had emptied my satchel and tossed away my drugs, my pocket knives and even the medication Elish had given me for my night terrors. He had even found his chimera necklace which I had taken off of his body back in Donnely. I got a lot of hell for that one.

Now I was nothing more than a slave, though occasionally Perish would tell me to walk beside him so he could talk to me. For the most part though, I stuck behind him and walked with the three remaining slaves: Danny, Edward, and Teejay.

It was hard to keep pace with Perish. He was powering ahead of us, rifle in hand, taking long strides that were almost impossible to keep up with. He was keeping at a gruelling pace that the slaves struggled to maintain.

So I was trying my best to keep their health up.

Perish glanced behind him and I saw his face twist in discontent. "I suggest you don't waste too much time watering them," he quipped with a sneer. "I would be surprised if they even made it to where we're going."

I ignored him and passed the blue cup to Teejay. He seemed to be the weakest one of them all; I had already given him some extra socks I had.

"Drink… hurry…" I whispered.

Teejay's nervous eyes glanced behind me. Suddenly his eyes widened, and a moment later, I saw a hand appear, smacking the cup out of his grasp.

I whirled around, my rage for Perish outweighing the cold fact that this wasn't the Perish I knew.

I pushed him hard. "That wasn't fucking necessary!" I snapped. "It's water and he can drink as much–"

A hard backhand threw me off of my feet. Teejay caught me, and with the other two slaves help, they steadiest me.

Perish's cold, icicle eyes stared me down. His face holding a caustic malice that I had only seen on this *Mr. Fallon*. A look that held with it a sanity I had never felt more uncomfortable with.

It was eerie… watching this happen to him, and me only a spectator witnessing his descent from the sidelines. This neurotic genius, my half-crazed scientist with a nervous tick but such a sweet disposition when he was around me.

Now… now? Now I couldn't understand just how someone could change so much, not just mentally but physically. How could a man to who I knew every tick, eye-shift, and movement become such a stranger to me? No longer rubbing his hands, no longer unable to make eye contact. He now stared me down with two slabs of ice for eyes, ones that held a coldness that rivalled Elish's.

I bit my lip, refusing to whimper as my cheek stung. I couldn't stop the tears springing to my eyes though.

"Stop being so fucking weak," Perish snarled. He grabbed the blue cup and threw it at me. "It is a marvel that Reaver deals with you at all. Get up. We have more ground to cover."

"Alright," I whispered. I rose and Danny handed me the cup back. I put it into my satchel and all four of us picked up our pace.

There was acres of forest ahead of us, long, thick black trees that rose several storeys into the air. Thousands of them, some even able to support leaves though they were so thin and dry even the slightest touch broke their papery skin.

Below the expanse of trees was the grey ash of the wasteland, but it was only a thin layer, mostly we walked across bone-dry rocks and small patches of bushes and brush. We had left the last of the snow behind yesterday and now we were deep in the valley, rolling hills on all sides of us and roads that were almost invisible in the grey.

I had never been to an area like this before, with so many trees, most hiding actual bushes that seemed to still be alive. Though none of them held green or even yellow. Everything was charcoal or grey; the trees so close to one another it dazzled you if you looked at it for too long.

I looked at the blue cup in my satchel in almost a solemn reminder that the colour still existed. Sometimes you spent so much time around this monotone slate, you almost could convince yourself you were colourblind.

Perish gave me another withering look. I stared back.

"Walk up front with me," he said, then turned back around.

I closed the distance between us and we walked side by side. Absentmindedly, I rubbed the chafed spot underneath the slave collar he had put on me. I knew where the key was, it was in his blue bag. New Perish was smart though, not the easy-to-manipulate, absent-minded professor I had seen as my friend. There was no amount of sucking up or sweet talking that could get him to take this collar out from under my chin.

Thanks Leo... I don't know what you were trying to find out, or even how you got Perish's O.L.S, but thanks.

Jade is dead because of this.

My eyes started to sting again, and because my mind was cruel I immediately saw Jade laying on the roof. His yellow eyes staring into nothing as the flakes fell gently around him. The snow underneath his body getting redder and redder.

Jade... Jade, I'm sorry. I should have listened to you. I'll never forgive myself. I'll never be able to look Elish in the eye again. How will I tell him that I saw his husband slowly dying underneath my feet?

Fuck. I closed my eyes and tried to blink the tears away.

"When we run out of food, I'm going to kill them one by one." My eyes opened as Perish said this to me, in a cold but matter-of-fact voice. I looked at him just as he turned his own head to look at me. Our eyes met.

He smiled. "Unless you can convince me to keep them alive."

I couldn't keep his gaze. Sometimes I would wait until Perish could make eye contact with me so I knew he was listening, but now...

"What do you want me to do?" I asked calmly back, though I knew the answer. I wondered how much of Old Perish's desires remained in New Perish. He had three slaves behind us though and they wouldn't kick and scream nearly as much as I would.

But that's probably what he wanted.

And what was my reaction to this? What was I going to do?

Keep myself alive... keep myself alive until Reaver found me.

A felt a catch in my throat. I stared at the ashy ground and watched my grey-stained army boots walk one in front of the other.

If I ran... how far would I go before the collar activated?

"You will tell me everything I ask."

My brow furrowed. I was certain he was going to pressure me for sex, or... or something like that.

"Like... like what?" I replied slowly.

Perish looked ahead, a thin, closed mouth smile on his lips. "I will know if you are lying, Killian. You realize that, right?"

I nodded.

"You know who my brother was, right? Do you remember?"

I nodded again. "His name was Sky... he was your identical twin." I stared at Perish and for the first time I realized that, in turn, I was also staring at Sky. The boyfriend, the love of Silas Dekker's life, the immortal who had killed himself.

"Yes, he was my younger brother," Perish responded, his voice taking a turn. I saw a fresh wave of hostility sweep his eyes. "I loved him a lot, until the power went to his head. Then he was not my brother anymore. He changed, just like that piece of shit Silas."

It was such a small piece of brain and yet I had a feeling most of the memories and emotions in that small device contained nothing but rage and malice.

"I loved you, Perry," I whispered. Taking my chance, I held out a hand and rested it on his shoulders. "If you hate Silas so much... why did you take me and run? Why not continue with Elish's campaign?"

My attempt to win favours with Perish were dashed as he jerked his shoulder away from my hand.

"Because I have promises to keep–" Perish's face twisted into a dark scowl. "–and miles to go before I sleep."

I looked at him, not knowing what to make of those words. "Where are you taking me?"

Then another smile and another cold chill pierced my heart.

"I know you love me, Killian... I know you loved who I was and I love you too." He stopped and turned to me. I froze solid and tried not to cringe as he traced a gloved finger down my chin. "You were the first person to treat me like a real human being, even though I was broken. Do you have any idea what you proved to me... when you killed me? That you loved me so much... you would put me out of my suffering?"

But like he had suddenly realized he was showing affection, he recoiled his hand and quickly started walking again. "We need to hurry... we need to hurry..."

I rubbed where he had touched me and gave him a puzzled look. The brain piece had made him sane, it had knitted back together the chaotic and sporadic thoughts that were in his mind. But there was no question that something was still extremely wrong with him.

I shot a quick glance behind me. I saw Danny, Edward, and Teejay struggling to keep up with us. They were staggering behind about ten feet away; I wondered if they could hear us and wondered even more if they thought we were both insane.

"I just... please tell me what you want," I said to Perish. "Maybe I can help."

"I want you, Killian," Perish replied simply. I felt the hair on the back of my neck start to creep up. "It has always been about you... you don't understand that?"

I stared at him dumbfounded. "I love Reaver."

Perish gave me a grave look. He stopped and reached his hand out again to touch me. He lifted my chin up and tilted my head to the side. It brought to me such an underlining feeling of terror it took all of my will not to recoil and run. "Yes, I am sure you do. The clone of King Silas, with strands of my own brother's DNA. How could you not love him?" He smiled. "I am looking forward to seeing the reason he lusts after you. You're such a pretty little thing."

I wrenched myself back from his touch, immediately the blood started to boil underneath my skin. "I would rather die than touch you."

I was expecting it, but I wasn't quick enough to brace myself against his backhand. With a cry, I stumbled backwards, my back slamming up against a rock shelf we were walking underneath.

"You will do as we say, Killian Massey," Perish replied coolly. "Everything we fucking say."

My mouth filled with blood but it was nothing compared to the blood I could feel roaring in my ears. So much anger filled me I thought I was going to burst. "Who the fuck is *we*? Are you that fucked in the head, Fallon? It's just you, Perish."

He barely batted an eyelash at my remark, he only stared at me. Cold and calm.

"I would watch your tone."

I felt Reaver's influence stain the adrenaline rushing through me. I stared Perish down and took a step towards him.

"Fuck you."

He glared back at me, and in that moment I wondered just how many more minutes I had left on this earth.

But to my surprise, he walked past me. I turned around, still feeling the rage ravage my body. My fists were clenched for a fight and my feet pivoted as if expecting the next backhand across the mouth.

Then Perish took out his combat knife and grabbed Edward's hand.

I screamed, but at my sudden outburst Perish's cold smile only grew. In a flash, the knife swept down on Edward's fingers, severing three of them off of his hand.

Blood squirted from the stumps where his fingers used to be. The slave cried out and pulled his hand away, tucking it into the crook of his arm with a whimper. His face was stark and pale as his entire body went into shock.

I realized I had my hands clasped over my mouth. I watched as Perish bent down and picked up one of the fingers. He brought it to his mouth and nipped some of the flesh clinging to the bone, a drip of blood running down his chin.

"Say that again, Killian?" Perish asked calmly. His tongue poked out of his mouth almost like a reptiles to catch the running blood.

The fear began to overshadow my brief moment of bravery, followed by the distinct feeling and realization that I was nothing more than a mouse underneath his boot now. With Edward's stifled cries of pain like a sore on my heart, I swallowed down my anger and said calmly:

"I will do what you… ask of me."

All I can do now is buy time.

We were a small flare of light in the inky darkness that night. Perish had decided to make camp in a farm house he had spotted in the distance.

The slaves were tied up in the living room like dogs. Not even Hopper had treated them this badly. He might've fed them that disgusting Ratmeal and made them walk, but it was nothing compared to what Perish was doing to them.

The reformed scientist was standing by the fire he had started, warming his hands, white and wrinkly from being inside gloves all day. Beside him, roasting on a spit, was several pieces of arian meat sizzling and spitting as they leaked fat into the fire below. Perish had made sure to take meat from the slavers, mostly Hopper who I don't think he liked that much.

I was just glad he had left Jade to die in peace. I couldn't eat Jade – I would rather starve.

"Sit beside me; grab some meat," Perish said as he glanced over to me. "Did you feed the slaves?"

I nodded. The slaves got raw meat, the disgusting Ratmeal was far away in the resort we had left behind. The slaves were happy and thankful to have some real food, though I still couldn't look them in the eye after Perish cut Edward's fingers off. It was my fault, I should've obeyed him.

Reluctantly I sat beside Perish and picked up a skewer of meat. The skewer was an old radio wire we had found inside of this building.

Perish saw me staring at it. "The televisions stopped working..." he said suddenly. "But radio was still working. That was the only way we could get updates, to figure out what was happening. And where the Russians were dropping the bombs."

That's right; of course he was around before the war. A silly realization since I had known he was Silas's age, but hearing him talk about the times before the radiation... there was only one other person left in the world that could tell you about those times.

"Was that because all the electronics got fried?" I asked. The sestic radiation fried the electronics and now every one we scavenged needed to be manually fixed before it could work again.

"That came later." Perish shook his head and started chewing on his piece of meat. "The Government started to control the media. In retaliation, the people rose up and started bombing buildings and causing havoc. They were accusing the Government of padding just how devastating this second Cold War had become and their plans to bomb the Kremlin. In response, the Government shut all media down and government services. And when the war got even worse, the government said *fuck it* and shut down too. After that all we had was radio." Perish looked around the house. "Silas, Sky, and I stayed in a place not too unlike this house for a long time. Until we decided it was time to put a stop to all of this. We decided to try and stop the bombs."

"Did… did the Government make him release the radiation?"

Perish shook his head. "No. What Silas did and what Sky did… it was all them."

"How did they do it? How do you release all that radiation? I mean… it covers the entire world now. It killed or mutated everything that wasn't in Skyfall."

Perish stopped for a moment; his lips downturned.

"Fear," he replied slowly. "Hatred, fear, and just finally… being done."

I remained silent but there was no silence to the eerie feeling that was creeping inside of this room. It seemed to scream inside of my head a thousand cautions as Perish continued to speak. "All of us held the ability to create sestic radiation. Silas knew about his abilities and when he found us… he taught us too."

Then he smiled. "He knew we were real born immortals when he doused us with his sestic radiation. We didn't die from radiation poisoning he knew we were also born immortals. He was thrilled, it had been a long time since he had found other born immortals."

Then Perish chuckled. He looked at me and I saw a glint in his eye. "Did you know you can make a greywaster immune to sestic radiation? It's tricky but with the right dosage at the right time…"

I stared at him confused. In response, he grabbed my hands and stared down at them.

My confusion grew as my Geigerchip suddenly started to hum. At this, he chuckled again before removing his hands from mine. As quickly as it came, the radiation warning stopped buzzing.

Then he carried on, "After the Fallocaust happened, far from Skyfall, Silas and Sky came back. I was looking after the survivors underground, safe from the radiation; I kept them in the sewers. Oh, I remember how different Silas and Sky were. I remember the radiation radiating off of them It almost looked like they were… they were glowing white."

Perish paused and I watched the creases on his face deepen as he dove deeper into his old memories. Memories that I knew must've belonged, at least in part, to Sky.

"I remember it was then that Silas climbed to the top of Alegria, to clear away the radiation surrounding Skyfall. Sky was with him? Yes, I believe Sky was with him. I remember there was a white… there was a white light that I could taste on the air. I ran out of the sewers and looked to see a figure on top of Alegria, drawing in this invisible radiation like he was a black hole drawing in galaxies. It was beautiful. So powerful – Silas is so powerful."

Perish stared at his hands. "Silas died clearing out that radiation but, of course, he came back."

Perish reached a hand up and stroked my face. I was too shocked by his words to do anything other than stare. "Silas was a lot like you back then, Killian. Which is why I love you, and which is why I am going to have to let *him* do this to you. If only because the reward outweighs your pain."

I pulled away. "Who? Who's him?" I didn't understand.

Perish didn't move and I wondered if he wanted to tell me, but I knew he wouldn't.

Sure enough, not an answer, or the beginning of an answer, broke Perish's lips. So I decided to turn the conversation. I didn't know if it was a smart thing to do, to get him to continue talking, but I felt compelled to.

"Why did Silas end the word?" I asked. "We were told Silas ended it because it was already ending… he just… quelled its suffering."

Perish stared at the fire. "We wanted to do good." He glanced around, at the collapsed ceiling above us and the burnt-out studs around the living room we had made shelter in. "And we did. Though no one but Silas and I know how bad the war was. So to everyone else… we're just evil. They didn't see just how bad it got. How destroyed the world was before the Fallocaust."

He smiled thinly. "The world deserved what ended up happening. We just showed it what it had done to us. We showed the world our hurt."

Then Perish held his palms out to the flames and I watched the orange fire lick his pale hand. "I wonder what you'll do to the world, to show it what it had done to you? I wonder what Reaver will do, when he finally realizes what I plan on doing to you."

"You won't do a thing to me or Reaver," I suddenly said. I flinched away as Perish's eyes shot to me.

I swallowed the fear inside of me and against my better judgement I said to him, "I won't let you."

But he only smirked. I cringed as he raised a hand and touched my lips with a brush of his finger. A hungry look in his eyes; one I knew all too well.

"I love you, Killian. I know as time goes on I will stop showing it, but I do. I'll never forget when you proved to me how much you loved me too."

I knew he felt this way, but him putting his own feelings into words always made my gut twist. I knew I had to choose my words carefully, and I knew that the truth was not welcome here.

"I love you, Perry."

I casted a sideways glance at Perish and watched his face, though there was no change not even when he spoke.

"I know, and you don't deserve to suffer in this world so, which is why I need to do this to you. I will end your suffering, Killian, as you tried to end mine." Then his expression changed. I could see his calm face darken and twist, until it became like a black pit, pulling all the light into him and making it dark.

"You don't need to... to do this, Perry," I said in a calm but subdued voice.

Perish's dark face seemed to burn away the fleeting glimpse of love I had seen. And when he opened his mouth to talk to me, it was as if a new person was speaking through his lips. A dark person with a deep, sneering voice that sent a cold chill up my spine.

"You're an idiot, Killian," Perish suddenly growled. "Reaver and Silas belong together. The strands of Sky that he has guarantees that. These born immortals... they belong together. You'll see it as I had to see it. Deities that will always draw each other like magnets. No matter what... they will be attracted to each other. Just like Silas's chimeras will always be attracted to him. Silas will get Reaver, no matter how much it hurts you. If you are smart–"

I jolted away as he leaned in to kiss me, surprised by not only the kiss but his sudden attitude and topic change. But a moment later, Perish grabbed the back of my head and pushed me into his lips. I gasped, and he took full advantage of my open mouth.

I stayed still and let him, I was too scared to move and I didn't know what would happen if I did.

Finally after what seemed like forever, he separated our lips.

"You should give into me quickly. It'll hurt less this way," the dark voice inside of Perish growled. I had an eerie feeling inside of me, a feeling that I wasn't speaking to Perish right now.

I pulled away from him quickly. I couldn't hold back the disgust at the mere suggestion. "Get away from me... what you want isn't going to happen. We're not going to be together, Perish. I love you as a friend but…"

Perish grabbed me, his hand grasping behind my head. He pulled me in for another kiss but this time I shoved him away.

"If you don't let me kiss you, I'll make you sleep with me." Perish's dark tone dropped, plunging into those dangerous octaves I knew all too well. The once tense but quiet atmosphere around us suddenly becoming hostile. "So I would just go with it until I teach you to like it."

I got up, walked out of the living room, and started walking up the stairs.

"Last chance, Killian," the dark voice inside Perish called. I ignored him and continued up the stairs, daring a single tear to come to my eyes. I was stronger than that now.

Then I heard rustling beside me and suddenly a commotion. I paused to listen, and to my horror, I started to hear the slaves screaming.

Panic rushed through me. I flew back down the stairs and burst into the room we had been keeping them in. I cried out as I saw Perish beating Danny with the wooden leg of a kitchen table.

"Stop!" I shrieked. I tried to grab the table leg out of his hand but Perish swung it at me, catching me in the shoulder. I cried out and grabbed my arm, watching as his blazing blue eyes stared me down.

"Okay… okay!" I screamed, tears running down my face. I fell to my knees, clutching my throbbing shoulder. I saw Danny in the corner of my eye groaning, blood covering his face. "I'll let you kiss me just… please stop hurting them."

Perish glared at me; he took a step towards me, the table leg still firm in his grasp. I clenched my teeth as he put the piece of wood to my chin and made me look up at him.

Then Perish knelt down in front of me, and with a soft smile he ran his hand along the welt now forming on my shoulder. In a disturbingly caring way, he soothed the pain with his hand, now iced cold to the touch.

I whimpered. Perish shushed me as his touch became colder and colder, quenching the hot, throbbing hurt from his own hand.

Then he leaned in and kissed me on the lips. His mouth then opened, and I felt his tongue graze mine.

I choked and stifled another sob. Feeling my chest well with shame, I met his tongue with my own. With tears streaming down my face, we kissed deeply, the slaves' eyes staring at us in the darkness.

CHAPTER 39

Reno

THERE WERE LEGIONARIES ON THE WALLS OF ARAS. I think that above everything else disturbed me the most. There shouldn't be legionaries there, it should have been sentries. Sadii, Matt, Jess, Owen…

Reaver.

Instead I saw the black combat armour and the blue uniforms underneath. All of the stone-faced legionary soldiers holding their assault rifles, staring off into the greywastes.

Staring at me.

It was silent when I approached them, the realization as to why that was was obvious. The deacons were all dead or maybe they had escaped into the wasteland, I wasn't sure.

Either way… Aras had changed, and at this point I wondered if I would ever see it back at its past glory.

"What's your business here?" a soldier asked crisply. He looked down his nose at me and I heard the familiar noise of people drawing their guns.

"I used to live here," I said back. "I am Reno Nevada and I want in."

They exchanged glances. I let out a breath, feeling my shoulders slump.

"And what is your business here, Reno Nevada?"

I stared at the chain-link gate, and behind the crisscross wires I could see the structures off in the distance, the ones I used to explore with Reaver. We were only two and four when we first started going into abandoned buildings together. Seeking out anything and everything we could use to entertain ourselves.

My view of the inside of Aras was broken up by another figure. He was standing behind the fence with his arms crossed.

"We asked you your business." This one's voice held more hostility to it than I felt okay with. I swallowed hard and shrugged my shoulders.

"I... I don't know... I just wanted to..."

I had just wanted to go home. I had only wanted to go and knock on Reaver's tank hatch, curl up on his couch with some drugs and Mario Kart so we could hang out like we used to. Feel him relaxed and content, with Killian sitting beside him bugging the cat or strumming on his guitar.

Despair tightened my throat, filling it with that tingly feeling that told me I was seconds away from losing it. I felt like the butt of a cruel joke right now, that the universe was beholding my ironic misery with a right-fucking chuckle.

Here I was in front of Aras... in front of the only home I had ever known, and I had never felt more lonely, more lost... more homesick.

I stared at the empty deacon cages, then at the legionary on the walls. I felt like I was going to crumble with the amount of despair I felt on my shoulders.

"Nothing..." I whispered with a shake of my head. I could never go home, because Aras was no longer my home. It was Silas's now. "I'll... I'll be going now."

I just want to go home. I just want to be in Aras with Reaver and Killian.

Unable to contain it anymore, I let out a stifled sob. I put my hand over my mouth and turned away. I started walking back towards the bunker.

They laughed at me.

"Did he leave his balls behind? Maybe that's what he forgot!"

"What a fucking loser."

Yeah... yeah, I know.

I walked back into the bunker feeling worse than ever. It had been a stupid idea to try and see Aras. But having it so close-by...

Maybe I was hoping it would still feel like home.

I looked behind me only once, to the rocky crags that held my old cabin inside of it, now being used by my older brother Vegas. I didn't even want to try to go there; I knew it would be the same feeling if not worse. Vegas and my siblings shared my humour and need to not take things seriously. They would fucking tease me even more than the legionaries did.

I opened the steel door of the bunker and went inside.

Even the bunker held too many reminders.

Reaver, as I now knew, had been brought to his bunker when he was a newborn and here he lived for the first two years of his life. It was obvious now as I became more familiar with this place – there were bite marks on everything.

I had been stuck in this place for several days now and not having someone to talk to was driving me crazy. I was used to being around people; they're what gave me energy. I wasn't all… deep-thinker-introvert like Reaver was. I needed that constant stimulus or I was just alone with my own thoughts, and my own thoughts were boring. I didn't have much of an imagination; TV was my imagination.

I walked down the narrow hallway to my bedroom. I had completely ignored the left wing of the bunker. It was locked but it hadn't taken long for me to find the key. I peeked in and immediately knew I had made a mistake. That was where they had left Perish and it was nothing but rotten, brown blood stains, and dirty torture tools.

Leo had done that… or Lycos the chimera. That most of all disturbed me. This whole time he played himself off as being a kind mayor when in reality…

I shuddered. They had bloodied scalpels in that room, bone-saws, and bloodstained rope still holding bits of skin… they had done a complete fucking work-up on that crazy guy. Our mayors…

Chimeras were scary.

I flopped down on the bed and put my arms behind my head.

I stared up at the ceiling. I had learned quickly that chimeras were scary people, but I think the reality of it was starting to hit me. Even the kind, sciencey, smart chimera types had that mean streak to them. I had unfortunately seen that in my ex-fiancé. The one chimera I was sure had been different.

The one who had grabbed me and chained me to the bed…

My eyes burned, and because no one was inside this bunker to judge or laugh at me, I clutched my pillow to my chest and cried. I cried so hard it would put Killian to shame.

I was a homeless, fiancéless, friendless idiot. And I was so fucking depressed and lonely – I didn't know what I was going to do. I wanted to go home so bad, but my home didn't exist anymore.

I jumped a mile high when the phone Elish had given me rang. I looked around, my heart banging inside of my chest, and picked it up.

"Hello?" I sniffed. My heart pulled for it to be Reaver on the other end, telling me that they had Killian and Jade.

"Reno, we need your help." My heart sank, it was only stupid Elish. He continued talking even though I was sniffing like an idiot. *"You must find the key for the cell Lycos was keeping Perish—"*

"I already looked," I replied sullenly.

"Does it look like he performed brain surgery?"

How the fuck was I supposed to know? I asked him this and I felt his temperature start to rise. He had no patience with my attitude and I had no patience for any chimeras right now.

"Is there medical tools? Anything that suggests he—"

"Yeah," I replied. "I saw a bone-saw, scalpels; they were torturing him pretty good."

Reaver said something in the background. My heart lurched at his voice, and more tears burned my eyes.

Elish responded to Reaver, *"No, he disabled all cameras and hid all the proof, if that is what he did."*

"What's going on?" I sniffed. "Do you have the boys?"

"No," Elish said sharply back. I clamped my mouth shut and tried to force down the constriction in my neck that told me if I spoke any more words I was going to start sobbing like an idiot.

They hadn't found the boys yet… but why did they want to know if Leo performed brain surgery?

Elish was talking to Reaver; Reaver didn't sound happy at all. I stayed on the phone watching my boots become speckled with tears.

I hated it here, I hated being alone.

"Elish?" I croaked. "Can I take the quad to Tintown? I don't want to stay here."

Why was I asking him permission? Maybe I was used to answering to chimeras now.

"Yes, I insist that you do. Go to Tintown and keep the phone charged and ready. We are tracking Jade and Killian now."

Did that mean they found signs of them? I knew better than to ask.

"We'll keep in touch. Don't travel to any location that doesn't have cell reception and don't take the blocker off of the phone either," Elish

said. And with a quick goodbye he was gone.

And here I was alone again, but at least there was some light at the end of the tunnel, no matter how faint. I could get out of this bunker that I felt was slowly squeezing the life out of me.

So I was a vagabond, but at least I had a lot of money and a quad, so maybe in a way I had just emotionally freed myself. If there was one thing I had going for me it was that being in the company of chimeras gave me a lot of fringe benefits. Though black cards were as good as worthless in the greywastes, I had a couple thousand dollars stuffed on my person.

There were no teary goodbyes to the bunker, or to Aras. As I rolled the quad out of those steel doors, I realized I had been saying a slow goodbye to my home for the last couple of months.

I rolled into Tintown three days later. A town twice the size of Aras, with large walls made up of concrete blocks, rusted sheets of metal, and old cars. There were no deacons, but like Aras they had sentries, dozens of them. Standing like crows behind the rust-streaked walls, all of them wearing thick wool jackets and ear-flapped hats.

"Hey, mate! I haven't seen you around before." I smiled to myself as the cheerful boy looked down at me with a friendly grin. It was such a contrasting response to what I got in Aras I felt my spirits get lifted. This might not be home, but they had greywasters on the walls and right now that meant the world to me.

"My name is Reno, formerly from Aras," I called up to him. "That place has gone to shit and I need a town to bunk in for a little while and a place to stash my quad."

The young man nodded; his eyes squinted as he looked up at the grey sun. "Yeah, we have been getting a few of them since legion law came into play there. Come on in and make yourself at home. Paul stashes the vehicles for travellers, just leave it where it is and you can collect and pay once you leave. Half a buck a night, is that alright?"

I nodded. We had similar arrangements in Aras. "Sounds good, bro."

The sound of rusted metal scraping together could be heard. In front of me two flat pieces of sheet metal reinforced with a bolted on chain-link fence scraped open. It was like the rusty old gates of heaven opening up for me, though anything that wasn't that bunker was heaven.

I walked through the doors and was immediately greeted by the smell of smoke, rotting meat, and dirt. There was nothing more greywaster than that; it put another smile to my face. Skyfall smelled like fucking flowers and pretention, and I was more than happy to get back to my roots.

I gave the gate keeper an appreciative wave and walked into Tintown, deliberately taking in deep breaths as I found the main street. It was a single road with concrete medians that acted as fences. Abandoned structures stood in their dilapidated state behind these medians, most with collapsed roofs and sunken in faces. It looked like the occupied, repaired houses weren't for another half-block down the road.

I walked past a couple of kids, two girls, swinging their feet as they perched on these barriers. Both of them giggling and whispering things to each other. I had twin sisters so I knew annoying girls well, they were always whispering and laughing at shit.

"Hey... where is a good bar?" I asked one of them.

They looked at me and laughed some more, before one of them jumped off and pointed ahead of us. "Dust Devil... it's down there," she said. She wasn't scared of strangers at all, the kids here were either little morons or perhaps it was just that safe here. "And there's Tazzy's way, way back near the east entrance."

"Thanks." I dug into my pocket and found one of the chocolate bars I had stashed in my jacket. I gave it to her, and with a girlish squeal, I made two best friends. They jumped up and down screaming in each other's faces. With a shake of my head, I continued on my way. My younger brother and the sisters were all older now. Though I had a couple nieces and nephews somewhere out there but we didn't get a chance to visit that much anymore.

I checked out some of the people walking up and down the streets, most dust-covered greywasters with a few uniformed officers in the mix. No legionaries to be seen though which put me at ease.

Tintown wasn't a block; it was a free town so some of them could be a little rough around the edges. I had never been to this town but I had been to Anvil visiting relatives and so far I was impressed. The structures here were mostly one or two storeys with the market district contained in a strip mall separated by a four-lane road with street lights still standing. I could even see separate buildings, not made from refurbished buildings but jerry-rigged together with walls from houses and slabs of concrete.

One of them looked like an ammo store. I might visit that place just to stock up, though I liked it here you never know when you have to piss off and run.

I walked into the bar, busy and noisy with a billow of smoke above everyone's heads. The ceilings were stained with brown and the walls held the drippy run offs from the remains of the rainy season. There were pictures on the walls too, half-naked men and women showing off bikinis and tight-fitting underwear, and framed pictures of landscapes and old world people wearing ruffles and powdered wigs.

I weaved through the bar tables, most holding drunk men and women smoking cigarettes over half-full bottles of beer, and found a place in a corner to sit down. I chose one underneath a poster of a twink-looking boy with a sheepish grin, tugging on his grey underwear. Reminded me of Tinky.

I think I missed a golden opportunity not calling him Twinkerbell. I wish I had thought of that.

A guy my age realized I was there a few minutes later. Wearing a black apron and too much gel in his hair, he gave me a smile. "What can I get you?"

He looked kind of cute; I decided to turn on my charm. "One beer and a shot of whisky for starters. It's been a long trip." I winked at him. Even though I technically just broken off an engagement I was really too miserable with my life right now to care. Flirting would make me feel better. "When are you getting off?"

I watched his face, either he was going to behold me in absolute horror because I had the wrong thing between my legs, look at me like I was an ugly cockroach unworthy of his company… or he was going to smile.

And he smiled and shook his head. "My family owns this bar; they don't pay me so I can sit down when I want. As long as you don't slip anything in my drink that is."

I pursed my lips and slammed my hand down on the table which made him laugh. He shook his head and disappeared into the cigarette smoke. As I waited for him to come back I lit myself a cigarette and brought out a chocolate bar. It was warm in this bar and with my body heat they would melt soon, even with it still being winter.

The kid came back with my order plus a bottle of beer for himself. He sat down and looked me up and down. "You're a Skyfaller, aren't you?"

I stared at him helplessly, but I gave him a bit of leave because my hair was still mostly silver and my clothing, though now sweaty and dusty, were still good quality.

I gave out a loud sigh and cracked the seal on my beer bottle.

"I'm from Aras, but I… got shot and I had a Skyfaller friend who had good docs. I then…" I paused; I didn't want to say escaped. "Well, I left my fiancé and I missed home and… Aras isn't quite my home anymore."

His eyes widened as I lifted up my shirt so I could show him my war wound. "Holy shit… we heard what happened in Aras too. King Silas shot the mayors and it's under legion law now. Are you going to settle here? You don't have any family?"

I have tons of family, just my biological family is doing their own thing and my real family is off being heroes.

I shook my head. "I'll be staying here until I heal up, I guess. This seems like a friendly town. Aras was too far off to be a drop-in town like this place. You guys get a lot of travellers?"

Since Aras was so far away from the other greywaster towns, and too close to the blacksands, we didn't really get people dropping in. If you came to Aras you usually stuck around or were looking to settle.

The kid nodded and brushed his hair away from his eyes. Sandy-coloured hair on a triangle shaped face, gaunt from missing too many meals, like a proper greywaster.

"Yeah, most of our money is from travellers," he said. "The locals have their own taverns and the travellers or merchants have separate ones. You came to the right one."

I took another drink, the cold beer doing a number on my mood. There really wasn't many things alcohol couldn't cure, at least temporarily. "Yeah, some little girls pointed me in the right direction."

This made him laugh; he had a cute laugh. "That's Tiara and Misty, my cousins. Most of the shops here are run by some cousin, or aunt, or uncle. We're the Saint James family." He held out his hand. "And my name is Jesse."

I snorted and with that I got my first narrowed eye look. I waved a hand at him. "Sorry. Jesse Saint James sounds like a comic book hero or something. Are you a super hero, Jesse?"

"Far from it!" Jesse Saint James tipped back in his chair and waved one of the lady bartenders over. "Get us some meat chips, Maya."

Oh, meat chips. Ground up rat meat mixed together with salt and flour, pounded and cut into chips and then deep fried. In Skyfall we had potato fries but here we made due. I wouldn't say I missed greywaster food but the nostalgia was still there.

And he was being friendly which I appreciated. I had a knack for picking out the more cordial of greywasters, and if they were cute, well that was just a bonus. Anything to try and snap me out of this slump.

Maya came back with a plate full of brown chips which I shared happily with Jesse. I also insisting on paying for it but he haggled me down to me just buying him his beer.

Over the next couple of hours hanging out with him I learned that indeed a couple of our residents had abandoned Aras in favour for a free town. None of them were my friends though which I was almost glad for. I didn't want to have to tell Sadii, Matt, or any of the other sentries that Reaver was a mutant clone fugitive, and we couldn't find Killian.

Which was another thing that I learned. The Legion had been coming in and out of Tintown and the smaller surrounding communities looking for Reaver Dekker, Perish Dekker, and Killian Massey. Which I obviously knew nothing about. They had a rather big bounty on their heads, over ten thousand dollars. Though that was pocket change to my ex-fiancé.

By the time the bar was closing we were too drunk to do much besides tell dirty jokes and laugh at the other drunk patrons.

"Where are you sleeping tonight?" Jesse leaned up against the closed bar; his frozen breath falling from his mouth in short puffs of smoke.

I shrugged. "Got a hotel somewhere? Probably there."

"I'll walk you there, my Grandpa runs the place," Jesse said with a smile. He took a step and stumbled. I had no motor-skills to help him though, so I concentrated on keeping myself up.

We stumbled our drunken asses over the cracked pavement, leading down to a tall three-storey hotel. One of the tallest buildings in Tintown, it towered over the other smaller structures.

A small bluelamp hung its welcome in front of the grey wood building. Each sun bleached piece of paneling a different combination of grey than the one next to it. It looked solid and well repaired though, so I trusted it.

I walked in. Grampa Saint James looked up from a worn-out green chair facing a tube TV and rolled his eyes. "Who did you find, Jesse?"

"This is Reno. We're friends now." Jesse smacked me roughly on the back. "He needs a hotel room and I'm showing him where it is."

Grampa didn't look impressed. He slowly got up on arthritic knees and grabbed a cane. "He looks like he has money. Five bucks a night, twenty a week and seventy-five a month, comes with cleaning services and delivery but no meals."

Sounded close enough to Deider's rates so I nodded and we shook on it. Then I reached my hand into my jacket and brought out the money. I might have paid him for a whole month, I wasn't sure; I just gave him a bunch of money and stumbled upstairs with Jesse.

I walked into the modest hotel room, with full intention to bid Jesse goodbye, but it looked like I was a man who didn't take flirting well.

What I thought had just been two guys getting drunk and chatting, turned into something else quickly as Jesse's lips locked with mine.

My drunk mind immediately submitted, my own loneliness getting the better of me. It had been a long time since I had even a friend to talk to, longer since I'd had consensual sex. My body was craving attention and my mind human affection.

So he pushed me onto the bed and our clothes were soon lost. I looked upon that non-chimera body, with its beautiful flaws and drank him in. He was a slender thing, with sporadic hair on his chest and a normal-sized uncut dick. As stupid as it was, I had never had normal, the first dick I had sucked was Reaver, and the first consensual fuck I'd had was King Silas. They both had cut, beautifully flawless cocks.

I kissed Jesse and started to rub his dick, pulling the foreskin before I retracted it. Jesse moaned and started sucking on my neck, sending off sparks inside of my chest. He started to kiss lower, sucking on my left nipple before he got to my navel, and then finally I felt the soft brush of his hair against my dick.

This... I missed this, I needed this. But as much as I hated it, nothing would ever compare to the sex I'd had with 'Asher'. Though maybe if I had gotten the chance to sleep with Garrett...

Garrett... I flinched and almost pulled back. I had left my engagement ring behind; I had essentially called off our engagement. If he wasn't willing to let me rescue my best friend...

"Ah – damn," I groaned. I separated my knees as Jesse's tongue tested and licked my head, then gasped as he breathed a stream of warm air onto it. Soon it was fully in his mouth, and in my drunken, horny, and lonely state, my ex-fiancé faded into the background.

I was a dog and I had never pretended to be anyone different.

My arm flopped over my face, the alcohol permeating my system making my arms heavy. At least I could get hard though.

I closed my eyes and let him take me in, and after that the events of the evening blended into a drunken, hazy blur. At one point I had the kid on his hands and knees, his moans matching my thrusts as I fucked him. Then sometime after that my mind recalled him riding me; his hand rapidly stroking himself off.

The next morning I woke up with a pounding headache, covered in stickiness that I could only assume was cum. I stumbled to the shower before collapsing back into bed. The kid was gone, maybe he hadn't gotten hit with the hangover bug like us old men got. I never really asked his age but I pegged him at about eighteen or nineteen.

I first checked to make sure I hadn't been robbed. And when I made sure all of my money, my remote phone, and my weapons were still there, I decided he must've had to go to work. So I stayed in bed and felt sorry for myself and my shitty hangover.

While I was nursing my headache, I went over the events of last night and what they possibly could mean. I probably could date that little knucklehead if I wanted to.

I didn't know if I wanted to though, him being a rebound guy and all of that emotional crap. If I was going to make him my boyfriend then it was only for the sole reason that Garrett had fucking hurt me.

Okay, I knew I was being unreasonable, and I knew maybe I shouldn't be so mad at him. But when it came to Reaver and Killian's safety…

Garrett had restrained me and kept me captive just like the Crimstones had. Except he did it in our own apartment, and chained me with his own hands to prevent me from helping with Reaver's rescue.

I sighed, wondering if I had just made a huge mistake. But what did it matter? I was only here to heal, and once I was, I was joining Reaver again. Eventually joining Reaver had been my end goal from the start.

If Garrett had wanted me to marry him, if he had really loved me… he would have let me get Reaver. Hell, he would have helped me.

And with that in my head, I crawled out of bed in the early evening. I had started to feel a bit better, or well, I hadn't thrown up in a couple hours.

I got dressed and deliberately made myself look good, just to, you know, impress Jesse a bit. Since I was in town and not in the greywastes I could dress a bit better, though 'dress a bit better' to the greywastes was a clean'ish t-shirt and pants that didn't smell like death.

When I decided I was hot shit I strolled out of the hotel into the cold winter night. I couldn't help having a small smile on my lips as I walked down the uneven and broken pavement towards the Dust Devil. I guess getting laid did that to a man, it had been a *really* long time.

And I had someone to talk to... finally. A boy I could dote on and love, what Reaver had had for the last seven months, or how many months it was in total since they hadn't seen each other in a while.

I sucked on a cigarette as I passed the meandering greywasters, walking back home or perhaps to a restaurant for some food. Everyone still seemed so relaxed and at ease, I really could call this place home.

I could hear the faint music and the buzzing of bar patrons as I stepped onto the deck of the bar. I walked in, greeted once again with the smell of stale smoke, and found my usual spot underneath the Tinky poster.

Maya was waiting tables. I called her over and ordered a drink.

"Is Jesse around?" I asked.

She smiled at me, but my brow furrowed as I saw a bit of annoyance on her face. I wondered if he had told everyone we had slept together after knowing each other for about four hours. "No, he's... made a trip to Springton with his father. He won't be back for a week at least."

Disappointment washed over me. He hadn't mentioned that last night. "Oh, alright," I said. I gave her a nonchalant shrug to keep up appearances but I was really put out by that news. "Just bring me a beer and a can of something, I guess."

Well... that was unexpected. I didn't think last night had gone badly, but maybe he was the type of kid to feel ashamed after. I was the one who just broke off an engagement to a chimera mogul, if anyone should be feeling ashamed it was me.

So much for not being lonely, I had been so close too.

Maya came back with my food and I ate in lonely silence. A few other good-looking guys came in and were milling around but I wasn't interested. I wasn't a slut or anything like that; I had never been looking for the physical side... I was just fucking lonely.

People came and people went. Even a few little kids came bounding in to pick up wrapped packages full of food orders. I sat and watched them; no one bothered me and I didn't bother them.

Finally I had enough. I paid for my food and went back out into the night. But before I went back to the hotel room to cry a bit, I decided to relieve myself in the alleyway beside some trash cans.

But just as I was giving it a shake and tucking it back in, I saw none other than Jesse. He was holding a trash bag and wearing his black apron, walking towards the dumpster.

When Jesse saw me he was so shocked he dropped the trash bag.

"What the fuck?" I said, feeling my temper get tweaked. "She was lying? Why the hell are you avoiding me?"

Jesse stared at me, I saw his face pale. "Don't make a big deal about it… just, ah, I don't want… I don't want you talking to me anymore."

"What!?" I threw my hands up in the air, feeling more than just a bit offended. "Why? I wasn't that fucking bad. I was drunk!"

Jesse took a step away from me, shaking his head back and forth. His eyes were wide, he looked under an incredible amount of stress. "Just stay away from me, alright? My family runs this town and I've already told them—"

"Are you fucking kidding me?" My anger was pressing its toxic weight down on my brain, and the rejection was filling my heart with a bitter feeling. I was getting pissed. "I didn't fucking do anything to you, asshole. You were all over *me* first; my dick was in *your* mouth, fuckhead."

Jesse's lip tightened. He looked behind him, and then oddly, above him. Then, without another word, he turned to walk back into the white back door.

I stalked up to him and grabbed his shoulder. I pulled him back towards me before shoving him away. "In my town we don't fucking play mind games," I snapped. "If I find out you stole something from me, or did something to me, I will fuck you up, greywaster. Do you understand me?"

Jesse's eyes were wide and I could see him trembling in front of the door. The rage was rushing through me though and I couldn't contain it. I was too hurt, too tired of this shit, and too lonely. I had been being rejected by men all my life, and I had just left the only one who hadn't.

So I pushed Jesse again opened my mouth to give him more hell… when to my grim surprise, the kitchen cooks appeared.

"Get inside, Jesse," a tough looking darker-skinned one snapped.

"This doesn't involve you." I turned to him and gave him a push as well. The anger, ripping up my body like lightning, was filling me with a need to fight. He reciprocated and soon three more were behind him.

And though I was a greywaster, whose time with the Crimstones had toughened me up even more, I was still no match for four greywasters. I got a couple good swings in, but by the time they left me a crumpled heap in the alley, I was spitting out tooth fragments.

Feeling lower than dirt, I staggered back to the hotel. Thankfully Grandpa didn't give a shit or hadn't heard the news that I was a pariah. He didn't even look up from his god damn television set.

All my fleeing hopes that I might have someone to keep me company disappeared like the shredded wisdom tooth now a sharp jagged shard in the back of my mouth. I was alone once again, and judging that I was now in the Saint James family's bad books, I would probably have to leave town.

I ran my tongue over my tooth and made plans to buy some pliers tomorrow. Then I gingerly dressed the injuries I had on my face and body.

I glanced at my remote phone and wished I could call Elish to tell him I was fucking done healing now, but I knew he had more important shit to do. Instead I curled back up in my bed wishing I were dead. Confused, shunned, and more lonely than I had been in the bunker.

I hated my life, I really did.

CHAPTER 40

Jade

THIS PLACE... THE SMELL ALONE WAS ENOUGH TO make you want to vomit in your mouth. Though after a while your nose just committed suicide and you smelled nothing but your own slowly decaying body. That was what it was like here; it smelled bad and it was dark. But to my surprise they were smart enough to know how to start a fire. Not even by matches or lighters either, they could make fire by the tree limbs if they needed to. That perplexed me most of all.

I was in the back of their den, or what they called a den. In reality, this place had once been a motel, with a gas station on the other side of a parking lot and an old vitamin store behind it. It had been called Cobbleton Motel, I had seen it as they were helping me walk inside.

Yeah... helping me...

I glanced up as the leader, who I called Big Shot in my head, leaned down and offered me a large chunk of calve to eat. Raw. Even though they had fire they ate everything raw. I didn't complain... I had been eating raw meat for a long time now.

To say thank you, they bowed their heads and made a coughing, hissing noise like *kah!* I had learned that the first day I was here. So to be the polite person I was, I said thank you. As was custom, he put a hand on my head to show he recognized my gesture, then walked back into the conference room that was his own personal quarters and left me to eat in peace.

I was weak and every time my mind started to succumb to sleep I fully expected not to wake up. Sometimes I was disappointed when I did, but I was starting to get used to being here. It was an improvement to where I had been, I guess. Though the ravers' health plan wasn't that great, the back of my head had been healing and hadn't gotten infected. My arm was rather nasty as well, but by some stroke of luck it remained infection-free.

Even though ravers still got injured like a normal human, they didn't feel pain; they also healed slowly, if at all. Infection as well wasn't a problem for them, the radiation had soaked so much into their bodies it killed the infection-causing bacteria.

But I wasn't a raver, and I could see the raised pink scar of my Geigerchip. I could get infections but that hadn't happened. I was healing, and as they brought me offerings of raw meat, I was slowly gaining my strength. No matter how dangerous these creatures were, they had saved my life.

I started eating my chunk of meat, no longer caring for any manners I may or may not have had in my previous life. I chewed and thrashed my head back and forth like an animal to rip and devour every sweet bit of flesh, savouring the fact that I was finally eating decent meat.

While I was eating, I heard the floorboards creak and bend. I looked up and saw a younger woman, her stringy hair matted against her radiation-browned skin, beside her was a boy probably her kid. He was holding a red and yellow toy car in his hand.

It was strange to not be scared of them, but I had learned their movements and ways of communicating quickly. I watched her out of the corner of my eye as she stood with her kid in the doorway, their ragged, tight breaths filling the silent room I now called my own. I knew I wasn't to address her or acknowledge her or the kid's presence until she made herself known.

Sometimes it took half an hour, I think it was their mental capacities that made them slow to do certain things. Running and eating things alive were instincts, and something they did fast and quickly, but communicating was different. It took some of the slower ones a long time to do things.

And she seemed to be one of the slower ones; Big Shot was the smartest which made sense considering he was the leader. Or one of the leaders. I think they thought I was a Big Shot too now.

I guess I was the smartest? Or at least the one with the magic whistle.

Sure enough, almost a half an hour later the female *ksst* at her son.

The boy took the red and yellow truck and placed it beside my crossed legs. I lowered my head and *kah'd* at him, and as was custom, he put his hand on my head and walked back up to his mother.

Then they both left the room. I picked up my offering and examined it. It had a few teeth marks on it but what attracted them most was the bright colours. They were enamoured with things that were colourful, I was getting a pretty high honour receiving this truck.

I put it beside me and continued eating, filling my queasy stomach up with meat. After I was finished, I laid my head on a dirty, chewed-on pillow with the synthetic stuffing half-missing and went to take a nap. I slept a lot.

Sometime the next morning I was woken up by another agonizing headache. I buried my head into the fetid-smelling pillow and screamed my pain into it. The pounding and all-consuming pain always seemed centered right behind my left eye, and without meaning to, I always found myself pressing down on the eyeball and hitting it to try and quell the pressure.

Screaming and thrashing was nothing new to the ravers so they left me alone, though usually by the time the mind-shattering pain was done a bunch of them were watching me through the doorway. I could hear their quickening, rasping breaths, like they were wheezing rather than breathing.

I don't know where these headaches were coming from, all I knew was that they were getting worse. When I raised my head this time blood was pouring from my nose and mouth, leaving it glistening against the cotton stuffing of the pillow.

I needed some fresh air. I got up and stretched my legs, relieved that I was getting the strength back in them.

The ravers cleared to the side as I stepped out of the doorway, and bowed their heads saying the *kah* sound as if pleased I was doing something other than sleeping, eating their food, and screaming. I zipped up my jacket and stuffed my chapped and raw hands into my pocket and walked outside.

I was greeted by severed heads put on sharpened sticks and pieces of rusty rebar. There were over two dozen of them, all in various states of decay. Some of them nothing but brown and green skulls, infested with black flies and their writhing larva.

These were greywaster skulls, since I don't think ravers killed each other unless they were sick or mortally wounded.

I walked past the rows of skewered skulls, my boots scraping against bare ground. The snow had almost entirely melted now. Though where the snow had once been, greasy, brown-streaked bones took its place, and various shreds of clothes or personal items.

Big Shot saw me and bowed his head, I put my hand on his head and walked past him towards the fire. I sat down on a plastic patio chair and tried to warm my hands, taking big inhales of cold winter air.

When they had first brought me here I was too sick to look at where I was, but really there wasn't much to see. I was in the greywastes, with rocky hills and black trees around us, the highway no longer in sight. There was only a double-lane road behind the gas station and past that was just more trees and greywastes. I really had no idea where I was.

That being said, even if there was a big map with a sticker saying YOU ARE HERE! I still wouldn't know where the fuck I was.

Or *who* the fuck I was.

Several ravers were around the fire, all of them dressed in shabby winter clothing. Ravers never changed their outfits, they just put on different articles of clothing until they were warm. And once the clothes fell off of them, from rotting away or ripping off, they just added more. They also loved their body part trophies: scalp headdresses, severed ear necklaces; if you could cut it off and make it into something to put on your body, you did it.

I watched Big Shot walk out of the camp, and as my eyes travelled to see what he was doing, I saw that he was walking towards another raver. I had seen this one, an actual dark-skinned one, not just dark-skinned from the radiation. He had a necklace made out of human teeth and his earrings looked like shrivelled, old eyeballs. That raver was a hardass, that you could tell from looks alone.

The black-skinned raver tapped his hand on Big Shot's shoulder and pointed. Then he grinned, showing off teeth that looked like they had been chiselled down. Behind him, two more ravers appeared, a female with her lips and cheeks ripped off, making her look like a walking skeleton, and a young male that was missing his scalp and ears.

Big Shot spoke with all of them before he nodded; one of the only human ways of communicating they seemed to have. He turned away from the small party and suddenly let out a bloodcurdling scream.

I jumped a mile high and almost screamed myself. I put my hand against my heart and took a deep breath. I'd been used to hearing their screaming now, but this one was different.

This was the one I heard when they had found fresh human prey.

Sure enough, ravers starting spilling out of the motel rooms. I could hear doors slamming and the heavy pounding of footsteps. Around me the ravers of all ages and genders started running towards Big Shot.

My chest stirred as I saw the mob, and inside of me I felt the first spurts of adrenaline. Before I could stop myself I rose, the inner feral that I think had always been a part of me winning the fight against my rational mind.

I ran with the ravers and soon I was side by side with Big Shot. He acknowledged my joining him with a *kah!* and I returned the gesture. Together the two leaders ran ahead of the group of ravers they controlled, sprinting past the dilapidated gas station and into the greywastes in front of them.

Big Shot screamed his hair-raising scream, and not able to help myself, I screamed too. Fully aware that I was slowly losing myself to the nature of a raver, but in truth, I had lost myself weeks ago. I didn't know who I was, where I was from, or why I looked different from the humans I had eaten or dreamed of. My eyes were yellow, my teeth half metal and sharp, and my endurance strong. Perhaps I was a raver, or maybe I was their leader and I had just found my way home.

Either way, I think at this point I embraced it. Because I had nothing else in the world, my only other ally was the dog who had made friends easily with the ravers. These mad men accepted who I was, fed me and gave me warmth. So I think now I was their king. The King of the Ravers…

Why not.

The greywastes became a blur around me, and the wind blasted against my face as I ran with the group, screaming and howling as I kept pace with these irradiated humans.

I glanced behind my shoulder once and felt a swell of adrenaline when I saw over forty of them behind me. This was a large raver group and I was in control of them, all of them.

The black-skinned one sprinted ahead of us before glancing at Big Shot. He threw both of his arms ahead of him and screamed. A signal that we were close.

The horde behind me became alive with activity, like a thousand tightly woven wires now frayed and alive. To my surprise, I could see the electricity surrounding them, swirling around the group like ribbons, radiating off of them like heat waves on a hot roof. Some of them had colours but most of held nothing but monotone madness.

I was pleased to see Deek running pace with me, his red tongue lolling out in excitement and his amber eyes fixed forward. He made friends with whoever I was comfortable with and I was glad. I didn't want him to kill my people and I didn't want them to hurt him either.

A steep incline was ahead of us. I watched as Big Shot and the dark-skinned one leapt off of the ridge without care as to what was below them. Dismissing all reason and instincts of self-preservation, I jumped off of the ridge too, landing on my feet onto a gravel embankment which I skidded down.

Rocks sprayed up on both sides of me as my right foot pivoted to steady my body. I raised my arms out and slid down the gravel with the two top ravers ahead of me. I landed cleanly and continued to run, my ears picking up the sound of disturbed gravel and more shrieking as the forty behind me leapt off of the ridge. As a last thought, I reached into my pants pocket and grabbed the claw rings I had found when I woke. It looked like I was missing one but I slipped the remaining ones onto my fingers and felt the metal clink around in my pockets.

Then I saw them.

We all screamed and picked up our speed as we saw the greywasters in the distance, making camp by a large bonfire. There must have been at least half a dozen of them, all jerking their heads up at us. I could see the whites of their eyes and their mouths drop open in shock. There were men, women, children.

There were meat.

Fresh meat.

What was I letting happen to me?

Bloodthirst rushed through my body like my own brain had caught fire. My mind telling me to stop, but it was speaking a language I no longer spoke or needed. Instead of heeding its distant pleas to remember myself...

I am Jade.

... it fell onto ears that had been beaten deaf weeks ago.

The group shouted at each other; a child screamed and a woman ran with it. I clenched my claw rings in my hands and pushed forward, ravers running ahead of me with their arms outstretched, anticipating the first bite of living flesh.

We ran down another smaller hill, jumping over a fallen black tree. I could see their cart tracks, one of the wheels was broken. They had been stranded here, that would be their last mistake.

Big Shot got to them first. As the men and women drew their guns, shouting hysterically and stumbling to get their ammo, he jumped onto the cart and used it as a platform. He leapt off of it and landed on a middle-aged woman and pinned her down. Immediately Big Shot clawed her face with the sharpened bone that were his fingers, before sinking his teeth into her flesh.

A lightning crack of gunfire sounded, I ignored it, fearing nothing. I saw a flicker of grey out of the corner of my eye and watched as Deek lunged at an older man holding a gun. The man got one badly aimed bullet off before he fell to the ground.

I jumped on him.

"No... no! Please!" His voice was a high octave of desperation, breaking under the weight my body pressed into his chest. I leaned down and opened my mouth and sank it into his windpipe.

Like Siris in Stadium.

Like Loni...

Shadow Killer.

I paused. I pulled away for a second, wondering who those names belonged to, and whose faces I was seeing. I saw a man in his middle twenties, with short black hair and a square face. He had purple eyes that gleamed with bloodlust... he was... surrounded by cheering–

I gasped from surprise as the man threw me off of him, but a split second later Deek was on him. The dog's head thrashed back and forth on the man's neck, opening him up and spilling his blood onto the grey ground.

"Deek, that was mine!" I protested. The dog only gave me a tongue-lolling look before he ate the chunk of skin. Then, forgetting the recall I had just had, I rose and turned towards another gunshot.

Another man was holding his smoking gun, two ravers dead beside him. He was looking around with wild eyes, shouting something I couldn't understand.

I sprung up like a cat and pounced on him. This time there was no hesitation. I swung my clenched fists and shredded his back with my metal claws, splitting the thin, white skin like an overstuffed sack, spilling more blood onto the greywastes.

The smell was intoxicating. I allowed the bloodlust to overtake me, and on its command, I jumped onto the man's back and sunk my teeth into the side of his neck. Then I drew my hand to his neck and opened his throat with a quick slash of my claws.

I became aware of the other ravers around me as he dropped to the ground. One... two... three, they all swarmed around the wounds I had created and started eating him as he thrashed and spasmed. I spit and snapped at a younger raver who was getting too close to my area and proceeded to eat from one of the wounds I had created.

The air was saturated with the smell of blood, blood and the distinct taste of people who had died in agony. I feasted in ecstasy and let myself be taken by the intense, electrified air around me, feeling myself more a part of this hive than I did the world itself.

I consumed the sweet meat, the carcass moving and shifting as the ravers around me devoured it. We were like a pack of lions, our faces bathed in blood and our stomachs full of food that, this morning, had been a part of a human being.

When I had eaten enough I rose and looked around at my comrades. Those who had eaten their fill had started hovering around the bonfire, their bodies coated in a wash of blood. I noticed a few of them had fresh body parts hanging from their belts and wrists now.

I looked down and decided to commemorate my descent into madness. I grabbed onto a still intact ear and pulled it off, then the next one. I held them in my hands and pulled off what remained of the man's shirt.

I stood beside the bonfire with the others and started to make myself a necklace.

"*Kah!*" Big Shot said, praising me on my choice of jewellery. He was chewing a hole through a hand which I guessed was going to be added to his belt.

I put my hand on his head before wandering towards the cart. I tied my necklace around my neck and began to root through the supplies to see if there was anything I could use.

I found some brightly-coloured kids' toys. I set those aside for the children or perhaps an offering to Big Shot, then I spotted some blankets and grabbed those for my nest back in the motel.

The young man with his scalp and ears missing came into the corner of my vision. I offered him a pacifier which he took and started chewing on.

My eyes narrowed when I found a gun. I had wished on many occasions when Deek was pulling me that I had a gun to keep me safe... I might not need one now but I wanted it anyway.

I put the strap over my chest and grabbed a Ziploc of candy. Ravers probably didn't eat candy so I shovelled that into my already stuffed stomach.

Then I found something interesting.

I unfolded what looked like a hand-drawn map. There was a line scrawled in crayon that seemed to have originated from a town called Mariano. The pink crayon led a trail from Mariano to the highway, but veered off an inch or so into the greywastes.

They must have been keeping track of their travels. I glanced around at the other locations.

The nearest one to where we were was called Velstoke. So near...

I glanced up towards the direction I thought the town was.

I walked over to Big Shot, stepping over a half-consumed raver body, one of the fucks who didn't make it. I showed him the map and pointed to Velstoke.

"Town," I said to him.

Big Shot stared at me, his yellow clouded eyes more alive than any of the other ravers but still only holding half the intelligence of an arian. He took the map from me and traced his finger over the pink crayon. He breathed out of his nose at it, impressed by the colour was my guess.

"*Kah*," I said back and folded the map into my pocket. I heard a scraping noise behind me and watched the other ravers start to pick up the deads' body parts. They were swinging the half-chewed torsos, legs, and arms over their shoulders to carry back to camp. I did the same and even made Deek help; he ate more than any of us.

We made a big fire that night, and to celebrate our successful hunting mission, we foraged for pointy sticks and made six new spike-heads. We replaced a few of the more green ones and tossed their skulls to some of the younger children to use as balls. They liked to kick them around or use them as bowling balls.

Evening found me finally taking off the soiled and smelly bandage I had wrapped around my head. I threw it into my garbage corner and gingerly ran my hand over the scab. It was a rough and thick clot that was itching like all hell, but I didn't touch it. It would fall off in time. At least I knew I was out of the woods now. My arm and head were healing and my endurance was quickly advancing to where it had used to be. Or where I had assumed it had been.

I was warming my hands by the fire with the others when Big Shot walked up to me. As he often did he got down on one knee and I put my hand on his head. When Big Shot got back up I saw he was holding a belt in his hand; he thrusted it into mine.

I put it on, and as I looped it through my jeans, he started tying items on it. A severed hand impaled by scratchy, brown rope, a string which held an eye and an ear sewed together, and oddly, what looked like an old McDonalds toy which was bright blue and pink.

When he was finished I thanked him and admired my offering. It was putrid, it was going to smell like high heaven in the next couple days and it was grisly, but I was too deep into this now.

I might only know my name, I might not know who I was or where I had come from… but one thing was for sure.

I was a raver.

King of the Ravers.

Tonight I dreamed of that man again.

The one that always made me wake up feeling anxious and sad.

I didn't know who he was, or why his face made me stop in my tracks. I just knew whenever I saw him I felt like running towards him like a child runs towards his parent when he had become lost.

But he wasn't the man I had seen earlier, the one surrounded by the audience, or the scared man in the alley. This man was like no other. He had long blond hair that shone like the sun before it got its cloak of ashes. And purple eyes that took in every shred of light in the room. He was beautiful, tall, and held an elegance to him that seemed foreign to this world around us. An unworldly anomaly with grandeur unmatched.

This man held in him such beauty I knew he couldn't be real, and that hurt me most of all. It was like beholding the face of a god and then being told none had ever existed. A tease almost, though you valued just being able to behold this towering personification of perfection.

Though I knew, deep down, he never existed. Because the universe would tear itself apart if such a beautiful figure had to gaze upon the wild, dirty wretch that was me. Such dignity and grace, a perfectly clean, untainted wonder… would never give something like me a second glance.

So why was he in my dreams? Why did he offer me comfort when my feral mind wanted only bloodshed and pain? I didn't know, but my heart ached every time I saw that cold face.

Then, in an instant, his face disappeared. I jerked up from my blankets as the first scream forced its way into my dreams, banishing this white figure and bringing forth the cold, dark reality that was my new home.

I stood up and made a hissing click of my tongue, an inquisitive 'what the fuck is going on?' noise I had learned from my ravers. I grabbed my claw rings and exited my room, watching as several ravers ran past me.

I made the noise again and one stopped. His milky eyes were narrow and his half-missing teeth snapping together.

It looked like we had trouble… or did Big Shot find another caravan nearby? Armed and ready, I ran with the group as we spilled like insects into the parking lot.

I stopped in my tracks.

Torches, dozens of torches lit the greywastes in front of me like a thousand small omens. I hissed and lowered my head, a swell of anger shooting through me. On both sides of me, ravers started running out of the motel rooms, screaming and thrusting their hands forward.

There was a cracking of gunfire and the young man who I had just talked to fell to the ground with a screaming hiss.

I turned around and narrowed my eyes, then I ran back in and grabbed the gun I had salvaged. I loaded it, tucked several clips into my jacket, and ran out into the parking lot. I reached the overturned tractor trailer, and as the people with the torches started to rain the motel with bullets, I climbed up the front of the trunk and jumped onto the cargo bed. I then flattened my stomach against the cold metal and started picking them off one by one.

I was a good shot… how was I such a good shot? And my night vision. I had, of course, noticed it before, but only now that I was getting perfect head shots did I realize just how unworldly good my vision and aim were.

I was a god, I was a deity… I was their king.

Maybe I was king of the fucking world.

As they came closer, and their torches bathed their faces in a bright blue glow, I could see they were dressed in greywaster clothing; their hair messy but adequately groomed and their guns polished. They had ammo belts over their chests and no bags or supplies could be seen. These were townspeople and I bet they were from Velstoke.

I peered into the scope and sniped them one by one. There were a lot of them, shouting orders and dodging my peoples' attacks with quick movements. They knew their weaknesses, the ravers had trouble with sharp movements, especially zigzag; but whenever I saw one trying to run away or lose the raver's pursuit, I sniped them in the head.

The parking lot was alive with the thunderous cracks of gunfire, and the chest-rattling shrieks and screams of the ravers. With the bonfire as a backdrop, the battle raged on, soaking the parking lot in red.

"What the fuck? Someone's shooting?" a man screamed. He raised his gun and showered bullets onto three of the ravers who were consuming one of the dead townspeople. The man looked around with perplexed eyes before his head snapped back, a red glistening crater visible once he fell lifeless to the ground.

The man who was standing beside him looked down and then looked at me. His eyes widened further. "Who the fuck... you're an arian? How..."

Another shot. I shuffled off of the truck to reload my weapon.

Then I saw movement. I looked up and spotted another man. He raised his arms in a surrendering gesture. "What the fuck are you doing here, kid? You're not one of them..."

I growled at him as I shoved the clip into the rifle.

"I know you can talk. Your eyes have pupils and no fucking raver can use a gun. Come back with us. They'll end up eating you. Fuck knows why they haven't–"

I dropped the gun and jumped on him, my mouth open and my metal teeth exposed to the cold winter air. Before he could let out a scream, I clamped my teeth against his windpipe and crushed it with as much force as my jaw could manage.

The growling noise faded as the sound of his frantic breath filled my ears. Each wheezing and desperate gasp brought another string of bloodlust and adrenaline to my veins. I closed my eyes and pressed harder, until I felt both of my teeth meet.

Then I ripped out his throat and let his blood spray over my body. I let go of the chunk of flesh and grabbed my gun, then crawled back up on top of the semi.

Anger coursed through me when I saw the townspeople still shooting down my ravers. There were five of them left but they were successfully dodging the ravers' attacks. Deek was even useless, a silhouette off in the distance, chasing one of them from what I could see.

There were bodies everywhere, dead corpses surrounded by shining blood. Both townspeople and my ravers alike, so different when they walked the earth but now the same blood soaked into the ground underneath them.

I started sniping them off, growling and hissing my anger at the amount of casualties I could see. We had lost at least ten of our own, but it looked like…

Yes. As I sniped three… then four… I smirked in spite of the horror that was going on below me. Yes, we were going to win.

Big Shot took out the last one, sinking his claws into the greywaster's soft flesh and pulling out the man's bright entrails. They spilled onto the floor like coils of sausage before the man keeled over, desperately trying to push them back into his body with a low groan.

I jumped down, still holding my gun. The ravers who had lived were standing over the dead, too full from the meal earlier today to do very much eating.

Big Shot was staring forward, and though at times it was hard to see any expression of emotion on a raver's face, I could tell me was angry. He looked to his left where I was and *kah'd*.

I did the same back and looked around at the carnage.

"They'll come back…" I said to him. "The town is close to our home. We need to move…" I thought of the resort. "I know where I can take us, a place that will be safe until they stop hunting us."

I didn't know how much of this he understood, if any of it. He only stared forward, his face still troubled and soured. I stood with him as our people started dragging the dead back to the motel.

I kicked one of the townspeople with my boot and I got an idea. A farfetched one, a crazy one… but…

In spite of my mind telling me I was stupid, I picked up the man's gun. I held it out to Big Shot, and when he took it, I took out my own.

What if they only needed someone to show them? The thought filled me with morbid curiosity, so I slapped his forearm to try and communicate that I wanted him to follow.

The slower ones might not be able to grasp it… but…

I raised the gun and pulled the trigger, a loud crack split the night air. I put my hand on Big Shot's arm and squeezed it. "You... shoot."

Big Shot looked down and shook his head. He tried to give me the gun back but I insisted.

"Shoot!" I said more forcefully.

He looked uneasy and I could tell he was about to shake his head, but curiosity got the best of him.

Big Shot glanced down and adjusted his grip. I put my hand on the barrel of the gun to make sure he was shooting into the greywastes and nodded my head.

Big Shot's brow furrowed; his faint eyebrows moving up and down as he made the odd facial expression. The leader of the ravers then adjusted his hold again and shifted himself.

Then he pulled the trigger.

"Kah!" he exclaimed in such a surprised way I actually laughed. With a nod, I shot my own gun again and he reciprocated with another pull of the trigger.

"Get the smart ones... get guns, all the guns," I said to Big Shot. I rested my hand on the gun and then kicked a hunting rifle resting a few feet away. I picked that one up and looked around for the dark-skinned raver.

I raised my arm and swept the area, then grabbed my gun, trying to communicate what I wanted him to do.

"Get the smart ones guns... get them all guns," I said.

Then another idea took hold of my mind, a nefarious idea that tickled the lower levels of my imagination. Something that might be crazy, might be my own death trap, but in the same vein... something I so dearly wanted to see.

Because why should my people be pushed from their home? To a resort miles away from where travellers and caravans could be? I wouldn't let them starve, not when they had me as their other leader. I was smart, I was an arian. I had enhanced night vision, a sniper-like shot, and I could think, talk, order...

And I could teach.

I could teach all of them.

The corner of my right lip raised in a smirk. Big Shot stared at me with his half-vacant eyes but I could tell that he was watching me and he was listening to every word that I said to him. He was smart enough to know what I was doing and he trusted me. I had the magic whistle, but on top of that… I had firepower, brains, brawn, and a thirst to dominate and control.

I looked at him and he looked back. Then I put my hand on his head, and as the silent night was broken up by the sounds of bodies being dragged across the pavement I said to him:

"I'll train tomorrow… and after…" I dug into my pocket and pulled put the map. I pointed to Velstoke.

"We're getting ourselves a new home."

CHAPTER 41

Reaver

BENEATH EVERY PERSON IS A THOUSAND LAYERS, each one a clear, thin film almost impossible to pull back. They walk around seemingly see-through, giving off an air that they are an open book if you ever did have questions.

Then you start to peel back that film, layer by layer you remove the clear skin. And once you got several sheets in, you realize that the film was a cover, a mask to hide a secret person you never knew existed.

Leo was the mayor of Aras and the husband of Greyson Merrik. That was who he was from my earliest memories. Always the smart alec, always the kind man ready to teach you anything you wanted to learn. Leo had taught me how to read when Greyson taught me how to shoot; he taught me how to be a better person, when all I wanted to do was raise hell.

But underneath those layers laid a man with a thousand plans in his head and twice as many secrets. Never the greywaster, never the mayor... he was a chimera of extreme intelligence, with a plot in his head fed by his brother Elish Dekker.

But the chimera scientist had swayed from Elish's plan, though whether he had changed their plans or wanted to betray Elish I didn't know. What I did know, was that in that bunker he had gotten the device that held a piece of Perish's brain. He'd done this without Elish knowing; without anyone besides him and Greyson knowing.

And because of that... I was here. In the corner end of winter, searching along a highway with a man I never thought I would be walking the greywastes with. Looking, with matching weights of dread on our chests, for our partners. Two men who, from an ironic twist of fate, had found common ground and a mutual respect.

Sometimes one of us would veer off of the highway, thinking we had seen something, any sign of one of the boys, but eventually we would come back and not a word would be spoken. Then, with the foreboding even heavier on our shoulders, we would keep walking. Deciding with an unspoken understanding to not even ask if they had seen something.

In front of us was endless highway, though the valley to our left had disappeared. Now there were just grey hills, holding only the remnants of the snowfall.

We had spotted several structures and had checked out each one, but none of them held any sign that one of the boys had been there, or anyone for that matter. Everything was covered in either snow, frozen dust, or both. It seemed the slavers were the only ones insane enough to come up here, no matter the season.

It made for fair scavenging at least. With each building Elish and I looked in, we ending up coming out with at least two cans of food and our choice of utensils. The snow was easy to melt into drinking water with Elish's thermal touch, so we were able to keep up the energy we were burning while we looked.

And we were combing the entire area. We made sure to not just walk on the road, but check out every side road and shoddy trail we could find. Highway walking was slow-going but the trade-off was worth it. It would be devastating if the boys had found a cabin or something to keep shelter and we walked by it. We might never find them then…

Might never find them.

I glanced over at Elish who was walking along the edge of the highway, a shallow incline that dipped down before rising to a series of rocky slopes. I knew he was checking the ditch for one of them. The prospect, as it always did, made me queasy.

He was still holding the fire poker, which he used to check out the buildings we found. Probably hated touching things since it seemed he was just as much of a clean freak as Killian. I don't know why he felt like carrying it around though, he had a perfectly good assault rifle on his back. I did as well, my M16 on my own back where it belonged. It felt good to have the old boy with me, but the fact that the last person to touch my gun was Killian was rather sobering.

No, not sobering… it made me angry.

And as my thoughts took me to my own current reality, my teeth clenched.

"Why the fuck did you bring Perish along for this?" I suddenly snapped at Elish. And when he looked at me with nothing more than a disinterested glance, I carried on, feeling my anger start to rise to the surface. "Killian and Jade would have been fine if Perish wasn't with them."

He brushed off my tone like he was brushing snow from his shoulder. With his eyes fixed forward, he said to me coolly, "Jade's empath abilities were the only way for us to find out where the O.L.S device was hidden. Without Jade being around Perish, we would never know."

Elish took the fire poker and used it to lift up a rusted trunk lid. He glanced inside; his impassiveness grated on my every last nerve. "I was not aware that Lycos–"

"His name was Leo!" I snapped.

"I was not aware that *Leo* was planning on betraying me," Elish replied, dropping the trunk lid. There was a heavy *clunk* that echoed off of the sheer rocky cliff we were currently walking past. "If I had known Perish's O.L.S had already been implanted, I would have never let him near my pet."

I don't know why but his words just infuriated me more. I tried to press it down with a swallow but I was frustrated and angry. Angry that this is where we were right now, angry that Elish allowed this to happen. He was supposed to be in control of everything… he was supposed to be some hyper-intelligent mutant.

"When I get Killian… I'm leaving," I replied. "You obviously don't know what you're doing."

I glared at him as I heard him snort.

"Oh? You think this is a video game or something, Mr. Merrik? That once you pass the first level you slid easily into the next? This is real life, Reaver. And if there is something my ninety-one years being on this grey earth has taught me, it is that things do not always go as planned. Thankfully, to our credit, we literally have all the time in the world. We can not only fix the grievous mistakes you made, we can correct Lycos's as well."

I growled.

"It is a sad thing when my pet shows more restraint than you."

"Shut the fuck up," I said. "If you were so cozy with Leo, why did this happen? He obviously thought you would betray him."

Elish's face didn't waver but I saw a slight darkness come to his eyes. "I have the most to lose with this seed I have planted. If anything, it was my own doing for trusting that slippery scientist in the beginning. I should have known he would eventually try and go above my head."

"Don't you ever say anything bad about him!" I exploded. In the back of my mind I knew I wasn't going about this the right way. I was better than this, better than losing my temper. That wasn't me, at least it didn't used to be me. I was the calm, seethe in silence type.

Or at least I liked convincing myself I was.

Of course Elish didn't even flinch. "Just because Lycos is dead, does not absolve him from what he had done while living. This stunt, this foolish belief he had before he died, almost got us all encased in concrete for eternity. Grieve for him all you wish, I don't begrudge you that, but don't insult your own intelligence by trying to sell him to me as some sort of angel. He was neither, and neither was his husband."

"Yeah, well, neither are you."

"Did I ever try to convince any of you different?" Elish seemed amused. I glared at him and debated opening my mouth to get pissed at him further, but I shut it. What was important was looking for Killian and trying to challenge Elish was distracting from that. So I clamped it shut and carried on.

I was surprised that Elish didn't try and pick at me some more. I glanced over at him and saw that his eyes were fixed forward. I looked to see what he was staring at.

It was a small derelict cabin a few yards off of the highway.

Then the smell hit me.

"Something dead is over there…" My heart dropped, without thinking I broke into a run. The sweet and putrid smell of rotting flesh was crawling up my nostrils, though this time the languid smell didn't seep and nip at my brain, it clutched onto my emotions and filled them with apprehension.

Killian… what if I was smelling Killian's body.

I saw movement out of the corner of my eye. I didn't need to look, I knew it was Elish, running just as fast as me.

Inside I could feel every one of my muscles constrict and tighten around themselves, gripping my bones so tightly I was half-expecting them to snap under the weight. Such emotions used to be foreign to me, but now whenever Killian was in danger that deep sepulchre of madness seemed to bubble up to my surface. It was becoming harder and harder to force it back down.

But the oddest feeling of all was the darkness taking over corners of my mind, corners that used to collect light. Because though the flame where I held my love for Killian continued to grow, the places where my boyfriend's presence did not touch grew darker and more cold. Instead of my sporadic, fleeting emotions being spread over my body, they were slowly being chased to a single crowded room.

He had always been my lantern in the darkness.

When I saw the rotting carcass of the carracat I could physically feel the weight get lifted off of my shoulders. I rested my hands on my knees and didn't bother to hide the relief on my face. I could tell from the lurch in Elish's heart we were experiencing the emotion together.

"Wait..." As I was staring down at my boots I saw something...

Prints...

"That's Deekoi's paw prints," I said. I looked around, and when I saw the boot prints in a small patch of remaining snow I swore, and to my own inner madness, I started to laugh. "And boot prints... boot prints... they were here!"

Elish's purple eyes widened, and his jaw tightened. Wordlessly, he turned from the rotting carcass and walked onto the cabin's porch and then inside. I followed him.

We both stepped inside the old, musty cabin and looked around.

The floor looked disturbed, someone had made a bed beside the pot belly stove. My eyes scanned the garbage on the floor and stacks of crates, trying to find any sign that some of it was new.

Then I saw it, and so did Elish: bloodstained cloth... used as bandages.

Elish leaned down and picked it up. He brought the bandage to his nose and I watched, feeling almost coy, as he closed his eyes in relief.

"This belonged to Jade," Elish said quietly. "He was here."

But what about Killian?

"Jade would not have left him," Elish replied simply, even though all I had done was look around the room; he seemed to know what I was thinking. "If the snow had remained we would've been able to track them easier, but it doesn't seem like they've veered off of the road."

I was still looking for any sign of Killian. He would have written me a note or something, that seems like the type of thing he would've done. But there was nothing, just disturbed trash, a few prints here or there, and a blood-soaked strip of cloth.

I kicked an old coffee can with my foot, spilling cigarette butts of an unknown age over the floor. I left after that; I had nothing more to say and we had no reason to remain here.

Once I was back outside, I started to quickly walk down the highway.

Now more than ever I felt aware of my surroundings. The black trees and sheer cliffs offering nothing to me but places of ambush, or places where Perish could be stashing Killian. If he was tied up and gagged… how could he hear me?

But the dog…

I started doing the soundless whistle as I picked apart and analyzed every rock and rusted out car. Then, with Elish keeping pace with me, I started to climb the cliffs to our left to get a better view. I also kept my nose alert for any fluctuation in smell.

We got into our regular routine after that, the adrenaline filling both of us. Elish stayed on the highway always on watch, and I scaled every bluff I could find to survey the landscape.

To our benefit, there were a lot of sentry points right beside the road. They were mostly hills sheared in half by blasts of dynamite to make room for the highway, leaving their many layers of hardened sediment exposed and naked to the elements.

Unfortunately though, we nothing; even a couple hours after finding the small cabin I still could see no sign of them. But was that a good thing? If Perish veered off of the road there was no telling where they could be… or where he could be taking them.

"As for now, I do not know," Elish replied when I had asked him that question. Darkness had banished another day into oblivion, leaving the both of us with only our night vision to aid our trip. There was an unspoken agreement between the two of us that we would not be resting much this evening. But whether that stemmed from hope or just fear, I don't think either of us wanted to know.

We walked at a quick speed the entire night, only resting for an hour before we were back on our feet. The sun was just peeking over the hills when I started to notice chunks of compacted snow and scrape marks, all lined up perfectly one after the other.

Elish was also eyeing them curiously. "That is out of place, but what it is... I am unsure of."

"It looks like something was being dragged, something heavy," I said. Once more I looked ahead of us, then let out another silent whistle. "We have to be gaining on them. Killian wouldn't be able to keep up this speed. Jade wouldn't either if he was nursing a head injury."

Elish nodded his agreeance but that left us with no relief, only more questions. "Keep climbing... keep your eyes peeled. And I will say this now... if you see Perish, snipe him. I know you have the skills to hit only him. Kill first and ask questions later."

I liked how this man thinks, and my sniper scope would allow me to see further ahead than my own vision would. I started climbing up the incline to our right and started scaling the first thick tree I could find.

Elish was just a small figure below me when I got to the last usable branch of the tree. I used my height to look over the grey landscape around me.

"I see a town," I called down to Elish. There were clusters of structures everywhere but this one not only had a wall around it, but it also had smoke coming from the houses inside. There was also a single paved road leading right up to the gate. "The road that goes to it should only be a couple miles ahead."

I looked down and saw Elish staring back up at me. "They would need supplies... but I'm unsure if Perish would've even known this town existed. However we'll check it out; we'll be needing supplies ourselves if we want to keep up this speed."

My eyes picked up other buildings in all the cardinal directions but none of them looked occupied. I wanted to check them out once we got back to the highway though.

I climbed down the tree before letting myself drop the rest of the way. Then, with a skid, I slid down the embankment and back to the highway. Elish was already starting to walk down the road, more broken up and cracked than the previous areas. It was rough going, but at least there were no carts and no more bosen to slow me down.

But still we were faster than them... I just hoped they decided to stop in that town.

We both carried on down the highway, still meticulously checking out the forgotten cars, though nothing was ever found in them but chewed-up seats and bare metal coated in rust. We didn't find any more tracks either but that was expected, the lower we walked the more the snow disappeared. In all respects, it was gone.

Like we'd thought, there was a single road branching off of the highway, immediately bending into a thick thatch of trees. It was taking us west, however neither of us knew the town's name. Elish didn't even know, which I wasn't overly impressed with.

"Lots of colonies sprout up. Unless they register themselves with the ACL and become blocks there is no way to know where they are, what their names are, or how many people have taken residence," Elish commented after I voiced my displeasure with him.

"So chances are Perish wouldn't know where this road leads…" I sighed and glanced behind me at a bullet-riddled highway sign we'd just passed. It was advertising the Coquihalla highway and how many kilometres it was. It looked like we were officially over the mountain.

Elish looked down at the pavement we were walking on, half-covered in gravel washed up from a small river we could hear to our right. "This road is newer… the pavement that is. It was made after the Fallocaust. This colony was made to attract merchants, or at the very least, travellers going to Melchai. It would be a newer town, perhaps only four or five years old."

"So it's not Melchai?"

Elish shook his head. "No, I am familiar with Melchai. That town is another two weeks by foot if you stick with the highway."

This peaked my interest. "How do you know Melchai?" I offered him a quil which he took, and lit one myself. I don't think I could handle everything right now without them. It was bad enough my drug suitcase was missing and Killian had my heroin. Though at least getting killed had detoxed my body. Still though… I hated being sober.

A puff of smoke erupted from the red ember as Elish took his first drag. It seemed odd to see Elish smoking my hand-made cigarettes; he wasn't the robe-draped, sparkly clean god I had seen in the greyrifts. Elish was now dirty like the rest of us; his long blond hair tucked into his grey duster, and his hands caked in ash and dirt. He even had a short beard now which made him look even more rugged. I don't think I would have recognized him if I saw him in Skyfall.

It made me feel more at ease to see him become a greywaster. Not only was there the familiarity aspect, but it just showed how, deep down, his appearance and how he presented himself to me didn't matter when his husband's life was at stake. Elish Dekker was a bona fide greywaster now, with dirt-caked nails and wood-fire smelling, ratty clothes.

"Sanguine is more familiar with Melchai than I. It is a strange town. Sanguine spent some time in it as a child," Elish explained. "He had no good things to say about it, but apparently it has grown to be a farming town. It used to be full of meth addicts apparently."

"But that means... Sanguine was given to a greywaster? Isn't that dangerous, especially for such a rare scientific abomination such as him?" I asked. I had never personally met Sanguine but the pictures were enough for me to do a double take. Though his facial features were normal, the normal chimera hotness anyway, his eyes were deep blood-red and his teeth like piranha fangs.

"Yes, but Silas wanted him to grow up with a hard nose, he wanted him to be strong. Silas decided that if he survived he would come to Skyfall the tough-as-nails bodyguard he had designed him to be." Then a faint smile could be seen on his lips. "Unfortunately, it didn't work out as such. Sanguine is a rather sweet man, though confused and is still confused to this day. He fights with himself every day over whether he wants to be good or bad."

"Which is why you swayed him?"

"I have not swayed him; he is just extremely intelligent and decided to align himself with us. Though he is one of the ones who does not want to see Silas die. I had to promise him I would help Silas, not kill him."

Interesting. "And you agreed to this?"

Elish nodded. "I agreed to help Silas, and I have a perfect way of helping him."

"By killing him?"

"Of course."

I laughed and saw the corner of Elish's mouth raise. It felt strange to laugh; even though it was more of a scoff than a laugh it was still more than I had done in a long time.

We carried on down this one-lane, newly-paved road, and a little over two hours later, we started to see the walls in the distance.

It was the same type of walls I had seen in Aras, made up of anything that offered a thick shell of protection: medians, raised pieces of pavement, old cars, and chain-link fence. It was stacked two men high, and from the looks of it, seemed like it was in a constant state of being improved.

There was a rusted iron rung gate that was unguarded, but as I looked closer, I couldn't see a lock on it. This place seemed to be almost the size of Aras, but in the same vein, it was obvious that the town had only been really broken in over the last couple of years. Everything still had that green feel to it, the feeling that they hadn't perfected anything but building a small wall. I could take over this place in a second.

"Think of a name for yourself. Or do you want to stick with your roots and go with Chance?" Elish asked.

I nodded. "Might as well."

"I will be going with my usual James." Elish then looked up and said loudly, "We're travellers, we need to buy supplies. We'll be spending the night."

There were two of them, though they didn't address us from the walls like we did back in Aras, they climbed down on steady feet, their shotguns strapped to their backs. Two young men, one with glasses and one not.

"Are you ravers?" The one without the glasses looked suspiciously at us.

I could taste the annoyance coming from Elish. "Do I look like a raver, boy? Do ravers talk?"

The kid, no older than thirteen immediately shrunk under Elish's cold stare.

"I guess not." The grinding of rusty hinges in desperate need of oil filled the air around us. The young man stepped back and let us in, though he seemed to be watching our every movement. "What's five times twelve?"

I blinked and hoped that question wasn't directed at me, because fucked if I knew.

"Sixty," Elish replied coolly. "Now where is your store district?"

He was still eyeing us like we were aliens who had just landed on earth, but he didn't press the subject further. Instead, he pointed straight ahead. "Just follow the road. We made this town around a plaza; the store is inside the Save On and the bar is as well. The hotel is also in the same area, made in an old retirement home. We put up signs just last winter."

Elish nodded. "Yes, I suspected this town was new. What is it called?"

"We named it after our founder: Mantis."

To my surprise, Elish did a double take. "Mantis? Is that man here now?"

The boy shook his head. "No, he left last year and hasn't come back. We are hoping perhaps he will come in the summer, he is the mayor after all."

"Is he now?" Elish muttered before his eyes shot to the road the boy had pointed us down. "Well then, let's go, Chance."

I was not a stupid person, though at a few points in time Leo and Greyson had both told me the other had dropped me on my head as an infant. Either way, I might not be the most colourful crayon in the crayon box, but it didn't take a rocket surgeon to figure out who Mantis was.

"Another greywaster chimera?" I asked nonchalantly.

I got a look for that. "Do not mention that word here. We can discuss it tonight in the discretion of a hotel room," Elish said under his breath.

I let it slide, because though I was curious, finding Killian was more important. As we walked to the plaza I kept my eyes peeled for any blond heads belonging to my little boyfriend but no one came even close to Killian's appearance. I knew my boyfriend inside and out and it didn't take long for my hopes to fade.

The Save On was an old grocery store. The building had been patched with sheets of metal streaked with rust, and held together by bad welding jobs and loose screws. There were windows too but most were hidden behind shutters made from plywood and metal.

We crossed a broken parking lot which was buzzing with people. Some were wheeling shopping carts full of junk but most of them were keeping to themselves, either eating or drinking bad-smelling liquor. This place was more occupied than I had initially thought it was, this area was definitely the hub of the town.

I kicked an old can with my foot; it bounced forward with a series of clanks before resting beside an old shopping cart corral. An old man looked up from his dose of heroin and gave me the stink eye but didn't say anything to me. I was tempted to ask him where he got his smack, though I might settle for robbing him tonight.

Elish lit another cigarette. "Killian and Perish are normal in appearance, but I hold hope my cicaro's eyes will make him stand out." We both stepped onto the concrete walkway and started towards two open double doors, I could hear faint music and the buzzing of voices inside.

I didn't like it here, even though there was nothing in particular I didn't like. I just knew Killian wasn't in this place, and I wanted to get out of this town so we could continue to track them.

Perish wouldn't let anything happen to Killian... I sighed as I said those words over and over inside of my head. It filled me with bitterness to know I had to rely on Perish's devotion to my boyfriend to give myself that hope that he was okay.

Admittedly though, Killian might not be okay, there was no telling what Perish would do to him. But on the same hand, if Killian was alive… that was all that mattered. The thought of Perish touching him filled me with rage but it was nothing I couldn't help him get through.

My teeth clenched as a rush of that very same rage washed through me. I hated that the fact that my boyfriend might get raped was okay with me, but right now I was worried about more extreme things, like him being dead. No matter how I twisted it in my already darkening mind it was my fucking reality that Perish fucking him would be the least bad thing that could happen to my boyfriend.

I felt like shit for that, but it was better than him being gone. If he had to pretend to be Perish's boyfriend again, I could live with that. Killian excelled at manipulating that retard.

No… he wasn't a retard anymore. I don't know what he was but apparently he wasn't the hyper, shifty scientist I had known.

Just be okay, Killian. We can get through our issues together. I can make you feel better by telling you the several weeks of hell I experienced.

Fuck, I needed a drink. I don't think I knew what I was saying anymore. I didn't know how to handle these feelings of desperation and helplessness. Great fucking Reaper I was.

Elish and I walked inside of the bar. It was dark with the stale smell of body odour and old liquor The building inside was also just as bad as the outside, but they had made up for it by nailing old highway and street signs onto the walls. I even saw a couple pre-Fallocaust licence plates and some store signs. Well, make do with what you have.

We sat down at the bar and ordered a beer for both of us. I could tell Elish was trying to hide his displeasure at the taste. I assumed they had premium beer in Skyfall, or maybe he was just missing his tea.

After a few minutes of drinking, Elish glanced towards the bartender. "We're looking for three men," he said in the most casual voice I had heard from him. "One of them you would recognize if you saw him. He has yellow eyes."

The bartender, a man in his thirties with red hair, shook his head. "We get a lot of travellers in these parts and most of them want to remain anonymous. But I can tell you with honesty I haven't seen any yellow-eyed ones."

My heart sank. I tried to hide my disappointment by taking a deep drink of beer. I put the glass down with a clink and got up off of the bar stool. "Let's go then." Back to the highway, and quickly.

Elish shook his head and slid my beer glass back towards me. "No, we're spending the night here. It's already too late in the evening."

We're spending the night in a hotel room? For all I know Killian is miles and miles away being fucked by that psychotic scientist. The thought made my teeth grind together, and the anger start to churn inside of my chest.

"You would be a fool to rely on one person for intel, Chance. Now drink." I hated how that asshole talked to me like I was his kid. No wonder Jade was how he was.

But Elish didn't care. He looked at the bartender before reaching into his pocket. He pulled out a folded wad of cash and raised it to the bartender. "This is five hundred dollars. I don't care who you ask, but ask. If anyone in this town has seen a young man of eighteen with black hair and yellow eyes, I want to know. He would be travelling with a boy of eighteen, blond hair, blue eyes and a man of twenty-four, black hair, light blue eyes. Now do you have the people and resources to get this done?"

The bartender looked at him a bit perplexed, the look of a man who had thought that today was just going to be another normal day. He stared at the folded up money and then back at Elish.

"Are they wanted?"

"It doesn't matter... are you going to do what I want or not?" Elish replied coolly.

The bartender swallowed and nodded, looking with hunger at the bills. "Yes... names?"

"I doubt they would be using their names, the boy's odd appearance will be enough." Elish drained his glass and rose. "We'll be staying in the hotel for the evening. I'll be giving the man or woman in charge instructions to let you and only you knock on our door. Get the word around quickly, we will be leaving at first light. Get me a solid lead and the money is yours, but don't try and falsify information. I will know if you're lying."

There was a *clink* as Elish set his beer glass down. The bartender was still giving us confused looks but he was smart enough to just nod. We left silently after that and went towards the store to stock up on our supplies.

"I don't want to spend the night here," I said darkly to Elish as we checked into the hotel room. It was late in the evening now and we had our knapsacks full of supplies and ammo. "They could be getting further from us as we speak. I have energy, we can make a couple miles on the highway before we need to rest."

Elish put down his bags and started picking out some of the things we had bought. "I know your body, as I do mine. We have been running off of an hour of sleep here or there for a long time. Our bodies need a satisfactory rest and after we can continue our gruelling pace. If we go to that highway with the garbage we have been eating and twenty-one hour days we will not only be intolerable to each other, our minds will start to deteriorate, and yours is fragile enough as it is. I know more about this than you, and I want to find Jade as much as you want to find Killian, but I will not go out there half-asleep when we need our wits about us."

I unwrapped a brown package which contained some restaurant food we had picked up and started eating. He was right and I knew he was right, so I didn't say anything back. This wasn't in my nature… to… listen to people, but I had to push aside my own hot-headed, hard-nosed, asshole ways and do what I knew would help us find Killian.

I sat down and automatically put a chair up by the window, more out of habit than anything. I was a sentry after all.

Well, I *had* been a sentry.

I sighed. My heart ached for my old life. One I had never appreciated until it had been snatched away from me. I missed being a sentry, I missed Aras, I missed… my dads.

Automatically the barriers inside of my mind snapped shut, as they most often did whenever my mind grazed on the raw and festering wound that was my fathers' memories. It had been months now since they had died, months since that day in Aras when I had seen them get shot. And I still hadn't been able to deal with it. Anger helped… hating them helped… but I knew that was just me trying to protect myself.

And now where was I?

Fuck, Killian… I'm sorry. Though what choice did I have? If it had been Kessler torturing you when he had me prisoner… I would've told them everything.

I had to leave you… I just wasn't aware of who I was leaving you with.

I cracked open a bottle of whisky and took a long drink. I tapped it against my knuckles before automatically the bottle touched my lips again.

"You don't need to sentry. No one knows we're here," Elish said behind me. I saw his hand reach and grab the other wrapper of shredded rat meat that we had gotten from the restaurant. He then put a kettle of water on with his free hand.

"I thought that last time," I muttered under my breath, then said in a normal tone, "Do you think this Mantis guy will have any idea where Perish might be heading?"

"No. I don't believe Mantis has spoken to Perish in a long time. But once we find Jade and Killian, I will try and reach him. He has been absent from the family for many years and it is time he gets over his problems with us. He is an odd man."

"You all are," I said under my breath.

Elish ignored me. "He and I have a bit of a past and he's been living in the greywastes for quite a while. He is on our side and an ally, though as of right now, I don't know where he is and I see no way that Perish could know where he is either."

"Is he a chimera?"

Elish shook his head. "No, he's one of the few arians to be made immortal and adopted by our family. He used to be a psychologist for the Dekker family but events led him to take his leave from Skyfall. Now he lives in a house of an unknown location, and though he has called once or twice... I don't hear from him often."

"Are you sure Perish wouldn't find him?"

"No."

I was surprised at that.

Elish continued, "But even if he did, I still wouldn't know where Mantis was. Since he isn't here and I don't know where to find him... he is irrelevant."

I let out a breath. I thought Elish had tabs on everyone but I guess this greywaster immortal was different. I took one more drink of whisky and set my M16 down on the bed beside me.

I put my hands behind my head, but no sooner had I closed my eyes did I hear an odd noise.

The snipping of scissors.

I opened one eye and saw Elish snipping off his long blond hair, leaving only six or seven inches of it, barely enough to fall past his ears. I remember he had his hair cut short once when he came to Aras.

"Why are you doing that?" I asked curiously.

Elish took another handful of hair and snipped it away, before throwing it into the fire. "It's getting in the way, and I don't have the time to take care of it."

My brow furrowed. "I thought your hair was like your glory or something. It always made you look so regal and important. I assumed you took a lot of pride in having it so long and… shiny."

Elish's cold face didn't waver; he snipped off another chunk and threw it. "Do you know why my hair was short when I came to Aras last winter?"

I shook my head.

"I saved Jade from certain death at the hands of King Silas. I refused to leave Jade with him, and to humiliate me, Silas cut off my hair in front of my brothers," Elish explained. "To dehumanize me, to make me appear lesser… to cause me a great shame."

Another snip, the fire start spitting and snapping as more hair was thrown onto it. Before I had a chance to ask him why he was doing that now, he continued. "My brothers and Silas, and you apparently, think I take such pride in my hair. That it is some sort of status symbol I carry around to flaunt my greatness… or some nonsense." Another snip. "When really, it is more of a decoy, and I don't mind cutting it off once it becomes a hassle."

I stared at him. "Decoy?"

Elish glanced behind him to try and get the scissors right. He was doing a bad job of it. I got up off of the bed and took the scissors from him. Elish didn't raise an objection so I started finishing off the job.

"Once Joaquin angered King Silas, and do you know what Silas did to him? In front of our brothers?" I could see his smirk from the mirror he had positioned in front of him.

"What?" I asked curiously.

"Silas severed his penis and his testicles, and forced him to remain that way for a year before he let him resurrect them back."

I choked on the laugh that burst from my lips. I was smart enough to take the scissors away from the back of his head. "I understand now. You gave him something else to cut off, something that will grow back on its own?"

Elish nodded his head. "Indeed, I learned that trick many years ago and I have remained intact ever since. In truth, my hair is a hassle, but to cut it short now would only raise suspicion. There are pills available from Skytech that will have it grown back to its usual length in three months. So until I am home, I'd rather have it short."

I started snipping away at the last strands. "Joining the greywasters one small alteration at a time. You have a beard now and short hair, besides those eyes no one will be able to tell who you are."

"That's the idea, but no one will recognized us here. Mantis is gone and any person who might have, at one point, seen me has been dead for decades." When I was finished he stood up and dusted the remaining hair from his coat.

Elish looked entirely different now, but the coldness on his face and the way he carried himself was something physical appearances couldn't change. He was still Elish Dekker and still a chimera.

"Let us sleep now. With our strength up tomorrow we should be able to cover good ground." Elish got into bed with his boots still on and closed his eyes. "It will not be long now… we will catch up to them."

The nightmares came back that night. The ones that sunk into my brain like poison and stuck to my every last hope like glue, telling me with all the confidence in the world that I would never hold that boy again in my arms.

So much anger… those voices taunted me, poked at me, and laughed at every single mistake I had made. I felt like a bear in a cage surrounded by a dozen laughing kids prodding me with long sticks. It made me want to tear myself out of my own skin; I was so frustrated and mad.

I woke up with a start and realized that it was still dark out. But there was an orange glow reflecting against the stained ceiling, one that was drawing a brightness to my closed eyelids. I immediately jumped out of bed and saw that, at the exact same time, Elish had woken up too.

We both wordlessly walked to the window and saw half a dozen men with torches. I stared down, and for a moment I thought it was people looking for us, but it wasn't.

There were six people shouting at a group of men, loudly. We both grabbed our guns and ran down the steps and into the cold night air.

"What's going on?" Elish demanded.

One of the men looked our way; he was holding a torch with a white knuckle grip. "Ravers… ravers killed our chief officer's sister in Velstoke, and her children! They were travelling by caravan. We're organizing a group and we're killing them tonight. They're at the Cobbleton Motel."

Elish stared at him for a moment. "Are ravers active here?"

The man nodded. "They move into the abandoned hotels and resorts during the winter. We usually ignore them but… they're getting bold. We're putting a stop to it before it gets bad. Velstoke's men are several hours away now. We will be joining up with them."

"Where is Velstoke?"

"Ten days walk past Garnertown but the men have already started rallying."

I looked at Elish. "I wouldn't mind letting off some steam."

But he shook his head and turned around to walk back into the hotel. "No. Though I have all the faith in your abilities, if you get eaten alive by ravers it could take you months to resurrect. We're going back to sleep for another couple hours and we'll be on our way. This is not our fight."

I looked behind me at the sea of torches, the men and women's faces stern with determination. I wanted to go with them, I needed to kill something, let off some of that pent-up aggression. It had been too long since I had tasted blood, tasted the life leak out of someone.

But he was right, once again I knew that asshole was right. This wasn't about me, it was about finding the boys.

Still though…

I turned from the active scene behind me and followed Elish back up the stairs, leaving the villagers to their frenzy and their, most likely, certain deaths.

CHAPTER 42

Killian

LITTLE ROADS, FIVE OF THEM, ROADS THAT WERE drag marks on a mirror. Drag marks that started out in thick straight lines, but as they drew down they started to warp and bend until the dust enclosed on them once again.

I looked at the stranger. His ash-covered face stared back with dead eyes, the thin reflective ribbons contrasting with the grime seemed to encage him like he was behind bars.

Iron rungs of hardened dust and mirror, staring back at me with a sullen gaunt sanguine.

I held a pale hand up to the streaks in the mirror and rested my finger in each of the lines, imagining who made them though they were never good images. There was no blood here however, no bodies. Death hadn't reached this house.

Perhaps the next house, or the next, or the next we would find something to eat.

A shuffling of clothing, dry cloth rubbing against dry cloth, crackling paint and plaster crunching under my feet. I pressed my foot deeper and twisted it around. The sound reminded me where reality was, or where it should be at least. Perish had taken most of my reality from me, only the slaves gave me hope of getting it back.

Not slaves… they were my friends, because I was a slave too.

I looked behind me and saw Teejay holding an empty, rusty can in his dirty hands. He looked just as hopeless as I did. Though he had been a slave longer than I.

I think he had lost hope long ago.

The house we had found was aged and tired. Time had blanketed it in black spots of mould, with gouges taken out of it that suggested a beast rather than natural wear. I wouldn't be surprised, the radanimals here were huge. Just last night Perish had shot an urson with his assault rifle, he had spotted it from a telephone pole that had climbing rungs on it. He had told us to climb up them too. Me first.

Unfortunately it had ran away once it had been shot in the shoulder. We could've eaten it if Perish was a better shot. I kept that information to myself.

There was a *clang* as Teejay dropped the empty can onto the floor and started pulling out wooden drawers to check inside. I saw sawdust and ash rise up from every drawer he disturbed, making him cough into his hand.

"I think he would taste the best." I jumped as Perish hissed that into my ear. Automatically I started walking away from him, down a hall with a ripped up yellow carpet.

If we don't find food, we're eating one of them.

If you don't find food, Killian, it will be your fault.

I walked into a living room, with cream-coloured curtains dotted with blurry, black spots. The grey sun shone through the curtains bathing the room in a yellowy hue. Around it was warped, twisted paneling and the yellow carpet littered in chunks of plaster and insulation fluff. A soiled couch was in a corner, missing its cushions, and beside it a table lamp without a shade. The entire house gave off a musty, stale smell that seemed to take residence in your nose.

Even though I didn't expect there to be any food, I walked around and pulled open the drawer the lamp was resting on.

Old papers, stiff and brittle with age… but behind it I saw a small disk-like can. I picked it up and twisted it open.

Breath mints? I shrugged and popped one into my mouth. I turned around and saw Perish staring at me from the doorway. His arms crossed over his black duster and Garrett's old school hat on his head. The scientist didn't look happy, he never looked happy. The old Perish…

Was gone, stop thinking about it, Killian. I went up to him and held out the tin. "Want one?"

Perish stared at me before taking a mint, his eyes never leaving my face. "You four have five more minutes until we're leaving."

Yes, we had fifteen minutes in each house and we had a few more to look into before we went on our way. The area we had found had nice, two-storey houses on each side, separated by a quaint two-lane road. The black trees were tall, with thick limbs that hinted to being maple or oak at one point. We could climb them if needed be, in case we encountered another urson or even ravers.

I nodded at him, and with my head lowered, I left the living room and started to check the basement.

The basement was spooky but my life was already full of nightmares and horror stories so I walked down the wooden steps without fear. I brought out the flashlight Perish had given me and swept it around the basement.

It was a finished basement, not a decrepit lower room full of bare brick, chains, and concrete floors like my imagination had suggested. This one had carpet too, but grey not yellow, and what remained of plaster on the walls. In all corners were stacks of brittle boxes holding plastic dishes and old papers, all of it coated and covered in dust.

Though just a minute ago I was telling myself how brave I was, as the light of the upstairs faded I started to feel a bit spooked. It was pitch black here after all, and who knows what had been down here last.

I screamed from fright when I saw a pair of glowing eyes. I took a step back but once I saw that it was a radrat my greywaster instincts suddenly kicked in. I dropped the flashlight and started chasing it around the basement.

The thing ran quickly but it must have been too surprised and scared that I had found it to know how to get out of the room. As I chased it around, it ran to a closed bedroom door and doubled back, before ducking behind a tipped over filing cabinet.

I looked around and grabbed an old phone book. I threw it at the rat and got it on its head, then as it stood there stunned, I dashed over, out of breath, and smashed it on the head with my boot.

Crunch… crunch… Ugh, I hated the sounds of bones breaking. The radrat twitched and thrashed, but with one last blow, I finished it off.

I breathed a huge sigh of relief and grabbed onto its tail. I sprinted up the stairs and found Perish waiting for me at the top.

He stared down at me coldly; he had been getting more closed off towards me as time went on. New Perish was just… he didn't seem at all like the Perish I had once known.

Can an O.L.S really change someone that much?

"I killed a radrat… that will feed us all for a day." I held it up and forced a small smile. I had been trying make it appear that I was warming up to him. It was a slow process, I had to make it believable and I knew this new Perish was smart. He knew my tricks.

The scientist looked at the creature and made a face. "Barely," he replied. "Give it to Edward to cook. We'll forget the other houses and keep moving on foot."

I nodded and saw Edward sitting down on one of the chairs. His missing fingers hadn't gotten infected but they still caused him a lot of pain. I had been doing my best to take care of him. I felt so guilty for what had happened.

My pride regarding Perish shouldn't get in the way of keeping my friends safe.

"Hey, Edward, look I found us some fresh meat!" I forced another smile. I forget when the last time I had actually smiled was.

Edward looked up and took the radrat from me. He had been a cook before he had been sold. He loved to cook anything that walked.

"Thanks, Killian… if I can find a river we can make soup. It'll fill us up more." His eyes were dull but they seemed to shine at the prospect of getting food into us. Or maybe it was because the slaves were safe for another day.

If we don't find food, we're eating one of them.
If you don't find food, Killian, it will be your fault.

I wouldn't let that happen. We would find food… lots of food…

Somewhere.

Our small party left the dilapidated structure behind and soon we were back on the road. The scenery around us was different than it had been in Aras or even the highway. We were in the greywastes again, where all you could see was grey and black, occasionally broken up by a tall tree or a large industrial building or hotel. There were more houses here than I was used to, but most held nothing inside but disappointment.

We made camp once the night started to take the greywastes. Perish decided to branch off to check out different houses which always made me nervous. The slavers also had the same fears I did, that the scientist would forget that we were on an invisible leash and our collars would activate.

So where Perish went, we went. We hovered around the house he was checking out and tried to make small talk with each other. They liked hearing stories about Aras and Tamerlan which I indulged them in, adding more positive things to even the most boring of stories to lift their spirits.

Perish emerged from one of the houses and looked at us with annoyance. I had just finished telling them about when Reaver got Biff, and how I had made him go *Here kitty kitty!* They, of course, knew my tough boyfriend so they thought it was just great.

"We're staying in here tonight," Perish said. "Get a fire and cook the rat."

We all filed in and I dragged a couch over a scorched tire rim that the last traveler had used for a fire pit. I shook out the two remaining cushions and sat Edward down first. I wanted the slaves to rest; they had less energy than I did.

The rat meat tasted like butter, the grease coated my mouth with a delicious taste. I savoured every bit of it but it was gone before I knew it.

Perish put the bones in a pot and emptied one of the bottles into it. Thankfully, we had many rivers that had formed from the melting snow, though the water was extremely irradiated. All of our Geigerchips buzzed whenever we took a drink from the water.

All of the water that fell from earth held amounts of radiation and we usually had Dek'ko filters we installed in whatever rig we had set up for running water. But, of course, we had no such luxuries here, not even Iodine pills to help counteract it.

Perish boiled the fresh bones and I threw in the spine I had been chewing on, Then, to my amusement, Perish cracked open the radrat's skull and started poking at its brain.

"No matter what… you'll always love your science," I said with a smile, trying to get another brownie point from him in my slow campaign to win his trust.

Perish had a scalpel in his hand. He slowly cut the rat's brain down the middle and gently separated it with his fingers.

"Radrat brains are about the size of a second trimester fetus brain. Usually I had a microscope or something on my glasses to help me, but I can still see well," he murmured, his tongue was sticking out of the corner of his mouth. "I have dissected a lot of them, to see why they died. There was one baby before Reaver was successful, the last one before Leo handed off the research to Elish to try. He had curly black hair though so Silas would have never been happy with him. Though as long as he got his clone, I suppose he would've kept him."

Perish's tongue stuck out more. He lifted up a small piece of brain tissue and smiled at his achievement. "This right here. The root of the brain beside the thalamus is where we resurrect from... but, of course, it is just normal on the rat." He showed me before he popped the piece into his mouth and kept digging.

"Reaver is a clone of Silas... but I guess like all the chimeras, Silas can make them look how they want?" I asked curiously.

Perish nodded. "That is what makes Reaver a chimera too. Though his DNA is how Elish wanted it. Silas wanted a Sky replacement so Elish put in strands of Sky's DNA. Then we added chimera enhancements because, really, it is easier to do them there than surgery when he's older."

"I guess Silas wouldn't want a clone that reminded him of himself, since Silas hates himself so much," I muttered. I watched as Perish held up another piece of brain.

He nodded. "Yes, Silas really does hate people who remind him of him, especially who he was before the Fallocaust." He leaned over and showed me the new piece. "This piece right here is where the memories are, long-term anyway. This is what Greg took from our heads... how he was able to just find those memories..." Perish's brow furrowed. "He was a mad scientist that one and a troublemaker. I'm glad he's long dead."

As was custom apparently, Perish ate that piece of the brain too, and continued to dig.

"Perry, why are we going to the plaguelands? You know the radiation is going to start overloading our Geigerchips, right?" I said. Perish seemed at ease, I wanted to take advantage of that.

"Born immortals have an immunity to sestic radiation," Perish said casually, scraping his small knife over the rat's open brain.

"So you don't care that this is going to kill me?" I asked soberly.

Perish paused, my words seemed to scald him because all he did was glare at the rat brain he was dissecting.

Oddly he was silent, but his eyes remained two focused blue pits. I wondered if I was going to be punished for drawing light on this reality. Though if he was in denial about my eventual fate, maybe I did need to remind him.

"Months ago, I got through to Reaver... I told him that he only had a limited time with you and he should treasure you, protect you," Perish began slowly. His movements were still frozen like he needed all of his concentration to say these words. "He put you in danger anyway. My Killian, my precious boy. My sweety, who did such a kind yet horrible thing for me in Donnely."

I stared at him. "You want to hurt Reaver by killing me now? Through radiation exposure?"

"Someone has to protect you, Killian. Someone has to protect–"

Perish suddenly stopped, his voice stopped, his movements stopped, it was like time froze around us.

"I have the right formula... he found it for me on the laptop," Perish murmured. He held up a hand before resting it on my arm. Oddly it went warm but not the warmth that Jade's thermal touch had, it was different.

Then, just a fleeting moment later, I felt my Geigerchip hum.

Perish's face got dark. His eyes shot up to me, and as he stared me down, they narrowed.

"Stop asking stupid fucking questions," the scientist, or whoever he was suddenly snapped. "Go to bed. I'm tired of looking at you. I'm tired of hearing you."

And that was the end of that – whatever that was.

That night with the slaves asleep in the other room, I laid next to Perish as was my duty as slave. This had been something that I had been forced to do since the night he had bludgeoned Danny, and I had stopped protesting. Perish liked to spoon me, or make me lay my head in the crook of his arm. It was... it was awkward for me and I hated it. Mostly because in the middle of the night, when the night terrors took me, I woke up thinking he was Reaver.

But it wasn't, though Perish soothed me all the same. It was only in the dead of night, in the middle of nowhere with a thousand terrors in the darkness, that I let him comfort me. No longer the hyper voice, no longer the rapid-speed consoling, now he held me close to him and shushed me, telling me it was all in my head and that I was okay.

No, I wasn't okay... as soon as I heard his voice I no longer cried from the nightmares in my head, but because I was once again far away from Reaver.

That night I woke up with a start and asked for him to turn the flashlight on so I could make sure no one was here. Something I had done many times in a half-lucid state back in Aras.

"I haven't fallen asleep yet," Perish said quietly. "No one's here."

I sighed and took in a deep breath. "It's late, why haven't you slept?"

He shrugged. "Sometimes I like to watch you sleep... I missed it when we were separated."

When we were separated... like we were two people who should have never been apart in the first place. That wasn't true and it had never been true.

"Well, I'm right here," I whispered. He always seemed so much kinder in the middle of the night, during the day he turned back into a cold, prickly jerk. "Go to sleep."

I closed my eyes and tried to force the fear from my mind, but a moment later the fear was replaced by horror when his lips press against my forehead.

He kissed me again and I felt his hand slowly stroke my stomach. "You know what else I have been thinking of?"

No, no no, not tonight... not tonight. Don't let tonight be the night.

I was frozen solid, my body so coiled in on itself my muscles hurt. Unable to hold it back, I let out a scared whimper.

"Shh... come on, I'm not going to rape you, Killian," Perish whispered. His hand slipped underneath my shirt and I felt it start to rub against my right nipple. His hands were rough from being out in the elements, not the soft, delicate hands he had in Donnely. "I would never do that to you."

"Then what are you doing?" I refused to open my eyes; I only squeezed them shut tighter as he twisted the pec between his fingers. "I don't–" No, I can't make him mad; he'll beat or possibly kill the slaves if I do.

"Take your pants off, I won't have sex with you," Perish said. I saw a burst of light through my closed eyelids.

I opened my eyes and saw he had turned the flashlight on. I swallowed and made eye contact with him. "Promise?"

He nodded, but to my unease, he started taking his pants off too.

I didn't trust him, but he had never expected me to trust him. Perish only expected me to obey, and what promises I got could be taken away as quickly as they were given.

With my heart pounding and the silence deafening around me, I removed my pants and underwear, seeing Perish's hard penis pop out of his own underwear as they were slid off of his body.

I was soft and untrimmed, and the cold air wasn't doing me any favours. I looked at the small space between our still laying bodies and tried to force my mind to be somewhere else. Anywhere but here, just like when Asher, or Silas, raped me with the dildo and made me do those horrible things to him. I had to close my eyes and pretend I was somewhere else. Let him do what he needed to do to his body to get his release, I would be his visual stimulation if I had to be.

"Your body is so perfect... I remember that body. I remember you." Perish's voice caught and he took in a ragged breath. I glanced up and saw his hand between his legs, slowly rubbing himself. "I missed you, Silas."

Silas? I blinked and stared at him.

"I'm... I'm not Silas," I said to him slowly.

"Touch it, get it hard."

What!? My eyes shot up to him, I immediately felt tears well.

"Please, no," I begged. "I... I'm not Silas, I'm Killian, Perish. Is the... O.L.S making you think I'm someone else?"

Perish's eyes were full of desire, his mouth open as if he was unable to breathe through the lust he was feeling. He held out a hand, his chest rising rapidly, and gently stroked my soft shaft.

He didn't answer me, and I wondered if what was going on inside of his mind was preventing him from acknowledging my words.

But when I let out another whimper, he retracted it. "You don't know how much I'm restraining myself right now. I could do worse to you, so–" He groaned and pulled on his dick. "–so much worse."

My mind raced, going over a thousand different ways I could get out of this, but none of them were plausible. I blinked away the tears and tried to reason with him any way I could. "I'll... kiss you, make out with you while you... do it to yourself."

Perish shook his head. "You have ten seconds to start touching it... or else I'll do it myself."

The thought sent a wave of sickness through me. I remembered how my body responded to Silas and I didn't want that to happen with Perish. Ignoring the screaming inside of my head, I took my dick into my hands and closed my eyes. I tried to imagine I was with Reaver and started stroking it.

It had been a long time since Reaver and I had had sex. Our last time was in Mariano before he had been taken, since then I obviously hadn't done anything.

I kept stroking it, my teeth clenching together, trying to get it to harden in my hands but nothing was happening. I was too scared.

Then I heard shifting. I kept my eyes closed more out of fear, but when I felt his hand touch mine to stop me I opened them. I watched him staring hungrily down at my penis before it disappeared into his mouth.

"Perish," I cried. I put my hand on his head in a desperate attempt to push his head off of me but he stayed between my legs. His mouth firmly suctioned around my dick, his tongue licking and rubbing against the head.

And it was working. I put my hands over my face and let out a sob. With every slow lap and drawn-out movement of his mouth, my dick got hard.

Perish removed his mouth and stroked his hand down the shaft. He stared at my dick with insatiable hunger and groaned; his fully hard penis rigid, standing erect between his bent knees.

"You… have no idea how long I have wanted this," he whispered. Hunger seemed to be taking over every part of his body. "Thinking of you… being intimate with you. I would die happy if I would have you just once."

Me or Silas? I was confused because this was something Perish would say to me but… he had called me Silas.

Perish put his mouth back over my penis and continued to suck on it.

"This is what King Silas did to me," I said quietly. "I hope you know that."

"Then should I fuck you instead?" Perish suddenly snapped.

The shifting in tone sent warnings off in my mind. I shook my head and separated my legs further, realizing that I was about to dig myself an even deeper grave. Perish approved of this and continued to work his mouth on me. I forced myself to relax and just get it over with.

"Put your mouth over mine," Perish said, the cold air stinging my sensitive head as he removed his lips. "Don't suck on it. Don't distract yourself from what I'm doing, just put it somewhere warm."

I think I knew that was going to happen, and I was thankful he wasn't going to lose control and fuck me which I was afraid he would. So without complaint, I took his penis into my hand and put my mouth over it.

I could taste the precum on the tip. I put my mouth over the head and left it there, ignoring his moans of pleasure and the motion of his hips as he automatically tried to push it in further.

Unable to contain his lust, Perish started to enthusiastically suck me. My stiff dick slid deeper into his mouth as he took in every inch; his hand stroking it in rhythm as he eagerly tasted me. The pleasure was intense and soon my breathing was rapid, so rapid that I couldn't hold back the small moans that came with every exhale. I was moaning into his dick, he could feel every vibration of my mouth and I could tell from the precum still forming on his head that it was driving him wild.

But there was no inner thrill of being able to control him like this, only shame and fear. I was walking a razor's edge right now and I knew if I didn't play my cards he would fuck me right here, tonight. Would he do it after I came? Could he hold himself back once he heard the sounds break from my lips, or the cum shoot into his mouth? I felt horror burn inside of me, and then the stark reality of what I had to do once I came.

And it wasn't long after that that the tension in my groin started to build. I gripped my jacket, the crown of his dick still in my mouth, and pursed my lips. As the pleasure gathered inside of me, I took in a sharp breath and broke my mouth away from his penis to let out a strangled moan.

His mouth rapidly licked up the cum shooting from my dick. I didn't look, but I could feel his tongue collect and gather the spurts as he devoured it hungrily. I could hear his rapid breathing through his nose as he kept up the tight seal.

When it was over I took a moment to catch my breath, then I did what needed to be done and started sucking him off myself.

Perish swore; his voice edging shock and surprise. He continued to lick and clean the bits of cum from my dick as he let me blow him.

I closed my eyes and in my head it was Reaver. Their dicks were similar anyway, thick and long, perfect in every way. I blocked out Perish's moans and his light thrusts into my mouth and replaced them with the intimate moans my boyfriend made when I was giving him this kind of attention.

Perish got up from his laying position and kneeled in front of me. As I continued to suck on him, he weaved his hands through my hair, moaning and taking in sharp breaths until I could feel his dick start to twitch in my mouth.

Then he came too. I let the cum fall onto the carpet below, feeling my pride drip down with it.

When the last spurt fell I laid back down without a word and put my pants on. Tears streamed down my face as I got back under the covers.

Perish didn't protest. He laid down beside me and put his arm over my chest, pushing my back into his stomach.

"Couldn't hold yourself back?" he purred into my ear. His fingers wiped the tears from my eyes.

I shook my head, exhausted and done I closed my eyes.

He laughed at this. "Lies… but it's alright, I won't tell Reaver."

Perish knew I was Killian again, I guess that was a good thing. I would treat this incident as a hook, another hook to get him to trust me.

But as I sliced away pieces of my pride to gain his favour; I wondered just how much of me would remain.

It became a regular thing for us after that. Over the next several days as we walked down the two-lane road I became less of Perish's slave and more of his personal object. I was what he used to release himself at night.

The next night when we had camped inside of an old video store he made me masturbate in front of him as he stroked himself. I considered myself lucky that that was all he made me do. Though at the end, when I had forced myself into orgasm, he couldn't resist his mouth over my dick to catch my cum. The night after that he gave me head again and to once again fend him off I did the same back.

Last night was worse even though, for the most part, he kept our clothes on. While he was spooning me he started grinding himself into my backside like he had done in Donnely, but his dick was out and he pulled my pants down over my backside. He thrust the hard piece of flesh into me until he brought himself to climax. No penetration, no innocent slip, just skin on skin.

I cried but he ignored it. I even choked and gagged when I felt the warm, stickiness spill from his penis onto my backside but he ignored that too.

Perish was going to fuck me soon, and I knew it. This thin razor I was walking on was getting slighter and more sharp. On one hand I was getting him to trust me, but on the other hand it was always going to escalate and it would continue to escalate. Perish was going to try and get sex out of me, and all I could do was try and think of ways to satiate his sex drive.

I knew the sex drives of men, Reaver was no different. When he got horny he was bringing out the handcuffs, the leather. He was nipping, licking, and biting me with throated growls full of vulgar dirty talk. He was wild, and the more riled he was the more he wanted to fuck me hard, try different things and kink it out. But once he had his session, once he orgasmed his last time and was done, he was done. The fantasies disappeared by morning, and bringing them up during the day would bring blush to his cheeks and have him disappearing into the tunnel to hide his embarrassment. Reaver was a man for the moment and Perish was too. Once I made him cum he remembered himself again and backed off. It was bringing him to his peak before he stepped over that line that was my job.

I had been with Perish for a long time now, however it seemed like longer. But to my credit, even though every night I was leaving more pieces of me behind, I was gaining his trust again. And I had to keep his trust to keep me and my friends alive.

"You can still pick up things at least," I said to Edward. He was wiggling his thumb and index finger, the only two digits he had left on his left hand. "And it's not your dominant hand, right?"

Edward nodded and made a show of making a pinching motion. He was slowly starting to get his strength up. I had been doing a good job finding food for everyone. Even yesterday I had spotted a small scorpion and Perish had managed to kill it. The meat was insect meat which tasted like dirt, but it was good meat with a lot of protein.

I took Edward's hand to make sure the stumps were healing well and they were. He was lucky that they hadn't gotten infected or he might have become food.

No, they won't become food…

Danny appeared beside me, scratching the chafed area underneath his collar. "Do you think you could try and convince him to let us search a pharmacy? Teejay's leg is starting to bother him; the bruise is getting bigger not smaller."

My face burned with guilt. That had been my fault. I had told Teejay he could eat the last scorpion leg which I hadn't realized Perish wanted. Perish had thrown rocks at him and had gotten him in the leg and the hip. The poor greywaster, a man in his thirties with such a kind disposition, had been limping and struggling to keep up with us.

"I will… just try and keep a lookout for a good walking stick for him," I said under my breath to Danny. I glanced at the trees around us but the ones we had the strength to rip free wouldn't support his weight.

Danny nodded and I sprinted up ahead to where Perish was walking.

Ahead of us was an abandoned town, one of the once 'sleepy towns' they had here before the Fallocaust. No huge buildings or skyscrapers, just houses, shops and the occasional bigger office building or apartment. There should be a hospital here, or a pharmacy, and we were so deep into the greywastes I held hope that they hadn't been picked clean. I didn't think so; we hadn't seen a single soul since we had left the resort and any sign of them looked ages old.

"Are we staying in that town tonight?" I asked Perish.

Perish glanced over at me. He looked so different now with his short beard and I did too, but my facial hair grew in patchy and weird. It was starting to fill out at least.

"Yes, I want food for the next week. We won't be seeing much in the way of towns, so unless you want fresh meat you better find some good food," Perish replied crisply. New Perish was an asshole but during the day he called me Killian and understood who I was. It was at night that I occasionally became Silas to him.

I still hadn't figured out why – I just assumed it was the O.L.S giving him confusing memories.

"Could we check out a pharmacy or a hospital? I want to get some treatment for Teejay's leg and for Edward's fingers as well," I asked nicely, bumping up my voice to a higher octave to try and curry his favour.

Perish glanced behind him. I did too and saw Teejay hobbling along with help from Danny. We had all formed a bond over the last several weeks and we did our best to help each other.

"Yes, I can allow that. I would like to check out a hospital, especially one this deep into the greywastes. Perhaps I can find some interesting tools." He looked up. "We are into March now. The weather will soon start to warm."

"How long are you expecting it to be until we get to the plaguelands?" Where I'll die.

"A long time. Weeks. Maybe months."

My heart plummeted. "I… I don't think the slaves can make it for that long, Perry."

Perish's face hardened; his facial hair and the bangs framing his eyes, giving him even more of a menacing look. "I don't expect them to. They are only here until we need food, Killian. Why do you think I have them?"

He turned around and glared down Teejay. "Hear that? You're only here until Killian fails to find food, and then we eat you. Do you realize that?"

THE GHOST AND THE DARKNESS

The three of them, sunken-faced and gaunt, just stared at Perish, knowing that arguing with him wouldn't do any good. They continued to walk.

But Perish always had to press them, like in Donnely he seemed to get pleasure from bullying those under his control. "Did you hear me?"

"Yeah," the three of them murmured.

Then the scientist put a hand on my shoulder and patted it. "See? It's all on you, Killian. You are in control and you decide who lives and who dies. All up to Killian. If they make it to the border maybe I might let them live. Do you want that, slaves? If you make it alive to the border, I let you live. It's all up to–"

I put my hand over my mouth as the tears sprung to my eyes. I turned from the slaves and kept walking towards the town. My shoulders were shaking and my throat tightening around the boulder of guilt that was growing with each passing minute.

This was all up to me…

But I could do it. I wiped my eyes with my sleeve and tightened my lips, forcing the guilt and sorrow down. I was Reaver Merrik's boyfriend. I had killed King Silas and I had killed Perish. I was strong; I could get everyone out of this okay. I had already failed Jade, and I wouldn't fail these slaves. I would get them all out of this alive.

I would get out alive too. I might get radiation poisoning but if Elish was with Reaver I could get detoxed in Skyfall – I could still make it out of this alive.

Or maybe, since it would be weeks to months, Reaver would find me? If I wanted him to find me… I was scared of what Perish had in his head. The entire reason we were out here was because the O.L.S held the secret of how to kill immortals.

The O.L.S that Perish was implanted with.

I glanced up at the sky and focused my ears to any noise that might be a Falconer. Right now I might even prefer the Legion to find us, because at least Elish would then know I was here. But there was nothing above me but sky and a sun hidden behind hazy grey.

We were alone, just the five of us.

And no one knew where we were.

Perish put his arm around me but I ignored him. I knew if I opened my mouth to say anything I would start to cry again.

"I know why you're looking at the sky, Killian," Perish whispered into my ear. "And I guarantee you – he's in Skyfall right now with Silas. They're making love every night, getting to know each other in intimate ways you never dreamed of. He's not coming for you, Killian. No one is coming for you."

I started to cry but he continued to dig into me. "You're mine." He wiped the tears from my eyes. "And it would be in your own best interest to just accept that. The slaves' best interest too."

"He isn't with Silas," I said wiping my eyes. "And... I'm not..."

I stopped myself before I went too far, but I saw his eyes narrow.

"Where do you think he is, Killian? He isn't here, is he?" Perish chuckled. His eyes shone with a darkness that had been a part of his face since the resort. "I wonder if Elish knows I murdered his little pet. I wonder if I'll get to see him cry like a fucking child."

Deep inside of me something happened. It wasn't the flicking of a switch, or the snapping of my sanity. It was the burning anger inside of me I had been keeping caged in a glass bottle. The one I refused to let out because I knew the punishment.

But I was only human. I was just one man with emotions already a wildfire inside of my chest. I didn't have steeled restraint. I didn't have control over myself, and most of all: I didn't have the armour needed to fend off Perish's words.

And with that inside my head... I ripped my shoulder away from Perish's arm and punched him right in the mouth.

Perish stumbled back and fell on his backside onto the greywastes' floor. I glared at him, my chest heaving up and down to accommodate the adrenaline ripping through my body.

"Reaver isn't in Skyfall and he isn't with Silas!" I screamed. I kicked him in the ribs at that point, tears blurring my vision and stinging my eyes. "He isn't with Silas! He'll find me and fucking kill you! And Elish will make you pay for killing Jade." My voice broke. I raised my leg to kick him again but to my surprise Perish raised his own leg and kicked mine out from under me.

I fell to the ground hard; my head cracking against the ashy dirt. Automatically Perish was on top of me. I kicked and screamed as he straddled me before wrapping a hand around my neck.

Perish's face was a blank expression but his eyes held ice and fire. He stared down at me, before raising his free hand and backhanding me several times across the face.

In retaliation I spat blood at him, and tried to hit him again but the next blow he dealt threw my senses out of me. I could only cough and gasp for breath as the blood pooled in the back of my throat.

Then he got up. I quickly scrambled to my feet and went to face him, when to my horror, I saw him walk up to the slaves. All of them huddled together, staring at him like scared children.

Then screaming, more screaming, echoing inside of my head as he started bludgeoning them with the handle of his combat knife.

I grabbed onto Perish's shirt and pulled him back, crying and begging for him to stop. Promising him everything in the world as he rained blow after blow on whatever slave was closest to him.

I did the only thing I could think of, the last desperate act of a man who had lost everything. I grabbed onto the belt of his pants and pulled him towards me.

"Drop it... drop... drop the knife and come here," I whimpered, taking advantage of his brief pause I slipped my hand down his pants and grabbed him. "Come here."

Perish was still, though his eyes were a blaze of anger. I unbuttoned his pants with trembling hands, and when he didn't make a move to push me away, I unzipped his fly.

I took out his penis, and with the tears running down my face I kneeled down and put my mouth over it.

I started to suck on the head. In full view of the slaves, out in the open, I did what I knew would save my friends.

And another piece of me falls away.

I didn't have many pieces left.

CHAPTER 43

Reno

AND WHAT A SORRY FUCKING SIGHT I WAS. I HAD been a sorry sight since I had gotten shot in Aras, constantly nursing injury after injury. I was either being shot, beat, yelled at, raped or beat some more.

Now I was on the floor groaning; the root of my back molar on the ground pinched between a set of pliers. I was drooling blood, or bleeding drool… either way, I was in a fucking lot of pain.

This was my life right now. Fiancé less, friendless, and hated by everyone in this damn town.

I rolled onto my stomach and drooled on the floor for a few more minutes before I got my pathetic ass up. Then I took another big drink of whisky and sat on the bed. I was wearing nothing but my tighty-whiteys because whatever, I had stopped caring a few days ago.

I almost gagged as the whiskey got into my open tooth wound but I managed to swallow it down with a shudder. Then I laid back in bed with my mouth stuffed with a washcloth and felt sorry for myself some more.

Since I'd gotten the snot beat out of me I hadn't really felt like leaving the hotel room, so I had been sending off Trixie and Mitzie or whatever those little girls' names were. They didn't hate me like the rest of their family so they were more than happy to deliver me food for chocolate bars. It was a nice arrangement and I could probably take them if they tried to beat me up like everyone else seemed to want to.

Probably being the optimum word.

But even though I had food to eat, I couldn't eat properly right now anyway. I just tore off pieces of sandwich and nibbled on the ratchips with my front teeth. My back molar was just a crater and the one beside it felt like it had a crack in it or something. Too bad I no longer had Skyfall to help me with my teeth, greywaste medical care consisted of exactly what I had right now: whisky and pliers.

I spat another mouthful of blood into a plastic bucket and laid in bed until the crater started to clot. Then, with my stomach full of whisky and self-pity, I got up and went down the hotel stairs to wander around outside for a bit.

It was dark out, and considering no one liked me I probably should stay inside, but I was bored and my social meter was low. I needed to talk to people. I wasn't like Reaver... I needed to talk and mingle or else I just went crazy.

The dusty, paved streets had several people milling around but it wasn't full. Most of them were carrying flashlights to see their way until they got to a more populated area of the town.

All the lights in the direction I was heading were turned off. It was behind me that was more lit up. That's where the restaurant and pubs were but I don't think I was welcome there so I branched off to explore a bit.

I had an old flashlight so I clicked it on to light my way, shining it down alleyways but all that greeted me back were glowing eyes of stray and wandering cats. I missed our cats in Aras, most of them were wild and a bit dickish but the tame ones were awesome. Like good ol' Biff, who was probably sporting his own sengil outfit now.

I wish I was a cat.

The whisky bottle found its way to my lips again. My movements were already stumbly but I wasn't drunk, just a tad buzzed.

I felt my pockets for my remote phone. I was tempted to try and get a hold of Elish but I knew if they had found out anything they would ring me and tell me. So chances are if I called those guys all I would get was yelled at. If the phone was even...

I scowled. I turned around thinking I had heard someone beside me. I raised the flashlight and swept the area, I was walking past another alleyway, but all I saw were trash cans.

Odd.

I shrugged it off and branched off in a different direction. This area was just greywaster homes and some park land. I didn't think I would find many people but maybe I would luck out and find someone getting drunk in the park.

Well, it wasn't much of a park. There was no green grass, just a stretch of greywaste dirt and rock and the occasional twiggy bush or tuft of yellowy grass. In Skyfall…

"Gah!" I said out loud and put my hands on my head. I shook my head back and forth and sighed. "You need to stop thinking about that place, Reno Nevada. It won't do you any good at all."

With an angry sigh, full of self-disappointment, self-derision, and a lot of other selfs, I walked on with my flashlight lighting my way. I strolled through the dusty park and sat my ass on an old spinny-go-around thing and lit myself a cigarette. I took a moment to enjoy the smoke killing my lungs and absentmindedly chipped a few loose pieces of red paint from the metal bars.

This shit would only be temporarily at least. I would be reunited with Reaver. I just had to keep healing and stop getting myself more and more hurt. Reaver needed a friend right now; he would probably be going bananarama in the head worrying about Tink, and Elish too worrying about Biter. I had to be mediator; they must be ripping each other to shreds both physically and verbally by now. I couldn't imagine them getting along.

And Reaver was also in a bad space mentally over what had happened with Nero. I would hope Elish would know how to handle that but Elish was a bit of an asshole when it came to being empathetic. I think Garrett had sucked up all the empathy genes in the first generation.

I shone my flashlight on a black tree as I worked through my cigarette. My bored mind was pleased to see a black cat in a thick branch, peering down at me with reflective eyes.

"Hey, buddy," I said to it. I decided in that moment he would be my new friend. I held out my hand and rubbed my fingers together to try and coax him over but he only glared at me. "Where are you from? Me? I'm from a town far away."

The cat, of course, didn't answer me back. I gave up with a sigh and shone the flashlight elsewhere. Trees, more trees, an old swing set that looked like something out of a horror movie, and a rusted slide with blue spray paint.

This was boring. I took another drink and got up and went to find another bar I could sulk in.

I decided to cut through a few alleyways on my way back to the more populated parts of Tintown. So with a flashlight in one hand, my whisky in another, and a cigarette dangling from my mouth, I left the park and crossed the street.

Once again I jumped as I heard a noise. This time a crashing sound above me, like someone had accidently hit an air vent or something. I glanced up and shone the flashlight to investigate but still there was nothing.

This was getting weird... I glared at the flashlight beam as I slowly trailed it along the edge of an old industrial building. I saw nothing but grey, aged wood and some loose tar paper.

But I didn't move. I stayed still, my tipsy mind trying to mull over this strange occurrence I was experiencing. It seemed like right after I arrived here odd things had been happening. First with Jesse deciding I was the scum of the earth all of a sudden, then getting beat up, and now with these noises.

I had liked that kid. He was a normal non-chimera who wasn't completely fuck-nut insane. I had missed normal; I hadn't been around anyone normal in a really long time. He was supposed to be sane-of-mind, easygoing, and just... normal! But nope, he ended up being a bigger fucking douchebag than the douchebags I had–

Another fucking crash! I whirled around in alarm as I heard a gasp and a yelp, before suddenly something big and black fell from the roof. It landed right into an open dumpster with a crash that sent several cats dashing off into the darkness.

I stared. I stared because I recognized that yell...

A smile crept to my lips. I sighed as I walked over to the dumpster. I peered in and saw none other than Garrett struggling to get to his feet.

"You're the worst chimera in the world," I said to him, still holding the smile. "Reaver stalked Killian for months and I don't think that kid knew he was there most of the time. You were clanking around like you were wearing a pair of lead shoes."

Garrett was flushed with embarrassment and looking flustered. He started stammering and stumbling over his words which made me laugh.

Then he paused, I saw his lips purse together.

"I missed your laugh," he said quietly.

I shifted my eyes away from him, remembering why we were apart in the first place. I shone the flashlight beam on the ground, knowing it would be more blinding with his vision than helpful. "What are you doing here anyway?" I replied.

"I miss you?" Garrett said with a half-hearted shrug. "I love you? I owe you an apology and I couldn't just… make Elish tell you for me? I… had to tell you in person."

I helped him out of the dumpster and dusted him off. He was still wearing a suit and tie, horrible greywaster attire. "Are you hurt? That's a good ten feet you fell."

Garrett looked at me, that kind of look that tugged on every heartstring you had. I had erected many walls inside of my mind since I had left Skyfall, but I swear those green eyes always seemed in the process of tearing them down.

"You care?" he said back, a hint of confusion in his voice.

Do I care? Who did he think I was?

"I… I don't hate you, Garrett," I said. "I just…" I glanced behind me to the end of the alley, only a faint bluelamp on the other side of the street lighting our way. I turned the flashlight off and put it inside my jacket.

"I just had to help him."

Still the shy boy, with self-esteem lower than my own, Garrett nodded and started to walk out of the alley.

"Where are you going?" I asked him quietly. I started following his steps as he quickly made his way to the street, his head lowered.

Garrett kept walking. I sprinted up to him and grabbed his arm. "You came all this way… did you really just want to follow me around for a while?"

"I'm… my apologies I just wanted to make sure you… you were alright. I'll go home. I, ah…" He rubbed the back of his head. "I left you some more money in your hotel room… it's under your bed. Also, Sanguine is here and he will do some repairs on your quad and… ah…" His voice was starting to wobble and with each shaky octave I started to feel more and more guilty.

What had I done to him? My poor little Garebear.

The guilt welled inside of my chest as I saw his eyes shift around uncomfortably; his lower lip had disappeared into his mouth with his teeth firmly clamped down on it. His eyes were so wide, and though it was dark, I could see the faintest glisten to them.

He was… such a horrible chimera. Look at him.

I laughed as I thought this. And when he gave me a crushed look, I opened my arms. "Come here, baby."

Garrett's face fell; he gave me one last heart-wrenching glance, a glance that held ninety-one years of sorrow, before he walked into my arms.

As soon as I heard him start to whimper I lost it too. Together in this dark alley that smelled like trash and piss, I held him in my arms and we choked back tears together. Looking like lunatics to all that were watching, though the biggest spectators were our own crumpled up emotions.

I sniffed back almost all my tears but one as I held onto him, his suit smelling like fresh laundry soap. A smell so fucking foreign to this place, it made me miss home.

"I love you, I'm sorry," I whispered to him. "I was being an insensitive asshole. Can you forgive me?"

Garrett pulled back, his face reading a look of shock. "You? You're sorry? Lutra, I... I mistreated you. I am the one apologizing. I should have helped like I promised."

Look at him, such a silly creature. Or maybe I was the silly one, or the idiot anyway. One look from him, one single pure emotion and all of my feelings for him came rushing back.

I brushed back his hair and kissed the corners of his lips. "You came here for me, that's all the apology I need."

Then his lower lip stiffened before it disappeared as he held his hand to his mouth. "I... I have to apologize for something else as well. I promised I would do it as soon as I saw you."

I raised an eyebrow and when his eyes got a bit wider, I narrowed my own. "What did you do?"

Garrett shifted his feet around, his hand still covering his mouth. "I'm sorry... Reno, but...it was me who made Jesse avoid you. I scared him a bit."

For a moment I just looked at him, probably with a blank look on my face. Garrett withered under my gaze.

That was the reason why Jesse wanted to get as far away from me as he could. Garrett had fucking threatened him!

Which meant...

I swallowed my own guilt, but it shot back up my throat and filled it with a lump of cold regret. "I... I'm so fucking sorry... I was lonely and..."

He held up a hand and the corners of his mouth raised in a smile. "I don't care... I fucked him bloody in the adjacent room as soon as you passed out, so we can just call it a threesome."

My mouth completely dropped open.

"Are you fucking serious…?"

Garrett glanced up at the stars above us and moved his pursed lips over the side of his face.

I hit him on the shoulder, my mouth still open in shock. "You manic fuck! You *are* a chimera, I knew you were! You're fucking nutso!" When Garrett saw I was smiling, he grinned and tried to fend off my repeated assaults.

"You raped that poor kid?"

"I was angry at the time!" Garrett protested, holding up his hands as I kept up my onslaught of domestic violence. "This way you won't feel guilty for doing it! Right? We're… we're even! I was jealous! And well… now you don't have to feel guilty. Really, love, I did you a huge service. I knew you would feel terrible for doing it."

I laughed, wondering if I myself was starting to become a chimera since I found his confession kind of funny, in a morbidly-disturbing-yet-endearing way.

"You're… you're crazy. That poor kid," I chuckled.

I lowered my hands and smiled at him. Garrett smiled back and I could see the relief pouring off of him. His actions reminded me of something Reaver would do, and I hated to admit it but… I liked that.

"Come on, psycho chimera…" I rested a hand on his face and stroked it. "Let's get the fuck out of here. I hate this fucking town. You have a plane, right?"

"Really?" Garrett said. His head tilted towards my touch. "You… you want to go back to Skyfall?"

I smiled and nodded, then I took his hand and started pulling him out of the alleyway. "Well, I certainly don't want to stay in this shithole, and Aras is pretty much fucked too. Where else would I go? The only time I've been happy over the past several months has been when I was with you."

Garrett gave me a shy smile and let me pull him off the road. We started walking towards the hotel room. "I didn't expect you to welcome me back… I thought I would just be following you around for the rest of eternity."

Like how Reaver would just follow Killian? I wonder if that was a chimera thing; always the silent stalker out of the corner of your eye. A constant thing in your life until you want to look upon it.

But this chimera was different. I let out a long breath and opened the door to the hotel room. We walked upstairs and I started packing everything. The more I shoved my dirty clothes into that bag the more I realized I was anxious to go back to Skyfall. I don't know what that meant in the long run, but I knew right now... I needed Garrett and he needed me.

I think this entire time I had thought he was being the jerk, but now that I look back on it... I was the one being a complete and total prick.

I looked over at Garrett. Unaware I was watching him, he was quietly folding my dirty shirts and placing them neatly into a bag. His lips tight and his eyes still welling; I wish I could hear his heartbeat.

He came here to get me. Garrett might not have broken the Morse code, he might not have busted me out of the shack in Cypress... but maybe I was a dick for expecting that from him. If he was that type of chimera, I wouldn't love him the same.

I loved him, because like me – he had his faults, but fuck he always tried to do the right thing.

"Gare?" I said.

He looked over at me, and like every time I called to him, his eyes lit up.

"I love you... you know that, right?"

Garrett stopped, clutching my old Iron Maiden t-shirt in his hand. I thought he was going to tear up again, or say it back, but instead he replied quietly, "Then why did you leave me?"

My heart gave a guilty jolt. "I... I was mad and still fucked up from the Crimstones," I replied honestly. "But... I did a lot of thinking here and I realized I was expecting you to act like Reaver. And you're not Reaver."

I didn't realize the weight my words held until I saw him stiffen. "I am not Reaver, or Elish... far from it." He picked up my bag and put it over his back. "Come on, love. Sanguine has the plane... let's get you home. I can smell that wound inside of your mouth and your face is so bruised." He reached out and gently touched my cheek, the crater that was once my molar still raw and aching.

I gave him a look. "Which can also be blamed on you."

Garrett gave me a guilty glance and an apologetic mumble before he turned and grabbed my last bag.

I chuckled and shook my head.

We both walked downstairs and I said a fleeting goodbye to Grandpa who gave me a wave. *Happy Days* was on the television and even if a talking bear walked through the door and asked him for a cigarette he would just give him a wave. I loved that old man. If I could pull it, I'd ask one of the chimeras to deliver him one of those giant fucking televisions and really blow his mind.

We walked back into the cold night, hand in hand. Garrett was leading me to the east part of town, an abandoned area much like the old West Aras, covered mostly in half-cleared streets and debris from fallen structures and broken roads.

It was quiet until we turned a corner, a metal sign with spray paint telling us this area was off limits to children. Behind the sign I could hear the rumbling of a Falconer, and the higher octave motor of what sounded like my quad.

"I guess when a guy with red eyes and pointed teeth ask for a quad you give it to 'em," I said amused. Sure enough, I saw the outline of a slender figure, Sanguine obviously, steering the quad up a lowered ramp. His tongue was sticking out of the corner of his mouth as he tried to keep the tires on the shoddy slab of metal.

Garrett nodded and gave Sanguine a wave. "Well, yes, Sanguine is a better tracker than I. He was raised in the greywastes after all. I wasn't sure if you would go to Anvil or Tintown. Jack is having a nice time in Anvil doing his paintings. We will pick him up on the way back."

"You sent out the dogs, eh?" I said. Sanguine jerked the throttle on the quad and with a roar it sped up the ramp. I saw the plane shift as the quad hit the other side and then an echoed laugh.

Garrett looked embarrassed. "I had to make sure you were safe... though we did a rather bad job since you did get hurt. I... well, I think I may have been drunk in the plane when that happened."

"I deserved it anyway," I said with a shrug. Sanguine closed the plane door and disappeared into the cockpit. I walked over to sit down on the bench, still seeing the faint bits of blood from my injury months ago. It was kind of sobering and sad in a way that it was the same plane, the last place I had seen Killian and Jade.

But Garrett grabbed my hand and led me to the front of the plane, then sat me down on his lap and put his arms around me. I felt him lean his chin on my shoulder with a relieved sigh.

"Never do that again, ever," he mumbled. "I was so worried about you. When Elish said he had you... I can't explain to you the relief I felt. You're mortal, love, please remember that."

"Normal people are mortal, Garrett." I felt him kiss behind my ear. "Normal people die sometimes..."

"Not you, never."

I smiled at this. "Are you going to make me immortal like Elish wants to make Jade?"

Garrett stopped kissing me. "Why would you think I wouldn't? Once Elish is king... he has promised us we will all get our partners. I choose you."

I get to be immortal? I shifted myself on his lap so I was sitting more length-wise. "Can you do chimera surgery on me and make me all fucking badass Super Man?"

Sanguine chuckled from the pilot's chair; his blood-red eyes purple as he checked on the Falconer's control screen.

Garrett nodded and traced his finger along my jawline. "I'll do whatever you want. If you want to have the enhancements you can. Though I don't think we have ever put them in a non-chimera since Mantis. Have we, Sanguine?"

Sanguine shook his head no. "Not since Mantis. Reno might be an interesting human to experiment on. But, of course, it could go wrong and he could be disfigured for life or mentally stunted."

"I'm already mentally stunted so I don't mind that." I reached inside my jacket and pulled out my whisky. I took a long drink and handed the bottle to Garrett. "Could you make me strong enough to whoop Reaver's ass?"

Garrett took a drink and passed it along to Sanguine. "No, love, but since Silas is probably going to mutilate and murder Nero, perhaps you can replace him in Stadium? I can see my love pull convicts heads from their bodies." He continued to dote on me by tickling under my chin. I missed human touch so much. "You can be whatever you want to be."

"Right now I just want to go back to Skyfall and have a hot shower and some proper food." I yawned and rested my head on his shoulder. "And see Sid or Lyle. I need one of them to do a root canal on me. My cracked tooth is starting to ache."

"Of course, love," Garrett said sweetly. "Whatever you–"

Sanguine made a disgusted, choking-type noise. Garrett gave him a look that could peel paint. "Just fly the plane, clown."

Sanguine laughed and shook his head. "You might need to take over. I think I may throw up over the controls from all this sickeningly sweet doting you're doing."

Garrett raised his nose up in the air and squeezed me tight. "Well, get used to it. You're going to hear me love and dote on him for all eternity. And when you and Jack finally admit you're soul mates, I shall laugh just as hard at you."

At this, Sanguine scoffed and I saw him press a couple buttons on the display screen. "Do not get me started on Jack. However we will be landing to pick him up soon. Hold on, I see Anvil in the distance."

"Oh my god, I missed this place!" I walked out of the steamy bathroom with a towel over my waist and shook my hair like a dog. Garrett laughed and held up his hand to shield himself from the spray.

"You look wonderful, lutra. Did you want to turn your hair silver again?" Garrett asked. I could smell the delicious aroma of hot food, immediately I looked around for it. When I spotted two plastic bags full of containers I rubbed my hands together and walked over to attack them.

"Nah, I want to transition back into Reno. I think I'll be less depressed that way." I rooted through the bags and opened up one but it was only green beans, pah. I started digging through some more. "It was fun being the hot, silver-haired cicaro but... I just want to be me now. Silas knows I'm here anyway, I have no one I'm hiding from."

I opened another container and found potato fries. I cheered and picked up a handful. I started shoving them in my mouth.

Garrett hissed at me and shifted the container away from my greedy hands. "Slow down! Chally, get us some plates."

Chally? Sure enough, as I turned around the small blond kid was hiding in a corner giving me those scared eyes. Now dressed in a sengil outfit with his hair neatly cut and styled. He was holding a duster in one hand and his other was nervously clenching the sides of his trousers.

"I thought you would give him the boot after the information he gave me," I said. I smiled at Chally. "We found him. We haven't found Killian yet but Reaver is out looking for him. He'll never forget what you did for him, bro. I can tell you that."

The former slave and now sengil gave me a kind smile back and signed a few quick signs at me. I looked at Garrett for help.

"I told him this once I spoke with Elish, and he's happy to hear that.

He did like Killian a lot," Garrett said. "He also wants you to know I haven't mistreated him. Well, of course I haven't." Garrett shook his head.

"Is he okay being a sengil?" I looked at Chally. "We can send you back to your town if you want. Sengils are technically still slaves just… better treated."

Chally shook his head and continued to sign.

Garrett translated. "Chally is happy being our sengil. He and Luca have become best friends and that poor boy needs a friend. He is so lonely in Olympus and misses Elish and Jade dearly. Also Sid wants to check out Chally's vocal cords to see if we can get him to talk. Apparently Sid suspects he has a neurological disorder."

I shrugged and grabbed another handful of fries. "Most greywasters do. When did you stop being able to talk, Chally?"

"Ten," Garrett responded for him. "I have him going over there tomorrow morning. Since we have tea with Silas the day after that I would rather Chally be out of the skyscraper. Why dangle meat in front of a dog."

I groaned and disappeared back into the bedroom to quickly change. King Silas was someone I wasn't looking forward to seeing. I never knew if he was going to torture me, electrocute me, or give me a hug. That guy was exactly what Garrett and Elish called him: a mental shapeshifter. It was exhausting being around him because you never fucking knew what to expect. Though I didn't miss the greywastes and I was happy to be back with Garrett, at least Silas wasn't a constant dark threat over my head. That was one thing the greywastes had on Skyfall.

When I emerged Garrett and I took our food and ate on the couch, sitting beside each other and picking apart our hamburgers like we always did. As per our agreement, he got my tomato and I got his pickles. I was sure it wouldn't be hard to just order our hamburgers without the ingredients we didn't like, but well, it was kind of cute.

After we had eaten and Chally had vanished into his bedroom to play video games I snuggled with Garrett on the couch, a movie playing on the television.

He was petting my hair back, I was half lying on him, half lying on the couch.

Garrett kissed my neck, then my cheek bone, then my ear. "I love you. I'm so happy you're home and not angry with me."

I turned around so I was facing him. "You won't do it again? You know… stop me from helping Reaver? You know… once I'm healed…"

Garrett's face became grave. "Never will I disappoint you again. I will be going with you. We can help them together. We are partners now… which… actually…" I moved off of the couch as he got up and watched him go into his office. He returned a few moments later and I saw he was holding my engagement ring.

"How about it?" he said with a smile.

I laughed at his choice of words and held out my hand. Killian had told me how Reaver had asked him to be his boyfriend and I had, of course, told the cute story to Garrett. "Alright… since you seem to have learned your lesson, chimera. Go ahead, make an honest man out of me."

How could I have ever been mad at this man? There was a stupid grin on my face as he slid the engagement ring back onto my finger, but it faded as he leaned in and kissed me.

The butterflies came back, like the first time we had kissed. I opened my mouth slightly to take him in deeper, and with the fireworks exploding inside of my chest, his tongue met mine.

The movie continued to drone on but we weren't paying attention. We made out on the couch, our hands going everywhere but where I wanted them to go but that was alright with me. I respected Garrett and I still felt guilty for fucking Jesse, even if Garrett had had sloppy-seconds.

His skin was so soft. I had loved Jesse's rough greywaster physique but there was something about Garrett's smooth, lotioned skin that drove me wild. I found myself kissing and sucking on his neck just to fill my senses with as much of it as possible.

It was driving me crazy, I was fully hard and he was too. Coyly I pressed my groin against his and used this opportunity to nip at his neck.

Garrett let out a small moan, and I felt his body rise and fall as he took in a deep breath.

"I am not as strong as I think I am," he whispered, pulling himself away from me. I leaned in and kissed his lips again and was surprised when I felt his hand, which had been resting on my chest, creep down my pants.

I pulled back and looked down. My mouth opened in a gasp of surprise as he started touching my hard dick. My chest shuddered and started to tighten as his warm, soft hands started to gently touch and fondle it.

He was watching me, taking in every expression on my face. I closed my eyes and groaned, feeling my ears go hot with adrenaline and want. I knew if he pulled away this time I wouldn't be able to handle it. I wanted him.

My hand strayed, I moved it down to his own pants and slipped it in, past his underwear and down to his groin. I felt a brush of his pubic hair until I found the hard member radiating heat. I took it in my own hand and started stroking it up and down.

We kissed; only breaking away to let moans escape from our lips, each of us touching and rubbing each other as the heat reached the inner core of my mind. I could almost see the energy seeping off of our bodies, encasing us in a lust no hotel fling could match.

"Take me to the bedroom," I whispered, rubbing the head with my thumb.

Garrett nodded and at his acceptance, at the glaring fact that he wasn't putting a stop to this, my chest quaked.

I got up off of the couch and he rose too. Then, without a word, we went into the bedroom we had once shared.

I threw the last of my clothing onto the floor and sat down on the bed. I looked up as I shifted myself into the middle of his king size bed and watched him remove each piece of clothing from his flawless body.

Toned arms, actual abs, and just a slight wisp of chest hair on his firm body. I shook my head and looked down at my own horrible physique. I might have had some muscles but I was pale and still bruised.

"You're just beautiful."

I looked up and flushed with embarrassment as Garrett whispered those words to me. I rubbed my nose and looked away to try and hide my red face. "You know I'm not."

Garrett got onto the bed and crawled over to me on his hands and knees. He grabbed my chin and made me look at him. "No… you're perfect and your body is perfect. Don't let me ever hear otherwise."

I blushed some more and felt him kiss the corner of my mouth. I waited for the kiss on the lips but he started to slowly lick my collarbone. I put my hand between his legs and took his dick into my hand and started to stroke it, admiring finally being able to actually see it.

So chimera bodies weren't that bad. Maybe they did have a lot going for them.

Garrett kissed me, and leaned his groin into mine. Like I had done to him before he kicked me off of him, he started to grind and rub himself into me.

"You know, I'm rather versatile," Garrett purred into my ear. "I could go either way. What would you like?"

What would I like? "You're my big tough chimera aren't you?" I smiled at him and started grinding him back. Garrett laughed at this and kissed me again.

"Sure, but if you think you're going to get away with not showing me how good greywasters fuck you have another thing coming."

I gaped at him, before giving him a smack on his thigh. "Language! We're making love, asshole, and it's going to be wonderful and magical and we'll still be talking about it five hundred years from now."

"Mmhm, I guess we do have an eternity to rip each other to shreds. I know you well, lutra, and I know you're just waiting to release all of that energy," Garrett said. He slipped down until he was between my legs and took my dick into his hand. He locked his eyes with me before sticking his tongue out and giving it a hard lick. "I'll give you your love now, *amor meus*, but rest assured… I am going to be ravaging every inch of your body."

Chimera talk? What little Tasmanian devil had I awakened in my sweet fiancé? I cocked an eyebrow, but before I could question just what I had done, he put his mouth over the head of my dick. Instead I leaned back and let him do his work, taking in every moment of what I knew would be an unforgettable evening.

His mouth worked me over good, showing off skills that reminded me of good ol' King Asher. Though as I felt that talented tongue lick and massage the head and shaft of my dick, I realized they had all probably learned their skills on him and each other. I wonder how many of his chimera brothers he's had in bed?

Well, I had fucked the king, I would always be proud of that one.

"Ah… wow," I gasped, spreading my legs apart as I felt his finger start to probe lower. Then to my shock I felt his tongue beside that finger, both teasing and licking my hole. I closed my eyes and groaned from pure ecstasy. I couldn't get over how good it felt and how gentle he was being. It felt like he was lighting small fires with just his tongue and his touch.

Now *this* I have never experienced before.

I liked it and I showed him I liked it. I took my dick into my hands and stroked myself slowly as he licked and lapped the tight opening between my legs. My mind was being blown right now and after several minutes I had to force myself to stop stroking.

Though I didn't want this to be one-sided. I moved my body away from his tongue but no sooner than I had he grabbed onto my knee and tsked me. "Nope, all you. Lay back down or I'll handcuff you to the bed."

"You kinky little fuck." I relented and back went his tongue, but soon it found its way to my dick once again. "You do take control when you want to, don't you?"

He didn't answer me and I didn't say anything else. I closed my eyes and let him lick me until I felt his tongue pull away.

Garrett kissed my neck before lifting himself partially off of me. He opened the night table drawer and flicked open a bottle of lube. My chest gave an anxious and nervous quiver, all of a sudden I felt like a teenager again about to lose my virginity.

"If I hurt you, just tell–" I kissed him to shut him up and took some of the lube from his open palm. I prepared myself and fell back onto the bed, pulling him with me.

I took in a deep breath and clenched my teeth as I felt the pressure between my legs. With a push, he eased the head in, and before I could even get used to the intense feeling, he slid his entire length inside of me.

Garrett's forehead, clammy and hot, rested on the pillow beside me. His quickened, rapid breathing only inches away from my ear. I heard him groan and say something in his chimera language before I felt his hips start to move.

It had been a long time since this had happened to me in a consensual way. All the way back to King Silas in the greywastes, and if you didn't count him… fuck. Well, at least my non-consensual times had left me able to take it even during the first few painful minutes. So with that in mind and my body relaxed and under my fiancé's protection, I let him slowly thrust his hips.

They never got this close to me. As Garrett moved himself in me, kissing me on the lips, chin, neck, anywhere he could reach, I realized this. Jesse had been a full bottom, Silas liked it rough, quick and multiple times, and Bridley, well…

Garrett though, he was right on me, his body pressed against mine, one hand gripping the pillow and the other holding back my left knee. He was gentle, attentive, and emotional, all without saying a word to me. Everything he was trying to say was in his movements, and the invisible energies of our bodies mixing together.

I think I realized in that moment I was making love for the first time.

I drew him in for a kiss and slid both my hands down and grabbed his backside. I pushed him into me and started encouraging him to go faster. He knew what I wanted, we were perfectly in sync. Garrett sped up his thrusts, taking his hand off of the pillow to hold my other knee back.

The pleasure built and my hand found itself between my legs. Garrett watched me; his eyes focused and his mouth open as the moans fell from his lips with every thrust. A part of me wanted to try a new position just to see what it was like, but I didn't think any position could be more intimate than this one. I could see him and he could see me, with our bodies intertwined together.

Every time I sped up my hand, still stroking myself off, he sped himself up too, taking every one of my movements as a cue. It was so different than what I was used to. He wasn't fucking me, he wasn't trying to get himself off… he cared about my experience. He wanted this to be special.

I tried to hold myself off as long as possible, but soon I had my knees back as far as they could go and my hand rapidly jerking myself off. Garrett seemed with me on our mutual agreement, he tightened his grip on my knees and started to quickly thrust himself inside of me. His moans now being drawn through clenched teeth; his chest and body glistening with sweat.

My body filled with a rush of heat as I heard him reach his climax. An intake of breath before he shut his eyes tight, then with a sharp thrust he opened his mouth and let out a loud, strangled moan.

I grabbed onto his back as he fell into my arms, his hips still thrusting through his orgasm. That was all I needed to reach my peak, with his stomach almost pressed against my hand still working myself over, I gave it a couple good strokes before I came as well. I could hear him swearing beside me as I gasped through it, feeling his hand reach down to rub and pull on the head.

We laid there breathing heavily as our orgasms subsided, leaving fatigue and exhaustion in its place. After several minutes Garrett separated our bodies and laid down beside me.

He kissed my shoulder. "You have fifteen minutes to recover before I take you again."

I blushed and moved myself onto my side. Garrett gazed back at me, his eyes full of love to the point of worship. He brushed my still half-silver hair from my eyes. "You're so beautiful. You'll spend eternity with me, Reno?"

It wasn't often he called me by my real name. It made me blush even harder, feeling like a love-sick teen. It was a unique talent that this chimera could make me feel so vulnerable but cherished at the same time.

"Why wouldn't I?" I smiled.

His face turned serious for a moment, which made me frown.

"Some people think immortality is unnatural and they don't want it. I was worried you might be one of those types."

I scoffed at this. "You know when Reaver was all emo about being an immortal demigod I told him he was being a retard. I always hated when the super heroes get all angsty about having super powers. I would fucking love the shit out of being immortal… think of all the adventures we could have, Gare. We could like… explore the outlands and the Dead Islands. We could go to the plaguelands! We have forever to… explore the world, watch the radiation disappear!"

Garrett laughed as he saw how excited I was getting. I couldn't help it though, I was kind of getting worked up about it. "We could become greywaster super heroes! Like the opposite of Reaver and Jade, or we can even have super battles with them! Like in the comics!"

Still laughing, Garrett stroked my cheek. "This is why I love you… this is what I missed about you. You're just… everything makes you happy, everything excites you. Never change, love."

I jittered with excitement. "Do it tomorrow!"

Garrett rolled his eyes, his face holding his classic smile. "No, not tomorrow, goof. We need to wait until Elish becomes king, then we can. It must be a born immortal to do it. So unless we can snip a bit of Silas before Elish outlaws him, we–"

"Outlaws him?" I stopped Garrett. "Reaver is going to kill him… remember?"

Garrett's face changed again, but just for a brief moment, after seeing his apprehension it shifted back to his smile. He kissed me to try and hide it further. "Not now, love."

I pulled back, and at that gesture his lips disappeared into his mouth. "Gare… he raped Killian. He killed Leo and Greyson. He… he wants Reaver for himself. You said you were loyal."

Garrett looked pained. "Yes, but loyal does not mean I want Silas to die. Everyone who Elish has turned, besides the greywasters, have an agreement with Elish that we will just… send him away to recover." At my expression my fiancé smiled sadly at me. "Lovely, do not judge Silas so openly. You don't know him like us…"

"He's crazy and insane… he's killed so many chimera lovers and–"

"And he's my master, Reno. You love your crazy and insane boy. Would someone on the outside looking in not see Reaver as just as bad of a person? But you see his heart, no?"

I stared at him, he might be making sense but… "Does Elish know this? And he has agreed to this? Because right now he's in the greywastes trying to find out how to kill King Silas."

"Perish will never tell him, it's physically impossible for him," Garrett said simply, and when I opened my mouth he put his hand up. "Please, Reno, not tonight. I have lived with Silas for ninety-one years and I understand him and his struggle. Silas will pay for what he did to Killian, Lycos, and Greyson. But… Perish *loves* Silas and is devoted to him, even if he could somehow manage it, which is impossible, he wouldn't."

"He might now that he has his brain piece back," I muttered.

Garrett suddenly recoiled from me, his eyes widened. "What?"

Oh shit. Good one, Reno. Bravo.

"Nothing," I said quickly before slapping my hand over my face. "Don't look into that… jeez. Elish didn't tell you?"

Garrett put his hand on mine and pulled it away from my face. "How did he do it?"

"Lycos did it… we have no idea how he got a hold of it," I said, hoping I didn't just fuck Elish over in some way. "Do you… do you even know why Elish was in the greywastes?"

Garrett blinked at me. "He's in, or was, in Kreig to… get files… and, ah…" He scowled at the wall. "Is he there trying to get… to get Perish's O.L.S?"

I leaned in and slowly kissed him. "Fifteen minutes is up."

But Garrett pulled away. "You must tell me everything."

"No, that's Elish's job. You know you can't ask me that shit…" I kissed him again and this time he let me. "Don't get me more involved in this than I have to be. You ask Elish. Now come here."

Garrett let out a long and haughty breath from his nose and kissed me back. "Very well, it's probably for the best anyway. You win – for now."

CHAPTER 44

Jade

THE MOON WAS ALMOST FULL TONIGHT, SHINING ITS silver light down onto the grey ash around me. It trimmed rocks, trees, and bushes with its brilliant hue. Moonlight always did seem to give objects its own texture.

My vision only enhanced it; my entire world tonight was black, silver, and blue. Even the lights in the distance were small orbs of illumination, seemingly floating around like omnipotent spectres, but I knew what they were… the twinkling lights of a town called Velstoke.

A town with no walls, a town new and ready for conquest.

My town.

I glanced behind me, and though I heard almost nothing, I could see dozens and dozens of eyes. Eyes that drank in the moonlight and reflected back opal spheres. Eyes of my people. A sea of creatures following me obediently, their heads lowered and their usual screaming muted. Each of them carrying guns on their backs or knives in their hands. All walking with a stealth normal ravers didn't wield.

Because they were not normal ravers… no. These were *my* ravers, these were Jade's ravers.

Big Shot was beside me with a leather strap across his chest, an assault rifle on his back, and a belt of bullets on his waist. On his collarbone was a bloodied gouge which held the Geigerchip I had implanted in him. I'd harvested fifteen of them from the townspeople we'd killed and from corpses they'd already partially consumed.

I had chipped fifteen of the smartest ones and those were the ones that

I kept right behind me. All of them carrying on their irradiated, scabbed bodies, guns, knives, and ammo.

They improved at the hands of their king. I had armed them, chipped them, and befriended them. And now I, the King of the Ravers, was leading them to their first victory, their first conquest. My thanks for saving my life, when I was only days from death.

Tonight we would become the stuff of legends. Tonight a raver colony would not only destroy a town, we would take it over and make it our first in what I knew would be a revolution.

Big Shot pointed to the town and I nodded to him, confirming we were in the right area. I made him watch as I pointed to a thatch of thick trees off to the north area, and told him that that was where I wanted half of them to go. The stupid ones, because I knew their chances of survival would be lower. They would be our distraction, a normal raver attack to draw all the fire power as me and the smart faction branched off to silently infiltrate the town.

Scout, or that was the name I had called him, had shown me where the town was yesterday. From the looks of this place there were about one hundred residents living in it and at any point in time five officers with firepower scouting the outskirts. My ravers would silently pick off those officers after the distraction.

I had said this over and over to Big Shot, Scout, and the black-skinned raver I had nicknamed the Beast because he was huge and powerful. I had made them draw out the plan on the grey ash dirt several times to make sure they understood.

So far so good. The Geigerchips had been slowly doing their work, and Big Shot was getting smarter by the day. I wasn't sure how much of an improvement the Geigerchips would make because, well, I don't know if anyone had ever done this before.

My chest was full of adrenaline, fuelled by the cold night air. The town was right in front of us. It was so close I could see each individual board on the houses.

I climbed up a gnarled black tree and turned to my warriors.

The sea of eyes gazed up at me. So many of them, all obediently following my every word, or as much as they could understand. I must've had thirty of them. Each one holding a different level of intelligence.

I raised my right hand and pointed to the center of the trees feeling a small thrill as the ravers I had hand-picked obediently split from the group to await the massacre.

They didn't know how to count but they knew signals, and beside me, with his hot breath breaking up the last weeks of winter, I knew I had the perfect signal.

Deek was quiet but his tongue was out. He would be eating well tonight too. A dog as big as he was would make for a terrifying enemy. I was glad he was on my side and smart enough to know ravers were our friends.

"Let's go," I whispered to Big Shot. I nodded to him, Scout, and the Beast, and the four of us branched off. The remaining would take the east and west. We would have the city surrounded, and on Deek's signal the ravers in the trees would attack, and on Deek's second signal – *we* would attack.

My claw rings clicked together as I ran silently with my faction, weaving in and out of the trees until we hit a stretch of bare greywaste dirt. We ducked our heads and held our arms to our sides as we steadied ourselves, hugging the grey boarded-up buildings and watching the bare car-less street come closer and closer.

I turned to Big Shot and put my hand on his head. "No bang… right? Just teeth. Quiet. No bang."

Big Shot nodded at me. His milky yellow eyes were starting to clear; I could see the hints of black pupil start to form. Underneath his scalp headdress he had a narrow triangle-shaped face and I think, long ago, dark brown hair just starting to grow thick again.

I saw three cloaked figures talking to each other, not even aware of what was behind them. I clenched my fists, feeling my claw rings clink together and started to run towards them.

Suddenly there was an eruption of gunfire.

I swore and looked to my side. Big Shot was grinning from ear to ear, fire and sparks coming from his gun as he rained the officers in bullets.

My hands raised and I grabbed Big Shot by the shoulder. He stumbled and stopped firing, then looked at me with a wide, shit-eater grin.

"BANG!" Big Shot exclaimed.

I stared, before, in spite of the danger we were all in, I erupted into laughter. His voice was a dry, broken rasp but it was words, actual human words.

"Yeah, BANG!" I grabbed my gun and whistled to Deek. "Big Bang, Big Shot. Hey, Deek?" I said with a shout.

The dog perked up and looked at the four of us.

"Sing for me." I grinned.

As the sounds of guns clicking from their holders filled the night air, the deacon dog looked at the moon in the sky and howled a long, drawn-out howl.

Then shrieking. Lots of shrieking.

In the darkness I closed my eyes for a brief moment. Hearing the sounds sweep over my body like a cold blanket, sounds that once terrified me but now they were the songs of home. The songs of my people, following my orders to the letter. In that brief pause I took them in, feeling myself more present, and more in reality, than I had since my lucidity had come back to me.

When my eyes opened I realized my hands were shaking. In front of me I could see people starting to run down the street holding bluelamps and torches, running towards the thatch of trees.

"Sing, Deek," I whispered.

Tonight was our night.

Big Shot, Scout, and the Beast ran ahead of me. I stayed watching them, and slowly walked down the dark, shadowed road. My chest was rising up and down in anticipation; my mouth could already taste the blood.

Taste the blood.

I spat on the pavement and did a double take as I realized it was red. As I stared, it was followed by several droplets, crimson liquid that shone like small crystals in the moonlight.

I wiped my nose and mouth and looked down at my jacket sleeve.

Blood… lots of blood.

They were screaming, raver shrieks in the distance and suddenly gunfire. I took a step to start running towards them when my left leg suddenly gave out in front of me.

I gasped and fell to my hands and knees. My eyes, blurry and unfocused, stared at the pavement as more shining, purple spots appeared.

Blood.

Then images in my mind, memories.

I was in a backdrop of hundreds of abandoned structures. Ones with alleyways in between their burnt-out frames.

I dragged the bodies to my lair, and tied them up like slaughtered livestock. I made them sway back and forth in the darkness. In the darkness, in an underground house full of dying, gaunt faces. Needles and trash. I was in a dark room, feeling a sorrow I had never experienced. Again and again I wished for death.

Then a man in white with hair that had stolen the yellow of the sun. He picked me up with caring hands and held me to his chest.

Mint and nutmeg.

An ear-shredding scream ripped through the vivid hallucination taking reign in my head. I looked up and saw Big Shot and the Beast tearing a man limb from limb. Behind him, more ravers, jumping on the backs of residents as they mangled and dismembered whoever they caught in their grasp. Blood ran like water down the streets, even the dog was picking off whoever he could reach before the ravers.

Madness. Pure madness.

I pushed past the weakness my body had temporarily succumbed to and I ran towards my people. I saw Big Shot, stooped over the man he had just killed, eagerly eating his stomach, spilling organs onto the street that steamed in the cold.

When he saw me he stood up. "Kah!"

I put my hand on his head and said to him, "We eat when they're all dead. Kill all of them. All of them. Tell everyone that. Kill now, eat later."

Big Shot turned around and made a series of hiss-like shouts. I saw each raver pop their head up from the kills they were devouring, their faces soaked in blood. Obediently they rose and took their guns into their hands; the sounds of gunfire singing through the cold air in the distance.

Then we ran to the other side of the town. Me, Big Shot, and the Beast in front, and Deek taking our flanks. We sped towards the gunfire and came upon the most grisly of scenes.

The officers and over twenty residents were in an old parking lot, a large mall behind them which had been quickly boarded shut, and the glow of a bluelamp visible through hastily erected boards. The men and women who had remained were holding guns in their hands, shooting and dodging ravers as they relentlessly chased their warm prey. I could see the panic and horror in the whites of their eyes, made only brighter in the moonlight. The smell of fear was thick on them, so thick it washed over my senses like a potent drug.

Without barking orders, without sending my men first, I charged. My mouth already salivating at the prospect of feeling their own blood pump into my mouth. I had to kill, I had to taste their flesh slip down my throat, feel their life drain from their bodies in the most savage and grisly of ways.

Shadow Killer.

I lunged with a snarl just as a man turned, gun in hand. The gun went off with a crack as he stumbled under my weight, falling to the pavement with a *thud*. He put his hand to my face and shouted from fear.

My claws dug into his shirt, piercing his flesh. I raked them and snarled like the raver I knew I was.

The man closed his eyes and screamed, his hands on my face temporarily weakening. I took this chance and clamped my mouth over his throat, snapping them down and breaking his windpipe.

There it was… yes.

In ecstasy, my eyes shut as the warm blood sprayed from his neck and into my mouth. A thrill ravaging my body that bordered on sexual. I half-groaned, half-growled as I let it cover me, counting each weakening heartbeat as he died in the jaws of the beast.

Then a blow to my back that had me flying off of him, a piece of his throat still in my mouth.

I twisted my body and held out my hands. I managed to press them against the concrete and steady myself, doing a partial back flip that landed me back on my feet. I whirled around with an angry shriek and charged at the person who had hit me.

A young man stared at me with his eyes wide. He turned to run, but before he could make it two steps I pounced on his back. I reached in front of him and opened his throat with a slash of my claw rings before I leapt off, landing behind another one.

My heart was a hammer inside of my chest, not a single ounce of pain being felt in a body relying solely on adrenaline. I didn't even notice the blood still streaming from my nose and mouth as I whirled around for more victims.

The hall.

I stared at it, ignoring the gunshots and screaming behind me. My bloodied face split into a grin as I reached down and picked up a fallen torch, still holding a brilliant flame. I started crossing the parking lot with a low chuckle.

"Bang!"

I turned around, torch in hand, and saw Big Shot holding his assault rifle, the same shit-eater grin on his face. I looked past him at the activity and saw that every single fighting townsperson had been killed. Their bodies lying both splayed and crumpled, some left dead in the cold, others shaking and twitching as the shadow-cloaked ravers devoured them alive.

"Burn them." I looked behind me and held up the torch.

"BURN THE HALL!" I screamed. "KILL THEM ALL!"

Big Shot stared at me for a moment before he bent down and picked up a snuffed torch. He slowly walked towards me and lit his torch against mine.

"Burn?" The torch made a low roaring sound as he waved it in front of the large, looming structure, the flames only temporarily turning the scene yellow before it went back to the black and silver-blue.

Big Shot looked back at me for confirmation; his eyes holding the small rubies of the flames inside of them.

I nodded. "Kill every single one. We don't take prisoners."

The raver leader nodded to me and held his torch up in the air. "BURN!" he said and let out a long, piercing shriek. Every raver in that vicinity rose and started screaming with him.

I turned and ran towards the hall. I grabbed onto the loosely erected boards with my free hand and started pulling them off of the windows. Inside I started to hear scared screaming and then the cracking of gunfire.

The bullet whizzed past my face; I could feel the wind and the heat against my cheek. I ignored it and pried the board down, then I flung my torch into the hall of people.

Beside me the sounds of wood scraping against metal could be heard. The ravers were all pulling the boards off of the windows. The barriers fell and were quickly followed by a blinding flash of light as they threw their torches inside. Once their hands were empty, they ran back to the parking lot to retrieve more.

They all ran back and forth like ants retrieving food for their nests. Each one ran and got a torch, and if they couldn't find torches they started trying to burn the wooden boards we had just pried off. Anything that could catch a flame they took and threw into the windows as the screaming drowned in the night air.

Then the door to outside started to shake and rattle. I looked and realized that it was chained from the outside, a thick, rusted lock and chain that was unlatched.

Because ravers had never been smart enough to unlock or open doors. A closed door puzzled them and only if they saw you run in did they know to look for you there.

But not *my* ravers.

I walked to the door, pulsing with their desperation, pushing out and then back in like the building was trying to take its own desperate breaths. Then, as it heaved, I saw the first trickles of smoke start to spill from its cracks.

"Shoot whoever comes through that window," I shouted to Big Shot and the Beast, they were several feet in front of me holding torches in their hands. Their faces were calm, but my own bloodlust was ravaging me alive. I kept looking in all directions to see if I could spot anyone alive. I wanted to kill; I wanted all of them dead.

Why? They hadn't done anything to me.

I didn't have an answer to that. I just knew my drive was stronger than what morals I may or may not have had in my previous life.

I stood with my people and watched the smoke start to spill from the open windows. Ravers around me branching off to watch the other covered windows, some running and shrieking but my smarter ones had been able to hold their calm, emotionless demeanor. A trait I suspected had never been seen in ravers before, but one I found most fascinating.

When the smoke started to spill out of every crack in the building, the people inside got desperate. Unable to find a suitable escape, or perhaps what was awaiting them outside was less scary than inside. Either way, the first desperate woman started to crawl out of the window.

When she looked out and saw all of us watching her, her face went pale before dissolving into tears. She put her hands up to beg as her foot touched the ground.

Then behind her I heard a bellow and a man shouting. He pushed the woman out and made her fall to the concrete with a heavy *thud*. He himself started climbing out. I could see smoke coming off of his clothes.

Then more. The fire had reached them. I grabbed my assault rifle and started picking off each one that tried to escape the death trap I had made for them inside. Each time a face appeared, usually red with burns, and later on, black, I picked them off with a bullet to the head. I did this until no more men or women could spill from their prisons… because their bodies were blocking the exit.

I stepped back and looked up at the hall. The smoke was now spilling in thick, black billows from the roof, rising up in the air like they were the ghosts of the newly dead.

I walked backwards from the parking lot, and as I did, I saw the first flickers of orange peek out from the tarmac roof.

Fire.
The pub back in Moros.
Sanguine loves fire.

This memory made my body temporarily freeze, but my brain was too fixated on the inferno in front of me to delve too deep inside my own mind. Instead, with my gun in my grip, I continued to walk backwards, the heat getting stronger against my face and the night sky above me becoming more red by the passing minute.

My ravers walked along the edges of the parking lot, some holding limbs but most only their assault rifles. The bodies of the townspeople piled up against the windows, roasting in the flames, filling the burning air with the delicate aroma of cooked human flesh.

It was transfixing, like I was staring into Hell but in this Hell I was the king, the chosen one dropped from above to reign my terror down on the innocent. I might've woken up as nothing, but tonight I felt like I was king of the entire universe.

They all gathered around me, twenty of them left. All staring at me with milky yellow eyes that captured the red and orange of the flames in front of us. They looked at me as my gaze drank in the flames and carnage of our conquest.

"Eat," I said to them and slung my gun over my back. "Eat, and make yourselves at home."

I sat comfortably on my throne. It was a wing chair made out of a dull blue cloth, one that had the look of something repaired many times. But it was the best and most comfortable chair we'd found in Velstoke, so I had decided that this would be my throne.

I had taken up my kingly residents in what had once been a coffee shop. The sign was still hanging on it, but the links were rusty and threatening to fall off at any time. Still though, it was intact and almost in the center of town, with lots of windows so I could see everything that was going on.

I'd made myself comfortable here, commanding the ravers to bring me a nice queen size mattress and the most thickest of blankets. With that on top of our continuous supply of fresh meat... well, I was doing rather well for myself.

When I saw Big Shot, I rose to greet him. He had presented me yesterday with a crown of finger bones chewed clean. With his intelligence returning to him more and more each day, he and a female raver had crisscrossed the bones and held them in place with the thorny vines of a plant found around the town. I wore this crown on top of my head and I wore it proudly.

"Jade." Big Shot's voice was still raspy and broken, but he was starting to remember more words. How much of his intelligence would return and how much had been permanently damaged by the radiation, I didn't know, though I had noticed peculiar things starting to happen to their bodies. The areas where the ravers had chewed their fingers to the bones, or had chunks of their flesh missing, were not healing. I had expected them to, since the sestic radiation was the reason these wounds didn't get infected, but instead of healing they were starting to almost calcify and harden.

"Yes, Big Shot. How are they doing?" I put my hand on Big Shot's head to welcome him and he did the same for me. Even though I still called him the leader in my head, he was, in reality, more of my second-in-command.

"Come." Big Shot looked behind him with a smile; a chunk that had always been missing from his chin had grown a hard grey callous on it. The rest of his face had started growing facial hair again and his eyes were now starting to turn green. He was, in all respects, the first and most advanced half-raver in the world.

I walked with him to the grey sun outside. One week after we had taken the town and so far no repercussions. We'd had several scouts from different towns come in but we had made short work of them. This town's ammo and gun cache hadn't been hard to find and we had distributed the firepower and armour evenly through all of the ravers. We'd even had a small colony join us and increase our numbers to forty-six. Actively we had three groups finding other colonies to join us. I would need the numbers when we decided to invade the next town.

The grey sun was shining down on us, the threat of snow far away and the promise of a warm spring that was just around the corner. The perfect weather for our conquests.

Big Shot led me down the street, barrels full of fire centered on every block for my people to warm themselves. They didn't use houses, or beds, they slept on the ground beside the fire and only went inside of buildings to have sex (most of the time anyway), or to stash and eat their food. So to keep them busy I was teaching the smarter ones to board up the buildings, mostly to appease myself. I would eventually reach a hand out to trade with the humans once we established our rights as a town and as people.

That might be in the far future, and it depended on what these Geigerchips could do, but I had great plans for my people. This wasn't just about killing and taking things over.

Big Shot led me to the fast food restaurant which we had been keeping our prisoners. Though I had adamantly said no prisoners while taking over this town, we had found a cache of twenty people, men, women, and children, hiding out in here.

"Are they eating raw flesh yet?" I asked casually. I opened the door and held it for Big Shot, seeing the Beast and several others standing guard with shotguns and revolvers.

"Yes," Big Shot replied. We crossed the dirty room, ripped up booths with metal tables on either side of us, and behind them windows streaked in mildew and dirt. The ceiling above us was missing most of its push-paneling, leaving wires to spill out like loose intestines, dangling over our heads as they swayed in the darkness.

We went into the kitchen and I opened up the first freezer door, handgun in hand, ready to shoot any of them if they still had their bravery.

But as soon as I looked in I knew that wouldn't be a problem.

In a single week you could already see the effects of the sestic radiation on them. The ten we had in this room were covered in purple sores that sunk into their flesh like craters. Their hair had also fallen out already; it now covered the floor that was rank and putrid from their own waste.

With hollow desperate eyes they looked at me, trying to inject any kind of sympathy into a man they knew was an arian human, but their voices had gone. The radiation had paralyzed their vocal cords so all they could do now was shriek and scream.

"In another week I think they'll be ready to join us," I said simply. "We'll do this from now on. Take out their chips and save them, or give them to the intelligent ones. We'll leave them without chips until I deem them ready to be implanted again." This was all experimental, but I had many arians at my disposal. I could experiment as much as I wanted; I knew what my end result was.

I turned to Big Shot as he nodded.

He was my ideal end result.

Big Shot was wearing newer clothes now. However the trophies of our victory last week were still rotting on his belt and on his head. I myself had my own: my necklace of ears, the hand-belt Big Shot had presented me with, and, of course, the crown on top of my head. Even though arians usually shower and keep themselves clean, I had fully embraced the raver inside of me. Our clothing had been replaced by newer articles, but we were still ravers through and through – just a bit more advanced.

"Is there anything else?" I asked Big Shot after we had checked on the other freezer full of turning arians. We were walking outside now, passing a fire barrel that was surrounded by four ravers, their arms outstretched to warm themselves even though the day was rather mild.

He shook his head no. "All good."

I chuckled at this; it would be amusing if I could ever get him to speak real sentences.

I put my hand over Big Shot's head and held it there. Then I patted it and gave him a smile in return.

"That's right, Big Shot. All good," I said with a smirk. "Everything's all good."

CHAPTER 45

Reaver

  I HAD NEVER BEEN APART FROM HIM FOR THIS LONG. Ever since he arrived in Aras I was always near him. Whether it was the distance between my basement and his cul-de-sac house, or the distance between us when I started following him. He had never been far from me and I had never been far from him.
  Now he was gone from my line of sight, I had left him with my parting kiss, a sleeper-hold. Grabbing on of the slim chance they wouldn't find him; that he could go back to the group and be safe.
  I know if he was caught by Nero he would probably be dead by now, but my lesser of two evils had turned just as sour. I didn't know if he was still alive; I just knew I had to keep following the trail.
  The last days I had with Killian were spent arguing over that stupid slave.
  I sighed, ignoring the aching in my chest. I made a solemn promise in that moment to never fight with him again. Killian could win even if I knew he was wrong. Whatever made him happy.
  The town called Mantis was far behind us, several days walk. We'd left quietly that morning without incident. We'd cleared the stretch of highway we had wanted to check out and were now doubling back to inquire in a town one of the Mantis residents had mentioned: Garnertown. There was that town and then Velstoke and we were planning on checking all of them for any signs of the boys.
  I looked over at Elish who had been chain smoking all morning. Admittedly though, I wasn't much better. We had almost run out of

cigarettes so we made sure to buy a couple cartons in Mantis. Now we were rarely without a cigarette between our lips, I even got the novelty of seeing Elish light them with just his fingers.

The town we were heading towards was the center of what used to be a larger pre-Fallocaust city. However, all the buildings surrounding the town had been burned or dismantled.

We were walking through a house graveyard right now, just open shells and floor plans still intact surrounding us.

But we still checked every one of them, even though we hadn't had a solid lead since the shack on the highway. There was nothing, no sure sign that they had even been here.

And no sign of Killian at all. That had been Jade's bandage. How did I even know they were all still together? It was obvious that Perish had wanted to kill Jade.

I changed out the cigarette for a bottle of whisky and passed it to Elish. I heard his lips seal over the bottle before he passed it back. We had already drunken half of the bottle and he had a good share of it. I knew I couldn't search as well drunk, but my nerves were starting to shred my mind like a thousand small paper cuts. I needed the break and Elish did too.

I heard him take another drink of the whisky before the amber bottle came back into my view.

"I'm learning something new," Elish said in a flat tone.

I took another drink and wiped my mouth. I noticed his purple eyes were just a bit glassy, I think mine were as well. "Oh?"

"I understand why greywasters are either drunk or high all the time."

I chuckled and took that opportunity to have another drink. While the bottle was to my lips I craned my head to check inside one of the burnt building's windows.

I broke the bottle away from my mouth. "And that was normal life, not even the shit we're having to deal with now. I told you I was smart to buy all this whisky and rum." And he had told me I was an idiot too.

"Well, I'm not one to indulge myself to excess." There was a *creak* as Elish lifted up the board that had been put over a shattered window. "But, quite frankly, I know they're not here. The deacon dog wouldn't be hiding from you, and I'm confident they're travelling with him."

I could see Perish getting him to stay so they wouldn't draw attention in the town; the dog was getting pretty huge. But Elish was right, Deek wouldn't be hiding from me. That dumb dog flipped shit when he saw me after I had been gone for an hour; he would piss himself if he heard me now.

"Every day you're out here I see you become more normal," I suddenly remarked, the drink starting to make my ears warm. "It's not a bad thing."

"I have more important things to concern myself with," Elish replied simply. "What little transformation you may have seen just comes with the environment. It's human and chimera nature alike. We all transform and adjust ourselves according to what is around us. You yourself have changed."

I snorted.

"You're not the wet-eared, arrogant shit I saw over a year ago," Elish said with a smirk. "Perhaps love has tamed that beast?"

My brow furrowed at that. I remembered a conversation Killian and I had had, our last night together in Mariano.

"Did you send Killian to Aras on purpose? To catch my eye?"

Elish was silent for a moment. "Yes."

My eyes widened. So Killian had been right... "Why?"

"Because I knew you two would be a match and that it would be a mutual benefit for you and Lycos," Elish replied, tipping the amber liquid back and forth in the whisky bottle. "You needed someone to calm you down, teach you patience and control, and Lycos and Greyson needed to see that you weren't a lost cause. They needed to see that this dark chimera could still show empathy and compassion... even if it was solely isolated to just a single person."

I was their 'lost cause' because they kept trying to make me into a human instead of a chimera. I wish they hadn't been so naïve.

Then another question popped into my head. "Why Killian though?"

Elish drained the bottle and threw it into the shell of a small shop we had been passing. "In time."

That wasn't that great of an answer, but the heat from the liquor was spreading from my ears to my face. I shrugged it off and cracked open another bottle. We were both starting to slip past tipsy. Though the greywastes might be dangerous, it was empty now, and even if we did see something... we were both fucking immortal.

And I needed it. I was out of pills, out of quils, and long out of heroin, liquor was all I had.

I took another drink, my taste buds fried and raw from so much whisky. "Your king used to get me drunk and drugged, then try to fuck me. Did you know that?"

"One of his many perks."

We skidded down a steep incline, hitting the backyards of a row of houses at the bottom. I stumbled a bit but I managed to make the whisky not drop. I think I saw Elish stumble too.

"What way do you want to kill him?" I asked.

Elish threw his cigarette butt down onto the ground and walked into a half-standing rancher. I followed him in and quickly walked the area to check for any signs.

"I'll burn him alive," Elish replied. He opened up an old closet, and didn't even flinch when a dry, mummified corpse was visible in the darkness. It looked like it was hanging by the neck from a belt. I almost laughed as Elish checked his pockets before closing the door. "Or perhaps roast him, not burn. A slow heat so the pain will last."

I checked out the kitchen and saw that the dust that covered the countertops and shelves hadn't been disturbed. Killian, anyone really, would check the kitchen first.

I pocketed a couple of cans and we both walked out of the house.

"I once tortured a man for two weeks. This time it will be four. One week for what he did to Killian, then one for what he did to Leo, then Greyson, then me," I replied. "The fact that he'll return after is just perfect. I can do it all again."

"Yes, until the final blow."

"But… with Perish getting his mind back… does that mean he knows how to kill King Silas?" I asked. I dropped the whisky bottle onto the ground but thankfully it didn't shatter. I picked it up and swayed a bit. This stuff was really starting to hit me.

"I believe so. However, now that I will not be able to monitor him… I'm unsure just how we are going to get this information from him. I was not born yet when Sky and Perish's O.L.S's were created. I don't know what kind of person Perish was. I fear he is taking Killian and Jade to the nearest base to turn them in… but that being said, he could have an entirely different agenda. My pet has talents of his mind that, with training, could rival Silas's. Though on the same hand… that could be why Perish wanted him dead."

"Wait a second." I stopped in my tracks. "You have a piece of Sky, right? Why the fuck is he dead then? That's not dead..."

Elish shook his head no. "An O.L.S is an electronic device we place the piece in; it keeps it alive. Once out of it, the tissue would die. That piece was removed before Sky killed himself, so it is nothing but a piece of brain. Silas has coveted it and kept it safe since his boyfriend died, in hopes of resurrecting him one day. Perish's was removed by Dr. Greg Lenard after the fact and hidden far from Silas, by the twins' own request. Sky's has never left his skyscraper."

"And Leo got a hold of Perish's O.L.S somehow and implanted Perish?" I started stabbing the can with my pen knife. I smelled it when I got a good hole in it and was thrilled in my drunken state to find it was cherry pie filling. "Well, if Perish won't tell us we can just make a Sky clone, infuse him with the Sky O.L.S, and ask him." I shrugged. "Wouldn't that work?"

"Yes... I believe it would." I watched his eyes narrow before he looked over at me. I was busy trying to suck cherries out of a small pen hole. I handed him the can and he took it.

"Why wouldn't Silas just make a Sky clone instead of a Silas clone?" I asked. "Since apparently he hates himself and all of that shit."

"He tried, but the children were never successful and the cloned matter we had left, the matter not in the O.L.S, had run out. Silas did not want to use the O.L.S material since we had no guarantee it would produce a clone."

"So then you made me?"

"Eventually, yes. After I perfected it and knew it would work, I used some of Sky's O.L.S material with Silas's to make you."

I may be almost drunk, but I was sober enough in the head to catch the subtle admission in his words. "You perfected it? Before you made me? So where is that kid?"

"In time."

I rolled my eyes. He was saying that to me just as much as that 'indeed' word he loved so much. "So you know how to now though? Just you?"

Elish stared forward. Even though he was just as bordering on drunk as me his face remained the same. "Yes, I told Silas to scrap the project and that it was impossible. When in reality... I had figured it out and had great success. I know the formula now and I can make as many Silas and Sky's as I please."

"As many born immortals?"

He looked proud of himself. "Only I know how it's done. Not Lycos, nor Perish or Sidonius. I alone cracked the code."

"So you can make like a dozen me's if you wanted to?"

"I would never punish the world so."

I snorted but it turned into a laugh. Elish smiled.

But both of our smiles faded when we emerged from behind an old grocery store. Immediately we both froze in place and ducked back into the shadows.

Though it was more an automatic response. Elish and I glanced out from the back alley of the grocery store and saw what looked like a merchant and a bodyguard travelling alone. An old brown bosen in front of them pulling a cart full of supplies.

"It's just a merchant's caravan," Elish commented before walking out into the front parking lot. Half of the concrete was missing and the bare greywastes had started to take over the rest of the flat surface.

The merchant looked surprised to see us, the bodyguard looked ticked. They both drew their guns at us, but Elish raised a hand. "No need for guns, we're only looking for information."

The merchant's eyes hardened. "I have no information for you, Skyfaller."

Oh great, this was going to be a fun experience. I stepped in front of Elish, and since I no longer had death to fear and I was half-cut, I said to him acerbically, "I am not a Skyfaller, shithead. I am a greywaster and we're looking for three people."

The merchant, with greasy blond hair and a sour look on his face, pointed his gun up higher. "And I have no information for you. So unless you want to make an issue out of it, carry on your way. I don't talk to Skyfallers or elites. Purple fucking eyes don't occur naturally and I don't give a shit who you personally are. Now fuck off."

I glared him down and took a step towards him, until he was pointing his shotgun right into my chest. My drunken mind filling with a thousand creative ideas on how to murder them.

A smile crept to my lips and I moved to threaten him some more when something caught my eye.

The merchant had a ring on his finger.

A single claw ring.

"Elish… his hand." I felt my throat tighten around my voice box.

In a flash, Elish was there, and as time slowed down, several things happened at once.

I moved my chest away from the shotgun as the merchant pulled on the trigger; the heat of the bullet grazing my side. I spun around and grabbed his hot gun barrel with my gloved hand and raised it, then got behind him. I ripped the gun out of his grasp and pressed the barrel against his throat, hearing an agonizing scream spill from his lips.

Then another gunshot, and a flash of grey from Elish's overcoat. I looked over as the merchant struggled in front of me and watched Elish put a hand over the bodyguard's face.

Then the bodyguard started shrieking. I didn't understand why until I saw the smoke start to pour from his face. As the bodyguard struggled and screamed, I could hear the crackling of burning flesh.

"Where did you get that ring?" I snapped, pressing the barrel further into the merchant's throat. I could smell burning flesh start to tantalize my nostrils, both from the red-hot gun barrel and Elish's thermal touch.

"What fucking ring?" the merchant cried.

"Put him on the ground," Elish suddenly barked. I looked over at him and saw him drop the bodyguard. His face was holding a black handprint on it, even his eyeballs held wrinkled black bits from where Elish's hand had laid.

I dropped the merchant and kicked him down, before hearing a crack as Elish snapped the bodyguard's leg with the fire poker he carried around. At this gruesome display, the merchant started screaming and sputtering. I kicked him again and drew my combat knife.

I kneeled down and straddled him, feeling an intoxication hit me that was stronger than the alcohol.

Now this, this I missed.

"That ring... the claw ring," I snarled. I dug the tip of the knife into his throat. "Where did you find it?"

"He sold it to me for a fucking ammo belt!" the merchant cried, his eyes bulging from fear. He looked over at the bodyguard who was cursing and spitting at his injured leg.

Elish was already on him. With the poker dragging against the greywaste dirt, he walked over to the bodyguard and raised it. "Where did you find that ring?"

"Fuck you!" the bodyguard snapped. "I'm fucked now thanks to you, Skyfaller. Go fuck yourself."

"So you don't know where he found it?" I said to the merchant.

The man shook his head, looking relieved. He raised his hand and put it in front of my face. "Just fucking take it and get!"

Since you asked me nicely. I got my combat knife and grabbed onto his finger. Knowing what I was about to do, he started to scream and pull away, but I kept my grip strong and sawed his finger off with my knife. I put the finger into my pocket and opened his throat with a quick slash.

I rose and walked over to the bodyguard Elish was standing over, hearing the sounds of gurgling as the merchant choked on his own blood behind me.

I brought out the finger and handed the ring to Elish. "That's Jade's?"

Elish took the ring and held it in his hand. He nodded and slipped it into his pocket before roughly shoving the tip of the poker into the bodyguard's chest. Not enough to penetrate, but enough to slam him backwards onto the greywastes' floor.

"Do not make me ask you twice," he replied coolly. "You may think you have nothing to lose; that, either way, you will wind up dead. But my creation beside me has a knack for drawing out one's demise. I suggest you tell me what I want to know, or I will hand you off to him."

I didn't want to wait for an answer. I raised my boot and stomped it down on the guy's other legs, feeling my own patience start to trickle away from me.

The bodyguard screamed and continued swearing, grabbing his broken leg and rolling onto his side.

"Where did you get this claw ring? Where did you find it?" I demanded. I started to circle him, the burning darkness forming and growing inside of my chest. The fact that this man may have been near Killian, may have seen him, was filling me with rage. The same madness that had taken over me when I was interrogating those legionaries, when my future boyfriend had gotten kidnapped and sold.

The bodyguard coughed, a drip of spit falling from his mouth. "It doesn't matter, asshole. I found it where no human could survive. A motel that's been swarming with ravers."

A silence fell on both of us, though not the silence that can only be felt by your hearing. A dark, depleted silence. One that left you frozen in place, like every sense inside of you had been wiped out.

Ravers... he had found it in a ravers' den?

A scream broke my lips. Before I realized what I was doing, I picked up the bodyguard by the throat and thrusted him to my face.

When he saw me all his bravery slipped away. He stared back, his brown eyes wide and now filling with fear.

"Where?!" I snarled before shaking him hard. "Where's the ravers' den?"

The bodyguard's eyes shut; his broken legs dangling underneath him. I was holding him up off the ground. I growled and shook him again, trying to keep him from passing out.

Then Elish's hand came into my vision. I saw him grab onto the bodyguard's neck and a moment later I heard an electric snap reverberate off of my own hands.

With the electricity, the bodyguard opened his eyes, sweat dripping down his already badly burnt face.

"They're dead, it doesn't matter."

"Where – are – they?!" Elish bellowed. His hand snapped around the man's throat.

"Fine, go find their bones in the ravers' shit," the bodyguard said through gasping breaths. "Cobbleton Motel. If you follow the road we were on, you'll find it."

Cobbleton? The townspeople in Mantis had cleared that out over a week ago.

There was a burning glint in Elish's eyes that mirrored my own, overflowing with an adrenaline that told me he was thinking the exact same thing I was. I felt my body become encompassed in static-like energy. One that coursed through me, bringing a feeling I felt unable to control.

That darkness that covered my eyes and filled my body with a black energy like I'd felt in the greyrifts. The one drawn from the torture I had endured under Nero's hand. It commanded me to hurt; it commanded me to draw blood. It rushed into me, pushing bloodthirst in and forcing my sanity out.

I screamed, and like an over-fuelled engine, my body suddenly became alive. Before I had time to stop myself, I grabbed onto the merchant's head and pulled it from Elish's grasp. But I didn't stop there; I could never stop there. It wasn't in my nature, it wasn't in my makeup. Stopping this madness wasn't a language the darkness inside of me spoke.

Elish's hands slipped down to the man's underarms, and he held them steady so the bodyguard was standing upright. I held onto the man's head, and with a shuddered breath, like the quickened gasps before an orgasm – I started to twist.

The cracking of his neck bones reverberated through my own hands, tickling and massaging the dark, macabre feelings I had come to embrace. A rush of pleasure, no longer just bordering on sexual, flowed through me like greywine, and as I ripped the bodyguard's head off of his body with a rough jerk of my hands, I felt like I was going to climax.

Blood started squirting through the neck, tightening it like a corkscrew before the blood spilled onto me and Elish. Then suddenly the skin broke away and the twisting became easier. I wrenched it back and forth and heard a maniac laugh roll from my lips.

I gave the head one last hard twist, severing the spine from the skull, and watched the blood flow from the shredded stump.

My breath became short. I felt like my chest was twitching and tightening under this odd feeling. I watched with my mouth open, inhaling and exhaling, as Elish dropped the seizing corpse onto the ground.

Then something happened. Something I didn't expect or see, and in the heat of the moment – didn't understand.

Elish grabbed my chin and kissed me.

He kissed me.

Something stirred inside of me, a dangerous mixture of alcohol, bloodlust, and relief. It twisted and infiltrated my body and lit up my mind with such a brilliant light I found myself opening my mouth and accepting his lips. I didn't know what was happening, but as we fell backwards onto the greywaste ground, our lips locked, kissing deeply, I had never fucking wanted this to continue so badly in my life.

Elish was on top of me, his hand slipping up my shirt. Everything was happening so fast my brain didn't even have time to start screaming at me. It was too drowned in the whisky and too busy trying to slowly process just what the fuck was happening to the both of us. I was going by reflex and emotion alone – and that feeling was making me slip my hands down his pants.

My body wanted him in a way that, in the dark areas of my brain, scared me. Because I knew just how he would take me.

Then it wouldn't just be Nero, it would be someone I trusted.

Reaver, what – the – fuck?

Before I could pull away, Elish pulled away first. He swore, his breathing as ragged as mine, before he got up.

I quickly scrambled to my feet, and as I felt the trance-like feelings start to drain from me, I looked around the greywastes bewildered. Cold reality was a bitch. It snatched me from the warm lust ruling my mind and tossed me right back into the frozen jaws of reality.

I saw that Elish had the same surprised look on his face, but when I made eye contact with him, it disappeared as quickly as it came.

"Let's... never speak of that again," Elish said. His voice was cold but he spoke the words too quickly. I knew then what had just happened had taken him off-guard too. "That is... our engineering is to blame for that. Let's go and... throw that whisky away while you're at it."

My eyes looked around the broken up parking lot we were in, desperately seeking out a distraction so I didn't have to talk to him. I spotted the merchant's caravan and I walked over to it. My mind reminded me that it might have drugs and I accepted that as a good enough reason to raid their bags. I needed something to numb what Elish and I had just done.

Behind me I could hear chopping noises. I glanced over my shoulder and saw Elish hacking some meat off of the bodyguard. Dinner, I gathered.

I wiped my mouth and tried to swallow down the queasy pit in my stomach.

What the fuck, Reaver?

No, shut up. You get hot after you kill people and apparently so does Elish. It's our engineering and you're both bordering on drunk as well, so don't make a deal about it.

It happened and it wasn't important. I tried to push it out of my head and started going through bags, throwing the ammo I wanted into one of our knapsacks and any light food we could carry.

"Oh, thank the gods," I murmured when I came across a plastic container. I opened it up and found small baggies full of pills and powder. I dumped the entire container into the bag and also the one that held medical supplies.

I turned around as Elish put a large chunk of flesh into a sack. "He said follow the ro-" My drunken mind stopped talking as soon as Elish threw a pill at me. I caught it and looked at it before giving him an inquisitive look.

"It's Intoxone, a Skyfall drug that will sober you up. I carry a supply for when my cicaro's drunken antics start to become more annoying than amusing. Swallow it so we can start to sprint. I want to get to that motel before dark in case there are still ravers there," Elish said.

I was briefly thankful he was using his regular cold voice with me. I didn't want it to suddenly become weird between us. I wasn't that type of person and I knew neither was he, but emotions were running high at this point.

I would take his lead and forget it ever happened... it was blood, alcohol, and engineering.

Killian is going to scream so loud Skyfall will hear it.

And Jade? Well, Jade is going to rip out both of our throats, that I'll put money on.

Running helped us not have to think about it, so we ran; we didn't just sprint, we ran. As Elish and I kept pace with each other, I could feel the alcohol leave my system one hard step at a time, and by the time we saw the cluster of structures in the distance, standing in grey ruins against the rocky terrain behind it, I was completely sober.

With the liquor gone my emotions came back. I was looking forward to stifling them with drugs because I was starting to feel a clench inside of my heart. And it wasn't even about what happened between me and Elish... it was because I didn't know what we were going to find in that motel.

The smell hit me like I had ran through an invisible wall of rancid meat, and as we ran closer, I could see the outlines of heads on spikes and crucified arians. Soon the dirt underneath our boots was littered with chewed bones and half-buried trash, pounded into the ground by the ravers' feet.

The motel had been a ravers' pit, that much was obvious. Everything was putrid, half-rotten carcasses, shreds of soiled clothes, and the occasional pile of wood taken from buildings or black tree branches. The crucified men were rotting off their crosses, uneaten flesh hanging like curtains from their greasy bones and falling to the ground in a pile that was buzzing with black flies.

The entrance to the motel was open and exposed. The doors were gone and only a gaping hole that promised nothing but more grisly gore. Two crucified heads stared at us on either side of these doors, staring at us with vacant eyes and open mouths with a backdrop of spray-painted graffiti behind them.

But none of these were our boys. I looked over at Elish who was rolling a torso over with his fire poker.

"These bodies are over a week old," I replied, and as the torso flopped onto its back, a cloud of black flies burst into the air, buzzing angrily at our disruption of their laying grounds. "And they're not all eaten."

Elish nodded and walked towards an old fire pit, the coals white and long cold, half-covered in a dusting of ash the wind had blown in. "You know more about ravers than I. Do they migrate?"

I shook my head no. "Not with all this free food around. I'm starting to think these are the townspeople we heard about in Mantis. I don't think they were that successful. I mean, I'm seeing raver carcasses but not nearly enough of them to point towards some sort of stalemate."

My eyes travelled to the door of the motel. I walked between the two decapitated arian heads and into the rank, disgusting lobby. Elish was behind me.

The inside was just as bad as I would expect. Though the ravers could shit outside, they ate and made their messes indoors as well as out. The interior was covered in sticky, green-hued blood, and the bones were spread throughout the inside of the structure like the inside of a radanimal's den. It was everywhere, and now that the insects were coming back, it was loud with the echoing buzzing of thousands of wings.

This place had been abandoned for a while.

My mind started to race for an explanation. "They probably stayed here for a night and–"

"Jade would've never stayed here."

I stopped and felt my lips press together. "Yeah, Killian wouldn't have either…" I swallowed down the dose of poison those admissions brought and started checking rooms. Everything was just… disgusting, and disgusting by my standards was really fucking rank. This place was crawling with flies and death, chewed bones and severed limbs, all at least a week old. They had definitely cleared out of here a while ago.

I wiped my hands on my cargo pants after touching something sticky and walked into one of the back rooms.

My breath caught in my throat. I called for Elish and kneeled down in front of the nest of blankets. These were blankets I recognized, they were given to us by Elish before we left.

Shock rippled around me and the atmosphere suddenly became thick and weighted. I pushed the blankets aside, my heart hammering, and looked for any sign of Killian.

Anything, anything...

Elish was there; he picked up the blanket and threw it aside. He saw the bandage first and snatched it up from the ground.

"Jade... Jade was here," he whispered. "Jade made it this far."

The reality hit me like a freight train, a rush of emotions that hammered down on me, each blow bringing more depthless black into my eyes. With a scream, I threw the blanket and kicked the side of the wall.

"Just fucking say it!" I suddenly lashed out, feeling every ounce of pain and fear suddenly come rushing to the surface. "Go ahead and say it!"

Elish rose and looked at me. "We don't have time for–"

I screamed again and pushed him; his body firm in its stance and barely wavering under my weight. I raised my fist to punch him but he blocked it easily.

Though no sooner than he had done that, my other hand raised and this one connected with his face.

Elish's head snapped to the side and I saw several drops of blood spill from his mouth. With the direct hit egging me on, I grabbed his duster and tried to pull him onto the ground.

We struggled for a moment before, with a quick flash of grey, he backhanded me right across the face, in a manner that... reminded me of Greyson.

"Say it? Fine, I will say it. I don't think Killian and Perish are with Jade," Elish responded, his voice low. "But that changes little. Jade will know more than we know now. We must find him."

I tried to push down my own personal feelings but I found my eyes rising to meet Elish's. "Perish is going to hurt him and Jade isn't going to be there to protect him. He can't fucking protect himself, Elish."

I never realized how much that scared me until I said it. I had felt better knowing Jade was there. My brother was friends with Killian, they had bonded during their time with the slavers. He would've never let Perish touch Killian.

Maybe that was why Perish had tried to kill him.

"I know," Elish replied simply, "but Perish will not fatally hurt Killian, the same cannot be said for my cicaro. Now let's get out of here. I want to make it to Garnertown before dark. If Jade is alone... he could be staying there."

Elish left the room without another word. I felt sour and angry but I also knew we had to move on.

I left too and we both walked out into the rancid air. The outside air was still putrid and rank but it was nothing compared to the stale rot inside the motel.

"Are you leaving with Jade once you find him?" I asked as we started to walk towards the town. "Will that be it then? You find your beloved little husband and then you're going back to Skyfall to think of a new plan?"

"You think that little of me?" Elish murmured, kicking aside a severed arm after briefly checking it over. He carried on walking. "I would think our time together would raise your opinion of me, if only in the slightest."

This caught me off-guard and I hated being caught off-guard. I was pissed off and worried, still conflicted and frustrated and looking for a target to release some of those feelings on.

Fuck, I felt like such a weak piece of shit right now. I was tired of worrying and tired of losing my shit every ten hours. I was never like this before, and though I denied it through and through… I knew a lot of it was from what had happened with Nero.

I just… didn't feel like Reaver lately. I felt like an emotional wreck and I knew it wasn't all caused by worrying about Killian.

"What if he's hurt too badly?" I said back, after over a minute of silence. "We've seen those bandages."

"He's a strong chimera and I doubt he'll approve of me ditching him in the apartments while we have all the fun. No, Reaver, Jade will be joining our search and with his abilities he will be invaluable," Elish said. "I do not plan on leaving once we find him. I need to find both Perish and Mr. Massey before I return to Skyfall."

That filled me with a guarded relief over something I didn't even realize I had started worrying about. I could move fast and I could find Killian alone, but there was no doubt that having Elish beside me so far had been a benefit.

"I think it was Perish who tried to kill him," I said after we had been back on the road for an hour. We were passing through a congested section of road, with several jack-knifed semis that we had to travel around. We checked each one for Jade but there were no signs.

"I think so too," Elish replied. "I think the dog was dragging Jade behind on a sled, perhaps a piece of highway sign. That was the odd tracks we found. If the deacon dog is with Jade, he would have kept the ravers away from him. Which means Jade was in that motel after they left... I'm hopeful we'll find him in Garnertown. I suspect we only missed him by a week at most."

I nodded but my mind was just shot. I wiped my face with my hands and looked behind me.

All this time I had thought I had been tracking Killian, but now... no, all signs pointed that it was just Jade. But at least this meant... I mean, it meant that he was still alive, right? That at least he wasn't leaving a trail of blood like the pet was.

But where was Perish taking my boyfriend, and why? And what were we going to do now that Perish's mind was intact? Elish said he didn't know Perish before he had been compromised so we didn't know just who the fuck that mad scientist was now.

Was Killian more safe, or more in danger...?

What if it wasn't just about us finding him? What if the Legion or Silas found them first?

I reached into my knapsack and started sifting through the drugs. I popped a few opiate pills I found and checked out what I thought might be a higher potency Dilaudid pill. I'd be crushing that later.

While I was waiting for my therapy to kick in, I noticed the raver tracks I had been seeing on and off were starting to head right. It did look like they were going somewhere but at least it wasn't the town we were heading towards.

At least Killian didn't have to deal with ravers... and the flies meant maggots so he was spared of that too.

Maybe Perish just wanted to be with him... be his boyfriend again.

Is he that lucky?

Before I could stop it I gave a dry chuckle and shook my head. "My mind is telling me it's a good thing Perish loves him. That maybe... he will be taken care of even if I know he's probably terrified right now. Funny how that works."

"I went through the same thing when I dropped Jade off in Moros," Elish replied quietly.

It took be my surprise he was saying this kind of personal information to me.

"And was he?"

"No, but at least he stayed alive."

I nodded and hoped my overactive, racing mind would take that response.

"Do you regret doing it?" I didn't know why I was asking that.

"Yes, it was an error in judgment," Elish said back to me. "He suffers still from abandonment issues and many other problems I am still having to help him through."

"Yeah, he's pretty fucked in the head."

Elish gave me a cold look. "I could say the same for yours."

"I never denied it." I shrugged. "Though chimeras are prone to acting like whackjobs, unfortunately mine doesn't have an excuse."

Funny enough, Elish chuckled. "He has quite the excuse."

There was more behind those words than he was letting on. I opened my mouth to question his statement when suddenly I stopped in my tracks. In front of us, just becoming visible over a dip in the road, were over a dozen people. All of them were covered in bloodied bandages, hobbling on, slowly but steadily, towards the town.

I drew my gun. "We're travellers and we're going to approach you," I shouted. Obviously these fucks had been through the wringer, and from the looks of their wounds, the wringer was ravers.

One of them, a middle-aged man with his throat bandaged, looked at us in horror, but when he saw we weren't approaching aggressively he calmed down.

"We're just trying to get to Garnertown," he said. He had his arm around a little boy no older than five; the kid was missing his hand. "They... they killed all of them. We're all that's left."

"What did?" Elish pushed past me. "Ravers?"

The man nodded, a grim look on his face. He shook his head back and forth and pinched the inner corners of his eyes with his fingers. "I can't explain it. They've gotten smarter... we've never seen it before. They've learned how to use guns. They're evolving I think. They attacked our town in an organized fashion, with a plan. I heard the leader talk. He was an arian, but they were all obeying him like he was one of them."

At the same time both my and Elish's pulses jumped. I found myself looking at Elish, just as he looked at me.

Elish turned to the man, his face stern and unyielding, but I saw his hands were clenched into fists. "And this... *leader*... did you get a look at him?"

The man nodded slowly. "I could never forget a face like that. I hid like a coward to protect my son." He put a hand on the back of the boy's head and clenched his jaw.

"He was a demon that walks on earth. A man with yellow eyes and pointed fangs. He's commanding over thirty of them I think."

Elish's eyes widened, and the hammering in my heart travelled up to my head.

I stared. I stared until I couldn't take it anymore.

I burst out laughing, just as Elish put his hand on his forehead and swore.

CHAPTER 46

Killian

"HEY, LITTLE BEE, ARE YOU STILL IN THERE?"

"Killi bee bee bee." He laughed at his jingle. I think he knew I was out of it, so he was pushing the charm. "Killi… Killi Cat? Come on, it's time to get up."

But I was staring at the heater, my knees drawn up to my chest and my face tight from my own dried tears. I shook my head and buried my head into the pillow with a sob.

"No," I choked.

"Oh, Killian… come on," he whispered with a sigh. "Going to Greyson's will cheer you up. Come on, I'll piggy back you."

I sniffed and opened my eyes. I opened my eyes to Reaver smiling at me, an encouraging warm smile that held no darkness, no Reaper, just love. Inside this warm, comforting basement where all my happy memories stemmed from.

I nodded and wiped my nose with my hand.

"That's my boy. Can I give you a kiss, just on the cheek?" he asked. I nodded again, and because I was expecting it, my body didn't cringe away.

I smiled as his prickly skin rubbed against my own, and at the sight of it, he smiled too. "There. Reno has nothing on me. Okay, get up… Greyson's expecting us. I'll carry you there." He put a hand on my cheek and suddenly gave me a beaming smile. "But remember, Killian: if the food is gone, we're eating one of the slaves."

I recoiled back and stared at him, my eyes widening. "W-what?"

"If the food runs out – we're eating them," Reaver's voice dropped. A cold look crept to his eyes. When he saw the expression of horror on my face, he let out a laugh and slapped my shoulder, before grabbing it hard and giving it a shake. "And guess what, Killi Cat? If you don't satisfy me, every – single – fucking – night. I will rape you bloody. You know what right?"

"Right?"

"Don't you, Killibee?"

"Killi bee bee bee."

"Come on, Killian, you wanted to find a hospital…" Perish's voice broke through my living nightmare. He was holding his assault rifle in his hand and his blue bag in the other. "Or are you going to stay outside the building and hope I don't get too far away from you?"

"Killian?"

"KILLIAN?"

I screamed from shock as Perish grabbed my shoulder and shook it. I stared at him, suddenly feeling the cold, eerie quiet of the greywastes around me. I looked around, barely remembering where I was, and tried to suppress the scared noise on my lips.

"You're so fucking…" Perish muttered, "… weak."

"I want to see… see Reaver…" I murmured back.

"Yeah, well… Reaver's in Skyfall fucking Silas, now all you have is me," Perish snapped. He pushed me towards the entrance of the hospital. A row of glass, several panes still intact but most of it broken and crunching below our boots, all that was left of the entrance windows. "Come on, assholes, keep it up or none of you shit fucks get any medication."

I looked behind me and saw the three slaves, all of them giving me worried, sad looks. When they noticed I was staring back, they dropped their gaze and obediently followed Perish into the hospital. All of them were getting weaker by the day. It had taken us a week of travelling through the towns to find where the hospital was for the area.

But… but we found it.

It had been a week, right? Maybe it had been a month, I didn't know.

"Killian!" Perish snarled. I looked up and realized he was already twenty feet from me, the three slaves travelling obediently behind.

I looked around at the walls on either side of me, all with strips of their siding peeled away like burnt skin. But instead of pink, inflamed flesh, underneath these walls held the paints and panelings of the distant past. Greens and yellows, soothing colours that were supposed to calm their patients down.

Now this was a greywastes' fun house. Derelict to the point where the building itself looked mad. Whatever the modern humans had done to this place had started coming undone from its walls and ceilings, raining its failures down onto the floor to collect dust and garbage. Drop ceiling tile so easily disturbed, gyprock siding and rotten corkboard. Easy fixes for understaffed hospitals, but the Fallocaust held no mercy for structural shortcomings.

This building was scarred and broken. The floors rotten and the roof just waiting for the next rainy season.

We shouldn't be here. This wasn't a good place.

No place was a good place.

I jumped when I felt a hand on my shoulder, but Edward's voice soothed me. "It's alright, come on… let's start walking."

We were passing a door, through that door I could see a circle of hospital beds, all of their mattresses perfectly formed only holding a few water stains. The beds were metal frame and looked corroded but they were intact.

I took a step towards one of the beds. I wanted to lie down on it but Edward directed me away.

"We could rest there," I murmured, rubbing and tensing my hands together. "Do you think…?" I took a fleeting look at an old machine, covered in dust and standing vacant in the middle of the room. "That might be a heart monitor… we could see if it works."

Edward led me away and I let him. My heart clenched when I saw the look Perish was giving me. A look as cold as his ice blue eyes, eyes that seemed to glow in the darkness around us.

He handed me a flashlight. "Snap out of it already. I'm really getting sick of this way you're acting."

"I'm sorry," I whispered. "Want me to suck your dick and make you feel better ab-"

The slaves caught me after Perish hit me across the face. And as if taking advantage of the fact they were holding me up and I was still in his reach, he hit me again.

"Drop him," Perish snapped.

"He's losing his fucking mind, just let him be!" Danny suddenly shouted. I felt them lift me up and steady me to my feet. "How fucking manly are you to get off hurting this poor fucking kid? His mind is fucking gone."

No, no, Danny, don't... please don't make him mad. He hurts you to control me. He hurts you to control me.

Perish hurts you to control me.

I screamed when Perish hit Danny. The young greywaster dropped me as he fell and we both spilled to the ground.

Then Perish started kicking me. Me? Don't kick me.

A second scream burst from my lips and I covered my head, tears streaming down my cheeks. I tried to shield myself as Perish delivered a hard kick to my side.

"You like him, huh? He's your little fucking buddy too, eh? How about you three shits find food or else we'll fucking eat him? Would you like that, you fucking worthless shit?" Perish snarled and I felt Danny's body give a heave as Perish kicked him.

"Fine! We're going..." Teejay shouted. I felt someone grab the back of my jacket and pull me up. "Just calm down, no one here has to get eaten. We have food for the night. It's alright, we'll check the cafeteria."

I was staring at the floor but my eyes travelled up to Perish. His face was red and his jaw locked. He was mad, or was he stressed out? Maybe I should suck him off to calm him down. I couldn't let him get angry; he's scary when he hits that state.

I saw Perish nod, his jaw still set. My eyes then travelled past him and I realized behind him was a large pane of glass, more hospital beds and machines covered in dust and dirt. But more than just that, everything that had been above the ceiling, above the push paneling, had come down. You couldn't even see the floor anymore or what colour it had used to be.

"Are you coming, Killian?"

It was all just plaster and insulation, blanketing everything and covering it in a smell of raw, souring wood and dry must.

Someone grabbed my hand and led me away from Perish. I could hear murmuring but there weren't any more raised voices so I was alright.

We went down the hallway and Edward spotted a sign for the elevator. Beside it we found the stairs and carefully walked over to them, testing the floorboards for any weakness but this floor seemed stable. In some of the rooms though I could see dips and craters from where heavier machinery had fallen through, including a reception's desk that was half-

THE GHOST AND THE DARKNESS

sunk into the rotting boards.

"We shouldn't be here," I whispered as we passed it. I walked over and looked down. I could see checkered linoleum barely visible through the ash and plaster. I ran my fingers along the desk and looked at the three slaves. "Really... we need to leave now."

"Jesus... he's broken this kid – bad," Danny whispered. I looked up and saw ribbons of peeling paint curling from the ceiling. It made me nervous, more nervous than all the other ruined sections around me. Something about the curls of paint being clustered together like this set me on edge, it made me anxious.

I looked away and left the room and started to walk towards the stairs, trying to push away the realization that the same curled paint was above me and around me on the sections of painted walls.

Musty, sour smells... I started to walk down the steps even though the flashlight barely lit my way. Down the stairs, down the stairs... I shone the flashlight in all directions, taking in the plaster so fragile even my footsteps were making it fall from the walls.

I coughed as the plaster tickled my nose, before sneezing into my jacket. I got to a landing and shone the flashlight outside, seeing nothing out of the window stained grey and black from age.

The slaves walked behind me, making more dust fall from the walls. I started wiping off a large sign and was thankful to see it had directions on it.

Danny read them out loud; he was the only one besides me who could read. "Cafeteria is another two flights down. Let's go. I want to eat as much as I can before we bring any to that shithead upstairs."

I shone the flashlight down the stairs, seeing an old Exit sign dangling from the ceiling, only being held up by several wires. We ignored the door it was pointing to and kept walking down the stairs, covered in a plastic no-slip covering that gave our boots good traction.

"When are we going to do it?" I heard Edward whisper behind me. I kept walking; shining the flashlight up ahead as much as I could to make sure nothing was going to ambush us. It was all just building though, crumbling, broken... dark building.

"We'll find knives in the cafeteria," Teejay whispered back. "We can make it quick."

I reached the bottom of the stairs and coughed again. Taking the lead, I cautiously walked through the door and looked around.

Dozens of chairs surrounding tables, plastic and perfectly intact like they were still waiting for the doctors and visiting family to fill them. The chairs were red and so were the tables, the brilliant colour only broken up by the dust and paneling that had fallen from the ceiling above.

My flashlight checked the ceiling but I couldn't see nests or signs of anything. Just more lights hanging like noosed convicts, and abyss-like darkness that swallowed up my light without care. At this sign I crossed the cafeteria, my boots and our breathing the only noise we could hear.

I gently touched the red plastic table.

"It's so red," I whispered and felt a smile come to my lips. "Reaver... loved the colour red. He used to... take home signs, especially Coca Cola signs, and repair them." I looked behind me, my mind deciding to ignore the grave and concerned look coming from Edward. The other two were off in the kitchen. I could hear rattling around. "Ever notice in the end... it's all just grey and red?"

Edward let out a long drawn-out breath. He looked like he was going to say something else, but instead he smiled and started directing me towards the kitchens. "Come on, we're going to find some food for us. Eat a shitload before we bring any back to that fuck."

I wanted to look at the benches some more but I went with him. We would have an extra flashlight that way.

"Why don't you tell me a story about Reaver again? What else did that crazy shit do that was funny?" Edward asked encouragingly. Danny and Teejay came into view, opening and closing metal doors, sending dust and the occasional loose panel onto the floor. The entire kitchen was filthy but the roof hadn't rained its remains down on it as much as the other ones. All the filth came from food that had been left out and stacks of pots and pans, even large racks. The food that had sat in those places were long gone of course, but they had still left a deep black stain that time hadn't erased.

They left in a hurry. They were running.

"Reaver..." Even saying his name out loud brought me close to the fringes of sanity, though in the same turn it filled my heart with sorrow. "Reaver used to pretend to hate our cat, but he loved him a lot. Once I got up to use the bathroom while I was sleeping. Reaver never needs much sleep, he's always awake it seems. Well, anyway..." I absentmindedly picked up a huge commercial size can and tried to dust it off. "I got up and saw he was sitting on the very edge of his chair making quils, like very edge so he was practically falling off. Do you know why?" I looked at Teejay who was right beside me and smiled at him. "Because Biff was asleep on that chair and he didn't want to disturb him. If I was awake, Reaver would've just..." Tears started to well in my eyes. "He would've just kicked him off to maintain his air of... his air of just being Reaver. But when no one's looking... he's so sweet to him."

"I wouldn't believe you if I didn't trust you," Edward said with a weak laugh. His hands came into my view and he slid the can I had found towards himself. I saw he'd found a can opener. That was something we would be taking with us, those were very valuable. "Reaver just seemed like well..."

"A bit of an asshole?"

All three of them chuckled.

"Yeah, but we saw what he did for that little one, the mute kid. You're right, when you're around he did seem different," Edward said.

Chally... are you still alive? I'm sorry Chally but if you did die... at least a quick death is better than what Perish is putting us through. I knew Perish would've brought you with us. I would've never let him hurt you.

My brow furrowed and I nodded; the sound of Edward opening up the can filled the room. "He once said I was his only tie to morality..." I paused and pursed my lips together. "He also said, no matter what happens... he would find me."

"Do you think he will?"

I nodded. "Nothing can keep us apart. We're meant to be together." I said that with a forcefulness to my voice. Maybe because I was used to saying it in the same tone inside of my head. Nothing will keep us apart. He told this to me. Reaver loved me and he would find me.

All four of us cheered in spite of my madness and their starvation. It was canned corn! We all took ourselves a handful and started shovelling it into our mouths.

Food, real food. The taste was so sweet, the texture made my mouth water. I started gorging myself on it, feeling tears well in my eyes just from relief that we had some food.

"We should stop eating..." Teejay said, but his hand was reaching back for more. "We'll throw up; this is too much sugar. There is a lot here. We'll leave the can here and keep looking and slowly pick at it until Perish starts to hound us."

Edward let out a groan but nodded. He put the lid over it and I finished off the half-handful I had. "Yeah, you're right. Okay, let's keep looking. We aren't weak enough that we can't carry what we find. Then we can all stop worrying about becoming Perish's next meal."

'If you don't find food, Killian...'

I wiped my hand on my pants and picked up the flashlight. Without a word, I started to look around the cafeteria for more canned food.

Edward was right… if we find enough…

I started to feel sick. I took a moment and leaned up against one of the kitchen counters and closed my eyes, taking in deep breaths. I stayed there, listening to the guys rustle around the kitchen.

I heard an odd noise. I looked over and saw Edward trying to sharpen a knife against a long handheld sharpener. He said something to Teejay before he slipped it into his jacket.

My mind filled with alarm, but for reasons I didn't understand, I stayed silent. Maybe I just didn't want a fight, or maybe deep down I was aware that these were slaves who were constantly being threatened with death and cannibalism just like I was. I didn't want to ask questions. I was too lost inside of my own head to care what was happening around me.

But he made eye contact with me as he zipped up his jacket. I stared back at him for a moment before my mouth opened and I started to talk.

"Reaver once found a sparkly rock… in a park we were making plant beds in. Well, one of the townhouses," I whispered to Edward. "I would've never noticed, but he did. It was normal but inside it was just so pretty… like diamonds inside of it. He gave it to me."

Edward stared at me for a second before giving me a half-hearted smile. There was no other exchange after that; he went towards the rows of freezers and ovens and left me in my corner.

I remember when I had found out who Reaver was.

I was so scared for him – so scared of what my baby would become.

What was a chimera? Were they really as bad as everyone said? Elish hadn't been outwardly mean or cruel, he just seemed cold. Even the pet had been nice, though he was a bit sharp for my taste.

I remember trying to ask Reaver about his father and what he remembered. He tried to get me to have sex with him as a distraction. What a silly boy. Oh, I miss that from him.

I miss that…

Our steps echoed in the stairs as we travelled up them one by one. Still testing each step even though we had come down them only a few hours before.

I remember when I played him songs on my guitar.
There's bodies in the water
And bodies in the basement
If heaven's for clean people.
It's vacant.

We could hear Perish in the distance, whistling to himself but he wasn't whistling the song that had been playing in my head. I held onto the can I forgot I was holding and started walking towards the noise. I felt like a dog coming towards its master's call.

With the slaves behind me, I walked down the dirty halls, red brick now just barely visible under the many layers of paint, plaster, and pressboard. They were talking behind me, in hurried voices. I didn't know what they were saying but they were making a point to stay far back from me.

"Perish?" I called weakly. My voice was like the broken plaster around me. Done, dead, and cracked. "We found food."

The voices continued behind me, until as quickly as they came, they left. My face scowled to the point where my eyebrow started twitching. It was like they had pressed mute on themselves, suddenly everything had fallen into an eerie silence.

Perish appeared in the doorway. He was wearing an old lab coat he must've found. However it was dusty and the creases seemed to have bent the fabric from being folded for so long.

The scientist, now my slave owner, looked at me and then the others. "I found several things I was looking for. Well, we're not spending the night here. We'll find a house. I have antiseptic and antibiotics to keep you fucks alive for another week."

"Okay," I said, still holding the giant can in one hand and the flashlight in the other. I looked around the room Perish was in and absentmindedly started cleaning off the screen of an old computer.

"What did you find? You opened the corn? I should fucking beat you for that," Perish growled. "Go on... get the–"

Suddenly there was a scuffle. I whirled around and dropped the can onto the ground as I saw a flash of silver reflect against the flashlight. I screamed into my held mouth as I saw Edward raise the knife and stab Perish right in the back.

Perish was silent. His blue eyes filled with an inferno that made me back up until my back hit the wall. I stood there with my hand over my mouth as Perish slowly turned around, the kitchen knife sticking almost halfway out of his back. He glared down Edward as the slave gaped at him; his face tight and stricken, and his hands shaking.

No one but Perish moved. The scientist reached behind him, and with one pull, like he was withdrawing Excalibur, he slid the knife out from his back and looked at it.

"Killian," Perish said plainly.

My feet trembled in my boots. I looked at him and shook my head back and forth feeling my body sink to the ground. I kept shaking my head.

"Killian, come here."

Killi bee bee bee.

"Killian? I said come here."

The floor underneath my feet was filthy; I could see the tread from my boots perfectly in the plaster dust. The dust was everywhere, but it wasn't from the greywastes, just the ceiling above us. I scraped my boots against the dust to watch the treads.

"KILLIAN!"

I gasped from shock as I felt someone grab me. The person with his face twisted in anger pushed a kitchen knife into my hand and grabbed my head. He made me look at the slave named Edward who was down on his knees. His mouth was dripping blood and saliva.

"Kill him."

There was a man staring back at me in the knife's reflection. A blond young man with a scraggly beard, with dark blue eyes barely visible under the blackened circles. He was skinny, and his blond hair was long and not brushed. I wondered who this kid was and why he looked so terrified.

"If you don't do it… I'll cut his arm off and let him suffer."

"If you don't kill him now, Killian."

"Killhim Killian Killhim Killian."

"If you don't kill him, Killian. I will torture him first and then I will kill him. Do you want him to suffer?"

"Do you want him to suffer more, Killian?"

"Killian?"

"KILLIAN!"

A knock upside my head. I turned around in shock and saw the angry man glaring at me, injecting my body with his poison. I stared at him wondering why he had hit me.

I looked down at the knife.

"No," I whispered and dropped the knife. "Stop using them to control me."

The man backhanded me, then grabbed my neck and hit me again. With a hard push, he shoved me back into the corner of the room and I fell down, face first, into a hospital machine.

I crawled further into the corner, hearing a sudden burst of screaming from Edward and the other two slaves. One was in agony, the other two begging.

I tucked my legs up to my knees and watched, trembling in place, as the man raised his knife.

I could see the terrified whites of the other slaves' eyes. They stared in shock and horror but I also saw obedience.

I saw obedience because they were holding Edward's arms out like he was on a crucifix.

Mr. Fallon grabbed onto the forearm of Edward and gripped it hard, so hard I could see Edward's skin turn white where Perish's hands were clenching. He gripped it, and with his free hand, the one holding his knife, he started to cut through the slave's flesh.

The skin split open, red and grey, always that red and grey. The only white I could see was the bone when Perish stabbed his knife into it and pried it away from its socket. But even that would turn red soon from the blood rushing out of the stump.

Perish twisted the limb away but my ears couldn't hear the snapping or cracking. Even their screams didn't add torment to this living nightmare. Because all I could hear was a deep hammering inside of my ears, and that song playing over and over in my head.

Bodies in the water. Bodies in the basement.

Edward's mouth was open. His eyes were closed, and his sweaty face tensed in a pain I couldn't imagine. Beside him Perish loomed, holding the severed arm in his hand.

I thought he was going to kill him, or cut the other arm off, but instead Perish kneeled down and held his hands out to Edward's shredded stump.

A sizzle and a billow of smoke erupted from his hands. Edward groaned but didn't scream, only when the heat radiating off of Perish's palm gave a flare did he make a wheezing noise.

Several seconds later, Perish removed his hand, bits of flesh sticking to his palm. Edward's face tensed and he cried out; his cauterized stump still steaming and smoking.

Perish turned around and threw the severed arm at me. It landed beside me and disturbed my boot prints, making a puff of dust flying up into the air.

"Take it. We're cooking that tonight. We can have it with the corn you opened."

I got up and picked up the arm, staring at the still warm limb. It was heavier than I thought it would be.

"Answer me."

"Killian."

"Do you want me to cut off another fucking arm, Killian? Really?"

"No." I found my voice.

"Then do it. Go."

"Okay," I whispered, my mind choosing to ignore the groans and cries coming from the group of slaves. I could smell the hot blood and burnt skin; it tasted odd mixed in with the stale smell of age. Though I think this had been the aroma most smelled after the Fallocaust.

Without looking, my mind continuing to jam on itself, I walked out of the room and down the hallway to the hospital.

"You're going to have to die, Perish."

"Not tonight and not in this town. You seem stupid enough to try and make a break with the slaves. You remember your collar will kill you if you stray, don't you?"

"Yeah."

I poked the last hook through Perish's upper back, wondering just how he was able to still stand and how he wasn't screaming in pain right now. The scientist was staring forward, glaring at the slaves sitting down in front of an old dresser. All of them stared back but Edward, who was weak and the colour of curdled milk.

Edward's severed stump was wrapped in a bloody lab coat we had found on a metal shelf. Red had now stained the white, and over the last several hours, had turned into a dark brown. He was still moving though, I didn't know how.

We were inside a house, one of the last houses before the town ended. Behind us, miles of structures and the hospital, now a looming omen in the distance. In front of us… just landscapes, a thousand shades of blacks and greys. I could see some structures, broken up smears of different textures, but for the most part, we had nothing to look forward to but wasteland.

"PAY ATTENTION!" Perish suddenly snapped, jerking his back away. He whirled around to hit me when he paused.

I was just looking out the window; it was only when I glanced down did I realize I had stuck the hook through a piece of his skin an entire inch away from his stab wound.

"Anyone home?" Perish patted my cheek. "You're really slipping, I see."

I winced as he stroked my cheek gently. "It looks like you need to relax," he murmured. "Want me to relax you, *bona mea*?"

Relax me? I knew what that meant. I knew what that meant.

I shook my head and put the last stitch into his back.

But I knew he was going to die; the knife wound was deep and it had nicked one of his bones, his ribs I think.

I was still holding the bloody wire in my hands when Perish turned around. He took it from me and brushed my hair back over my forehead. "Want me to hold you? Protect you? You know during the day I miss your cock, Silas."

Oh, I was Silas again.

Okay.

I didn't answer, and when he realized I wouldn't, he took the hook and wire from my grasp, before turning around to address the slaves. "Get a fire going and skewer that arm. I want it roasted and ready for when we come back."

I didn't want to go anywhere with him but I didn't have a choice. Perish grabbed my hand and led me upstairs to one of the bedrooms. Or what had once been a bedroom. It had cardboard boxes stacked one on top of the other and a mattress on a bed frame in the corner. The ceiling was intact but barely, like most ceilings in the wasteland its contents had spilled to the floor.

"Is this where you're going to fuck me?" I rasped. My voice was gone, it had been gone for a while.

Too much screaming.

"No," Perish said. He walked over to the mattress and kicked it, sending a plume of dust up into the air. "I want *you* to fuck *me*."

My eyes widened before they rose to look at Perish. He was staring back at me, his shirt and jacket already off of his body. His chest was blanched, sickly, and still holding smudges of blood from his stabbed back.

I shook my head no.

"You don't want to punish me for what I did to you? Punish me for breaking that fragile mind of yours? Come on, Silas." Perish walked up to me and grabbed the crotch of my jeans, I looked away. "Punish me. Fuck me until you kill me. You have my permission."

I shook my head again. Perish slipped his pants down and stepped out of them, his boots still on his feet. When he pulled down his boxer briefs my ears went hot.

I turned to walk out of the room but he grabbed my shoulder. "Come on, Si-guy. You think you're such a big man now. You don't want to take some of that inner anger out on me? You can tear me in half if you want to." He smiled as he started undressing me. I let him, there was nothing I could do but stare at the floor.

"Reaver decided at the end… that we could keep Chally." I looked down and saw my flaccid penis, I had never seen myself so ungroomed, I looked a mess. "He didn't want to; you saw how much he… was against it. But he decided in the end he loved me enough." I felt my face tense as my eyebrows knitted together. "He is such this… dark horse, but to me, he's my baby. He loves me so much."

It was cold in the room, but Perish's hands were warm. The next thing I knew he was rubbing and jerking off my penis.

I watched and said absentmindedly, "You know I'm not Silas. Right, Perish?"

He hit me again. I stumbled back naked and slammed into one of the stacks of boxes. They fell on top of me, raining their miscellaneous contents down, mixing in with the dirt and dust.

I coughed and felt him pull me out from under the mess by my leg.

"Get up, get it hard, and come here," Perish snapped.

I got up in a daze and saw him lay down naked on the mattress; his own dick hard as rock.

He spread his legs. "Do it, or you don't want to know what I will do in retaliation."

What he would do in retaliation? He would hurt the slaves again, my friends, the only friends I had. He had already cut off Edward's arm, the same arm that he was forcing them to cook right now. Those slaves had helped me even though my own mind was slipping through my fingers, and hadn't turned their backs on me even though Perish treated me better than them.

I couldn't let him hurt them, I couldn't.

My eyes stung as I started to stroke my own dick. I sniffed and stared at it as I pulled and tugged at the soft member trying to get it hard.

Nothing was happening. I stood there like an idiot and continued to try and force something out of it, but it was limp and useless in my hand.

Perish started yelling at me. He got up off of the bed and slapped me across the face.

I didn't fall this time. I stood there. "Reaver loved watching *Friends*. He would laugh so much but when I would come out of the bedroom and try and watch it with him he would switch it to *The X Files* and tell me I had been hearing things. It took me two months until he would admit he liked–"

"Shut up!" Perish screamed. He took my shoulders and started shaking me. "You useless, deranged idiot! Do you even know where the fuck you are anymore? You weak-minded, pathetic fuck! This is all your fault! All of this is your fault!"

My head snapped back and forth until he stopped. "I'm Killian... not Silas." I looked at him, my brow creased. "That's why you're being so cruel to me, isn't it? I thought you loved Silas?"

"You are Silas, you blond little dumbfuck," Perish snapped. "I remember you, I remember what you did. How could we forget? We said the radiation would stop the computers that were controlling the missiles, but now look at where we are. Look at what we did!"

Perish paused, his face blank. "Look at what we did. I asked you if I was right, you said I was right. You said it was the right thing to do."

"Oh," I said quietly staring at my boots and groin. I still wasn't hard. "You're just as crazy as I am, huh? I thought the brain piece was supposed to make you sane."

"Shut up and get your cock hard."

"NO!" I suddenly screamed. I ripped myself away and pushed him. "I am not going to touch you, you disgusting, sociopathic, fucking piece of shit! You sorry excuse for a fucking immortal!"

Tears sprung to my eyes. I pushed him harder this time, and before I could stop it, all the anger hidden inside of me started to spill from my lips like water.

"Greyson and Leo, good people… my parents… all these people die and pieces of shit like you get to walk the earth forever without fear. You're nothing, Perish Fallon! NOTHING! I will never love you. Silas will never love you. No one loves you, you fucking loser! NO ONE! I'm glad you're fucking immortal because you get to experience eternity being reminded that you're worthless! WORTHLESS!" I shrieked so hard my nose started to bleed but I didn't care.

I sunk down to my knees and started to sob.

My breath became short. I ground my teeth together and drew my hands up to my knees. I closed my eyes, feeling my teeth grind and squeak against each other, the sound echoing in my head matching the pounding in my ears.

Bodies in the water, bodies in the basement.
If heaven's for clean people.
It's vacant.

The anxiety attack came with vengeance, hitting me like a truck and leaving me nothing but a gasping, crying heap of muscle and bone. For a long time I felt like I had become nothing, lost inside my confused and pain-filled head.

Yeah, I was nothing. I was nothing.

I was hyperventilating, clawing my legs and crying, babbling like an idiot as the panic attack claimed every last part of my body. From my head to my feet, nerves to my blood. I was gone and the world around me was nothing but a distant memory. A haze of images that had once been clear, but were now so far away from my brain the grey sun seemed closer.

I came-to to the sound of grunting and crying, rhythmic noises like a song I would have skipped on the Discman. Noises that started out quiet but were soon pounding on the door of my brain, demanding for me to let them in so they could watch me scream in horror.

I looked up and saw Perish fucking Danny, the young man's face frozen in shock as Mr. Fallon fucked him from behind. He was doing him hard; his face sweaty and his eyes two slabs of ice. He was pushing into him, the sounds of flesh smacking against flesh replacing the hammering inside of my head.

My head stung and I couldn't catch my breath. My chest was on fire. I whimpered and tensed my hands, then felt something odd. Something odd, something odd…

I looked at my hands and saw they were stained red, and covered in tufts of bloody blond hair.

My hair.

I put my hand on my head and felt it warm and sticky. Not knowing what else to do… I clenched my hair again and pulled, ripping more out of my scalp. I chuckled at this.

Then the sound of hair ripping from my skull infiltrated my head, instead of them fucking.

That was better – much better.

So I did it again.

And again.

And again.

Laughing the entire time.

CHAPTER 47

Reno

"COME ON… YOU'RE BEING SILLY. I WON'T BE GONE for long," Garrett sighed. His freshly trimmed moustache twitching on his face as he gave me a sympathetic look. I don't know why he had dressed up; he was just going to the greywastes.

"No," I said stubbornly. I was leaning up against the door to the outside hallway. "How can you leave me with that guy?! He's going to string me up by my toes and torture information out of me."

Garrett kissed my cheek and grabbed his suitcase. "Silas requested it, love. And this is a good chance for me to go to the bunker in Aras without having to worry about him monitoring me. I must find out what Lycos did. Not only for my own reassurances, I am sure Elish wants to know for sure as well, and that in turn will help Reaver."

I gave him a heartbreaking look and got down on my knees. Garrett gave me a surprised blink but I didn't do what getting down on one's knees usually meant (though that was also a good angle), I grabbed onto his leg and hugged it tight.

Garrett burst out laughing and started dragging me around the apartment. "He's bringing Drake and he's bringing Sanguine, you know as well as I do Sanguine is in Elish's pocket currently. Love, I would never leave you here if I felt you were in harm's way. Please, he only wants to visit with you and get a more detailed account of your time under the Crimstones, especially where Kerres might be."

I clung to his leg tighter. "Will you bring me back something?"

He stared at me. "Like what?"

"A treat."

My fiancé stared at me before he chuckled and patted my head. As I slowly unwrapped myself from his leg he said, "Alright, I will bring you back a treat. What's a treat to a greywaster? A severed head?"

I thought for a second and stood up. "Actually... could you go into Aras and just walk by Leo and Greyson's house? Killian and Reaver's too? Just... make sure they're houses are still there and no one's touched them."

I knew the mood would take a turn after that but I didn't expect the sadness to hit me how it did.

Garrett gave a sympathetic nod and touched my cheek. "Sure, love, I will. I know where they are. Are you going to let your fiancé go now? The sooner I leave, the sooner I'll return."

I got to my feet and handed him his scarf; Skylanders loved their stupid scarfs.

"Alright," I said with an over-embellished sigh. "Go crack the chimera code and figure out just what Leo did to Perish. I'm sure you'll have fun on your adventure while I get emotionally ruined by the King of the Fallocaust."

"No such thing will happen and if it does Sanguine will help you," Garrett reassured, and after a parting kiss he was gone with Chally and I was left in the apartment. Even the new kid got to skirt King Silas's visit. Even though Chally couldn't talk he had been with Reaver and it was best to just not risk it. However the kid was pretty reluctant to go. I don't think he missed the greywastes that much.

I was just making myself a drink of rum and ChiCola (yeah, that was what they called it here, chi was short for chimera), when there was a knock on the double doors of the apartment.

For a moment, not as brief as I would tell Garrett later, I wanted to duck into our bedroom and hide under the bed, but I decided I had to trust Garrett and let the crazy king in.

I slunk to the door with a sigh and opened it.

Drake was staring at me, and as soon as he saw me his mouth opened and his tongue lolled out. Behind him was King Silas holding his leash, and beside him, the grinning face of Sanguine.

"Hey, am I supposed to bow or something?" I gave a nervous laugh and stood back as the three of them walked in. Immediately Drake threw his arms around me and gave off a happy squeal. Silas laughed and this and pulled his leash back.

"He has always held a soft spot for you. Get back, Drakey." Drake coughed as Silas pulled him back on his leash, before Silas handed the gold chain back to the fox-boy. The orange-eyed cicaro restrained himself but he was still buzzing on the spot.

Silas pointed him towards the television. "There. You go watch something on the TV. Reno follow me. We will be talking upstairs in the rooftop garden, where I am sure no ears will hear us."

I tried to push down the apprehension and managed to do so before it reached my face. I gave a cautious glance at Sanguine but he was looking at Silas with his arms behind his back, and that smile still on his face. The sengil bodyguard, wearing his usual bowtie and vest, wasn't even looking at me.

"Alrighty then," I said. I went to grab my jacket but Silas stopped me.

"Have you not been outside yet today? The sky is blue and the grey sun is out. Spring is coming to Skyfall. You will love Skyland in the spring. Artemis has been working very hard with Joaquin and young Jem. We have a lot of flowers coming up in Skyland this year."

"Oh?" I said casually. "I ate a couple flowers in the indoor gardens when I first came here. They don't taste as good as they look."

Silas chuckled and the door closed behind us; Sanguine and Drake both inside. I felt the well of apprehension grow as I realized I was alone with him.

"Nervous are we?" Silas whispered as we walked down the hall towards the elevator.

"I would be retarded if I wasn't, *Asher*," I said to him lowly. "You know our history. Would you really believe my act if I acted all happy as shit to see you?"

"Oh? Garrett didn't prep you or anything?" Silas pressed the up button on the elevator and the doors closed on us. I was trapped with him now, well, this was going great so far.

"He told me I was safe and not to worry, but Garrett loves you dearly. We, on the other hand, have a bit of a past," I replied honestly. "The fact that you're currently hunting Reaver doesn't win you any favours with me. Why insult your intelligence by acting like everything is okay?"

I might be digging my own grave today but I think I was doing the right thing. Silas was smart as fuck; he was over two hundred and fifty-five years old. If I acted happy to see him – he would smell the bullshit in my words.

And from the look he gave me I think I had done the right thing. We were silent as the elevator rode the single floor until we got to the garden area which was Garrett's roof.

When it had opened we still hadn't exchanged any more words. I walked out into the beautifully landscaped rooftop, complete with benches, fountains, and potted plants just starting to sprout green, and fake Astroturf that would be replaced with real grass once it became a bit warmer.

I walked over to one of my favourite benches and sat down; immediately I lit a cigarette and inhaled. The blue ember brightened like an electric blueberry and filled my lungs with the smooth biting taste of good-quality tobacco.

Silas lit one too and sat down beside me, still not saying anything.

We smoked together, but with each inhale of the smoke my apprehension grew. When I had killed the cigarette, I flicked it into one of the ashtray sculptures Garrett had up here and went to light another one.

"I miss him, Reno."

I stopped, the Zippo lighter burning the end of my smoke. I pulled the lighter away and took out the cigarette. "Reaver?"

Silas was staring forward, at the blue-tinged sky in front of us, the sun high in the sky bathing him in its faint warm light. Today was a beautiful day, and the golden-haired king seemed made for it.

He nodded slowly; his eyes looked troubled. "I enjoyed having him as my friend. Do you think that's strange?"

I shrugged and replied back honestly, "You know you could have continued to be his friend if you didn't… try and rape him, then molested and tortured Killian, and then stalked him and killed Reaver's parents. Just sayin'."

Silas snorted and looked over at me. "I admire your honesty. My subjects would rather die than speak to me in that way."

"I'm not a subject, just a dirty-blooded greywaster," I said back to him. "You could've been his best bud for a long time. You know, he loves Killian to pieces and he would never leave him for you… but you would've had a lot more success trying to just be yourself. Once you went crazy, you kinda lost it."

I looked to my side and he looked back. His eyes struck me, I never realized how vividly green they were.

I decided to press him. "Once you strip away all that… crazy shit about you, you're a cool dude. Why did you have to fuck everything up? You realize he'll hate you literally for all eternity now, right?"

"You know he belongs to me, right? And that I can treat him, and you, how I want, right?" Silas said coolly back. His body stiffened and I knew my honesty was starting to lose its charm. "Just like I saved your ancestors from the radiation."

That you fucking caused.

"Reaver doesn't belong to anyone," I said to him. "And you didn't create him. Leo did and he's dead now, thanks to you."

And that was it for our cordial conversation. "If you're going to be marrying my second born chimera, I suggest you start learning your place, Reno Dekker."

Reno Dekker. Jeez, he really knew where to prod me. I relented with a sigh and put my hands in the air. Garrett told me I was safe here but I don't think he was taking into account that I was an idiot.

"Alright, sorry. You can't blame me; you ruined my fucking life in the greywastes. I haven't seen or heard from Reaver in months, or Killian. I'm worried sick about them." I shook my head. "I miss him too, man. Fuck, I am so worried about him."

"It's not like he can die."

"Tinkerbell can."

"Tinkerbell *will*."

I dashed my cigarette ash onto the turf and watched a crow land on the railing surrounding Garrett's roof. It cawed at the both of us.

"Do you know why I want him so badly, Reno?"

Yes, I do. Garrett had told me and Elish had told me. "Reaver was cloned from you, which is why he's all psychopathic and murdery I guess." I shrugged. "You made him for the sole reason…"

"–for the sole reason to replace Sky," Silas finished even though I wasn't going to finish with that. I'd heard of Sky but I just knew he was Silas's boyfriend way back in the day. He was long dead, killed himself to get away from Silas, rumour has it.

"He reminds me so much of him sometimes." Silas glanced behind him when we heard a noise. I did too and saw Sanguine had joined us, but he was keeping in the shadows feeding birdseed to the crows. For all I know the sengil had been there since we had arrived. That chimera was sneaky and quick.

Silas watched the crow start to peck at the seed, it had red eyes which was creepy yet suiting. "The first time I saw Reaver, it was just like looking at my beautiful Sky. Same darkness, same air about him that seeps confidence and control. My Sky was a tyrant, an abusive, terror of a person. But when I had him alone we melted into each other's arms. I understood him, no one understood him like I did."

I cringed as Silas put a hand on mine. "Reno, I know very well where your loyalties lie and I have been kind enough to look past them because Garrett loves you. But I want you to consider something. Reaver was engineered from my own DNA, and I know myself more than I know anyone. Reaver needs me to help him learn to control his urges. He'll destroy Killian; he'll eventually kill Killian. Killian is weak, a wraith of a creature who Reaver will probably drive to insanity. As much as Reaver loves him, a born immortal cannot be with a greywaster. Reaver will eventually kill him or get him killed. If you want what is best for Reaver, let me train him and teach him how to control his impulses before it's too late. Let me make sure–" Oddly, the king paused, and to my shock, I thought I saw true raw emotion pass through his features.

"–let me make sure he doesn't end up like me."

I stared at him, feeling dumbfounded. Was he trying to get information out of me? I wasn't sure, but I felt awkward and uncomfortable with what he was saying.

No, it didn't matter though. Either way, no matter what he was doing, I knew he was wrong. Reaver was Killian's protector, not someone he ever had to be afraid of. He loved Killian more than anyone in the world loved anyone.

"And I loved Sky," Silas chuckled dryly. Once again I was thrown off balance; it was like he had read my mind. "Look what happened to my Sky, Reno. Look what I did to him. He was my... my everything and I miss him every day. He wasn't weak like Killian, Sky was strong. A beast, a monster... he beat on me, tormented me, and reminded me whenever we fought that it was my fault for ending the world. That I had caused it. I had thought–" Silas stopped himself, which I felt odd. The slippery king always had a way of crafting his words like he was shaping ivory stone, but he seemed to be giving me more information than he meant to.

"If he was so bad... I don't understand why you miss him so much," I said back. For some reason I felt the urge to spare him the backtracking after he'd caught himself giving too much personal information.

"No…" Silas whispered. "You wouldn't understand. You wouldn't understand just how much I loved him."

"So you want to bring Reaver here so he can smack you around? Call you names and treat you like shit. Why?"

"I would do it right this time," Silas replied, lighting another cigarette. "That's what he is to me, my second chance. I can get my born immortal and Reaver can get the man who he is destined to be with. We can rule Skyfall and the greywastes together… like it was always meant to be."

Sounds like you're a bit fucked in the head, buddy.

"Sounds like you have it all planned out." That though was what I said out loud; I wasn't that stupid.

"You'll see, Reno. I'm the only one who can control Reaver, who can tame him and help him. He will destroy Killian. A greywaster cannot be with a born immortal, they're too weak and that boy is even weaker."

I nodded and inhaled some smoke. I blew it out slowly. "Why are you telling me this?"

Silas was quiet for a moment. Then his dark green eyes, the colours of the sprouting plants around us, brightened. He smiled almost sadly at me. "Because I am patient, and I know you must have an idea as to where he is hiding." My heart froze, and at this, he laughed. I swore inside of my head and wondered if I'd just confirmed something to him with my heartbeat or if I could cop it up to just being directly called out on where he might be. "Just watch him, Reno. Watch and see for yourself. He's darkness encompassed, and this ghost belongs in darkness."

Silas rose.

"You say he's all bad because he was engineered this way. Well, if he's from your own DNA, he can't be that bad," I said with a shrug. "Because I knew you in the greywastes and before you took it too far… you were an okay guy."

The king froze and turned around. I was surprised to see I had touched a nerve, though it confused me as to what one.

"I am not okay, Reno," Silas whispered, slowly shaking his head back and forth. "And perhaps what this boils down to… is that I need Reaver to make me okay, just as much as I want to make him okay."

His words rattled me like he had just spoken an earthquake. Out of all the things he said to me, that, I think, had the biggest impact. It wasn't a subtle manipulation or a way to try and get me to sell out Reaver. I had this sinking feeling inside of me that, if anything, what he had just said was the truth.

Silas was the Mad King. We all knew this. We had all *seen* this. Would... would Reaver really calm him down? Perhaps...

I let out my last breath of smoke and flicked the cigarette off the top of the skyscraper. I... had never thought of it like that. What if that was the truth? What if Silas was actually speaking to me from his heart? If he knew I might know where Reaver was he could have tortured the information out of me, or tried at least.

I was confused; I felt butterflies start to tear each other apart inside of my gut. I didn't like this small portion of my brain and heart edging towards sympathizing with Silas, or at the very least, understanding it from his point of view. He was wrong and he was going about this wrong but... deep down inside I understood his logic and his reasoning.

Garrett had said Elish was promising the chimeras their own partners, even immortal partners once he came into power. Because King Silas became jealous when his creations had men to call their own, lovers that they might love more than Silas.

But if Silas had his lover...

FUCK, RENO! I clenched my teeth and forced it out of me, feeling a boiling anger and shame rush through my body. I started calling myself every derogatory name in the book. I was so ashamed of myself I felt like punching myself in the face.

How could I even... poor Tinky. Fuck, sorry, Tinkerbell, I didn't mean to think those thoughts. Please forgive me.

"I set your wedding date," Silas said as we rode down to Garrett's apartment floor. Sanguine beside us with his hands behind his back. "July, in the summer time. Elish's wedding was rather rushed, so I would like to hold a nice one for you two. I do love Garrett with all my heart."

The elevator dinged and when it opened Sanguine stood back and let us walk out first.

"In that time and after... think about my words. I'll be in and out of Skyfall seeking Reaver, but that is not new." Silas waited outside of the door as Sanguine slipped in. I could hear him talking to Drake. "Thankfully my chimeras are more than happy to pick up their brothers' duties. Which is good considering Jade is still injured. He certainly is a pathetic excuse for a chimera, but he is my creation and I love him." Silas's face brightened when he saw Drake. "There's my boy, did you have fun?"

Drake grinned and rolled back and forth on the heels of his tight leather boots. "Yeah, I watched *King of the Hill*. Can we watch it when we get home?"

"Of course." Silas brushed Drake's hair back caringly, before turning to me. "We will take our leave. Do remember my words, and if there is anything you wish to ask me… I will be there."

I nodded, still feeling the butterflies eat each other inside of my stomach. "Okay."

Silas put a hand on my cheek and smiled, before leaning in and gently kissing me on the lips. "You two will have to have me over one night; I do miss your body on top of mine."

I stared at him in shock and Silas laughed. I think that reaction was what he wanted because he kissed me one last time and left.

I felt physically exhausted after King Silas and the other two left. Silas and Sanguine both had a presence to them that just mentally drained you. Now that they were gone I downed myself a shot of rum and laid down for a nap. Chimeras were missing out with their unusual lack of napping. I wouldn't be able to survive being awake twenty hours a day. There just wasn't that much to do in a day in the greywastes, especially when I was stuck in the cabin. You can only jerk off so many times before things start to chafe.

My mind needed a bit of time to sort itself too. I was confused and rattled with what Asher-Silas had told me. I think the part that confused me the most was that I understood where he was coming from.

There was nothing I could do about it though. No way in whatever hells there were would I ever sell out Reaver and Killian. Even if Reaver had been going off the handle after what Nero had done to him, on top of the stress of everything else, who could really blame him for acting a bit loco. He had been through a lot over the past several months. Leo and Greyson raised Reaver and he had to watch them get shot right in front of him.

A thousand and one racing thoughts went through my mind as I lay in my and Garrett's bed. I didn't even realize I had drifted off to sleep, but the next thing I knew I could hear the sound of the television coming from the living room, telling me that Garrett was home.

I got up with a yawn and walked out into the living room to greet my partner.

But as soon as my eyes fell on my fiancé, sitting over the laptop… I froze in place.

Garrett's eyes were wide and his face holding a fear on it that made my muscles seize. I could see he was watching something, a video on his laptop.

"Gare?" I whispered. "What's wrong?"

His green eyes shot to me then he shook his head slowly. It looked like he was having trouble breathing. I realized from watching Killian that he was almost going into a panic attack.

"L-Lycos..." he stuttered. "Killian is in great danger, Reno." He turned back to the screen, and at the mention of Killian's name, I quickly walked over. I sat beside him and felt a stir inside of my gut as Leo's face was shown on screen. Older Leo, this was recent... possibly only weeks before he died.

Garrett, with a shaking hand, moved the video back before resting the same hand back over his mouth.

"I can't believe..." Garrett whispered. "I can't believe... Elish..."

"It's over, Elish." Leo stared at the screen. His face was hard and his hazel eyes even harder. I saw no cheerful mayor in front of me. I saw something more. Someone he had always hid from us.

"The plan is a failure and I'm putting a stop to it before it goes farther than it has to. I'll not give you my son. I'll not give you Killian either and, yes, I know you sent him here as a peace offering. I'll not say I know all of your underhanded tricks, but who's to know."

Leo rose, and a moment later, there was a swirl of whites and greys as he picked up the video camera. He walked through the hallway of the bunker, one I had just been in a few weeks ago, and opened the door.

The camera focused on a pathetic, sad sight. Perish was in a corner of the room, his rapid moving eyes focused on nothing yet staring intently at the same time. He was covered in blood and bruises, and I could see a nasty road of stitches on the back of his head. He looked sick, like he was going to drop dead at any moment.

"Let's make this a proper confession, shall we? Because I know once you realize what I have done, Elish, that you're going to kill me," Leo said acerbically. "But I don't care, because it's already too late. It's done and hopefully before you realize what I did... Perish will be in Sky's place. Silas will have Sky, he'll stop killing our brothers' lovers. You'll have no reason to kill King Silas and no use for Reaver."

What?

"I should've stopped this years ago. If I didn't listen to my idiot husband I would have too." Leo's voice dropped. "But, either way, it doesn't matter, I'm doing it now. I'll not send my son on this stupid mission to kill Silas. I won't risk Silas capturing him. You know more than any of us just what will happen to him if Silas finds out he's alive."

Garrett was silent beside me, looking green and in shock. I wiped my face with my hands and groaned.

Leo continued, "I've implanted Perish with Sky's O.L.S. They are both identical twins and with that device in place of Perish's own missing brain piece, I can make an even better replacement for Reaver. Silas will have Sky back, and your family will no longer have to suffer his insanity. All will be well and you will have no need for my son."

"Holy fuck…" My mouth felt like it had filled with cotton. I tried to swallow through it but I just ended up feeling dizzy. "That wasn't Perish's own device? That was… that was Sky's?"

The video paused and Garrett nodded grimly. He still had a hand over his mouth. "Reno, Lycos is an idiot. Perish and Sky were identical twins but… but it doesn't work like that. I'm gravely concerned for Killian. An O.L.S isn't some universal puzzle piece. Its synapses are different, it's entirely different. If Perish has that electronic in his brain, it will drive him mad. He isn't just going to all of a sudden become Sky, that is just some wishful, and incredibly ignorant, thinking. Thinking from some greywaster idiot who has watched too many science fiction movies." Garrett rose, his face sweaty and his hands shaking. I realized as I watched him that mine were too.

"I need to go to Silas's skyscraper and confirm this. If Lycos did get a hold of Sky's O.L.S… we must warn Elish and Reaver. Everyone is in danger, mortal and immortal alike."

My chest gave a sickening lurch. I tried to take a step but just found myself sinking back onto the couch. "How would Lycos even get a hold of Sky's brain piece?"

"I'm not sure. It was supposed to be kept under lock and key, in the lower levels of Alegria." To my surprise Garrett's lower lip tightened. "My poor Silas… he will be just devastated when he learns this. That is the last remnants of Sky's makeup that we have left. If something happens to it he'll be devastated."

I rose to my feet, feeling an all-consuming dizziness. "Let's go... to the skyscraper. Now."

Garrett nodded, and before I knew it, we were heading down the elevator.

My mind was a swamp, a fermenting pool that contained nothing but worries, each one trying to claw its way to the surface to fill my mind with a new wave of grim thoughts. I had so many worries in that moment, so many fears, I didn't know which one to focus on first.

"What do we do if this is true?" I asked him. "You'll help me if we have to go back to the greywastes, right?"

Garrett stared forward but nodded. "Yes, right now the immediate concern is Killian. Killian is alone with him, all alone. We don't know where and we don't know why Perish wants him," Garrett continued. "Perish is essentially... an unstable bomb of radiation right now. One that could explode at any time."

"What do you mean?" I asked.

"Sestic radiation comes from born immortals alone. It's a unique radiation that can erupt from a born immortal's body; it's how Silas started the Fallocaust." I noticed he was starting to go green again. "Stress causes these outbursts; intense, crippling stress. If you poke the bomb enough times..."

"It'll explode?" Another jolt of sickness.

Garrett nodded. "If Perish goes off, Killian will die immediately and anyone in a hundred mile radius will die of radiation poisoning. If he's implanted his mind can easily become unstable enough to release it. We were sure he couldn't access it anymore when his own O.L.S was taken out but... well, the part of the brain Greg removed was the same for both twins. Chances are he has that ability again."

I realized something. "What about Jade, isn't he in danger too?" The car started to slow down as the driver neared Alegria, Silas's skyscraper.

We both got out and started towards the glass doors, the thiens doing nothing to stop us. Once we were safe inside, Garrett spoke. "The *boy*..." Garrett glanced around and I knew it was now unsafe to use their names. "Was never with *him*. The *other two* are nearing reclaiming him."

A cryptic response, but I knew I would hear the rest once we left. It turned out I didn't have time to even think about it, quickly Garrett ushered me into a side elevator and pushed one of the lower buttons.

"Where are we going?" I whispered, looking around the elevator we were in. Even Silas's elevator was all fancy, with wood paneling on the bottom and some viney wallpaper on top.

"Basement..." Garrett said under his breath. "No one is here right now, well, no chimeras. Silas mentioned he was going back to the greywastes to search for Reaver. We're safe."

But still, even though he said we were safe, Garrett's hand slipped into mine. I squeezed it as the elevator lurched to a stop.

The doors slid open and revealed a large finished basement in front of us. A clean, dark-themed room with maroon-coloured walls and dark grey trim, all surrounded by a black and grey marble floor. In its entirety the room was empty, save for a single day bed and a black wooden cabinet.

I paused and gave Garrett a quizzical look. He smiled sadly and pulled on my hand as we walked down the hallway.

"I was young... perhaps only twelve. I had heard from Nero he was down here, so I came down, just wishing to request a fish tank to put my pet mice in. I walked through these very elevators and found him sitting alone. Holding in his arms this stuffed leopard. He was crying with it clutched to his chest." Garrett's eyes started to well. "When he saw me he leapt to his feet and as he did I heard a clunk as it landed on the ground. Do you know why?"

"It had the device inside of it?"

Garrett nodded. "I assume that was one of Sky's possessions, or perhaps something he had given to Silas before the Fallocaust. I never did ask..." Garrett walked over to the cabinet and put his hand on it with a sigh. "I was only down here once, but I always knew that whenever he was missing and we couldn't find him, he was down here with the last piece of Sky he had, mourning him alone."

My fiancé closed his eyes for a moment. He sniffed. "Reno, please believe me, Silas is not evil. He has a sadness in him... a deep sadness that age has calcified. He's sick but he can become better in time. I love Elish; he is my closest brother and my best friend and I will never betray him... but I will not help him kill Silas and I will stop him if he ever tries." He opened his eyes; they were so full of sadness. It made me think back to the conversation I had just had with Silas earlier that day.

Garrett looked at me. "I promise you, I will never let Silas have Reaver, but do not ask me to help them kill my master. *I love him* and I understand him. We love our monsters, Reno, both of us. And neither of us understand why the other one does, but we have learned to respect each other's hearts."

If you had asked me weeks ago what I thought of King Silas, I would have told you that he deserved a fate worth than death. For what we did to my best friends, my town, for what he did to Leo and Greyson, and the entire world.

If you asked me today... what I thought of King Silas Dekker...

I let out a long, drawn-out sigh; Garrett slipped his hand back into mine.

I would tell you I didn't know what to think anymore.

"Will you tell Silas... if the brain piece is missing? That it's in Perish?" I asked him. "It would mean Lycos had someone on the inside get it for him, possibly recently too."

"I... no, it would put Elish and Reaver at risk," Garrett responded. Slowly, like he was unsure and nervous about doing it, he opened the cabinet. "But... eventually I'd do it."

I looked into the cabinet as it opened and saw, sure enough, a little stuffed leopard lying with several other stuffed animals. All of them were lined up on a single shelf, and below them some loose papers and pre-Fallocaust items.

Garrett reached out to pick up the leopard, his hands trembling and a bead of sweat dripping down his brow. With a hard swallow, he grabbed it and I saw his eyes widen.

As if to make sure, he put a hand on top of the stuffed leopards head and felt around. There was a light rip as he opened up the back of its head.

He withdrew a small electronic device, the size of a pebble, but I could tell from Garrett's face that it wasn't the O.L.S.

"It's gone," Garrett's voice caught. "It's true. Lycos stole Sky's O.L.S."

I shook my head before glancing around the room. "I think the head honcho stole it for when he put the strands into Reaver. Lycos must've either stolen it from him... or it was given to him for safekeeping."

Garrett took the leopard and put it back in the cabinet. His eyes shifting from one direction to another. He looked uneasy, and I felt uneasy.

"What do we do, Garrett? We need to warn... *them*." Once we got into the elevator I dropped my voice. "We need to get Killian, and quickly."

My fiancé's face froze; his eyes fixed forward as he stared intently at the wall.

"Yes, yes we do," Garrett said lowly. "First though, I need to log into the security cameras to make sure they weren't rec-"

Garrett froze midsentence as the elevator doors opened.

Jack was standing in front of the doors, his hands behind his back and his face holding a devious grin I didn't trust. He stared at us as we gaped back at him in shock.

As Garrett tried to walk past Jack, the Grim put a hand on Garrett's chest, stopping him, then said with a smile. "Back inside, Garrett, back inside. Reno, push the blue button on top of the panel. We'll be going for a ride to Silas's apartments. He has some questions for you."

Garrett took a step back and let Jack enter the elevator, the tension high in the air. The Grim folded his arms and stared forward, a smug smile on his face.

Then in a flash Garrett pushed me out of the elevator. I stumbled back and turned around surprised.

"Go back to Skytowers," Garrett said quickly, blocking Jack's path when the Grim tried to step out to grab me. Garrett's other hand was rapidly pressing the blue elevator button. "Jack, he is not a part of our family yet, and as my cicaro he is free to leave." His eyes shot to mine and I saw that he was serious. "I'll handle this, love. Go."

For a moment I was frozen on the spot, my body jamming as it fought with itself. I wanted to go back into that elevator and support my fiancé – but I also knew Garrett needed me gone for this conversation.

So I nodded and took a step back as the elevator doors closed on the two, before turning around and quickly leaving Alegria.

CHAPTER 48

Reaver

THE WIND WAS BLOWING THE SMELL TOWARDS US and it was enough to make you want to vomit in your mouth. I had always been more than used to the stench of death and decay, but my nose had gotten used to smelling fresh air and greywaste dust. There weren't as many people in this area of the greywastes so I hadn't seen as many corpses.

Besides the ones Elish and I had made of course.

Though the smell was enough to make your nose curl, it was nothing compared to the gory displays of crucified men and women that we were currently weaving through. A sea of figures that, from a distance, I had thought were trees. But as we approached this stretch of greywastes we both saw that they were dozens of dead arians. All of them propped up and rising from the ground, hands outstretched and smiling through skulls just starting to peek through their rotting skin.

Below their bodies the natural process of decay had occurred. Puddles of guts, dried on the outside but squishy and squirming if you stepped in them, formed churning piles below the bodies, some even still connected to their hosts by a shrivelled brown piece of intestine.

It seemed that once King Jade had settled him and his people down in Velstoke they had gotten bored. For the entire quarter mile from the main road to the town, there were these human scarecrows on spikes. Green skin with black veins snaking through their bodies like lightning bolts, just starting to form the first blowfly maggots of spring. Before the Fallocaust they had green shoots to tell them spring was near, now we had blowfly maggots, different from the year-round flies, they were bigger and fatter.

I picked at an arm that didn't look as ripe as the others, just to see if I could eat it, but as I did a beetle crawled out. I poked it one more time and carried on, wiping my finger on my black jacket.

I looked over at Elish; his hands clenched and his head lowered. Every once in a while his heartbeat would speed up. I could almost guarantee that whenever that heart spiked he was imagining strangling Jade with his bare hands.

At least Elish knew where Jade was. I just wanted to go in there and grab the asshole and make him sing for me. He would know what happened to Killian and Perish; he could point us in the right direction.

Like a pissed off bee, my gut gave a nervous flutter; whenever I thought of my boyfriend I felt like I was going to throw up. Drugs had done a fair job numbing my worry but it was always there, eating me alive in a slow manner that told me it was enjoying every bite. However in a masochistic way I held onto that worry, because focusing on getting Killian back was helping me ignore my other internal issues. It was helping me put Nero behind me, my dads, and the fact that I was being hunted like an escaped rat.

If I could push it all down and pretend none of it ever happened…

Why couldn't I be strong enough to do that? And strong enough to know for sure that Killian would be okay.

Perhaps I had to have a bit more faith in Killian. In all reality the kid had been taking care of himself and me for months previous. He had gotten us out of Donnely, and fuck, he had even outsmarted and killed Asher when Asher had been fucking with me. Maybe I was selling him short, he really was strong.

Well, not strong… he had a pretty fragile mind still, but he had a hell of a lot of endurance.

I sighed. Elish heard and turned around. "We'll grab him quickly and be on our way," he said simply, knowing the origins of that sigh. "If Jade can give us a location we can quickly get a hold of Garrett and get a ride to the area. We can cover a week's worth of ground in an hour."

I nodded, walking past two townspeople who had been skewered, ass first, on a stake. I could see the blunt tip poking through the backs of their necks.

I glanced at them, my sadistic mind mentally noting that method for future interrogations, and said back, "That's if we can get Clig to lend us a plane. Silas probably has them all looking for me right now."

"I doubt they're searching this area," Elish said back. He looked up at the same skewered townspeople and I realized that he was falling into old habits and checking each one to make sure they weren't Jade. I wasn't checking them anymore; I've had enough of tormenting myself with that. Killian wasn't here. "Previously Garrett had said Silas was still searching the canyons and the surrounding areas."

Far away from where we were now.

Soon the crops of corpses started to thin. Besides stepping on a pile of guts that had fallen out of some poor fucker's asshole, we made it out okay. We left the sea of death behind us and made it to the double-lane road that led right through the city.

I got my gun out and so did Elish. I switched it on to automatic and started looking around. From the reports, there were about forty ravers living in this town and we had enough ammo to ice all of them if needed be. Admittedly, we didn't have that much time to form a plan, Elish didn't want to stop and neither did I. We were pretty much planning on Jade calling off his new people and then going with us. He would be shitting himself once he saw his master.

So we just had to… shoot until we found Jade.

Yeah, I know, our plan sucked.

"It looks like they had quite the fire too," Elish commented. I looked in the same direction he was and indeed saw the remains of a charred building. "Sanguine got my pet interested in the art of pyromania… I'm not surprised."

"Ravers never used fire, besides their bonfires at their dens," I said back. My hand was tensing around my gun; I had to make sure my finger wasn't anywhere near the trigger. I wasn't one to get trigger finger but I was also looking forward to contributing to my raver kill count. "They obviously never used guns either. How the fuck did Jade convince them not to kill him? That I don't get."

I watched Elish's face and saw its subtle change. I expected his eyes to grow cold, for the purple oculars to become steeled as he said something icy back, but to my amusement they almost softened. "He grows smarter every year. I'm not sure how he found a way… but he did. Jade found a way to survive certain death."

I smirked. He looked like a proud husband in that moment. Though we'd been getting along well so I knew better than to say it out loud. One day I would.

"I know ravers and their intelligence varies. I'll be interested in learning just how he…" I stopped and focused my vision on shadow of movement in an alleyway beside a large apartment building. Elish noticed my look and looked as well.

"What is…" I narrowed my eyes and we both stopped, our guns in hand and ready.

It was an animal and a fucking big one. I put my finger on the trigger and we both started walking towards it. But as we did, it looked like it spotted us.

Then the creature let out a hair-raising howl. I laughed, and in my joy of confirming who it was, I smacked Elish's shoulder. "That's fucking Deek!"

But my happiness was short-lived. As soon as the last octaves of the howl left my ears another sound was heard, a deep-throated growl that filled my chest with a vibrating percussion. Then, in the same instance, the deacon dog started charging towards us, his head lowered and his hackles raised.

A kick of dirt went up behind him as my own dog started to charge us. In an instant, he had covered half the ground that had separated us, leaving a plume of ash behind him as he pounded his huge paws into the dirt. He was fucking huge and had grown like a weed since I had last seen him. I could feel the ground vibrating under my boots as he came closer and closer.

A jolt of annoyance and anger pricked my brain. My own fucking dog was acting this way towards his master? Fuck that!

I found myself putting my gun back on its holder and stalking towards the snarling deacon dog as he covered the last twenty feet of ground. I could see his vivid yellow eyes open and fixed on us, his white teeth bared.

"GET DOWN!" I roared at him, pointing to the ground. "You fucking think you can scare me, asshole? GET DOWN. BAD!"

I watched as the dog's eyes suddenly widened with shock. Immediately more dirt got kicked up around him as he skidded to a stop and tucked his tail between his legs.

He looked up at me, finally realizing who I was – and relieved his bladder onto the wasteland ground.

I stalked up to him and gave him a hard, but satisfying, smack on the nose. "You think you're some sort of big fucking badass? BAD DOG! You don't fucking charge at me. What's wrong with you?"

Deek cowered down, his tail trying to nervously wag itself as it stayed tucked between his legs. I saw he still had his canvas jacket on him but it was covered in dried brown blood.

I narrowed my eyes but I knew he hadn't recognized me from that distance. So I relented and gave him a pat. "Alright, you're forgiven. Good boy." His tongue popped out at that.

Elish shook his head beside me. "He reminds me of Drake... a lot." He looked down at the dog.

"He's big enough now I could fucking ride him," I said. And was tempted to do just that, his head almost came up to my chest now.

"Yes, it's usually the opposite when with Drake," Elish replied casually. "Deek, *find Jade*. Where is Jade?"

Deek seemed excited at this command. He bounded forward towards the town before he stopped and turned back to us. We started following him, my gun back in my hand.

"Well, that confirms it... Jade's here. Let's get this over with," I said, patting my jacket and the bag I was carrying to make sure we had more than enough ammo, but at least we had the dog to–

Suddenly I chuckled.

Elish looked at me.

"I just got it. *It's usually the opposite when with Drake*. Because Drake is the one riding you. You can be funny sometimes."

Elish shook his head and continued walking. I was learning one thing about Elish: the longer I was with him the more of a person I could see under that sculpted granite. It didn't show itself often, but if you paid attention you could catch the small moments when he let his guard down.

I didn't get any more time to muse at this though. No sooner had we touched the fractured pavement did we hear our first shriek. Immediately the dog glanced back at us and then forward. I realized that he probably didn't know what to do. I'm assuming since Jade had made friends with the ravers, he had too.

Well, they weren't his friends anymore. I called Deek back to me.

"Stay here, you need to lead us to Jade," I reminded him.

My teeth gritted as the stupid dog started trotting off towards the ravers, now clustering around the buildings like a disturbed hive of bees.

I started sprinting towards him.

The dog walked over to the ravers and started smelling them, ignoring me completely. The ravers seemed used to him, but the fact Deek was there seemed to frenzy them. I think they could smell us on his fur.

Sure enough, one raised its head. I was mildly amused to see it was wearing actual clothing.

I raised my M16 and shot him right between the eyes. He flew backwards, and with that, over a dozen milky, yellow eyes shot towards us.

"And here they come," I murmured, pressing down on the trigger again. I picked off a young one near the front, then two other ones tripped over it and fell to the ground. I heard a crack beside me and saw an older one with stringy grey hair fall down dead.

The dog stayed behind, hanging near the apartment he had emerged from like he expected us to magically bypass the crazed subhumans to follow him. I cursed him internally and started shooting the other ones, falling back to give myself some more room as I razed the ravers with bullets. No longer caring for head shots, just as many fatal wounds as I could manage.

Then, oddly, they all stopped in their places. I shot down several more before I lowered my gun. Elish did the same and we watched the quickly shrinking first line of defence.

The ravers turned around and I looked past them to see a tall raver with a thin shadow of new hair on his head. He was dressed head to toe in clothing, a faded members only jacket and a pair of blue jeans. However he also had an assault rifle strapped to his back. My fingers itched for the trigger.

"Stop!" the raver suddenly rasped. "Stop. Bang."

Did a raver just fucking talk?

Elish and I exchanged glances before we both turned our attention back to the raver.

The more I looked at him the more I noticed other oddities. He had pupils, green eyes and black pupils. "Elish… that one's calling the others. Look at him, that's not a real raver. What the fuck is that thing?"

The leader raver continued to call the others in a fast voice, like he didn't want them to be killed by us. It was as if he knew we were different. Did he see that the dog wasn't ripping us apart and that tipped him off? I didn't know.

Elish swept the group with his gaze before his eyes fell on the talking one.

"I think Jade's been Geigerchipping them," he said.

My head shot back towards the odd raver. I looked at him and realized that was exactly what I was seeing. It looked like he had been slowly healing, even his skin was lighter than most of the others.

I needed to get to the bottom of this.

"You? Do you speak?"

The talking half-raver bared his teeth at me as I approached him, then drew his gun.

"Kah!" he said. He raised the gun and pointed it at me; his green eyes narrowed and his broken teeth clenched.

"I don't give a fuck about that. Is Jade here? Jade? Take me to your fucking leader. Jade," I demanded. In the back of my mind I was fascinated as all hell that I was only a few feet from these crazed ravers and they weren't killing us. They were standing still, the half-raver's words being obeyed to the letter. These weren't your typical retarded subhumans, this one was smart.

The green-eyed raver stared at me. "Jade?"

Elish's heartbeat jumped. I knew the clock was winding down on him. He might be letting me handle the ravers now, they were my forte after all, but soon he was going to start shooting everyone if I didn't lead him to the cicaro. Hell, I was going to start fucking shooting all of them.

But it would be quicker for all of us to just resolve this semi-peacefully. Getting Jade and fucking off would be quicker than murdering ravers and possibly getting our throats ripped out.

I nodded at the half-raver. "Jade is our friend. Bring us to him. We won't shoot."

He understood me... he actually understood me. To show I was serious I holstered my gun and heard Elish do the same.

The half-raver looked at us, then to his side where Deek was sitting, staring at the both of us with admirable eyes. The ravers all seemed comfortable around the dog.

Half-raver nodded and started making weird noises to the others that were still skulking around us. They dispersed, walking back to do whatever half-sane ravers did.

It was the oddest fucking thing I'd ever seen. Ravers chased you, snarling and snapping. They ate you alive and devoured your children in front of you – this was just fucking eerie.

Elish and I walked together side by side through the alleyway, passing a big pile of rotting bones buzzing with flies. We emerged to an area which held a couple stores and a parking lot, ravers milling around giving us cold glares.

Several times as we walked, the half-raver spoke to them, and once he even put his hands in the air to shoo them. Another very human act from a creature who usually just screamed and snarled. It made me admire the technology of the Geigerchip a bit more, but still left me with the question of how Jade managed all of this. It gave me an all new respect for him for pulling this off. The kid was annoying, and a bit of a shithead at times, but the proof of his chimera status was all around us. Like I had commanded and manipulated the townspeople to burn their own, this little fucker had organized his own raver army.

Not too shabby from a kid barely eighteen.

I smirked and glanced over at Elish, with every step his heartbeat was speeding up.

"Nervous?" I mused.

"Never." His eyes didn't waver. They were fixed ahead, glaring at the back of the half-raver's head. I realized as we walked that he was taking us towards an old Starbucks.

The half-raver stopped in front of the door and opened it. He looked inside and glanced back at us. "Stay."

Stay? I'm not a fucking dog. Elish had the same sentiment. He walked ahead of me and pushed past the half-raver. I kept pace with him and we both made our way into the old coffee shop.

Then I saw him. I saw the King of the Ravers.

King Jade was sitting on an old wing chair, or half laying on it, one foot up on the arm rest, the other on the floor.

The cicaro was wearing a crown on his head, which looked like a mess of small bones and twine. He was sickly and pale, with prominent black circles around his golden eyes. He was dressed in an old, stained jacket and the jeans he had been left with, but on his belt were a myriad of rotting hands and other severed body parts. It even looked like he was wearing a necklace of ears, though they were baked brown and dried out.

The cicaro was a raver now, which was obvious from just looking at him.

"Jade?" Elish's voice caught in his throat. He started walking towards Jade, but to my shock, Jade's eyes narrowed. He rose to his feet and raised a hand.

"How do you know my name?" Jade spat.

Oh shit.

Elish stopped in his tracks. I saw his body stiffen. Jade's face was cold and menacing. It was obvious just from one glance that he didn't know who the fuck we were.

"He lost his memory?" I stated the obvious. I looked back at Jade. "I guess Perish gave you a good smack in the back of the head. Eh, pet?"

Jade's amber eyes shot to me. I didn't think they could get any more hostile but when we made eye contact they did.

"Pet? I'm no pet, greywaster. I'm the king of this town and you're trespassing. If you wish to discuss trade negotiations stay at least ten feet from me. My people are uncomfortable with you being so close."

Elish chuckled and crossed his arms. "You know, Cicaro, when I asked if you were going to become a raver when I dropped you off, I meant it in jest. You really have been busy. Did you know your master has been looking for you for well over a month?"

King Jade stared at him. He took a step towards Elish and attempted to glare him down. "I have no master."

I could feel the tension from the ravers around us grow. They were getting uneasy with this interaction. There had to be at least ten of them looking on from around the coffee shop, most of them clustered around the glass double doors.

"Really? So you were just dropped from the sky like some prophet to guide the raver race to dominance over the arians? What do you think happened then, Jade? What was the first thing you remember? Does it happen to be the resort? Or perhaps when that carracat attacked you and Deek?" Elish mused.

Jade froze for a moment. His eyes widened just slightly as he looked at Elish, seemingly taking him a bit more seriously than before.

"You... you don't look like him," Jade whispered. "His hair was long; he didn't have a beard."

Jade took a step back and he looked past us to the gathering of ravers. "Are you hunting me? To make me into a slave again? I was a slave?"

"I've been in the wasteland for a long time now seeking you, Cicaro. Naturally my appearance has changed in that time," Elish replied flatly. "We were not hunting you; we are here to bring you home."

"Am I an escaped slave?" Jade asked again.

"You're not a slave. You're my…" Elish's voice trailed.

I elbowed him in the side, and at this gesture, he sighed.

"You… are my husband."

The cicaro stared at him, caught off-guard. Then to my surprise he smirked and gave Elish a dismissive wave. "I have no husband, and I am no slave. Even if what you are saying is true, why would I go back with you? I am a king now and this is my own town, the first of many. You have five minutes to leave my town or I'm sending my army out to crucify you with the others."

And that spelled the end of Nice Elish.

I saw his hands clench, but before he could strangle his pet, I put an arm out to stop him.

"What are you doing, Elish?" I said to him calmly. "You fucking know they're going to eat us if you hurt him."

An odd noise reached my ears and I realized Elish was grinding his teeth, but with a growl he stopped.

"Come, Jade, let's go for a walk," Elish said, his voice struggling to keep level. "We need to talk alone."

Jade recoiled from his suggestion and took a step back. "You need to… to leave now."

The cicaro was losing his nerve. I wasn't sure what was going on inside of that brain but I could tell he was starting to realize he did indeed know us. It was making him uncomfortable.

"Come on, Cicaro. One walk with me, and if you do not wish for us to take you, I will leave you be."

Internally I scoffed. Sure that would happen.

"No."

"Come on, Cicaro, just us."

"No."

"You would disappoint your husband so?"

"You're not my husband!" Jade snapped.

Elish took a step towards him, and to my shock and inner surprise, he put a hand to Jade's face and touched it. Then to further my surprise – Jade actually didn't recoil.

Elish stroked his cheek; his voice suddenly turned as sweet as honey. I knew he was switching gears, trying a different approach. "You don't remember the last time I saw you, maritus? I did this same thing. You were so upset, and I held you. You didn't want me to leave you because you were scared of the greywastes. I suppose you are not scared now, are you? My parvulus maritus, my little husband."

Jade's features softened. He stared back at Elish, his face uncomfortable and confused.

Elish pressed on. Seeing the first signs of weakness, he took another step towards Jade until they were standing next to each other. He stroked the leather collar Jade was still wearing.

"I did miss you, Cicaro."

And with that, Elish leaned in and kissed Jade on the lips, gently and lovingly. When Jade didn't pull back, Elish raised his hands and framed the cicaro's face. Taking him in in the oddest display of love I had ever seen.

Well, at least we could resolve this peacefully. I crossed my arms and waited for it to be over, because I had to find my own little cicaro now.

Then a sharp gasp and a flash of movement.

My head snapped back towards Elish and Jade, and as my mouth opened to swear loudly, I saw Jade rip his face away from Elish's with an animal-like snarl.

A large piece of Elish's lower lip was clamped in his teeth.

Jade held it like a prize. Elish swore and raised his hand to strike Jade, but the cicaro was quick. Though it wasn't just dodging the blow that the cicaro had in mind, in an instant, he spat out the lip, and before I could pull Elish out of the way, the King of the Ravers jumped on him and went for Elish's throat. The cicaro hit his mark and sunk his teeth into the front of Elish's neck.

Shit! I grabbed Jade and tried to wrench him away from Elish, the cicaro growling like a pissed off tom cat. But as I pulled, the other ravers around us let out a harmony of high-pitched shrieks, and I knew then we were both fucked.

Elish's hands were on Jade's face, trying to push the cicaro off of him. I was trying to pull Jade off of Elish, blood gushing over Jade's mouth like a dam had just broken. I could see his mouth flexing as he chewed the throat out of his master; red quickly covering the pale skin and pooling onto the dirty floor.

Then it was my turn. A blow knocked me off of my feet, sending me and the raver who had attacked me tumbling to the floor. I tried to grab my gun but I was fucking laying on it.

My chimera instincts kicked in. I bit the raver in the neck like my brother beside me and pulled out a chunk of his rancid-tasting meat. But as I pushed him off of me I felt a dull sting followed by the feeling of cold air on exposed skin.

Then another one; this one I could see out of the corner of my eye. It was the half-raver, and his nature had come back to him. With me trying to kill the first two ravers who were trying to eat me alive, he didn't have any trouble taking a chunk out of my stomach.

I screamed, not from pain but from rage. I raised my leg and kicked the half-raver, sending him flying backwards and into a metal booth.

I looked to my side and saw the image of Jade with his jaws clamped around Elish's throat. The pool of red around Elish's head was growing and, to my anger, he wasn't even fighting Jade off. He was half-heartedly pushing Jade's head away from his neck; his eyes shut tight and his mouth twisted in a grimace.

Though as I watched him die, I realized that there wasn't anything Elish could do. He wouldn't hurt Jade, even if it meant we were both dying meat.

Well, I wasn't giving up. I punched a raver trying to eat my shoulder and tried to rise to my feet. I looked ahead and felt my heart plummet as I saw over twenty of them now inside of the Starbucks, with another dozen looking in, waiting for their turn.

So this is what it's like to be eaten alive? It's weird knowing death was coming. However I'd gotten used to it with Nero.

Something hit the back of my body and knocked me to the ground. I shot to my feet again and grabbed the raver as two more clawed at my back. A bellow of rage fell from my lips as I grabbed his neck and twisted it, hearing the snap when I turned his head one hundred and eighty degrees. I let him drop to the ground and grabbed another one.

I fell back to my knees, my head going light.

The raver I tried to grab hissed and shrieked at me, their death noises filling my head with anger. There was no fear. I had nothing to fear.

No, I did.

Because I knew it was going to be even longer before I found–

A mouth snapped against my neck, and then another. I could smell fresh blood all around us, blood and rot. I tried to inhale a breath but all that filled my throat was a gurgling sound and the pounding of the blood rushing through my ears. Or was it my heartbeat?

Automatically my body gasped for air, and like a fish out of water I opened my mouth to try and inhale. I could feel the darkness creep the sides of my vision, and in that darkness I felt an anger inside of me, like I was about to burst from just sheer frustration.

I didn't need this... I had to get Killian.

I didn't need this.

The lights started to fade. I tried one last time to get up but I fell to the ground useless.

The last image I saw was Jade drinking Elish's blood.

CHAPTER 49

Killian

CRRRRKKK… CRKCRKK… CRRRKKK.

I looked down at my hands, stained with ash that seemed baked into my own skin. When it mixed in with the rusty blood it turned my hands red and grey. The lines in my palms acting like road maps, and the sores the free towns and blocks.

I got the whole greywastes, in my hands…

The Geigerchip crackled and snapped inside my collarbone, only Perish's touch could make it stop. I wasn't sure how… it was like he had a way to suck the radiation out of me.

Though other times when he touched me, it was like he was purposely filling me with radiation.

I didn't understand what he was trying to achieve, but he had a look in his eyes while he did it that told me he knew what he was doing.

"Snap him back out of it, hurry up!"

"I'm not going near him… he's fucking radioactive. What the fuck did you do to him? I fucking see you making that Geigerchip go off in the middle of the night."

A scuffle and a grunt, then a pull on my arm.

"Walk!"

I stumbled and looked away from my hands. I could see Mr. Fallon glaring at me, stabbing my head with those eyes. So full of hate. I didn't understand why he hated me so much. And if he hated me, why didn't he just kill me or leave me behind?

"I'll chain you to me if you don't start walking. I want to cover another three miles at least until we rest," he said, pushing me forward. I stumbled but maintained my balance.

In front of us we had seen a small town but it was in bad shape, most of the roofs were caved in and some only blackened skeletons, but we hadn't seen anything for days. The slaves were getting slower, they were all getting slower.

And sick. And sick.

Edward, Danny, and Teejay all were starting to develop sores on their bodies. What had just started out as a few hot spots on their skin had quickly been shredded by their desperate nails. They were almost purple in colour and risen from their skin, red and inflamed and the bigger ones leaking fluid.

Their hair had also been starting to fall out like mine, but I had pulled out mine too. Now on some parts of my head the air would make it cold. I had a wool hat on most of the time. Perish said I looked ugly enough as it is now.

Reaver wouldn't want me now. I was too ugly.

Maybe that's why he hadn't come yet.

I raised my hand and grabbed another handful of hair. I pulled it out and heard the strands rip away from my scalp. My Geigerchip gave off another low vibration of sound.

Why was that happening?

Because Perish was a born immortal... he could release radiation again.

Maybe he was trying to kill me?

Who knows.

I only knew how to put one foot in front of the other and even that I was getting bad at.

"Reaver read me *Cat Wings* in Donnely. He even tried to do the voices. He wasn't the best of readers but he tried and when he couldn't say a word I helped him."

Perish hit me and I cried out. My face was inflamed, hot and sore to the touch from Perish's repeated hits. It hurt to talk and it hurt to swallow. Everything on me ached, and every night when I took my boots off my socks were coated in blood. He was walking us too fast, too far; we could barely keep up anymore.

Where were we going?

The plaguelands.

It had always been...

"I don't want to hear about Reaver anymore. He isn't coming. He's happy with Silas and he's done with you."

I stared at the ground. "How did you meet Silas?"

I don't know why I asked this. And as my mind searched around my head like it was wading through soup, it couldn't come up with an answer either. Maybe I was just curious? I didn't know.

Perish looked at me, I looked back before my eyes jutted off into a different direction. I didn't like making eye contact with him for long. He had the mark of a beast all over him and I had learned long ago not to challenge him.

I wrung my hands and bit on my lower lip. I started to continue walking towards the town.

Then to my surprise... he talked.

"He found us... or maybe we found him? Silas once told me we were drawn to each other, that we would always attract each other, and it was true." Perish smiled. "But when was the first time I laid eyes on Silas Dekker? He was buying a medium coffee at 7-11 and putting in all these Irish Cream packets. I saw he had a duffle bag with him and he was filthy. I went home and he was always in my head. That night the first bomb dropped, but it was far away in Alaska, far away from where we were. I was barely following it, too young, too full of myself."

"What happened after?"

Perish's eyes seemed so far away, like he was staring into time itself. "I saw him on the streets and I took him home to clean himself up. Perish was living with me at the time."

Perish? I stared at Perish and wondered if I should point that error out to him. I didn't feel like getting hit again so I just let him talk. At least he wasn't calling me Silas, nothing good happened when he thought I was Silas.

"I learned he was an immortal, the thought fascinated me – I just had to have him; I had to study everything about him." Perish looked over at Edward, who was stumbling, half-alive, over a loose rock. Like that was a trigger to bring back the crazed mad man who had been tormenting me for the last several weeks, his face darkened. "Hurry up, three more miles. Get moving."

"Then how did you become an immortal too? Were you born that way?" I asked in a low voice. As if hoping that if I toned down my words it might give me more of a chance of him responding.

"Yes, me and Perish are born immortals," Perish replied. I kept up to his pace, making sure to not fall behind. "Like Silas always said: we find each other."

"How can that be though?"

Perish smiled at this, though I knew it wasn't Perish. "I don't know; it's too late to find out now. It might be a mystery forever."

I didn't know what to say to that so I just kept walking. My feet were starting to get wet, the blisters and sores had started to open up again. We couldn't get to the gathering of houses quick enough.

"You're a lot like Silas."

I glanced up and saw he was staring right at me. "I'm not him though." I still couldn't keep his gaze. I felt my ears go hot; I could feel his eyes burrowing into me.

"You will be eventually, when you decide you are tired of men abusing you," Perish said. "Like you let me so easily abuse you. It pleases me to do it but sometimes I realize you're not Silas, then I understand why Perish loves you."

I shook my head and sniffed. I didn't know what to say to that.

"I love Reaver," I said quietly. "Though I loved Perish as a dear friend."

My hand travelled up to my head and I started pulling on my hair again. I tugged until I heard the familiar twang as the hair slowly ripped out strand by strand. When my hand snapped away I looked at the fistful of hair, stained strawberry-blond from the blood of previous acts of anxiety.

I let it fall to the ground. I had nice hair once, now it was just greasy locks caked with blood and dirt.

"You're fucking ugly," Perish suddenly snipped. His mood once again shifted. "You used to be so cute too."

"I know."

"Would you stop it?" another voice said sharply.

I saw Danny's boots, walking towards Perish. I started kneading my hands together knowing what was going to happen.

"He's fucking gone. What kind of cruel fuck tortures a kid like this?"

"Danny... stop," I said, each hand wringing the other. I tried to look at him but I couldn't maintain eye contact. I didn't want to, bad things happen when I looked at them, when I looked at Perish. "Please."

"I don't remember asking you a fucking thing," Perish snapped.

I heard a smack. I continued walking feeling my eyes start to burn.

"How about instead of fucking him, I fuck you again? I heard you. You think I didn't hear you liking it?" Perish said.

"Whatever, fuck you," Danny spat, his voice rising with every word. "If it wasn't for this collar, I'd–"

"No! NO!" I ran over and started pushing the slave away; he was almost nose-to-nose with Perish. "Don't yell; don't yell… he'll hurt you."

"I don't fucking care!" Danny put his hands on my shoulders and stepped past me. "I can't sit back and watch him do this to us. Go ahead, Perish, or whoever the fuck you think you are. Kill me, go ahead. Kill me. I'd love for you to leave me behind so you can't eat me when you deem it the right time."

"NO!" I burst into tears, my teeth suddenly started to chatter together. I pushed on Danny's chest and started to cry. "Don't make him mad. Please, don't make him mad."

"Look at him!" Danny raised his voice higher. "Is that the kind of person you are? I bet you feel like a big man now, huh? Tormenting a fucking kid who's lost his mind."

I felt my knees go weak. I tried to clench my jaw to prevent my teeth from chattering but I had to open them, I couldn't breathe properly, my chest was too tight. Instead I grabbed onto Danny's jacket and pulled on it. I dragged him to the ground with me as he tried to hold me up.

"Don't make him angry, don't make him angry," I pleaded in a weak voice. I took a gasping breath, my fleeting embrace with sanity leaving me as quickly as it had come. Like an old friend only here for a cup of coffee, my mind had packed up and left me alone once again. I had no friends left, each now locked in their own personal battle. Though my fight had always been intangible and impossible to win.

How do you win a war with madness?

Before I knew it, or could react, Danny pushed me away from him again, harder than before. I fell onto the ground and watched in horror as the slave snapped. With a clench of his fists and a string of curse words, he swung at Perish and caught him in the side of the head.

I backed away from the scene until my back hit a gathering of rocks. I put my hands up under my wool hat and started to pull, scrape and pull.

Bodies in the water, bodies in the basement
If heaven's for clean people.

It's vacant.

There was a muffled grunt. I looked at my hands and tried to count the strands of hair. Singing the song I hadn't listened to in months again and again as I heard them, heard them fighting, swearing, and screaming.

The sounds of their fists pounding flesh echoed inside of my head. It felt like madness was knocking against my brain, begging for me to let it in.

I let you in a long time ago, you already have the key. What were you waiting for, crazy, a gilded invitation?

My eyes travelled through each crease in my hands. Something fell several feet from me but I didn't look. I was tired of seeing them get beaten. I was tired of –

A burst of light and a hard blow that knocked the back of my head against the tree I had been laying against. I fell to my side and gave a sob; automatically I held my hands up to my face.

Perish grabbed me and smacked me again. He rose me to my feet only to kick me in the stomach.

I didn't do anything.

I didn't do anything, Perish.

Sky… are you Sky now since you're beating on me? Am I Silas again?

"I didn't do anything!" I suddenly screamed. An incomprehensible panic coursed through me. I cowered and put my hands over my head in anticipation of getting hit again. My eyes stung and I shook my head back and forth, pulling and pulling. It was all coming out in tufts, so much greasy, bloody hair. I used to be blond. I was blond once. "Don't fucking hit me I didn't do anything, Sky! STOP!"

Perish grabbed my head and wrenched it up. His hand pressed on my jaw and he squeezed it hard.

"Got anything else to say? You seem pretty fucking comfortable with him. How would you like me to kill him, huh?" Perish screamed at them. His voice was loud, it dug into my brain and pulled out every lucid thought I had like he was disembowelling my own mind. I took a gasped breath and tried to pull away from him but my legs were rubber.

"We'll get you… mark my fucking words." That was Teejay. "You just remember what I said, Perish. Hide behind Killian all you want, and hide behind us when he pisses you off. Eventually we'll have a collar around your neck."

"It's four against one, and it won't be long." That was Danny. "We'll get you."

"No…" I managed to say. Where was my voice? Where was anything. "Don't piss him off… he'll… he'll use you to get to me. He'll use me to…" I looked up, seeing the three slaves staring us down. All men older than me, some in their thirties and one Reno's age. Scraggly and skinny, covered in purple sores and holding faces that told me they were edging insanity themselves. We were all crazy in the greywastes, in pre-Fallocaust terms. We were all insane here. How can this grey world hold anything with a sound mind? Every single one of us was fucked the moment we took our first breath of radiation.

I looked past the slaves, black hair, blond hair, brown hair, and saw the ruins in the distance. Ruins of broken houses that for some reason still remained standing. We were in the town right now, but all the other buildings had deteriorated. Now the only telltale sign we were in a town were the two-lane paved roads and lopsided sidewalks.

"Don't piss him off…" I said again. I looked and saw a red mailbox, still standing, behind it only the foundation of a house.

I walked up to the mailbox and opened it. I looked inside and closed it, everyone quiet behind me. No one was fighting anymore.

I looked behind me, unsettled from the silence. I saw the four of them staring at me as I held the mailbox open. Not able to take their oddly interrogating gaze, I closed the lid with a rusted *creak* and continued towards the town.

I led them; they stayed behind me, all of them. No one wanted to walk with me anymore; they didn't like how I made their Geigerchips go off sometimes.

How was I making that happen? Something Perish must have done to me. I would probably be dead soon. I didn't have any Iodine pills on me and soon I bet my Geigerchip would break.

I tensed my hands and wrung them together; loose strands of my hair in my palms. I crossed the road and cut across a parking lot, past that were the backyards of the houses we'd seen.

There was a tricycle in the backyard, and rusted remains of a barbwire fence. I walked along the edge of the house and without permission I went inside.

It was uninhabitable. I walked out but on the second step Perish was there again.

"Get back in, we're staying there tonight," Perish commanded.

"There's a better looking group of houses further on the road," Teejay's voice sounded from somewhere; I think he was walking along the side of the house. "If a radanimal finds us here we're fucked."

"That's east and we're not heading east," Perish snapped. I cowered when he glared back at me. "Get inside. Go be crazy in a corner where I don't have to fucking see you."

"Okay," I whispered and walked back inside. I found a patch of light where the roof had collapsed in on itself, and wedged myself in between a rain-warped dresser and something that had once had a metal frame.

I put my hands over the back of my head and stared at the ground, then closed my eyes and tried to pull up Reaver's image.

My face crumpled as I saw him in my head. Though it wasn't because I missed him, it was because his face was starting to get blurry in my mind. It was hard to remember what he looked like. I used to be able to bring up every detail. His little ears, his perfect nose, the small scar on his chin, and the remains of the scars on his back from when he rescued me. A lot of them had healed over when he resurrected but I had still traced my fingers over them in bed.

What did his body feel like under my touch? A cold body that no longer shied away from my hands. A body that melted into my own when we were intimate, when he was mine and only mine.

His face was distorted; the details were no longer there. Instead of him being a crisp image in front of me, he was now fuzzy; like a dirty VHS tape.

And his voice was gone too. I just remembered it was strong.

Perish had told me Reaver was with Silas but for all I knew he was still in a cell under the Legion's control. Under Nero's control. Maybe he was slowly forgetting what I looked like too?

Or maybe he won't even want you back when he sees you. You're ugly now, an ugly, crazed lunatic.

"No," I said out loud and I shook my head. "He loves me, and my hair will grow back. And I can shave my beard and bathe. I can be me again."

No, you lost yourself long ago.

And I was lost. I was lost inside of my own head, watching the background music of the slaves and Perish making a fire. We had no food though; we had eaten the rest of Edward's arm long ago. Edward had even eaten a bit himself. I wonder how that made him feel, or if he was conscious enough, and lucid enough, to care.

They found cans of things. It wasn't until later that Danny came over with a spoon.

He put the can on my lap. Behind him Perish was sitting on a plastic chair cleaning his gun, Edward was asleep or half-dead, and Teejay was warming his hands.

Danny wasn't leaving though. He kneeled down and looked behind him before glancing back at me.

"Eat… just don't talk," Danny whispered. "Stay as invisible as you can."

I stared at him; I could see red on the side of his face, another hot spot.

"He's leading us into the plaguelands." Danny took the spoon and scooped up some cream corn. It looked like he was trying to feed me. "We all have radiation poisoning. Killian, you're starting to get rashes on your face." He put the spoon up to my mouth. I took it, though even in my insanity it made me feel stupid. "We need to get out of here soon, kid."

"Don't make him mad," I whispered, staring at his pant leg. My eyes were dry; I tried to blink them. "Please, Danny. He'll kill all of us. He'll rape you again and me… and me."

Suddenly my throat tightened. I shook my head back and forth. "And me, and me, and–"

"Shut him up!" Perish suddenly snarled. Danny got pushed to the side and the can fell to the floor with a *clank*, upsetting the contents and spilling it onto the floor.

Perish kicked me in the side. I gasped and bunched myself up but he wasn't done with me. Perish grabbed me by my remaining hair and pulled my neck back.

"Are you too ugly for me to fuck, Silas?" His eyes froze me, encapsulated me in ice, every muscle in my body was tight. All I could manage was a whimper, a wheeze that escaped my lips. "Or should I just fuck one of them? They're better looking than you, you fucking ugly shit."

"Well? Well? Answer me?" He tried to shake me but he ended up dropping me instead. I fell to my knees and, knowing what he wanted, I started unbuttoning his pants.

"Jeez, look at you, you're such a little slut," Perish laughed. I hadn't heard him laugh, I didn't like it. "Can't help yourself, can you?" I pulled his penis out and felt the blood start to rush into it. I put it in my mouth and heard Danny start swearing at him. Calling him something, pervert I think, rapist... something, I don't know. I could only hear my own sucking. Getting it done like he wanted, distracting him. If I made him cum he wouldn't fuck Danny and he wouldn't fuck me. He wouldn't hurt us.

Perish swore back at Danny and I felt his hand against my hat, pushing my head into his groin. It got hard in my mouth and he sunk down to his knees.

I continued to do my job. I licked the head, deep-throated it and did all the tricks I had learned long ago, back when I had a boyfriend.

I no longer imagined it was Reaver, or tried to convince myself of some other fantasy to help me deal with this reality I was in. My imagination had left me with every other fringe benefit that sanity gave you. Now I knew very well what I was doing, what I was tasting, and who I was doing it to.

Then Perish removed it from my mouth. I tried to take it back in again but he pushed me back with his hand.

"Turn around."

I stared at it and felt the coldness crawl up my body. My ears started to burn, a fire that spread to my face and finally my brain. I shook my head and put my arms around myself. I squeezed myself tight knowing I had no one else in the world to comfort me.

"I'll give you two options," Perish said. "I can fuck you when I'm already close to my peak, or you can wait for me to do it tonight. Where I swear I will fuck you raw until the sun comes up. Either way, I am fucking you tonight, Silas."

I'm not Silas.

I couldn't move. My mind might be telling me I had no choice, but every muscle in my body had seized itself to rigor mortis. I froze, still as a statue, hoping that an asteroid, another Fallocaust, something, something would stop time, something would end the world.

Reaver would come bursting in, bursting in to save me. His M16, he would have it, and he would shoot Perish – No, he would keep him alive and... and...

Perish grabbed my hair again and pulled me towards the fire. I was dragged across the floor and I laid there, the warmth of the flames stinging my raw, chapped face. The fire warmed me to the point of burning but the pain only made me want to come closer. That was a pain I was used to. I... could deal with that.

I suddenly became aware of my Geigerchip. It was vibrating like it was an angry hornet, an insect trying to escape from my chest. I thought it was going to make my heart stop. There was radiation, there was radiation all around me and I didn't know where it was coming from. What was happening? What was happening to me? My body felt like it was covered in flaming static.

"Take his pants off..." There was silence before his voice raised to a booming roar. "DO IT!"

Someone, maybe Teejay, pulled my pants off of me. I felt the cold air on my backside, and with a whimper I pulled on my hair. Then I tucked my head down into my hunched shoulders.

I could pretend I was the Reaper too.

Reaver could be the Reaper. I remember when he told me about Perish saying he was a dinosaur, because they had no emotions. Then he said how he told himself... I am the Reaper, I am the Reaper.

What could... My eyes closed. I could feel him pushing my hip down, then the cold air on the inside of my cheeks. I squeezed my eyes tight, my mind drowning in the buzzing inside of my chest.

What could I be...?

Perish spat on me. I felt his fingers.

"Don't do that to him... for fuck sakes. What's happening to you? You were fucking normal when we first saw you."

"Perish, please, man-to-man... don't do this to him. He's lost his mind; he can't handle what you're–"

A scream, my scream. A cry, my cry. I clamped down on my bottom lip and heard a choking sob break through my locked jaw. The pressure of his fingers, many fingers, the overwhelming burning pressure like he was skewering me with a white-hot poker. I felt a hand on my head and one of the slaves pulling my hat over my eyes. Like he was soothing a scared animal by blinding them to what was happening around them.

He pushed his fingers into me and started thrusting them in and out, laughing like his master had done. Quick and brutal, without mercy, without care. I knew I'd feel his cock soon; there was no getting out of it this time.

Buzzing, buzzing... so much vibrating. It was burning everything, burning my face, my chest. I was going to die; I was going to die here from radiation poisoning.

I could feel the wool hat become damp with my screaming, my own heavy breathing. My whole face was on fire, but not from the flames in front of me, the ones I could still feel warm my face. It was my body; every inch of me was heating up, melting the bite of the air around me.

And my Geigerchip... crackling, vibrating, and snapping, getting louder and louder.

I could be the Reaper if I wanted. I just had never wanted.

The crackling swept itself through my body, not just remaining inside of my ears to knock against this broken fortress that had been my mind. It got into everything like it was the radiation itself. Permeating and infiltrating, destroying worlds, and gathering like paperclips to a magnet when it was focused on one spot. I could feel this crackling like it was solid. I knew as I felt and heard Perish behind me, that it was slowly collecting inside of my brain. Pressure and pressure. I didn't know how much more I could take. I felt like something was going to happen, something I didn't understand or know how to control.

I felt... I felt... fuck, like I was going to explode.

He was right against my ear. I felt his breath and then a faint, ragged whisper. "Take a deep breath, Si-guy."

I tried to take in a rattling breath but I ended up choking. I sobbed and inhaled as my throat tightened, awaiting what I knew was coming.

It was coming, this was it. He was going to fuck me – Perish would finally get what he had always wanted from me.

He was going to do it this time – he was going to do it this time. He was...

Silence.

Perish paused, his fingers still inside of me. A heavy void had fallen over every single one of us, like time had ceased to flow forward. There was no noise, no taunting, no screaming.

He was frozen; I felt a heat coming from his fingers but nothing else.

When I heard who I knew was Sky speak, it was nothing but a harsh whisper.

"The radiation is no longer sinking into you," I heard him say.

Then he chuckled.

"Well, brother, it looks like it worked. You got what you wanted just in time..."

"… I was so close too."

"Killian?" Perish suddenly screamed.

I quickly turned around, drawing up my hat, and tried to shift my body away from him; shocked by his sudden high-toned voice.

Perry?

Perish was looking at me in horror; his eyes wide and full of a terrorized fear. They jutted from left to right before he put a hand over his mouth.

"Sky said he wouldn't make me rape you; Sky promised me he wouldn't take it that far…" Perish stammered. The hand covering his mouth slipped to his head. He clenched it and looked around the room with a whimper. "Put your pants on. It's okay, it's okay. He got what he wanted. Maybe, maybe he'll let me stop hurting you. Prolonged, c-concentrated exposure, it worked. Put your pants on, okay? Okay, Killian?"

I stared at Perish in shock. "Perish? What's happening to you? Are you okay?"

His eyes shot to me as I said those words. He looked horror-stricken; I had never seen him look so scared. He gave me a slight nod before he turned away from me.

"Perish, you don't have to listen to him. You don't have to do what Sky says," I whimpered.

Perish shook his head and took a step away from me. "I'm… sit… I need to sit outside. I can't see you… just relax. Get warm… I'm - I'm sorry, okay? I have to do what he says."

"I have to do what he says, Killian."

"I'm sorry, just a little longer"

"Just a little longer."

CHAPTER 50

Jack

THE RIDE IN THE ELEVATOR WAS ONE OF THE longest ones Jack had ever experienced. It seemed that seconds quickly turned into hours as the red lights showing the floor numbers slowly climbed.

Floor six, floor seven...

"So did he see us on the cameras?" Garrett asked. "Or did he just know?"

"You know he knows everything that goes on here," Jack murmured back, and as suspected, this brought a shudder to Garrett's chest. "I hope you have a good excuse for sneaking into that room. You know that it is locked off to everyone. Above all, *your* generation knows that."

The elevator stopped with a lurch that matched the one inside of Garrett's heart. The second oldest chimera was starting to sweat; he had never been one to hide his emotions.

Though this display of anxiety was curious to Jack. What were those two doing in that room anyway? And why did Silas demand so quickly that Garrett come to Alegria?

Well, it's a common thing for one of our brothers to get into trouble. Garrett was such a well-behaved man though.

Maybe that was why Silas wanted to speak with him so quickly.

Dressed in his usual red bowtie and black blazer, Sanguine was waiting for them as they approached the open doors, his arms crossed and a smile on his face. Without exchanging a single word, Jack pushed past him and walked into the apartment of King Silas, an apartment painted in dark colours and trimmed with carved wood that boasted hand-crafted detail. It was a beautiful piece of architecture, and Jack knew this because he had renovated it himself. He had always enjoyed staying here.

But there was no space in Jack's head to appreciate his own creative talents. The Grim walked into the living room and saw the king looking out of his skyscraper window. A cup of bloodwine in his hand and a cigarette in the other.

"I have him, Master." Jack bowed before taking a step back and giving Garrett a hard shove towards King Silas. "He commanded the greywaster boy to leave; I had no authority to stop him." And he didn't. Silas had said to bring Garrett not Garrett and Reno, perhaps a small slip of the tongue but orders were orders and Jack did his job.

King Silas slowly turned around, his blond hair brushed back today, a golden backdrop to pale milky skin and ears adorned with emeralds to match his eyes. His face was soft though, which confused Jack.

No, it doesn't confuse me... it makes me uncomfortable. His own chimera snuck into his private quarters, he should be livid.

The king put down his glass of bloodwine and slowly walked up to Garrett; his eyes fixed on his second born.

The sound of Garrett swallowing hard reached all of their ears. "Silas... I know this is suspicious to you but I had my reasons. I had to be sure before I told you, because I knew it would... it would..."

Silas shushed him. He smiled kindly at Garrett and raised a hand to his cheek.

"My beloved, my smart, beautiful little man. You are so full of anxiety and stress. Tell me, why did you send Reno away? Are you scared of your king?" Silas whispered, his hand lightly caressing Garrett's clammy skin.

Garrett's face tensed; his prominent light green eyes wide. There was no move to hide his fear like his brothers would automatically do. No move to try and sway the mood or brush it off as mere nerves. Garrett was an open book, even when Jack was young he remembered his older brother being as such. In the beginning, before he found his place in Skytech, he didn't have an easy time with this ruthless family.

"Reno still loves Reaver, Master," Garrett said quietly, and at the mention of his betrothed, he showed the first signs of calm. "He would... he would hate me for what I must tell you."

Three pairs of eyes shot to Garrett: dark green, black, and red. At their glaring looks, Garrett swallowed again, before trying to stand himself up straight.

Silas's face didn't change but his hand dropped. "This is about Reaver? What did Reno say to you? Why did this admission from Reno drive you two to break into my private apartment?"

Garrett took a deep breath. "Master Silas... Lycos stole Sky's O.L.S."

A silence fell onto the room, but as Sanguine's jaw clenched and Jack's eyes widened, Silas only stared at Garrett.

"How?"

"I believe that secret died with him but it was many years ago," Garrett said calmly. "Reno was staying in the Aras bunker after we had a fight and briefly separated. Reno saw the tools for surgery, and once I analyzed the scene I found a confession by Lycos. Silas, the confession states that... Perish was implanted with the O.L.S. They knew who Perish was and were trying to... give him to you in hopes Reaver could live a normal life."

Silas took a step back. Jack felt a slight spark of unease as those piercing green eyes seemed to slay the room a thousand times over. Jack was glad he had left Juni at home.

"Perish... is implanted with my Sky's O.L.S?" Silas whispered. He put the glass of bloodwine down, and rested his hand on the table. Jack could feel his heartbeat speed up, and a slight tremble reach the tips of his fingers. An odd display of emotion but not out of character for when his former boyfriend was mentioned.

Only a small handful of us knew who Sky even was, and all of us were banned from telling Perish he wasn't a chimera. Never a word to leave our lips or the consequences would be extreme.

Jack was still as Silas absorbed this, knowing that just under the surface Silas's mind was racing. Solutions and problems that seemed to twist into a snare of twine, though if there was anyone to sort it out...

Jack jumped back as Silas suddenly picked up the glass of bloodwine and threw it against the window of the skyscraper. The glass shattered, showering the four of them in crystal shards, leaving a large, dripping stain of red that ran in torrents down the picture window.

"I need Elish!" Silas suddenly demanded. He looked past Garrett to where Sanguine was standing. "Sanguine, no excuses, no more taking care of that pathetic cicaro. I need Elish in Skyfall and I need him here by tonight."

Sanguine bowed and smiled kindly at the king. "He may be out of reach–"

To Jack's surprise, Silas stalked up to Sanguine and smacked him right across the face.

Sanguine's lips tightened.

"I didn't fucking ask for excuses, Sanguine," Silas hissed. "You have no idea how much danger Lycos has put us all in. But you wouldn't would you, *sengil*?" Silas turned around and looked at Jack. "I must find out if there's been any unusual radiation activity...." Silas clenched his fist. It wasn't often the king got angry. He was a controlled person, one who rarely showed an emotion outside of his smirking grace.

This immediately made the Grim nervous, which was an emotion he himself rarely showed.

Everything seemed different today, Jack's own voice mused inside of his head. Though in the middle of this thick situation Jack didn't appreciate his own masochistic quips.

"What do you mean, Silas?" Jack narrowed his eyes. "Sestic radiation you mean? Didn't making the O.L.S disable Perish's abilities?" As he said this Jack felt foolish, even though he knew the answer Silas didn't hesitate to shove the obviousness of it in his face.

"And the O.L.S Perish and Greg removed had Sky's abilities in it too. Which means he now has Sky's," Silas said, his words dripped acid; behind him Garrett's mouth fell open. "I need Elish here and I need Jade here, now. We need to find Perish and get Sky back before things turn catastrophic."

Jack nodded and took in a deep breath. He looked at Sanguine who now had a rosy patch on his cheek. However the sengil-chimera never flinched or made a move to rub what Jack knew was a stinging wound. He always stood there and took it, though it was his job.

They all had their jobs...

And Sanguine knew this. Jack's red-eyed brother slipped out of the room without a sound or a word, his remote phone in his hand. Garrett stood there still as a statue; his chin held high but his hands shaking at his sides.

"Silas... about Elish, I don't think you will be able to reach him. He's..." Garrett's mouth dissolved into mush as King Silas glared at him.

"Is there anything else Reno knows?" Silas asked sharply.

Garrett shook his head. "No, just what Lycos did with Perish when he recovered his body from Donnely. He... he told me right away, love."

"I need Elish here," Silas said again. The king standing tall in front of the bloodwine-coated window behind him, the moon in its grey glory framing him in its cold light. He looked almost ethereal in that moment.

I should paint that – I do love painting our king.

Jack pressed his sharp teeth into his lips and wished today had been an easy, relaxing day. But with the clone and the fractured scientist roaming the greywastes, that seemed impossible. Two pieces of someone long dead were now walking the earth and Silas would undoubtedly be even more vicious in his search for them.

I hope this will be over soon. Reaver can be found and our lives can return to what was once normal for us. I hate chaos; I hate this disruption.

Silas was on his own remote phone now, waving Garrett towards his personal bar to make him another glass of wine. Garrett's hands were shaking; he seemed to know how high the tensions were right now.

Jack took in a deep breath and put his hands behind his back, thankful that telepathy was never an ability King Silas developed. If he knew just a fraction of what was going on between most of his chimeras' ears he would have an aneurism.

"I'm getting nothing on my phone..." Silas snipped. He got the wine glass from Garrett and took a long drink. "You don't understand how dangerous this is. If Perish is within a hundred miles of Skyfall he could kill a lot of people."

Garrett turned, bloodwine clasped in his own hand. "What do you mean?"

"He's an atomic bomb right now with his unstable mind – any trigger could set him off."

Jack's eyes flicked up to Silas. "What?"

Silas's usual grace was lost; he was stressed and his grasp was firm on that wine glass. Jack watched him in an almost morbid fascination as his king stripped down his own ghostly armour.

"I don't know how Sky did it... and I don't know where Perish's own O.L.S is, which I think was always Sky, Perish, and Greg's plan. What I do know is implanting Sky into Perish... I tried it before." His grip tightened. "I tried it before; I tried everything to get him back. What I got back was a monster, an unstable hybrid of both Perish and Sky's worst qualities. On top of that... we came very close to starting a small

Fallocaust with the amount of radiation that poured from him."

Silas looked to the door, where Sanguine had left. And as a concerned expression slipped onto his face, Jack saw another piece of armour fall to the floor.

"That is why I specifically made my chimeras unable to produce sestic radiation as soon as we knew how. We removed the gene so that when stressed out – my beauties would not burn their towers down," Silas explained. "All of my chimeras have an immunity to the sestic radiation but no means of being able to create it themselves."

Jack raised an eyebrow and turned to Garrett who was nodding to himself. "Our first generation had the abilities but it got removed when we were made immortal… Perish on the other hand…"

"Is dangerous," Silas whispered. "Extremely dangerous right now."

Fascinating indeed. I'm sure enjoying this rare glimpse into Silas's humanity. I knew it was there but my king had been so cold as of late. So concerned with finding Reaver and, of course, it has been taxing running Skyfall with Elish gone and Garrett lovesick.

"So Lycos… didn't know what he was doing?" Jack replied calmly, his black eyes never leaving Silas's face. "He created a bomb instead of your new partner?"

The king shook his head. "No, Lycos didn't know what he was doing, and I don't believe he ever did. But in other ways he did succeed. I have my clone with all the qualities I had loved about Sky. Though the secret to how he did it died with him. Sometimes I regret shooting that man." Silas's face got dark. "Then I remember seeing the expression on Reaver's face and that regret goes away."

Yes, just as quickly as his fleeting compassion comes it disappears and our lovely Ghost King returns. He is never far, like the shadow that follows you around in the evenings, he is a part of Silas. Always stalking his steps, always whispering into his ear.

Jack glanced behind him to see Sanguine standing in the doorway, though his face held no Cheshire smile, it was cold and void of any emotion. His eyes however were staring intently at the both of them.

"I'll step up my search for Reaver and Perish now. Even though we are immune to the radiation, Killian is not. I care little for those savages, but I will be quite upset if Killian dies. If he dies, I will hold no leverage against my beloved *bona mea*. Killian must not die," Silas said, draining his glass. "I am disbanding our search for the remaining Crimstones and that red-haired bitch of an ex Jade had. All of our forces will be on hand, and I want the Legion on the lookout for radiation spikes." Silas's eyes lit up when Drake pattered into the room holding a ball in his teeth. The king put a hand on Drake's head and petted it. "Wouldn't you love that, my beautiful fox? Would you like Reaver to come live with us?"

Drake grinned and nodded, unaware or uncaring of the tense atmosphere in the room. "He'll throw my ball for me, I bet."

"Of course, and when he's bad you can rip him apart with your teeth."

Drake did a small shuffle-like dance at this, like a tailless dog trying to wag his backside. "I'm happy, and happy Jade will come back, and Elish. I miss Elish. Remember the time he gave me those chocolates that were supposed to be for Jade? And Jade accidently tripped me but Elish knew it was on purpose and he slapped Jade on the back of the head, and Jade swore and him and then Elish–"

Silas smiled and raised his hand. Drake stopped talking but he was still jittering on the spot. The Ghost King showed no other chimera the patience and love he showed his cicaro. Though mentally stunted and a bit weird, the orange-eyed cicaro held a tender spot in almost all of his brothers' hearts. It was difficult not to love the idiot.

Jack looked behind them to see when Sanguine was going to make himself known, but oddly the sengil had disappeared. The large wooden frames with the still open oak doors sat vacant; a painting of all four of the first generation as children hanging in the hallway behind where Sanguine had stood. Jack had painted it himself from a photo.

"M-master?" Garrett, who had been quiet in a corner, said, his voice stuttering and stumbling. "Please, can I have my leave? I... I have told you everything..."

Silas held up a hand and nodded. "You have pleased me with your honesty, Garrett, Reno too. It seems Reno will eventually join our side. I will–"

"Silas!" Sanguine suddenly burst into the room, remote phone in hand. "You need to leave now."

Silas turned around and so did Jack. Sanguine's face was pale and his jaw tight. There was an apprehension in his eyes that threw the careful milieu of the room off balance. Jack felt an unease clutch his chest.

"Why?" Silas asked lowly.

Sanguine swallowed and put his hands behind his back, before they disappeared Jack was shocked to see they were trembling.

"I just got off the remote phone with Caligula. He says Nero caught Reaver."

Silas's jaw dropped, but Sanguine continued, "Caligula saw him chained to Nero's bed. He doesn't know how long he's had him but Reaver is in horrible shape. Nero threatened Caligula's life and the life of his partner."

The king stared at Sanguine, dumbfounded, and for a few tense moments no one spoke.

Though the atmosphere spoke, and it was making the hair on the back of Jack's neck creep up. There was something about how Sanguine was listening in by the doorway, only to disappear once again, that made Jack wary.

"Nero…" Silas whispered. "Nero has my Reaver?"

Sanguine nodded. "Caligula has only been able to get a hold of a remote phone now. He's locked himself inside his quarters. He says he saw Reaver last week. King Silas… Caligula said he was naked, there was blood on the sheets–"

Jack grabbed Garrett out of the line of fire and pulled him into the corner of the room. He stood back and watched the king's head lower, his shoulders tightened.

"You are telling me… Sanguine… you are telling me my third born, is hiding Reaver from me?" Silas's voice dropped to a dark whisper. Jack's mouth was dry, full of needles, and tight to the point where his chest was starting to ache. "You're telling me… that Caligula is implying that Nero has been raping him?"

Sanguine didn't move, with his hands behind his back and his shoulders square, he stood tall as the Ghost King circled him like a predator sizing up prey.

"Yes, Master," Sanguine said slowly back. "Nero has Reaver tied to his bed. We've never known Caligula to be dishonest. Perhaps it's revenge over Timothy's death? Kiki, ah, I mean Kincade was in Tim's generation."

Silas turned away from Sanguine, and at one glance of the king's face, Jack stepped further back with Garrett. The two of them, all of them actually, old enough to know it was an intelligent move to stay out of the king's sight when he was upset.

But Silas only stared out the window; his lips tightly pressed together, his entire body tensed and radiating anger. This was the look that Jack was sure had started the Fallocaust, a look of pure hatred and madness. He was surprised his Geigerchip wasn't vibrating its protest, though Silas had trained himself long ago not to release radiation when he was upset.

"If I find out he took what is mine…" Silas whispered. "Nero will never see daylight."

Jack believed every word of that, he had seen it happen before. He had seen the back rooms of Alegria where no chimera or human ever wanted to go.

Back rooms where several immortal chimeras never came back from. They were still there to this day, encased in concrete tombs to spend their punishments in darkness.

"Drake… we're going to the Falconer; we're going to the Cardinalhall mansion," Silas whispered, before he seemed to snap himself out of his trance. "Garrett follow me. Sanguine stay behind."

Sanguine nodded stiffly and stepped aside to let Silas pass. There were no goodbyes or fleeting threats, Silas, Garrett, and Drake left in heavy silence.

When all was clear and Jack could hear the elevator leave its platform, he gave a sigh of relief.

Then something caught his eye. As Sanguine was shutting the double oak doors Jack could see… he was smiling.

Sanguine turned around and when he noticed Jack's eyes on him he chuckled and bowed. "I wish they still had Oscars."

Jack's mouth dropped open. "What are you saying…?"

Sanguine smirked and brought out a cigarette. After taking one out he threw the pack over to Jack. "Have a smoke with me, Jack."

The cigarette pack fell to the floor in front of Jack's feet, the silver-haired chimera not making even the slightest of movements to catch it. He continued to stare dumbfounded at his brother. "That was a lie? All of it was a lie?"

Sanguine shook his head and lit the cigarette with his fingers, a blue ember bursting from the orange flame. With a nonchalant sway and that same cocky grin, he strolled over to Jack and kissed his cheek. "You're adorable when you're confused, *diligo*. At least it got him from sending out all those legionaries to hunt down our dark brother, hm?"

Jack choked and realized he had been holding his breath. A heat that held an overwhelming dizziness swept him; he felt like he was going to vomit on the floor.

"What have you done? You've lied to our king? He'll never trust you again, Sami."

Sanguine didn't even flinch at being called his birth name, the name his own adoptive mother had given him before she died. Jack had a habit of using it on him when he was feeling scared or unsure. Sanguine knew this but still he didn't waver under its use.

"I didn't lie." Sanguine picked up the pack of cigarettes and took out another one. He lit it and handed it to Jack. "Nero did capture Reaver, and he held him for weeks viciously raping him. The difference is: I know Reaver escaped over a month ago. Though who will Silas believe? Caligula can mask his heartbeat; Nero never developed that control over himself."

"Caligula knew this?"

"Caligula rescued him."

Jack took the cigarette and leaned against the back wall of the apartment.

"Reaver killed Timothy…"

"And Caligula always hated his little brother. What's new?" Sanguine took another inhale and encouraged Jack to do the same. "No, Jack, my love. You have no idea what you've been blind to. However the question remains… do you want to know? Can you be trusted to know?" Sanguine put a soft hand to Jack's cheek and stroke it. He smirked through the cigarette being softly bit by his pointed teeth.

Jack stared at him; his eyes narrowed. But as he stared deeply into his brother's blood-red eyes, black and red like Sanguine's colour combinations, the pieces started to knit themselves together.

"I don't want to know," Jack whispered. He stepped around Sanguine and started heading for the doors. "The last game I played cost me… cost me…"

"Me?" Sanguine said behind him.

Jack stopped. He raised the cigarette to his lips and took a long drag to buy himself some time.

"You left me."

"And now I'm back."

"And I'm not a fucking doormat!" Jack suddenly snapped.

Soft boot steps could be heard as Sanguine walked over to Jack. "No, you're not. Which is why I wanted to wait until I pulled you close to me."

A shockwave rushed through Jack as Sanguine kissed his neck.

Immediately, like the chimera was lighting a small flame, Jack's skin became hot. He opened his mouth and let out a small breath.

"What are you saying?"

Another kiss, this one at the nape of his neck. "I am saying I grow tired of only having you as a fling every now and again. I miss you, and I miss what we used to be."

"You ended us, cruelly and without care," Jack said with a jerk of his shoulder. "You proved to me just how broken you were. That you were Silas's little slave with no will of his own. You're shattered, we know this."

"And what if someone put me back together?" Sanguine said. Jack could taste the smirk in his voice.

"Mantis?"

"Mantis is in the greywastes."

Jack whirled around, his patience failing him. "Who? Who then? Elish? Elish breaks toys he doesn't fix them. We all know that, I know that."

"Elish knows just what to promise. He knows my price."

"So what? What does it matter? So Lycos hid Reaver from us, big deal. It means nothing to me and nothing to you. What does any of this have to do with Elish? He didn't know either, Lycos hid that boy from all of us," Jack snapped, throwing the doors open.

"And who do you think helped hide Reaver all this time? Who do you think watered this seed, this clone of Silas? Really, lovely, it was right in front of you the whole time. Elish has been finding ways to gather us to his side. He promised me what I so dearly need… and once I have gotten what is promised, I will win you back. I will show you the same love and patience you showed me all those years ago."

Every degree of warm air in the room seemed to leave as those words spilled from Sanguine's mouth. Frozen on the spot, his hands outstretched, Jack was still.

More boot steps, and as they approached the seemingly frozen solid Grim, he heard Sanguine chuckle.

Jack could only stare before he sunk to his knees. Feeling like he was either about to throw up or attack Sanguine, he wasn't sure which. His own emotions, the primal rage and instincts that all chimeras had, starting to outweigh this tempered calm he had been honing since he had first reached his own personal enlightenment.

Sanguine rested a hand on Jack's side and rubbed it in a caring fashion. When Jack let him, he took his hand and kissed it slowly, before saying in a purring voice, "Come, my little silver devil… my *diligo*… it's time we have a long smoke on the patio."

CHAPTER 51

Reaver

IT WAS COMING TO THE POINT IN MY LIFE WHERE I was aware when I was resurrecting. The white flame that used to just be a dream inside of my head was taking shape, showing me as I became more aware, it knit my body back together. It always started with my brain and worked its way down to mend my flesh. Fingers grew back, blood vessels fused, and in the last final hours, my heart started to pump new blood through my repaired veins.

And in that time I counted every beat of my heart, thumping its rhythm inside of my brain, telling me I was fully aware though still trapped inside this motionless body. It was maddening at first; I remembered it frustrating me when I had been imprisoned by Nero. But now I was anxious to open my eyes and see where I was. I wanted to see how much time had gone by and how quickly I could resolve this situation.

The Reaper was done being nice about this.

Red started to seep through my vision and a thousand and twenty heartbeats later I felt my chest burn. I opened my mouth and took a long gasp and, to my surprise, I fell to the ground.

The greywastes met my face, snapping my eyes open as I inhaled quick sharp breaths to try and quench the flames that had taken hold of my chest. I tried to blink the blur away from my eyes as I rolled onto my back; my nose suddenly being attacked by the rank smell of long rotten flesh.

Finally my eyes focused, and I saw right above me the crucified body of Elish.

He hadn't come back yet. I slowly rose to my feet and put my hand over his chest. I listened and could feel the faint beating of his heart. My eyes travelled to his hands, still nailed to the cross-hatched pieces of wood.

Elish's hands had healed around the nails. I looked down at my own hands now holding tiny holes in the centers. It looked like weight and gravity had pushed me off of this crucifix, either that or my body had automatically tried to jolt me free.

And look at my hands. The digits I had re-grown were white with soft, new skin and the ones I had kept were still calloused and stained with dirt. It was an interesting sight to say the least, my hands and arms reminded me of a zebra.

To save his body the trouble, I pulled the nails out of Elish's hands and caught him before he could tumble onto the greywaste dirt. I leaned him against the wood we had been nailed to and left him to finish healing in peace.

I was done handling this the nice way. I was done talking and I was done wasting time while Killian fell further into danger. I didn't know how long it had been but there were fresh corpses around me, and those ones looked more than just ripe.

I checked my back but, of course, my gun was gone, our bags were gone too. All that remained were our clothes and the contents of my pockets. I might be able to get the grenade into a pile of them, but they all seemed to like clustering around their king.

I quickly walked towards Velstoke, leaving the crops of corpses behind me. There was no care left in me now, and no Elish to steer me into resolving this in a semi-peaceful way.

The town looked the same, nothing new had been burnt and I could spot several ravers in the distance perching on top of roofs. I was sure they couldn't see me given their eyesight, but since Jade had been Geigerchipping them, I didn't know if their eyes would've improved.

My jaw gave a twinge and I realized I was clenching it. A dark anger was festering inside of me, an anger I realized I had been holding to my chest since Jade's ravers had killed me and Elish. It was frustration mixed in with the distinct fact that I was tired of doing this Elish's way. He was having a grand time making me his minion but that time had passed. We could very well have been dead for over a month if they had eaten parts of us. I didn't know and I had no way of knowing.

I walked to the road and started checking out the rusted out cars for anything I could use as a weapon. I could locate nothing but two good-sized rocks.

Good enough.

I followed the road, both rocks in my hands, and felt my breathing start to shorten. Each strong inhale I took only lit more anger inside of my chest, and by the time I passed the first building and saw my first raver, my anger coated the last of my lucid thoughts.

The first raver looked at me and snapped its head back as it gave a loud ear-splitting scream. Then, with its arms outstretched, it started to run towards me. It must be a new one; this raver was acting like the normal ravers I had known around Aras.

I threw the rock at it and caught it at the side of the head. Then, with my eyes mentally scoping out two more coming on either side of me, I finished its head off with a single bludgeoned blow. I cracked its skull and picked up the fallen rock as it fell dead to the ground.

The raver closest to me gave out a snarl. I closed the distance between us and spread my arms. Like one of those monkeys with the cymbals, I dashed the rocks on either side of the raver's head, feeling an inner satisfaction as I watched the raver's face crush under my blow.

I whirled around as it fell to the ground, the third raver only several paces from me. I raised the rock as it lunged at me, teeth bared, and broke its jaw.

I stomped its head with my boot and carried on, my rapid breathing inflaming my body and filling me with burning adrenaline. Every sense inside of me was hyper-aware, I could hear each raver coming towards me. I could smell their stink and I could see them crawling out of the woodwork.

Bring it on.

I threw one of my rocks at a female one and caught her in the eye. Two more were behind her, and four more running in from a long stretch of road to my left. Five were in the buildings, and those five, I assumed, were Geigerchipped. They were smart enough to stay…

There was a thunderous crack followed by a blast of air and heat on my cheek. I looked into that building and, sure enough, I saw one with brown eyes staring at me, half of his face skeletonized but slowly callousing over. He was holding up an AK 101, a legion gun.

I whirled around as I heard several approach me. Snarling beasts with not a sane bone in their bodies; bearing broken teeth at me, and fingers either missing or chewed down to the bone. The sounds of their screaming deafened me, but it also fed the mania that had taken residence inside.

I punched the first one in the face, and behind it, I saw a raver with a half-decayed arm. The top part of his arm was skeletonized and the forearm scabbed and scarred. I ignored the other ones closely approaching me from behind, and with a hard shove, I pushed him to the ground.

Another bullet whizzed past me and caught a raver in the gut. I focused on the one I had on the ground and grasped the bone of his upper arm.

I could feel the tearing through my hand as I wrenched it from its socket. The raver hissing and spitting, no pain to be felt on their heavily irradiated bodies. I detached the arm and, not wasting any time, I whirled around and started beating the approaching ravers with it. I succeeded in bludgeoning them, and once they got onto the ground, I slammed my boots down to break their legs. Once the ones in biting distance were incapacitated, I ran into the house.

The next bullet hit my shoulder. I felt a growl rise to my throat as I grabbed the raver who shot at me's gun and pointed it away from my body.

The raver spat his mad language before he tried to wrench the gun away. Out of the corner of my eye I saw another one. So, before they could all mob me again, I snatched the gun away from him and shot him in the head.

Quickly I picked off the one in the doorway, and then a little one that was probably only three. I kicked his bloody body off to the side and picked off two women trying to escape out the back door. The Geigerchips were giving them fear again, amusing concept but of little interest to me right now. With a gun in my hand and the five in the house dead, I sprinted out of the derelict, dark building and back into the grey sun.

My eyes narrowed as I looked around. My finger held firmly on the trigger.

They were everywhere.

Fucking everywhere.

It must've been a month; I swear I must've been out of it a month at least. I swallowed down my annoyance as I saw the ravers spilling from the buildings and running in small clusters down the double-lane roads, weaving past broken cars and jumping over tipped over utility poles. They were all coming towards me like a single consciousness, some with their hands outstretched, snarling and snapping. Others holding guns, their pupils fixed firmly on me with the goal in mind of total eradication.

I heard a squeak and a small snap inside of my mouth, then a hard piece of tooth that pricked my tongue. I spat it out and held the gun firm in my hands. I took aim at the ones holding guns themselves. Then, with them all surrounding me, I opened fire.

One shot, two shot, red shot, blue shot. I picked them off one by one, hitting the ones who came close to me with the butt of my gun. With the armed ravers trying to make meat out of me, I tried to angle myself near the hordes of them approaching. It was obvious to me now that though they were recovering ravers, their aim was awful. So I steered their bullets where they would most likely hit their own comrades rather than me.

I knew I was close to being fucked, but my raging mind and the dark void inside of me was refusing to give into this suicide mission I had gone on. In all respects though, they were spilling from everywhere. Jumping down from roofs and lunging out of windows only to get up and beeline towards me. And the horde that was closing in.

Then one got another shot in. I grunted as my chest snapped back like someone had just punched me. I looked down to see a hole in my jacket, over the upper part of my chest. I swore and picked that raver off with a shot to the neck.

He fell off of the roof and crashed through an awning before tumbling onto the ground. To my luck, the group of ravers running towards me went to him instead, though that still left a good thirty of them chasing me.

I needed help. I looked around and tried to sprint towards where Jade's throne room was. My mind scanned through all the ideas I had of how I could convince him to call them off, but the only plausible idea I had was to call the–

Suddenly an impact. I was thrown backwards and fell onto the dirt. I screamed from rage as I felt teeth close in on my shoulder. I raised my hand and punched the raver in the side of the head before pushing him off of me. Fresh blood mixed in with the faint aroma of the greywastes, and the all too familiar stink of ravers.

The one who attacked me jumped off and I heard him give off a shriek. I tried to rise to my feet but another one got me from behind. I felt his sharpened finger bones slash my back before his own teeth sunk into my newly knitted flesh.

I rose and threw him off of me but they were closing in. I looked around for an escape route but all I had was my backup plan.

The stupid dog was my only hope now, and if he dared take the ravers' side I would take him behind these buildings and shoot him in the head. No matter how much Killian would hate me that dog would be toast. He was supposed to be our fucking guardian and he didn't get to pick and choose when he did his job.

I pursed my lips together and whistled down like Perish had taught me a lifetime ago in Aras.

Like I had suddenly become burning hot, every raver around me jumped back. I stopped whistling from pure confusion, and watched as they put their hands up to their ears. All of them letting out painful screams.

I whistled again and another wave of screams delighted my instincts. I rose, my lips still pursed, and watched in sadistic fascination as they started literally clawing their ears off with their fingers.

I picked up my borrowed gun and held it. I whistled as high as I could as the ravers shredded their ears to ribbons. Some even pulled them off of their heads whole, only to drop them on the ground as if they were the sole cause of their pain. After their ears were gone they shook their heads in agony, raining me and their comrades in ruby droplets of blood.

I kept whistling, walking down the street as the ravers made way for me like I was a god sent down from the sky, shaking their heads back and forth as chunks of flesh got ripped out of the sides of their faces. I didn't stop whistling, I didn't want to. I wanted to watch them tear their bodies apart by their own hands.

My eyes took me to the corner of an old industrial building as I heard a loud and hollow bang. A raver fell down dead to the ground, blood running down his head.

Then another bang and second one fell down. I watched the area and saw first-hand what was happening.

A female raver, with her hands coated in blood and her ears torn off, lowered her head and ran into the side of the building. I heard a low snap before she also fell down dead.

Oh, they're killing themselves. How unfortunate. I smirked and kept whistling, the echoing thunks and the sounds of snapping bones amusing every sense of my body. I watched them all with an almost orgasmic glee as they killed themselves one by one, unable to stand the high-pitched sound that no one but animals, ravers, and chimeras seemed to hear.

"What are you doing!?"

I looked to my right and saw Jade storming out of his Starbucks Palace. The half-raver was beside him... holding my fucking M16. "Stop tha-"

Jade froze when he realized it was me. He stared blankly; his mind unable to comprehend in what realm of possibility I could still exist.

But I had no patience for him or his questions. I stalked up to the half-raver and pushed him. "Give me my fucking gun or else I kill all of them."

Half-Raver stared at me, then looked to Jade. "Jade?"

Jade glared at me, bearing his teeth like the closeted feral he was. "If he gives you the gun, you get the fuck out of here, now."

In a flash, before any of them could react I snatched my gun from Half-Raver and pointed it at him.

To my surprise, Jade let out a fearful cry.

"No! Don't shoot him!" Jade cried. "Don't shoot him!"

So the pet made a friend. I glared at Jade and glanced behind me to make sure none of the ravers were going to attack me. It looked like they'd pissed off the moment I'd stopped the murder-whistle.

"I'm fucking done playing this game with you, Jade," I snapped. "If you don't come with me right now, I will make every single one of these motherfuckers kill themselves."

"Jade?" the half-raver said quietly. "He makes your noise. Your people?"

Jade's already pale face seemed to turn a new shade of white. He looked at me before his eyes shifted away. "I think so, Big Shot." But then he shook his head. "No, I belong here. This is my town and my people. I won't abandon them. Just leave me, I have made my–"

I grabbed onto his jacket and started pulling him towards the road. Jade screamed and wrenched himself away. "I said no! I don't know what you are, or why you're suddenly not dead, but... I don't care about my previous life. I'm not leaving them and I'm not leaving him."

The half-raver apparently named Big Shot looked on at the scene, a sad look in his eyes.

I grabbed Jade again. The feral continued to twist and thrash until I gave up and pointed the M16 to his head.

"Now."

"I don't care, he saved me!" Jade yelled. "He can't whistle like we can. What if as soon as he becomes human they attack him!? I'm not leaving!"

Like a toddler throwing a fucking tantrum. No wonder Elish beat this kid – *I* wanted to beat this kid.

"I don't fucking care, Jade," I said back. "I need to know what happened to Killian and Perish, and you need to get your fucking mind back so you can tell me. After, you can come back if you love being a raver. I don't give two shits. You'll be Elish's problem then."

"No!" Jade continued to throw a fit. I was about done so I put him into the same sleeper-hold I had used to knock out Killian.

Though he fought back more, but oddly his raver friend didn't attack me. Instead he turned around and walked back into the old coffee shop palace. Nice friend.

Jade's thrashing eventually died down. I let out an annoyed breath and slung him over my back.

I looked into the coffee shop and saw two shadows. Big Shot and a giant black one were standing beside the wing chair, watching me intently.

I let them be. The guerrilla ravers got off easy this time. They can take the twenty I killed and use that as a warning. I really didn't give an ever-loving fuck what they did with this town; a part of me hoped they took over more towns just because it would be amusing to see.

With Jade over my back, I walked into the coffee shop and spotted the bags Elish and I had been carrying; they were all resting unmolested against Jade's throne. I picked them up, and a bag that I think had been Jade's, and walked out of the glass doors.

I gave a whistle just to warn the ravers I was leaving. I saw over a dozen of them watching me from the shadows, flinching as soon as I whistled. They let me be and I let them be, mentally daring one of them to fucking shoot at me.

I walked towards the crops of corpses, and adjusted Jade on my shoulder. He might be a light, stealthy chimera but he was a ton of bricks against my wounds.

But as I walked down the road, half-covered in grey ash, I heard scraping behind me.

I whirled around and couldn't believe my eyes.

Big Shot was trailing behind; a blank expression on his face like this was just a Sunday morning stroll. When he saw I was watching him he stopped, but didn't move.

"Go home!" I snapped. I pointed towards the town behind us. "Come on, I heard you fucking talk, asshole. I know you can understand me. Go back to your raver clan, I got nothing for you here."

I kept walking and the scraping continued. I ground my molars and turned around again.

"I'll shoot you right where you stand," I threatened. "I will drop this little prick onto the ground and–"

"Jade," Big Shot said. He pointed to Jade. "I am his guard."

"I don't care if you're his pet dog, fuck off!" I was quickly losing my patience with talking ravers.

Big Shot continued to walk towards me. "I am King's guard. King Jade's guard. I go where he goes."

I stared at him. I closed my eyes for a second and said slowly, "I have more important things to care about. Do whatever you want to, buddy." I turned back around and started heading towards where I had left Elish.

The scraping continued behind me.

As I approached Elish I saw he was sitting up, looking half-conscious with Deek sitting beside him. Elish glanced up at me then did a double take.

Elish rose to his feet quickly; his heartbeat gave a thump. "Give him to me."

Gladly. I handed Jade off to him and started taking off my jacket. "I put him in a sleeper-hold; he'll be back in about five minutes. He still has no idea who the fuck we are, but I got him and the ravers are going to let us be."

"How badly are you injured?" Elish held his cicaro caringly in his arms, the boy limp with his eyes half-open and glassy.

"I can stave off death until tonight," I said. I put on my knapsack and carried Elish and Jade's. My shoulder was screaming its painful protest, and my back was scratched and bit to hell, but I had a high threshold for pain. One of Elish's death pills should have me healed by the morning.

Then Elish's eyes narrowed; he looked past me. "And why are you still alive?"

"He's your problem now," I said darkly, looking behind my shoulder at Big Shot. "He says he's Jade's guard and he won't leave him. Just shoot the idiot and let's go. I want good distance between us and those fuckers if I'm going to be dying tonight."

Elish adjusted his hold on the boy, still staring coldly at the half-raver. "How did he become your king?"

Big Shot stood there like an idiot, then to my surprise he actually answered. "We come to eat Jade. We take him back to den."

"Why?" Elish demanded.

"He was controlling them through that dog whistle Perish taught me," I explained. We all started walking away from the town, Big Shot still trailing. "I guess they were too afraid to kill him."

"How did you come to take over the town?" Elish said. The cicaro made a whimpering noise but remained still in his master's arms.

"Jade taught us to shoot and cut out skin for chip," Big Shot said. "Jade came with dog. He is family, my family. He said this to me in truth."

"When are you going to kill him?" I said to Elish.

I groaned when he kept on walking with Jade.

"We're not killing him. The more guards the better. If he can keep up we're taking him with us."

"Why!?" I demanded, throwing my hands up in the air.

"Because the more people to protect my pet the better. You obviously failed at the task," Elish replied crisply.

"You're the idiot who decided to kiss a raver," I shot back. When Elish didn't respond I decided to get to the real issue here. "Do you have any idea how to get his memories back? We don't even know if we're heading in the right direction."

"Yes, I do."

Well, I wasn't expecting that answer. To my confusion, Elish tried to make Jade stand on his feet, but since the cicaro was still half-dazed he was limp and couldn't stand on his own.

Elish motioned for me to grab Jade and I held him up. I gave Elish a skeptical look.

"I realized this while I was resurrecting," Elish said, noticing the look I was giving him. "The blow was to the back of Jade's head…" He carefully put his hand behind Jade's skull and started feeling around. "Jade has several chips inside of his head. All but two are currently deactivated since I needed his abilities. I think one of them malfunctioned. It's placed near where his long-term memories are stored, conveniently right by his tracking chip as well."

Elish slowly felt around the cicaro's skull as Jade started to writhe under my hold. From the times I had done this move, on Reno mostly when he wouldn't stop trying to touch me, he would be awake in under a minute.

But he wouldn't even get a minute. As Elish found the right spot, I felt a sharp tingling in my hands, and at the same moment, Jade yelped and went rigid. I braced myself as he tried to flop to his side and kept him upright.

The cicaro's eyes closed tight, his entire face creasing like he was in pain. I hoisted him up and tried to get him to stand on his own.

"Elish?" Jade suddenly whimpered.

Elish's pulse jumped, and until his cold countenance hid it, I saw a look of intense relief.

He took Jade from me and lowered him to the ground.

Jade stared at the ground and blinked slowly. Then surprisingly Elish suddenly took a step back from his pet.

I knew why a moment later when the cicaro's chest gave a lurch and he proceeded to throw up onto the ground.

Jade

I took in a sharp breath and threw up again. The next thing I knew Elish was holding me upright as I slumped over, my entire body trembling and my head pounding.

"Elish?" I tried to say it again. I was confused; my skull seemed to be ripping itself in half and I barely knew where I was. I wasn't even sure if that really was my master, he looked so different.

But he felt the same; his embrace was the same…

His hair though, it was so short and he had a beard. My Elish would never look like that, he kept himself obsessively clean. He only wore crisp, clean robes, or when we were at home, a button-down and trousers.

He didn't even wear the same socks two days in a row…

I threw up again, and saw his duster, now dingy grey, wipe my mouth gently.

"You know who I am now I see." His voice was gentle, though it held those smirking tones I had come to love – and miss.

I sniffed and tried to force air into my sore chest. I tried to get up and felt Elish steady me.

I turned around so I was looking at him, and felt my heart give a painful throb. To my own embarrassment and humiliation, I dissolved into tears.

I heard Reaver give an incredulous snort, but Elish didn't care and neither did I. When my master took me into his arms I melted and let him squeeze me tight against him. He held me so tight I thought my ribs were going to break; he had never held me this hard.

"I love you, I'm sorry," I whimpered.

He shushed me. "What could you possibly be sorry about? Are you sorry you got your head smashed in without my permission? Or are you sorry for ripping out my throat, and murdering me while consuming my blood?"

My heart fell; I had forgotten about that. Everything that had happened with the ravers seemed so far away now. Elish banished all other thoughts from my head.

I pulled away from him and looked at the greywaste ground. My ears went hot as the shame started to creep into my muddled senses.

"I'm sorry," I said. "I didn't mean to… I, ah…" I looked over at Reaver as if magically hoping he was going to help me, but he had his arms crossed over his chest and he was giving me a death glare.

"It doesn't matter, maritus. I'll punish you soundly when we get home," Elish said in a kind voice.

My heart jumped. "We're going home?"

"No, not yet… we have to–" Elish was promptly cut off when Reaver stalked towards me and put a hand on my shoulder. He jerked it back.

"Enough. You got your loving moment and now it's down to business. Where's Perish taking Killian?" Reaver demanded.

I stared at him for a moment. Then, as my past memories of long before I had met the ravers came into my head. I felt my knees become weak.

"Oh shit…" I whispered.

Elish held me steady but I felt like I was going to throw up again. I felt like my blood was slowly turning into ice water and yet my skin felt flushed and hot.

The last thing I saw before my mind had left me. I had to say it before anything else, knowing that was what Reaver was waiting for. "Perish does have him. Killian was unharmed when we were attacked, when the slavers were killed."

Sure enough, the relief could be seen on the man we had called the dark chimera. He looked at me and let me continue to find my words.

"Master, he said he was taking Killian northeast, that was the last thing I heard before I passed out," I said. "What's northeast from the resort? Were you there? I left your laptop in a safe spot. I didn't let them take it."

Elish looked at me for a moment before he turned to Reaver. "Perish... is taking him to the plaguelands."

Reaver, who was in the middle of putting on one of the knapsacks, stopped and stared at the two of us. "Why? Why would he be taking him there? The radiation will kill him, it will kill Perish too."

Elish stepped away from me and I used that opportunity to spit the rest of the puke out of my mouth. I was a dirty, greasy wreck and my head was pounding.

"Perish won't. Born immortals are immune to the sestic radiation and all chimeras hold the same trait inside of their DNA. All three of us will be fine." He looked past Reaver. "If Perish has him in the plaguelands the boy will not have long. Even if he has a dozen Geigerchips inside of him the radiation will eventually win."

Reaver looked to the north. I could see the demon that he was just crawling underneath the surface. The time away from Killian was apparent on the dark chimera, and that was without even looking into his aura.

That I didn't want to see.

"Why, Elish? Why is he taking Killian there?" Reaver asked. He started walking north, towards where the highways were.

After Elish made sure I could walk properly, we started to follow behind Reaver. I got a shock when I saw Big Shot trailing behind us, but I just gave him a smile and a quiet *kah*. I knew if I asked why he was coming along, interrupting Reaver and Elish's conversation, I would have my head bitten off.

"I don't know. I haven't the slightest idea why he would be bringing the boy there," Elish said calmly. "If he wanted to kill Killian there are much simpler ways of doing it. No, Perish has something planned for that boy – but at this point, I do not know what that is."

Reaver turned around. His face was tense and his black hair only making his shining onyx eyes look even more menacing. "If he starts slowing us down, I'm leaving you two behind."

I shot a glare at Reaver and felt a vibration in my throat, but I swallowed the words creeping to my lips. I knew right now saving my pride was the least of my worries, Reaver looked like he was about to kill all of us right now.

"He will not slow us down," Elish replied, still keeping his calm voice. I started picking up the pace absentmindedly. "If he falls into illness, he can do what you mused about earlier: he can ride the dog."

I blinked and turned around to where Deek and Big Shot were walking behind. The giant half deacon, half dog was getting big now. His head came up to my chest and his paws were huge.

"I could ride you, right, boy? I could get you a saddle?" I smiled and petted the dog's head, but not a moment later I felt my stomach lurch and nausea boil. I turned around and started gagging again.

Reaver kept walking but Elish stayed with me. He even helped steady me when I felt the dizziness start to send a heat to my face.

I let out an unimpressed groan as Elish picked me up and started carrying me. Another wave of heat sunk into my face but this one was from embarrassment. Just a couple hours ago I had been King of the Ravers, now I was back to being a sickly chimera in his master's arms.

"You've lost more weight," Elish murmured. "Do you think you will be able to keep up?"

I nodded. "My head is just a bit rattled…" I decided in that moment not to tell him about the intense migraines I had been getting. There was no way around it, I was going with Reaver and the group, so there wasn't much of a point in telling them. "I'll get some rest tonight. We have enough in our group we can trade off taking watch and all get some rest."

My master's eyes scanned my face, still looking so different than what I was used to. However I found him just as powerful and strong, maybe even more so – I kind of like that rugged look.

I looked back at him, wondering if he was looking for weakness, or just that he missed me. I decided to give him a smile before reaching up and tugging on his beard.

"James," I said with a smirk.

My heart soared as he smiled back at me, before leaning down and kissing me.

"Raver."

I smiled wider but I didn't laugh; I knew Reaver wouldn't appreciate that laugh. His boy was still out there and was still in danger. Even though right now I wanted to just cling to Elish and make him hold me tight to his chest, I knew we had to wait. Reaver seemed like a ticking time bomb, and he wouldn't take kindly to Elish and I showing affection to each other right now.

Killian was out there with Perish, with the man who had taken a metal rod to the back of my head.

At this mental admission, I looked up at Elish. "He got his O.L.S. I don't know how but he did."

Elish nodded as he stepped over a fallen telephone pole. "We know. Reno found out for us. He is safely back home with Garrett. Perish has his mind back, but what he is planning on doing with that greywaster boy I don't know. We'll find out though."

"Does Silas have any idea we're out here?" I asked.

Elish shook his head. "No, and I'll have to come up with some rather creative excuses as to why we've been gone for so long, but I'll do it. Or perhaps luck will be on my side and I can get that secret tucked so nicely inside of that O.L.S."

My eyes brought me to my friend Big Shot, walking with his green eyes fixed forward, obediently following beside me. "You let Big Shot come?"

A curious look swept Elish's face which, as usual, turned into a smirk. "Big Shot? You named him? Interesting. He insisted on coming along, I suppose you always made friends easily with the infirm. The half-raver will be your extra protection. You're still in the company of immortals and I would rather you have a guard."

I was happy he was coming along, but I would miss my ravers. My place was with my master though and there was no other place I would rather be.

"I think I can walk," I said to him after we had been silent for over an hour. I was starting to feel guilty that Elish was carrying me over this rough terrain. We were walking through the ruins of a small town, stepping over telephone poles and street lamps and making our way over dunes of greywaste ash. My master hadn't complained once but I could feel and hear it in his heartbeat that he was starting to get tired.

Elish let me slip from his hold and steadied me as I tested out my legs. I nodded that I was okay and he took his hand off of my shoulder before handing me several pills. I took them and popped them into my mouth before taking a bottle of water from him.

"Any blood?" Elish asked. Though it may seem like a vague question, I knew exactly what he was talking about. My empath abilities were slowly killing me. My brain, and the brain of any mortal, chimera or not, wasn't able to handle the stress of making my abilities work. A major reason why Elish wanted to make me immortal as soon as possible.

I shook my head, once again deciding to leave out my migraines. "No, but I have a nasty gash on the back of my head but it's mostly all healed. So is a carracat slash I got on my arm." I rolled up my jacket sleeve so I could show him.

Elish ran a finger up and down the thick and ugly scar. "You even look like a raver with these scars. Once we get home I will just move that scar removal machine into the apartment and treat you myself. What am I to do with a husband with such a disfigured body now?"

I didn't know whether to get mad at him for calling me disfigured or be happy that he called me his husband. Unfortunately my brain was still jamming on itself, so I just scowled and let out a huff.

Elish put a hand on my chin and rubbed it. "You look so adult now too. That beard on your face has aged you at least five years. Tonight while you tell me just what happened when I was away, I'll be shaving it off of you."

I scratched it absentmindedly. "As long as I can shave yours off. I don't think anyone would recognize us now. We're real greywasters."

"Walk faster!" The anger behind Reaver's voice made my heart clench. I looked ahead to see just what was going on with him, but the moment I saw the look on his face I took a step behind Elish.

The dark chimera was glaring at us, his shoulders hunched and his fists clenched tightly to his sides. He was standing at the top of a light pole and he was giving us all the look of death.

"Reaver, we are walking at the same speed as always," Elish replied back. His voice was low and calm, soothing tones like he was talking to an injured wild animal, and in truth he was. "Now that we know where

Perish and Killian are heading, we can get there quickly."

Reaver glared at us, searching our faces but for what I didn't know. I steered away from making eye contact with him; I didn't want to provoke him.

But I guess he would be provoked no matter what I did. I heard the shifting of ground as he jumped from his light pole. I kept on walking, staring at the ground.

Then movement in front of me. I looked up and saw Elish with his arm out, shielding me from Reaver who was only a foot away from me.

"Stand aside, I want answers from him," Reaver said, his voice was starting to become gravely and hoarse. "I want to know what happened while I was gone. How was Perish treating him? Was he being kind to him?"

Oh, that was what he wanted from me. I looked up at him, or up over Elish's arm anyway. My master was still forming his own physical barrier between me and Reaver.

"He was," I said honestly. "Perish was manipulating him pretty good, but Killian wasn't stupid. In the end, he knew Perish was playing us. Perish didn't hurt Killian at all; he was more interested in killing me and killing the slavers and the slaves."

As Reaver continued to stare at me, I could feel the dark feelings that came hand in hand with Reaver start to blur the corners of my visions. Different feelings from before. Unlike when he had killed Timothy back in Kreig, these feelings were infested with worry, an intense anxiety and helplessness that seemed to devour him right in front of me.

The clone of the king was being eaten alive right now. I was watching his own thoughts cannibalize all the positive feelings Killian had brought. And I knew that if I looked into that aura, I would no longer see the strands of light. It would only give me just as many, if not more, nightmares. Just like Killian's own aura had.

I decided to try and calm the beast. "He loves Killian; he won't hurt him. When Perish was raping me and drugging me, he was sucking up and protecting Killian. When he was bashing me over the head with a metal rod, he was protecting Killian from the ravers. Killian was worried about you. He's going to be more–"

"Perish did what to you?" Elish's voice sliced through my words making me stop in my tracks.

"Did he touch Killian?" Reaver barked, but Elish held up a hand for his silence. All eyes suddenly were on me. I felt my ears go hot.

"No, he didn't touch Killian or act like he wanted to. It…" I swallowed, too many glaring eyes were on me. "It was all on me. He was trying to get information out of me; he was using scopa and sex to make me talk."

I turned to Elish and shrunk down, feeling the brumal anger start to encase him like a tight glove. My shoulders started to tremble just out of sheer reflex. Usually when he was giving me that look I was ten seconds away from being knocked to the floor.

"What did he want to know?" Elish said coldly, his voice dropping. "What did you tell him, Jade?"

I shook my head back and forth, folding my arms over my chest. I glanced over at my master but I wasn't able to look at him. The fact that it was Perish making me fuck him made me sick; I didn't want to admit that to Elish. It made it seem more… more my fault. "It was confusing. He seemed to be pressing me for the passwords to your laptop and about the sestic radiation. He wanted to know the effects of something called prolonged concentrated exposure, I think."

I saw for a fleeting moment, a flicker so quick it was like a hummingbird's wings, a look of shock on Elish's face, before it quickly disappeared.

"Why would he need to know that?" Reaver asked. "What's in your laptop? He had access to the Kreig files; he was the one who got them."

Elish shook his head slowly. "My laptop has everything on it which is why I entrusted it to Jade. It has everything from clone research, the profiles of all the chimeras, to…" Elish was silent for a moment. "To everything to do with the sestic radiation."

"Yeah, but it was password protected, right?" I said.

Elish's mouth twitched; I could tell he was troubled. "Yes, but I don't doubt he was able to access it, which is why he might've decided to kill you." He looked ahead. "Well, let's get moving."

Reaver didn't move. He stared at Elish, his black eyes blazing. "What the fuck does Perish want? Tell me. I'm not an idiot, Elish. What did you just figure out?"

I was expecting Elish to verbally cut him down, or do something to stifle Reaver's attitude, but my master didn't waver from his usual calm. We both started to walk again, Big Shot and the dog still trailing behind.

"Sestic radiation is a remarkable thing, it can preserve as well as it can destroy," Elish responded. "I will not worry you with my theory nor will I give you false hope."

Reaver stared at him. "Fucking – tell – me."

My master was quiet; I could see the debate going on in his head.

"It is a risky thing to do, Reaver. And I am in no way saying this is what he is doing, or that it will work. But I believe that Perish is trying to make Killian immune to sestic radiation through something called prolonged concentrated exposure. As with Big Shot, and any raver, you can see the preservation effects prolonged doses of the radiation do to a human. When dosing a human with a concentrated amount at certain times for a short period... if done right, you can make them immune to sestic radiation. That might be Perish's way of protecting Killian while they're in the plaguelands. But as I said... I am not sure it will work and I am not sure this is what he is doing."

"Is Killian going to die if he does it wrong?" Reaver asked darkly.

"As Jade has said, and we all know, Perish treasures that boy. I'm sure he wouldn't risk it if Killian starts showing signs of radiation poisoning," Elish replied. "We need to move swiftly either way."

The dark chimera started walking again. "This would be a great time for you to reveal to me that Killian is a chimera and that this radiation won't affect him."

Killian a chimera? That would be one horrible chimera. Discount bin quality.

Elish shook his head. I was wondering if he was thinking the same thing as me. "No, though that would've made things easier – a lot easier."

Even though it almost killed me, I managed to keep pace with the group. By the time Elish insisted we take a couple hours of rest, my body was weak and my legs buckling with every step.

Reaver went off towards several still standing structures and Big Shot curled up by the fire with the dog. Though I was tired and I just wanted to sleep, Elish was sitting on a rock beside the fire and I was in front of him with my back facing him. My master was carefully tweezing and cleaning the gash on the back of my head, with a razor beside him to shave my beard off after.

I winced as he picked off a piece of my wool hat which had fused with the remains of the scab. To show his sympathies, he turned his touch cold to soothe the pain.

"How has Reaver been?" I asked quietly, glancing around to make sure the dark chimera wasn't in earshot, chimera earshot.

I felt cold antiseptic wet the back of my head before the softness of a bandage.

"Reaver has been having mood swings every ten to twelve hours where he flies off the handle. He was getting better, but I suspect with this new information he will now get worse," my master replied. "He has a lot on his shoulders right now, and he doesn't know how to deal with it. An easy life in the greywastes has not prepared him for the psychological repercussions that being involved in this family brings. It has been slow-going, but he listens to me and trusts me, which is the best I could hope for."

I scowled at the fire as he put my wool hat back on, before turning around to face him and the knife he was going to shave me with. "Mood swings? But... when you rescued him from the Legion, you two didn't know what had happened at the resort. Why would Reaver be acting like that?"

Elish started lathering up a mini bar of soap, before applying it to my dark facial hair. "Reaver endured a lot during his month being captive, and no, Cicaro, you will not ask what."

I stared back at my master, my mind turning over all the possibilities, but what Elish was implying was lost on me. Certainly they didn't...

As my eyes widened, Elish shook his head, as if warning me not to even voice it out loud. But that, in turn, gave me the confirmation I needed. The confirmation of just what type of abuse Reaver had endured.

"So King Silas got..."

"Cicaro."

"But that's important, did Silas have him?"

Elish shook his head. "No. Silas doesn't know Nero had him or what Nero did to him."

"*He* had him prisoner? NER–" Elish clamped his hand over my mouth. His purple eyes, two comets that had fallen from the sky, burned me with a white hot anger.

"Yes, Cicaro, and if you dare speak such information out loud, I swear I will..."

My lower lip tightened, I hadn't even been back for a day and he was already threatening me.

To my own surprise, Elish sighed, and moved the hand covering my mouth to my cheek. "Now, now, I am not angry with you. You must understand that Reaver has no tools to cope with what happened to him, that is obviously seen when comparing you and him. Your mention in passing of Perish's abuse of you shows just how different you and Reaver are."

I let him tilt my chin up, and smiled as he tenderly brushed my lips with his thumb.

He continued. "Reaver is at the end of his mental rope right now, if you speak aloud what happened that rope will snap. I cannot have him breaking off from the group right now. I need that boy near me. I need to watch him."

I nodded and I did understand. Elish had told me many times before that we needed him to be in Reaver's good books. Reaver didn't have many friends and it was essential for the future of the world that those two get along.

The future king of Skyfall and the future king of the greywastes.

"I'll behave," I said, tilting my chin as he started lightly shaving the scraggly hair. "I learned a few things from the time I spent with him. I think I know how much that would fuck him up – especially if it was... *that* chimera. That on top of Killian being gone... I'm surprised he hasn't started another Fallocaust."

Elish's eyes seemed to darken at that comment; he withdrew the knife and flicked the hair and soap onto the fire. "Yes, so far I haven't felt any radiation coming off of him which is surprising, but I will take no chances. Tomorrow I will get you to try out that dog. We need to move swiftly and you are in a horrendous state."

I glanced over at Deek, lying on his back with his stomach exposed and his head tilted back so his teeth were showing, he looked like a doofus. "I guess riding a giant dog would be cool. Reaver will cut my throat if I fall behind. I can sense a lot of bad things in him."

"Speaking of sensing things...." Elish put the blade back to my chin before he continued to shave off the hair. "Anything with Perish?"

"I learned the obvious thing, that he and Sky were twins. But you already knew that, huh?" I said.

Elish nodded. "Yes, that was known by the first generation and some of the second."

"I saw his aura start to knit itself back together, in hindsight I guess it was the O.L.S making those connections." I went on, "Reaver commented that he saw Perish act normal when they were being attacked by those

Kreig lizards. I was able to look into his head a few times but every time I did he flipped out and either attacked me or tried to attack me. Like he didn't want me to see what was going on in his brain."

"And when he raped you? You tell me he was asking for information regarding the sestic radiation?"

I flinched as he mentioned the rape between me and Perish. The heat started gathering to my face, and sure enough, Elish noticed.

He stopped shaving and stared down at me. "What is it?"

When he removed the knife from my skin I shook my head, the sick nausea bubbling in me again. He also sensed this and narrowed his eyes.

"He didn't fuck me. I… he, ah, kind of… got on top of me," I stammered. "He thought I was drugged. I switched out the scopa for water so I went with it, hoping I could get a look inside of his head."

Elish didn't look happy. "Well, I did give you permission to do what needed to be done. This news sits better with me than the thought that he violated you."

Then we both heard a crunch of gravel and saw Reaver returning, a severed leg being carried over his shoulder.

Elish and I both stared at Reaver as he laid the leg over the fire, balancing it on a large piece of tree branch we had been burning through. The leg still had a dirty sock on it and what looked like an old tattoo of an orca whale.

Reaver stared at us back. "What?"

"Where did you find that leg?" Elish asked, trying to hide his perplexity.

Reaver shrugged. "Found two people camping, decided I was hungry and sick of your shitty tact and energy bars. I have their bodies hanging a warehouse a mile back. We can't carry all of it but the dog will probably eat the remainders."

Well, Reaver will certainly always be Reaver.

CHAPTER 52

Killian

MY FINGERNAILS SCRAPED OVER THE RED PATCH ON my arm, again and again until the skin broke and started to bleed. I had sores on my body and on my face. Hot sores that stung to the touch; sores that seemed to have emerged over night.

Even my fingernails; they had turned black. I checked the dirt-caked fingers of the slaves and, sure enough, the same thing was happening with them. Though it wasn't dirt that was being forced into the soft undersides of my nails, they were black from being filled with blood. I had torn one of them while scratching my arms only to have it bleed all over me. Another effect of the radiation? I was too defeated and tired to ask; right now, I was just waiting to die.

Waiting for death to take me and give me the mental peace my life had failed to sustain.

Death for the mortal, a boy who, at one point in his life, had wanted to live so badly.

Perish was walking ahead of us, his black duster now grey from ash and the bowler hat on his head marbled with all the colours of the greywastes, mostly the greys and reds. The red painted on the canvas in spots and smears, a side effect from beating on the slaves as he most often did.

Behind me, falling behind, were my friends the slaves. Teejay stumbling ahead with Danny trying to keep up. Edward was growing weaker by the day, and though his stumped arm wasn't infected, it wasn't healing either.

His eyes were starting to cloud over too, and he wasn't talking as much as he used to.

"Killian? Come walk with me," Perish called suddenly. His voice was still strong and powerful, ours had become raspy and thin. The radiation, it seemed, were slowly eating our vocal cords, it was hard for me to talk.

I tried to speed up but Perish ended up slowing down his own pace. I approached him with my head hung low, my fingernails dripping blood from where I had torn them against my skin.

Perish lifted an arm and pointed. I looked in the direction and saw something yellow, a sign posted on a wooden beam.

As I looked, I saw that these signs were everywhere. I hadn't even noticed them but they surrounded me like sentinels on watch. All of them the same, yellow triangles holding words on them.

"*Radiation, stay out, by order of Skytech*," Perish read them for me. "We're in the plaguelands now, Killian. We're near where Sky died."

I turned my head to him and said in a dry rasp, "Sky killed himself here?"

Did Sky tell you this? I was too tired and sick to ask him that.

Perish slowly nodded, staring ahead. I looked to where he was looking and saw what had once been a highway in front of us, though the ash had been blown over most of it. Only half-exposed medians gave insight as to what this place looked like before the Fallocaust.

"Yes, his lab. Sky's lab... my lab," Perish said slowly. He slipped so often into thinking he was Sky I didn't even think twice about it now. "We'll be approaching it soon, where it will be warm, dry. Where you can shower."

I nodded slowly and felt Perish's hand brush my face. "Those radiation burns will heal. I had to give you a strong last dose but your body is working it out of your system as we speak."

Then the scientist glanced behind him and I saw his face darken. "If you live long enough to see it. I don't think you're going to survive. Or me. I think they'll kill both of us first."

"Who?" I asked looking towards one of the radiation signs; it had a blue ribbon still wrapped around it. "Did Sky make..."

Perish grabbed my shoulder as I started walking towards the ribbon and clenched it. "Don't tell me you've forgotten? The slaves want us dead, Killian."

I stopped, the grey world around me getting smaller as I narrowed my eyes trying to make sense of what he was saying. "No, not them... they–"

Perish *shh'd* me, which was odd. He slipped his hand, still resting on my shoulder, over to my side until he was half-embracing me.

The scientist pulled me close and whispered in my ear. "Killian, you forgot? Danny tried to rape you just a few days ago; he put his fingers inside of you. I managed to fight him off. You don't remember? You don't remember, Killian? How could you forget something like that?"

I took the blue ribbon and stared at it. I held it up to show Perish. "Look how blue this is, does it match my eyes?"

Perish smiled at me and put a hand to my cheek. I didn't flinch away as he stroked it; I had learned. "Killian... what do you remember from when Danny put his fingers inside of you?"

I couldn't make eye contact. I stared at the ribbon and said quietly to him, "You did that to me, Perish. You said Sk-"

"No, no... I'd never do such a thing." His voice became a higher octave, sweet and dripping honey. "I love you, why would I ever hurt you?"

"You always hurt me."

He glanced behind me as the slaves' boot steps started to come closer. He quietly led me away and we started walking towards the highway. There were no buildings here, everything was rolling terrain with mountains around us. I knew there had been fire here though, the medians were covered in scorch marks.

I touched one, my bleeding black fingernails leaving prints all over the scorched medians. It felt rough and uncomfortable underneath my hands, but oddly warm. Though the warmth could have been coming from my own hands; I felt warm with the radiation inside of my body. I wonder if death was warm?

No, it was cold. Winter might be disappearing from the greywastes, but I knew in my grave it could be cold and dark.

I looked around, wondering if there were any signs that winter was leaving, but the dense grey landscape never changed. Only the temperature of the air and small shoots of yellow grass could tell you which season it was; the flies never left, the desolation never left, the grey and red never left.

I left red on the grey, in the form of my own blood, and kept walking beside Perish.

"Can we rest?" Danny's dry voice sounded. I turned around and saw the ghost of the slave staggering on. His face was sunken, gaunt, and completely covered in flaking red blisters, several of which had burst, coating his patchy beard in hardened pus.

Their hair was falling out from the radiation. I didn't know if mine was; I had pulled most of it out.

Perish stopped and stared at him before nodding slowly. "Yes, you can share the can of dog food. Killian come rest with me up ahead. We'll sit on that median together."

I looked at Danny's hand, holding our sack of food. The dog food was the last big can we had left, then all we had was a smaller tin of mystery food. Smaller tins usually meant tuna or other fish we couldn't eat, though I got bamboo shoots once.

"Killian? Walk with me…"

I had never had bamboo shoots before, they didn't taste like much but I enjoyed the textu–

My heart jumped as Perish grabbed my shoulder, but it wasn't a forceful grab, he was only bringing me back to reality. I turned around and walked with him towards a median, scorched and crumbling off on the far end. In the distance telephone poles still stood, becoming more shrouded as they stretched off towards what the rest of the planet was now.

Nothing.

Perish handed me an energy bar, warped and twisted from the heat of his body. I took it with my bloodied hands and started eating it. Though as I chewed on the blueberry-flavoured bar, I saw Perish looking at me.

Then he looked behind him and I heard him take in a shaking breath. "Did you see how Danny asked us to rest? He wants us to take as long as we can to get to the lab; he's waiting for you to die. Danny, Teejay, and Edward are planning on eating you as soon as the last can is gone."

"And it's almost gone, Killian."

"The food is almost gone, and it'll be time for them to eat you. I've been holding them off right now, but I'm only one man."

Danny was sitting on the ground with the other two staring forward, holding the can of dog food in his hand, a spoon sticking out of it. Edward was facing him; I could see him the most. His eyes looked so strange now and his skin was getting darker and darker.

"See how he refuses to look at you?" Perish whispered. He stroked my neck before running the hand down to mine. I winced from pain as he grabbed my hand and held it. "Watch him, watch the way he looks at you, watch the things he says. He wants to kill you; he's already raped you once. We can't let it happen again."

He already... did it before?

I shook my head and felt my body constrict, like a sea anemone recoiling at a strange foreign touch. The memories of what had happened in that house were so fresh inside of my mind, but in the same thread of thought, they had become a haze. A blur of faces and physical objects, only the feelings and the fear were bright inside of my head.

The horror of feeling his fingers dig into me. The pain was nothing; I was friends with pain, but the disgusting violating feelings...

I shuddered and turned away, not realizing I had turned into the crook of Perish's arms.

Taking that opportunity, Perish put a hand on the back of my head and shushed me. "I'll never let them hurt you, sweety. I did all of this just so... no one would hurt you anymore. Look, sweety, not even the radiation will hurt you. Soon you'll be all healed."

"Kill me," I whispered. I shut my eyes but no tears came. I felt like my body had been sucked of all liquids, my mouth was dry, my eyes dry, everything was just dry pain. "Perry... show me the same love I showed you. Kill me."

Perish clucked his tongue, lips pressed against my forehead. "I'll show you that and more, you just need to trust me. Do you trust me?"

"Poor Killian, he's so confused. You're forgetting what everyone has done to you?" he murmured.

Danny in the distance raised the spoon to his lips before passing it to Teejay. Teejay weakly took it and held it frozen in his hand, as if he didn't even have the strength to lift the spoon to his lips.

Were they trying to kill me?

My face felt hot. I took in a sharp breath, my lungs burning.

Did I trust Perish? I tried to search his voice. I tried to search him for any signs of hostility, but oddly, I saw none.

Was I confused?

Danny took the can back and I heard scraping as the spoon ran along the edges.

Perish let out a breath at this and squeezed me again. "Look, he didn't even save any for you or me. That's our last big can of food and he didn't save any for us. They're only out for themselves now. You need to watch yourself, Killian, they're going to try and eat you."

I did watch them, like Perish had told me to. Three men passing around a can of dog food, all of them looking like they would collapse at any moment. Danny, it seemed, was the most conscious. Edward was the worst.

Was it true?

I tried to think back to earlier memories, now just smudges and stains on the crumbled, derelict walls of my mind. The memories were painful and hard to read, but I forced myself to concentrate on remembering them.

"He fed you creamed corn, then suddenly he jumped on you while I was tending to Edward. He had you on your stomach, his fingers thrusting in and out of you as you screamed," Perish whispered in my ear. "It was horrible, you were screaming and crying. He wanted to fuck you, Killian. I had to pull him off of you. Don't you remember what I whispered in your ear? I'd never hurt you, Killian. I love you too much. I forced Danny off of you, right when he was about to penetrate you. Don't you remember? Your Geigerchip died shortly after."

I kept staring at Danny. He took the can of dog food and threw it behind a scorched median with an echoing *clunk*.

Perish continued, "I feel so badly that I let that happen. But rest assured: I'll kill him if he even looks at you. I promise."

I looked down, feeling something wet, and saw that I had been clenching the median with my fingers. I groaned as I saw I had torn several fingernails off, their black shells hanging loosely by bits of red flesh. A sick nausea swept me and I felt like I was going to throw up.

Perish put his arms around me and pulled me onto his lap. He started rocking me back and forth, his grip tight.

"It's okay, sweety, it's okay. In the end, everything will be fine. I promise you, my sweet sweet boy. We'll show them all, Silas. I'll protect you, always."

My face crumpled, but no tears came. I might be in the plaguelands, I might be surrounded by enemies, but in that moment – I so dearly missed being held. It brought into my chest a comfort I had thought had been forgotten, memories and recollections of a moment in time I could no longer recall, but the feelings it brought I remembered.

Slowly, and if only for a moment, I relaxed and embraced the feeling; a small fleeting moment of security in this inner and outer hell.

Yes, I knew this feeling, I knew this feeling – even when my world was falling to black flames I would be held against him and it would all disappear. His tight embrace, his low but dominant voice, his smell, his... his small little ears, one that had once knitted itself back together after an explosion.

I gave into him in that moment; I gave into the feeling and held onto the only comfort I had. My mind drawing me to the feeling like flies to carnage.

Yes, I remember him. I remember that man. I thought I had lost him.

"You... you'll protect me?" I whispered. He held me tighter and my face twisted. Not from pain though, not from agony or fear – but from relief.

He was here.

"Of course... I'll protect you, Killi Cat."

My teeth clenched and a whine escaped my lips. I held onto him tight and sobbed.

I had him... was it really him? I don't... I don't remember him. I just...

He called me Killi Cat.

In the darkness, after we had made each other sweaty and tired, he called me his Killi Cat, his Killibee. He had so many nicknames for me but all I had called him was mine, my very own.

"We can be safe in my lab, my radioactive kitten, but we might not make it with the slaves. They're trying to stop us, they want to eat us, Killi Cat," the man whispered as he kissed my forehead. "You'll watch out for them?"

I nodded and buried my face into his jacket. "I will."

"That's a good boy; you just watch them. Watch how they look at you, watch what they say. You'll see, we're in danger," he whispered before pulling away.

I looked at him and searched his face. But looking into his blue eyes didn't bring me the same relief that hearing him did. It confused me but not enough to cause alarm. We had all changed out here, me most of all.

"Who are you?" I whispered to him. I reached out and touched his face. "You are so many people in one body – Who are you now?"

The man smiled, but his eyes didn't smile, just his mouth. He leaned in and kissed my forehead. "Silly, Killi. I'm Perish. The same man who has been protecting you for months now. It's just me and you Killian, just me and you, okay?"

I couldn't stop staring at him, wondering in my own madness if I could see the other one if I looked hard enough. The one named Sky and the one who held me.

I shifted myself back into him, not able to keep his gaze and let out a relieved sigh as he held me.

The signs disappeared behind us, left in the greywastes where people could see them. There were no signs in the plaguelands, or anything besides the burnt shells of houses and the same blackened roads and medians. Even the rocks here had burn marks on them, there must've been a great fire here at one point in time.

Perish was walking slowly with me, matching my footsteps so he wouldn't pull too hard on my hand. He was holding my hand now, gently with a soft touch, though I couldn't feel his skin through my bandages.

I had many bandages on me, snowy white ones, grey ones, and a blue tenser bandage he put on my feet. I had been wrapped like a mummy and I walked like one too.

He had decided it was to be done last night, last night when we camped on the side of the road because there were no houses around for us to sleep in. The burned skeletons of buildings in the distance offered no more shelter than a median on the side of the road so we didn't bother.

The can of food we had opened this morning was cat food, just our luck. I ate some and it tasted good. I think it was chicken and I could feel the ground up bones in my teeth. I only had a bit to eat before the slaves took the rest.

The slaves took all the food.

Perish raised my hand and petted it, shaking his head back and forth. "My poor thing, we'll get to the lab soon and we'll clean you up. How are the burns on your face? Do they hurt?"

I brought my hand to my face and brushed over the hot spots. The one on the right side was the worst, but I found they were slowly getting better. I remember someone telling me they would, but I couldn't remember why…

I just… had trouble remembering things now.

"Yeah," I mumbled, drawing my hand away from my face and looking at it. My skin was peeling off like I had a bad sunburn. My neck was worse. "Am I still ugly?"

He shook his head and leaned in to kiss my lips. I shied away but I was too slow. Perish kissed me slowly and only withdrew when I whimpered.

"You're beautiful, so beautiful," he said quietly. "Don't worry anymore, it's almost over. Sky will be gone soon."

What's almost over? I wanted to ask but behind me there was a noise.

We both turned around at the same time and saw Edward on his knees, his hand up to his face, cradling his head like he was unable to hold it up any longer.

"We need to rest... he's... I think he's turning into a raver," Danny choked, the emotion heavy on his voice. "Should... should we–" Danny's flaked and chapped lips pursed, barely visible under the matted remains of his beard. He turned away from Edward and staggered up to us.

He looked at me and then Perish. "Perish, just... put him out of his misery before he becomes a fucking raver. If his mind does that switch in the middle of the night and you're not fast enough he could kill us all."

Perish put a protective hand over my chest. "He's too weak to become a raver; he's going to die."

"Either way, he's toast. For fuck sakes, just have some mercy in you." Danny coughed into his jacket. I saw blood speckles. "You're almost at this lab, just let us go. Killian's going to die out here; we all are."

I'm going to die out here? My eyes widened and I took a step back. I searched Danny's face like Perish had told me and felt a percussion of anxiety go through me. I squeezed Perish's hand and bit my bottom lip. Was he right? Had Perish been right? Had it really been Danny who abused me?

Killian's going to die out here. What if he kills all of us? Perish was my only comfort, the only source of comfort I had. He had held me and... and I had recognized that touch.

His eyes had become blue but hadn't they been black? A deceptive black, like coffee, such a dark rich brown.

Not blue.

But his mind had changed; his eyes had changed too, I guess.

"Killian isn't leaving my side, never," Perish said acerbically. He squeezed my hand back. "I'll kill him tomorrow and we can have a good meal out of him."

"And what about us?" Danny coughed again. "Come on, just... just let us go, man."

Behind him Teejay had his hand on Edward's shoulders, giving them a supportive rub. These strange slaves. Who had been trying to overpower us. Who had been trying to kill us.

Danny reached out to touch me but I shied away, my heart jumping to my throat. He withdrew his touch and stared at me. "Killian? Are you still in there?"

"Killian? Hello?"

"He's fine," Perish said. "Get Edward up; we have more ground to cover."

Danny's face darkened, the lines in his face prominent with the dirt that covered every crease and crevice. He took a step away from Perish before narrowing his eyes at me. I didn't like that look, it made me move myself closer to Perish.

"Be careful, Killian," he said, before turning away from us and walking back to Edward and Teejay.

Perish tsked. "See, Killian? Did you watch his face? Look at how much hatred he has in him. Did you see that when he looked at you? When he told me he wanted to take you away? I could see it in his face, didn't you see it?"

"Did you see it, Killian?"

I... I had. I had seen it.

Danny walked away from us, his worn shoes revealing large purple sores on his heels, bleeding and weeping fluid onto the ground. He may have been weak, but...

Danny turned around and I shrunk back. He made eye contact with Perish and said to him in a dead raspy voice, *"I'm going to fuck him, as soon as I kill you, Perish."*

"Perry!" I cried. I turned around and Perish held me tight to him.

"What is it? What's wrong?" Perish whispered.

Hadn't he seen it? Hadn't he heard him? I had... hadn't I?

Hadn't I?

I let out a sob, though to my horror Danny's voice sounded again in my head.

"Killian, are you still in there? We're going to fuck you tonight, all three of us. We'll fuck you, and then we'll eat you. I bet you'll taste nice." The tones of his voice struck my brain like a sonic boom, blasting away what remainders of my mind I still held. They hit me in quick succession, one after another, pounding against me, pounding against me.

"It's okay, I won't let them hurt you," Perish soothed. "I'll protect you, everyone might want to hurt you but I won't, okay?"

"Okay," I whispered, squeezing my eyes tight as Danny's threats spread like a virus through my mind. "Promise?"

"Of course, sweety."

That night I slept in Perish's arms and he held me tight against him. He put his arms around me and drew me close, and I slept smelling his shirt and his neck. My own bandaged hand was on his side and the other bent underneath me so I could use it as a pillow. In my head were the nightmares that had become more my reality than the objects around me, but whenever I woke up I was with him, so I think I was okay.

I think I was okay because when I woke up he shushed me and kissed me until I fell back asleep. He called me Silas in the middle of the night, but I didn't mind. Sky came out at night; I was used to that now. He had stopped being cruel to me at least.

No... that was Danny.

Wasn't it?

There were no more Geigerchips going off, no more buzzing hornets underneath my skin to keep me up. Maybe I had ripped it out of my own flesh, I wasn't sure. There weren't many memories my mind let me keep, just the present hell I was now in.

"My feet hurt," I said quietly to Perish the next day. I had asked Perish if we could walk behind the slaves now, I didn't want my back to them.

"We're almost there, love." Perish beamed at me. He seemed to have a lightness to him this morning. I think it was because we were getting closer to our destination but I wasn't sure. He had pointed out a slab of metal a few hours ago that was nothing but a melted, deformed pool. Perish had said this place had once been a city but it had melted.

"I can rest then?" I massaged my throat as it cracked; my bare skin was so chapped and red.

Perish's face turned into a frown; he looked in front of him then lowered his voice. "If we make it... I think the slaves want to kill you soon."

I froze and Perish stopped. "W-what? They do?"

Perish nodded, his face heavy with concern. "Didn't you see how Danny was looking at you this morning? They can't stop looking at you, Killian." He leaned down and I felt his hot breath against my ear. "They're trying to decide who gets to break you in first. No one wants blood and someone else's cum. It's going to happen soon, they're going to kill me and fuck you, Killian."

"No!" I choked. I wrenched my bandaged hand away from Perish's and shook my head back and forth. I stumbled away but my legs became like rubber. I fell to my knees, still shaking my head. "No, they won't… that's…." My eyes closed. I was so confused; I didn't know what was happening anymore, or what to believe.

I looked at my hands, grey from dirt with brown circles from where my fingernails had bled through. "I… I'm…"

"Get up, Killian. We'll be there soon," Perish said soothingly. "I'm sure I can overpower them, but it only takes one to kill me. Then you'll be theirs to pass around."

"You just can't trust anyone anymore, Killian."

"Just me, you can only trust me. Everyone else is out to deceive you, out to betray you."

"Not me though, Killian, not me."

Bodies in the water,

Bodies in the basement.

Killi bee bee bee.

I raised my head, still no tears, no liquid, no nothing. I raised my head and saw the slaves all staring at me, their eyes fixed on me and their faces blank. They were like canvases, blank canvases, but they had all once been painted on, before someone had taken a scraper to their faces.

Now we were all empty, all blank.

Perish brought me to my feet and kissed my cheek. I didn't move until he pulled on my hand, encouraging me to walk like I was a stray bosen.

I let him lead me and I followed, my bandages wet and squishing between my toes. I scanned where we were walking and said to Perish, "Are we close?"

Perish turned around and nodded. The terrain was slowly changing, though not really the terrain, what we were walking on had changed.

Melted metal was now underneath our feet, lumps of it like what remained of a toy soldier after you put it in the microwave. When I brushed aside the dirt I could see it, warped and deformed and holding ash in its wrinkly crevices. It was surrounding us, some disguised as hills from the wind sweeping the ash onto it, others completely invisible until you walked past it. This place had once been engulfed in a fire so hot the city had bowed to it. How could a fire be this hot? How could it do so much damage?

"It took twenty years to cool. Sky had somehow rigged it to burn after he was gone," Perish said to me in a subdued voice. "It took twenty years for Silas to accept that Sky had really died." He looked ahead, to the metal sculptures and broken roads and dropped his voice. "He would go in there, and burn himself so badly I would have to put him out of his pain. Then once he resurrected he would go back in, picking up boiling hot metal with his bare hands, burning himself alive in the heavy duty equipment he would salvage. But he was gone… Sky had died, I knew he had. The last act he had entrusted me to do, so I knew – my brother was dead."

"Why?" I asked him. "Why did Sky want to die?"

Perish's face tightened and I saw a glisten in his eye, a shred of humanity I hadn't seen in a long time.

"Because Sky knew he was a bad person and he hated himself for it. He was cruel to Silas, the man who loved him more than anything, and he was tired of hurting him. Even though Silas took his abuse and loved him all the same… Sky couldn't stand the man he had become. He explained this to me and after years of watching him slip into his own insanity I finally agreed to help him kill himself. We found a way, and we did it."

Then like an old engine starting, my mind turned over and I remembered something from long ago.

"But you removed his O.L.S?" I asked. "You wanted to keep some of his memories?"

Perish nodded. "Greg removed our brain pieces and put them into his invention. Our O.L.S's held both our memories and our abilities. He removed mine so I wouldn't know how Sky died, so Silas could never have that information."

"And Sky? Why did Sky have his removed?"

"Because I couldn't let go of him. I told him it was the only way I'd agree to do it," Perish answered. "I loved that man. He was my twin; it was our jobs to protect each other, to make the right decisions when the other was no longer capable of doing it."

A hand rested on my head and I felt a soft stroke of my hair, or what remained of my hair. I had ripped most of it out and the radiation was going to take the rest, just like the slaves.

Slaves…

I looked ahead at the corpses, walking slowly ahead of us, hunched over with their weeping wounds spread all over their body.

"And why are we going to the lab?" I whispered. "What are you doing to me?"

Perish continued to rub my hair, soothing long strokes like he was touching expensive fabric. Up and down, soft and loving. Painting images on me, both body and soul, that I knew would follow me until the end of my days.

"Oh, Killi Cat, my Killi Cat… it will all be over soon, I promise."

"I promise, Killian."

"It will all be over soon."

"I'm sorry, I'm sorry for what Sky made me do but we had an agreement, an agreement."

"But I love you."

"I love you, Killian."

CHAPTER 53

Reaver

I OFTEN WONDERED IF HE WAS SCARED. I OFTEN wondered if he had lost hope. By now it had been months since I had seen him. Months since I had held him on my lap as we watched the town of Mariano through the window.

If I had known that would be the last time I held him, the last time I would lay down with him until he fell asleep – I would have treasured every moment. I would have…

My life was full of regrets now, and if I wasn't filling that dark void with the toxic substance that was me second-guessing my decisions, it was torturing me with the images of my boyfriend, alone with Perish.

What was I going to find when I found Killian? In what state would my boyfriend be in? He hadn't even had a proper amount of time to recover from Silas's mental games before all of this happened. We didn't have long at all in the greyrifts apartment and then all of this shit. Killian was going to be a wreck… what if I couldn't get him back this time?

This thought brought a frown to my lips. No, I was overthinking this again, I needed Killian to be alive, that was it. That was the only thing I should be hoping for, that Killian was alive. Everything else I could handle, death was final for a mortal, death was the only thing I didn't know how to fix.

I looked behind me and saw Elish walking beside Jade and Deek. The pet was riding on top of the dog, Elish's hands steadying him by holding onto the canvas vest Killian had made for the dog long ago.

Jade was slumped over, his face creased in pain and his heartbeat racing.

Elish put a hand on Jade's shoulder and rubbed it in a caring manner the chimera reserved only for his pet. The blond chimera and the man I saw as a friend hadn't left his pet's side. Just like I would've never left Killian's side if it was him I had found with the ravers. I didn't think any different of Elish for showing this side to me, in a way I felt honoured that the cold chimera was this comfortable around me now.

But perhaps, like me, he didn't care what side we showed each other. It wasn't about us; it was about the boys we loved. And I understood that, which is why I was patient with Jade's weakened state. Though I wasn't too nice about it in the beginning, after I took a couple days to cool off from my adventure with the ravers, I had become a bit more understanding.

And the idea Elish had come up with had worked. We had been making good time since we put Jade on top of the dog, but the pet was still deteriorating as the days went on. There was something wrong with his head, something extremely wrong.

Just then Jade gave out a strangled cry, in a flash, Elish grabbed him as the boy slumped over.

I ground my teeth. *Not again…*

I walked over and helped Elish lower Jade onto the ground.

The pet screamed and twisted around like a dying insect, thrashing and clenching his fists like he was having a seizure. Then, at once, he started bashing his fists against his left eye, hammering it hard like he was trying to bust his own eye socket.

There was no alarmed cry from Elish or myself, or even Big Shot, who watched beside the dog. We had been having to deal with this three times a day since we had gotten the kid back. The pain, Jade had told us, was focused behind his left eye, and in his pain-filled, delirious state he said pressing and hitting it distraction from the migraine itself.

Like a trained team, I grabbed Jade's hands and held them back. Elish put his hand over Jade's left eye and made his touch cold. His remaining hand was resting beside the boy's ear which he made so hot I could smell Jade's hair burn.

This was our routine; this is what we had to do until it subsided. It only took ten minutes out of our walking time so I tolerated it, but it still made my teeth grit in frustration.

Jade shrieked, and in my core I felt bad for him and I worried for him too. I took that as a win. Leo and Greyson would've been proud that I was feeling a bit of empathy for someone that wasn't Killian. I think it was because he had been protecting Killian from Perish while I was gone. I had learned he had known something was off with Perish and had been protecting Killian in any way he could before Perish tried to kill him.

After another minute the screaming died down and soon it was replaced by rapid breathing bordering on hyperventilating. I held the cicaro down for a few seconds longer before I slowly let go of his arms.

I looked at Elish and saw his face was tense, his purple eyes still fixed on his pet. He was worried, and I knew he was worried. We were a long ways away from medical attention for this kid. Even if we had a town close-by no one would know what the fuck was going on inside of his brain.

Cluster headaches were what Elish called them. He had told me Jade's brain was weakening, that he couldn't handle his abilities growing as quickly as they were. That and the stress of being in the greywastes, plus not having the medication Elish usually gave him – it was taking a devastating toll on the little yellow-eyed brat.

"Elish?" Jade murmured, and, as always, at his cue Elish took the boy into his arms and cradled him. The cicaro, an eighteen-year-old adult, curled into him, his long spindly legs and arms tucked up into himself like he was a toddler who had just found his parent.

I couldn't hold that against him. I was going to break Killian's legs when I found him just so I could carry him around like that without complaint. I was never letting him out of my sight.

And I would find him soon… since Jade had the dog to ride we had been making better time. Elish wasn't forcing us to rest for more than four hours a day. It was hard on Deek and Big Shot but they were managing.

Elish let out a breath and looked forward. "I'll carry him until we make camp. Let's go. The houses you spotted are not far away."

I nodded and started sprinting ahead. We had veered off of the highway several days ago and now we were walking deeper into the greyrifts towards the plaguelands. According to Elish's knowledge of this area, it was northeast. Elish and I had found Jade northwest so thankfully we hadn't been going in the complete opposite direction.

We would be completely bypassing Falkvalley and Melchai. Elish was sure Perish wouldn't be stopping in any of those towns. No, he was on a straight course to the plaguelands.

Where my boyfriend could die from radiation poisoning. We were now relying on this prolonged concentrated exposure, or whatever, that Elish had told me about.

But why? Why was he was taking Killian out of the greywastes? The plaguelands weren't mapped and any old pre-Fallocaust map would be outdated and almost useless. We had no idea what we would find there besides the usual abandoned destruction. All I knew was there had to be a reason.

But what reason? If this theory of making a greywaster immune to radiation didn't work would Perish love Killian enough to abandon his plan?

My heart gave a poisonous lurch. I felt the bitter liquid rise to my throat which I swallowed down with nothing but self-control. I buried my fears inside of my body and picked up the pace.

Big Shot appeared to my left, standing in the middle of two fallen black trees, both fallen on top of each other. He put out his arms and climbed up one of the trunks and looked ahead. He scanned the terrain for a moment before jumping down and sprinted towards me.

The half-raver looked entirely different than when I had first seen him. Though I was unhappy with it, I had let him dress in some of Killian's old clothes that Jade had in his pack. It was either that or he kept wearing the rank and disgusting, rot-smelling clothing he had come with. He was wearing a pair of jeans now, a faded black shirt with a cartoon spaceship on it and a member's only jacket he had been wearing before. It didn't smell as bad as everything else.

Physically he was still changing as well. His hair was dark and covered all of his head now, and his once milky eyes held no clouded film, just dark green with black pupils. He was probably Reno's age, if not a bit older, and fair-looking though he was still scarred and his once unhealed wounds held hard grey calluses over them instead of exposed meat and bone.

"No ravers," Big Shot commented. He pointed to where he had jumped from and nodded. "All clear, none at all going northwest. All clear."

"Good," I said. I was used to him sprinting beside me; he was my second watch since Deekoi had become a pack horse. I had gotten used to the half-raver helping me scout and he was used to me.

"Did you ever go this way? Towards the plaguelands?" I asked him.

Big Shot shook his head and I saw his eyes widen, the raver had a lot of weird facial expressions. I guess it had to do with how they communicated.

"In plaguelands, cable worms, big ravers, big beasts. Big, all bigger there," Big Shot said with a sober shake of his head. "Your boy... can fight them? Bang. Bang?"

My mouth twitched; he had never met Killian obviously. No one would ask that question if they had met Killian. "No, he's... he's small. I protected him from all of that."

"I protect, Jade." Big Shot nodded. "Small, sick, bad head."

Small, sick, bad head. Yeah, that was how it ended up for a lot of people who got mixed up with chimeras.

I left Elish and Jade behind and found an old single-lane road which led to the houses I had spotted. I slowed my pace down and started scanning the area, looking for anything that could be out of place, anything to show me someone had been here.

I didn't know their exact trail, for all I knew their trail was only a quarter mile from where I was walking, I didn't know. My best bet for finding any sign of my boyfriend was to keep checking these clusters of houses; something had to be here, some sign.

For fuck sakes, just give me a sign that Killian was here.

Only my boots crunching against the dirt could be heard, and as I approached a string of fallen down and half-burned houses, the sounds echoed off of their structures. I walked to the porch of the first one and tried the door, but there were no traces of footsteps, no disturbed dirt. I didn't bother opening the door I turned around and tried the next one.

Big Shot, Elish, and Jade were now at least half an hour behind me, and in truth, I preferred that. I wanted to be the first to check out this small abandoned cluster of houses, it was my boyfriend out there not theirs.

I walked down the road, houses on either side of me and the occasional fallen down telephone pole or lamp post. I even spotted a mailbox still standing, I walked to it and opened it – just because that was what Killian used to do. Even though the rusted hinges put my teeth on edge and made me question why I was making such a racket.

Come on, Killian – tell me where you are. Every house, every building with its wood stained a faded grey looked the same, but for all I knew one of them held the jackpot inside: the sure-fire sign that my boyfriend had been here.

Even if he's long gone, just knowing… just fucking knowing… I sighed and closed my eyes, and because my own inner masochisms would eat me alive if I let it, I shut that area of my brain off and slipped into the dark chimera I knew I was. I could be the boyfriend later when he was safe in my arms, but until then…

I couldn't be that man.

Methodically, I looked through every open window frame, and when there was an open door I looked inside and scanned the area for any signs of life. There was nothing though, just ripped up carpets, rain-warped wood, and the endless piles of crumbled gyprock and faded pink insulation.

By the time I was down to the last two dozen houses, the ones at the end, the rest of my travelling companions had arrived.

"Not a sign then?" Elish asked. Jade was walking again, giving Deek a break. The deacdog had made a beeline to a porch so he could lay on it; he was shit out of luck though.

I shook my head, not feeling like voicing it out loud, and decided it was time to pull out my wild card. "Deekoi. Killian. Is Killian here?"

The dog scrambled to his feet and started to smell the air. Inside of me my heart started to implode on itself as I watched the dog do his work, not knowing what was going to happen next.

Suddenly the dog looked at me and barked. My throat tightened and my limbs locked in place as he turned and started running towards the last string of houses, the ones I hadn't checked yet.

Elish whirled around, his eyes shooting from the dog to me.

I… I still hadn't moved. I couldn't move. Why couldn't I fucking move?

I only stared as the grey deacon dog with black legs sprinted down the road, before turning and giving the door frame a hard sniff. He started quickly smelling around it before his paws started to dig and scratch at the bottom of the floor.

"Killian?" I whispered. *He had been here? He had really…* I looked around the mess of houses and tried to push down the overwhelming emotions this realization brought to me. In a second I had control of my body again, and without wasting another second, I ran towards the dog. Elish, Jade, and Big Shot trailing behind me.

Deek jumped back as I threw my weight against the door. The half-rotten door frame came off and splintering as the door itself flew forward, landing beside a cabinet overflowing with boxes.

I ran inside of the house and looked around. I was in a kitchen with shredded floor tile and wallpaper that had come down in curls like an unravelled scroll.

"Killian?" I knew he wasn't there, I knew he wasn't but fuck... I couldn't... I didn't know what I was doing. "Killian?"

I looked around the kitchen and started opening up cabinet doors, my chest a frozen block of ice as I saw the dust-less circles that outlined the bottom of the cabinet like cookie cutter shapes.

There had been cans here and they'd gotten them... Killian had gotten them.

"Killi?" I yelled. I ran into the living room, the old carpet frayed and covered with dirt, the light from the outside seeping through the curtains to make the entire living room bright.

"Killian?" I hollered, wishing in the throes of my own panic-stricken insanity that I could just hear his weak voice calling my name.

But there was only silence, silence and the sounds of boots stepping onto the front deck.

I looked down, and saw outlines of boot prints.

"These are Perish's...." I called, knowing the others were here now. I traced them to the far end of the living room, nodding to myself. "These are Killian's... there are... the ones without the tread marks are the slaves. They must have brought slaves with them. Elish do you–"

I paused, the words on my lips lying forgotten as my eyes fell on something I didn't want to see. Something that I had tried to accept might be a reality, but once I had that confirmation in my mind – something I don't think I knew how to handle.

Blood... blood and semen. I could see it, and as every ounce of heat inside of my body drained out of me, I realized I could smell the semen too.

Before I could stop myself, I leaned down and brushed my hand over the dried blood. My face tightened and my jaw locked as I saw the shining reflection of a single blond hair.

Killian's hair, my Killian's hair.

"Reaver?" Elish's voice sounded behind me. "Is that..."

"He raped him." My own voice was a rasp in my throat, barely able to sound over the tight vice that was holding my breath hostage. "There is fucking... semen on the carpet, Elish."

I felt his presence behind me, my shoulders started to tremble as Killian's single blond hair slipped from my hand. It fell to the floor right beside a long string of dried cum, contrasting against the dirty carpet like it had been deliberately left there for me to find.

"Yes, I see that now. Reaver, this means Killian is alive, remember that," Elish said quietly.

I whirled around and heard a low vibration start to sound in my throat. I took a step towards him, my fists clenching.

"Perish fucking raped him, in this fucking spot!" I suddenly screamed. In an instant, I felt all my restraint and control fall from me like a shedded snake skin. I let out a scream of frustration and rage and took a step back, knowing that if I didn't I'd attack Elish.

I slammed my fists against the back of the wall, raining powdered gyprock on top of me. "How long since he was here? It could have been a month, Elish!" My voice broke, my brain automatically tried to make me inhale but I ended up choking on it. I scanned the room like a cornered animal, not knowing what to do, just knowing I had to do something.

I felt like I was going to explode.

"Yes, Reaver, but Killian – is – alive. He's alive," Elish spoke calmly to me. Such a perfect fucking statue of calm that fucking piece of shit was, but I saw his true colours, I saw the worry when Jade was in danger.

But no, no more worrying for that asshole. He got his partner back but where the fuck was mine? Getting raped every night by that fucking maniac of a scientist?

I couldn't handle it… I was helpless, I couldn't be helpless, not when it came to Killian. It was my job to protect him; it was my fucking job to make sure this shit never happened to him. I had failed.

I had failed to protect my dads. I had failed to take over Aras. I had failed to find out how to kill King Silas.

I was a failure, a failure.

"Jade, you will take the raver and the dog… and wait for us at the edge of the town. Now, Jade."

Right here, in this spot Perish had raped Killian. My Killian, my boy who had just started getting his mind back after being tormented by those fucking chimeras.

Tormented by MY family.

Another squeak and a crunch as I broke another tooth but my jaw kept clenching. My hands kept clawing at the wall, trying anything I could to get rid of this burning pain inside of my chest. It was filling me with heat, an overwhelming urge to do something.

I had to do something.

Then Elish's quiet voice. "Run, take the dog, tell him to continue on Killian's trail and run, Reaver. I have no one for you to kill to stem this rage you feel inside of you. I have nothing to give you. So run ahead, kill whoever or whatever you–"

"I don't need you telling me what to do!" I suddenly roared. I took a step towards Elish and to my surprise he took a step back. "*I am* the fucking Reaper, Elish. *I am* the clone of the man who destroyed the world. I give *you* orders not the other way around!" I snarled, not even aware of what I was saying, or understanding why I was saying it.

"You are MY creation!" I yelled, feeling a heat start to come to my hands. Instantaneously the same heat travelled up my arms and started gathering in the middle of my chest. "I own you! All of you! Every-single-fucking–"

The words kept flowing from my mouth, rolling off of my tongue like they were made of oil. Each one formed perfectly before spilling from my lips like a rockslide. I had no control over what I was saying. I was babbling, I knew I was…

Then a roaring inside of my ears. No, a buzzing… a buzzing around me. It came with the heat that I felt coat my body like a bad sunburn. It smelled… familiar, a stale almost chemical smell I recognized from when I would walk past Dek'ko dump sites, it made my chest burn. I didn't know…

"REAVER!" Elish suddenly roared. He grabbed me but suddenly recoiled away like I was burning hot. I heard him swear and look around for something.

I kept talking; I kept walking towards him as my lips moved. The deafening roar inside of my ears seemingly splitting my mind in half. The lights started to go out, one by one, places inside of my head that Killian once lit with his lantern snuffing themselves into darkness.

Only white haze and the building of pressure on my temples.

So much pressure.

I felt like I was going to explode.

Elish grabbed the only thing in his reach: his assault rifle on his back. He quickly took it into his arms, and without hesitation, he pointed it at

Reaver.

The man, full into his madness, was nothing but a radiant illumination, a brilliant white light that every surviving person before the Fallocaust had seen before their death. A light that contained in it a blinding fire that could melt steel like it was soft rubber. A fire that swept the terrain, burning everything to cinders for miles around. Where the fire did not reach, the radiation did the rest, dooming all that once lived to death or equal madness.

A light that had killed the world.

Elish pulled the trigger. Reaver's head snapped back and a spray of blood suddenly painting the crumbled wall behind him. All at once the light faded – but not the danger.

Without pause, even though the boy was still pouring out the last remains of the sestic radiation, Elish picked him up and ran out of the house.

He spotted Jade, the half-raver, and the dog walking down the road.

"RUN!" Elish suddenly yelled. "Get out of the town. RUN!"

Jade turned around in shock, immediately he took a step to run towards Elish but with a quick shout of *NO!* Jade turned around and started to run as fast as he could out of the small cluster of buildings, the half-raver and the dog running in front of him.

Elish's chest burned as each boot slammed against the dry earth, mentally scanning through all of his lessons about the sestic radiation, trying to figure out just how long they had. It was instant in some stories, in others it took minutes, all he knew was that he had to get the boys out and quickly.

Then a flash. As the sestic radiation pressed into the wood, into the metal and the pavement, it reached critical mass. An explosion behind Elish sounded and then a burning heat that made the assault rifle on his back become boiling hot.

'When it is concentrated it will explode into white fire, burning everything around it to cinders. Though in those ashes my radiation will remain to preserve the world and make it grey. That is what I was born with; that is what is inside of me.' Silas had once said.

In front of Elish the black trees, the telephone and light poles suddenly became illuminated, a washed out light like an overexposed photo. They glowed and blinded the chimera to the point where he had to hide his eyes.

Then the explosion, the explosion that Elish knew was the house he had just run from. He lowered his head, and kept on running as the debris flew past him, white fire eating every last shred of it alive.

CHAPTER 54

Reno

GARRETT WAS CHAIN SMOKING AGAIN AND I WAS right there beside him. Our ashtray was overflowing to the point where Chally had two out for us now. It seemed like all we had been doing for the past several days was smoking and stressing out.

My fiancé had told Silas that Sky's O.L.S was inside of Perish's brain, that was a hard thing to swallow but I didn't know enough about Sky or the chimeras to know if that was a bad thing or not. I didn't know what the fuck was going on; I had to trust that Garrett did.

I just knew that Killian was in grave danger, that though Perish might love my friend, he wasn't really Perish anymore. He was, as Garrett put it, two mismatched puzzle pieces being forced together. Perish was out of his mind, and with the radiation inside of him, he was literally a time bomb.

So we had been trying to get a hold of Elish, dialling his remote phone over and over trying to find him. Both of us had been taking turns, we dialled that damn number at least ten times an hour even when Garrett was supposed to be sleeping for work.

King Silas was out of Skyfall, in Cardinalhall where he was probably busy torturing Nero.

Sanguine had saved our asses with that.

"He isn't on our side though, not fully," Garrett murmured to me. I had just commented on the demon-chimera's clever distraction when Silas was getting ready to send out the cavalry to find Perish. "Elish made that clear, but he agrees with me that we cannot kill Silas. He would also not sell out Elish, this I know for sure."

I took an inhale of my cigarette; drug powder, loose smokes, and half-empty boxes of food surrounded us. Chally was in the kitchen trying to clean up after us, but the stress around the apartment was apparent. We were calling in Luca tonight to help the kid; we were both acting like pigs right now.

There was another faint dial tone and a long sigh as Garrett put the remote phone down.

"How are you so sure he won't?" I asked. "You guys all seem to have so much trust in one another and yet everyone is so fucking underhanded."

My fiancé considered this for a moment. He tapped his cigarette against the ashtray before resting his chin on his hand. He blew the silver smoke out of his mouth before dashing it again.

"Elish and I see it as an advantage to know each and every one of our brothers. He recently has become even more skilled at this with his empath husband. We know our brothers and we know which ones we can trust and which will deceive us. Sanguine might be slippery but he will never betray us." Garrett's eyes travelled to the window. It was dark out now, another day had passed without us reaching Elish and Reaver. "Jack is the one we have to worry about the most. He's close to King Silas and loyal to his king and his job. Unfortunately for us, he's Sanguine's ex-lover and they still fling it around when they're bored. I don't trust Sanguine not to slip information to him, and quite frankly, I don't trust Sanguine to not do this prematurely."

"Sounds complicated," I mumbled. "How does your mind not explode? Aren't you like... tired?"

Garrett laughed and I smiled, not because what I said was funny but because I still loved making him laugh.

He leaned over and kissed my cheek before leaning down and taking a hit of the china white. Yeah, we had been doing that a lot too. I had corrupted my fiancé. He might do a bump of coke here or there with the liquor, but influencing him to do the drugs was all me. He had kicked his own habit years ago apparently.

So I got my fiancé back on drugs.

Oh well, I never said I was a fucking boy scout.

"Yes, my head does hurt from time to time, it is a lot to remember," Garrett remarked then gave out a long sigh. Once again he picked up the phone and dialled the number and once again the angry tone thanked us for our failed efforts. "Oh, lutra... I'm so worried. Elish is either going to praise me or wring my neck. I… just… this is serious, so serious. Sky is dangerous, I know you do not understand this, but Sky is…"

I looked at him before giving his leg a loving rub. Garrett wiped his face with his hands and shook his head. "Sky could kill a lot of people, Reno, including Killian. I had no choice. Please understand I had no choice. Silas knows Sky. He loved Sky dearly; he can handle this better than we can. I'm afraid Lycos's deception plunged Elish to dark waters. I fear he's over his head with this new development."

I took some more of the powdered china white and leaned back. I put my head on Garrett's shoulder and watched another plume of smoke escape from his lips. "So what is Perish trying to do? Or Sky anyway? Is he just wandering around with Killian?"

Garrett was quiet for a moment before he rose and picked up his laptop. I watched as he started clicking folders and searching documents. Eventually he put the laptop on his lap and started pointing out things I didn't understand. "I don't know. I just know with that O.L.S, he is a crazy person right now. Stress is what releases the radiation, stress and sestic radiation have an odd and unique relationship. When the host is stressed out he can release it without being aware of it. Silas has his under control, and after the first and some of the second generations, he took out the genes he isolated that gave us that ability." Garrett highlighted some text, but it might've well been Mexican to me. "Perish is unstable and at any point he could explode."

Something suddenly occurred to me. "Wait, you're saying he could start another Fallocaust?"

When Garrett shook his head my shoulders slouched from relief. I didn't even realize I had tensed up.

"No, Silas was able to concentrate his sestic radiation when he killed the world. He was able to concentrate the radiation into a small area, no one knows where. He released it until the area he was in was full to the point of bursting, then, as the legend goes, Sky pressed a button and all of the concentrated radiation exploded. Not just Skyfall Island, not just what was British Columbia, the entire world was coated in it."

"But he saved Skyfall?" I asked. "How?"

"Because born immortals can clear it away too," Garrett responded.

Well, that was new. "They can?"

Garrett nodded. "Yes, Silas can absorb small amounts back into himself. It may kill him but he can. He cleared it away from Skyfall hundreds of years ago. I wouldn't be surprised if Perish and Sky helped him do it as well."

My eyes widened before suddenly I jumped. I hadn't even realized the cigarette I was holding had burned down to the filter. I flicked it into the ashtray before lighting another one. "Could he like… save the world that way? Like reverse Fallocaust?"

Garrett shook his head. "No, it's easier to release than it is to absorb. Which is why I'm sure he must have had Sky and Perish's aid when he was clearing away Skyfall."

"Which brings me to my other question." I tried to read the spread sheets and Word documents that Garrett was looking over but I still wasn't having much luck. "I can understand having one genetically-fucked born immortal, but how did he manage to find two more?"

Garrett pressed the buttons on the phone again; in the distance I could hear Chally in the kitchen putting dishes in the dishwasher. "That I do not know. Unfortunately there are secrets the king insists on keeping to himself. We were forbidden from speaking of Perish as a born immortal. When he brought Perish back and put him into the family we had to keep up the belief that he was just another chimera. No one who knew the truth spoke of it and no one asked questions."

"Oh shit!" Garrett suddenly exclaimed, about the same time my jaw dropped to the floor.

It was fucking ringing!

Then there was a clicking and a rustling of movement. I gawked at the phone, my mouth open and my pulse racing like I had just done an eight ball.

Garrett put the phone up to his ear. "Elish? Elish?"

"What is it, Garrett?" Elish's voice could be heard. Garrett's face was paled; I took his cigarette from him so he wouldn't burn himself.

"Elish, do you have them?" Garrett's asked.

The silence seemed like it was going to last forever. I was holding my breath and so was Garrett, even Chally behind us had gone silent.

"We have Jade… Perish is taking Killian to the plaguelands. We do not know why. Jade is sick but I am managing him until I can take him to Sidonius."

I had to put a hand over my mouth to stifle the groan. I couldn't believe he was taking Killian to the plaguelands. Nothing was there but horror and death, Killian would die from radiation poisoning. Though the lethal radiation barrier was slowly receding the greywastes only grew by like fifteen feet a year.

Garrett swore and wiped his hands over his face once again. "Elish, I must say this before the call disconnects. It's… it's worse than it looks. Perish is not implanted with his own O.L.S, he has Sky's inside of his brain. I found a confession by Lycos in his bunker. He thought he could just plant it into Perish's brain and he would suddenly become Sky. He was going to give Perish to Silas in hopes that would solve our problems with Silas's jealousy. Elish, Perish has his sestic abilities back. He… he could destroy the entire northern greywastes, Killian with it."

The silence descended on us like a thick blanket, bringing in its awkward darkness a weighted unease that made me feel like I had just gotten punched in the gut. I didn't know what was going to happen, what Elish was going to do, or if Reaver was listening to this entire conversation.

"You're sure?" Elish's voice broke through the almost solid tension around us. His cold voice sounded like a thunder crack in the middle of a deserted city.

"Yes, brother… I'm sure. I saw the video myself," Garrett said back. This time I did grab his hand, in response he clamped down on it like a metal trap. "What do you want me to do?"

"There is little you can do…" I swallowed hard at that comment. *"Reaver has been unstable. He is tapping into his own sestic abilities. No one was hurt but I had to dispatch him. I am not looking forward to telling him this news."*

Reaver could do this shit too? I guess that was obvious since he was a clone, but god damn why didn't they remove his abilities? Reaver was the most crazy and psycho out of all of them.

Without realizing it, my mind brought me back to the conversation I'd had with Silas on the balcony. When he had told me that Reaver was a danger to Killian, that only Silas could control him and teach him what he needed to know.

What if he was right?

Perish was a sestic radiation machine and so was Reaver… Perish was extremely unstable, but fuck, I had seen Reaver after Nero had raped him. Reaver had been really fucking unstable and this was proving it.

A chorus of swear words filled the room as the dead tone sounded from the remote phone. Garrett slammed it down on the coffee table and pinched the inner corners of his eyes with his fingers.

"This is a mess, Reno," Garrett whispered. I lit him a cigarette and put a rolled up fifty dollar bill into his hand. "We have two sestic bombs of radiation walking the greywastes and the plaguelands? Why would he be taking Killian to the plaguelands? This doesn't make sense."

When he didn't immediately go for the drugs, I obliged myself and leaned back against the couch with him. I put a hand on his knee and shifted myself close to him.

"I don't know…" I said honestly. "But if it's Sky's memories… what if no one knows because only Sky knows? His memories would be from like… when did he die?"

Garrett thought for a second, before leaning over and tapping around on the laptop some more, the smoke dangling from his lips adding to our already hazy apartment.

"I think he died about fifty years after the Fallocaust. I am unsure. Silas just never spoke to us about this." Garrett thought for a second before seemingly dismissing the idea. "No, I wouldn't have files on him myself. Skytech was in its infancy when Sky died and their record keeping was shoddy at best back then." He nodded slowly. "But I believe you're right. No one knows because no one was alive back then, except Silas."

"So we're fucked then? No one has any way of finding out why Perish is taking Killian to the plaguelands?" I wiped my nose and sniffed the drugs up into my brain. I hated that I was here sitting on my ass doing drugs while Reaver was in the greywastes miserable. I wanted to be with my bud, but I knew there was nothing I could do but slow them down.

"No one except Silas," Garrett said quietly. "Perhaps now that he knows it's Sky's O.L.S… he knows why? I do not–"

There was a knock on the door.

We both froze in place, immediately Garrett grabbed the remote phone and turned it off before putting it into one of the side table drawers. The two of us both rose to our feet as Chally came walking out of the kitchen, drying his hands on a hand towel.

I didn't think much of it; we were expecting Luca, and Teaguae had been wanting to discuss work stuff. Well, I hope whoever it was didn't mind all the drugs out. Chally hadn't…

As the door opened we were greeted by King Silas beaming at the two of us. Sanguine and Drake were both behind him with their hands behind their backs. All three were staring at us with the same smiles and the same looks, though I knew each one held smiles for different reasons.

"Garrett, my love." Like a hot knife over an ice block, he glided into the apartment, his sengil and cicaro behind him. Chally closed the door and gave us both paled, fearful looks before he disappeared back into the kitchen.

I tried to swallow the lump inside of my throat but it ended up getting caught halfway down. I coughed instead and plastered a smile on my face.

Garrett, I could tell, was just as nervous. "Silas, I thought you were in… in Cardinalhall." I saw Garrett looking at something on Silas's sleeve. I looked too and saw that his sleeves were covered in a grey chalk and his hands had bits of what looked like hardened concrete on it.

"Oh… shit," Garrett moaned. He put a hand on his head and shook it, before turning him away. "How long?"

I looked at my fiancé confused; I saw his eyebrow twitch over his tense face. He suddenly looked like he was in physical pain. I didn't understand why.

"Until I miss him, so quite a while," Silas said, his tone dropping. He held up his sleeve and smiled at it, before his eyes flickered up to mine. "Do you know what this is from, Reno?"

I shook my head like an idiot, my feet firmly planted on the floor. Even though he was rather nice to me the last time I saw him… he still scared the fuck outta me.

On silent feet that knew no noise, Silas walked up to me and held his sleeve up for me to see. A crisp purple dress shirt with silver buttons and black cuffs; the entire cuff and his hand holding the thin hardened concrete.

"Just so you don't think I have no retaliation against my immortal chimeras," Silas whispered. He leaned into me and kissed my neck; my heart clenched. "When they displease me, I encase them in concrete for as long as I see fit. Tell me, Reno, my second born's fiancé and my dear dear friend, can you imagine what it would be like for an immortal to be covered from head to toe in concrete? I put in air holes for their nose so they can breathe, and sometimes I even put in a hole for their mouth so I can be lulled to sleep by their screaming."

Jesus fucking christ…

"I keep them in there, for years sometimes, listening to them slowly starve to death, only to resurrect right back where they were. Trapped in their own tombs, unable to move, unable to see, unable to do anything but breathe and scream." Silas pulled away from me and I saw a burning glint in his eyes. "If I am feeling generous, I let their former partners visit them, though there is never that much catching up… just endless pleading." He narrowed his eyes and reached a hand up to touch my face. I was frozen to the fucking floor so I made no move to get away from him. Every word that came from his mouth stunned me like it was a poisoned barb.

"Remember that, yes? Remember that…" Silas turned around and I looked behind him towards Garrett. My body got another shockwave of anxiety when I saw the look of terror on his face.

Silas noticed it and glided up to Garrett. He patted his cheek before taking his chin into his hands. He gave Garrett's trembling lips a quick kiss.

"So… Nero's gone then?" Garrett said through a raspy voice. "He… he really raped Reaver?"

Silas pulled his hand away from Garrett's chin like it had suddenly became hot. "Yes," the king replied. "Nero had my Reaver, and not only did he rape him, beat on him, and humiliate his future king… he let him escape."

I looked past Silas to where Sanguine was. The blood-eyed chimera was watching his king with that squinty smile on his face, his hands still held behind his back in his usual prim and proper position. He had no reassurances to offer me; I just hoped he would do something if this was Silas's way of putting Garrett in concrete.

"Did he?" Garrett said quietly. "I am sorry that happened, Master. I know you wanted to take Reaver for yourself first."

"Indeed, I did," King Silas murmured. He turned around and I saw his face tense and angry, but then, like someone had switched discs on a Discman, he suddenly smiled. The king walked towards Sanguine, and oddly, he pet his hair back. Sanguine smiled at him and tilted his head towards his touch, not unlike what Biff used to do.

"Garrett, I need to speak to you in private, where this greywaster cannot hear us. It so happens that at the same time I have been rather busy, too busy to satisfy the needs of my sengil and cicaro. Sanguine, Drake… show Reno a good time while your king speaks with his second born."

I was certain that I had just suffered a stroke. No way in hell could Silas be insinuating what I think he was. I looked at Garrett but he just stared at me, sweat glistening on top of his forehead.

Sanguine then took my arm and started pulling me towards the bedroom. I stumbled forward and looked around confused.

"W-what?" was all I managed to say.

Garrett watched me go. Silas looked rather pleased with himself.

"It's… it's okay, lovely. Have a good time with them. Do-do not feel badly, this is… normal for our family. Enjoy yourself, lutra." Garrett's mouth moved, he was saying those words but it looked like he had turned into a robot in front of me. He was gaping at me, seemingly shocked by this entire situation, just as shocked as I was.

Sanguine pulled me into the bedroom and shut the door, Drake behind him who was turning on the lamp beside the bed.

"Sanguine… what the fuck is… what do we do…? I–" I pulled away as he tried to kiss me and shook my head. "No. What's Silas going…" I gasped as Sanguine put his hands down my pants, before his lips started lightly pecking my neck.

"Sanguine!" I gasped and pulled away. My face flushed red, all of this was happening way too fast and I had no idea what I was supposed to do. I looked behind me and got another shock as I saw Drake stepping out of his tight leather pants, a visible bulge showing through a black thong. As the pet walked towards me I tried to pull away from Sanguine again. The demon-chimera growled at this and let out a low chuckle.

Sanguine grabbed my shoulder and wrenched me towards him. As he continued to kiss my neck, Drake appeared by my other shoulder and started kissing me too.

I flushed even harder, my heart racing and my pulse rising higher and higher. I didn't know what the fuck I was supposed to do. In all respects having two hot guys all over me was a dream, but this was confusing the fuck out of me. What did Silas want with Garrett?

"Mmm… Drakonius, it seems our little Otter needs to relax," Sanguine murmured. He rubbed his palm against my dick and started playing with it. It felt good, fuck, of course it did.

Drake slipped away from my vision and the next thing I felt was him unbuttoning my pants. Sanguine held onto my shoulders as the cicaro pulled my pants down and then my boxer briefs.

"He's uncut!" Drake exclaimed. I sucked in a breath as I felt him grab onto my still soft dick, and felt the air sting the head as he retracted my foreskin.

Then he licked the head. Shit… that was it for me.

"Oh, look at that. I wonder if that will be fixed," Sanguine mused. He rubbed my shoulders and started kissing and sucking on my neck, each kiss sending a spark down to my gut. I was quickly starting to not care about what was going on outside these doors. My mind was telling me with solid assurance that Garrett was fine... that everything would be... okay.

Then the mouth... fuck, he put his mouth fully over it. I looked down and saw my dick disappearing into the orange-eyed cicaro's mouth. The entire thing. The pet swallowed it before pulling his lips away with a smirk. He stared up at me with a smile.

Making eye contact the entire time, Drake stuck his tongue out and gave it a long lick, then swirled the tongue over my head and down the shaft. Then, once again, he took it into his mouth and started generously sucking me off.

"There, see? Nothing bad," Sanguine purred.

I heard scraping of one of Garrett's stuffed chairs he kept in the room. I saw the chair out of the corner of my eye, then a hand on my leg. "Put your leg up."

I did what he asked, one foot on the chair the other on the ground. I looked down and saw Drake eagerly sucking my dick, and a moment later, Sanguine separating my cheeks.

I expected a finger, so when I felt the sengil's warm tongue flick around my opening I almost fell down. Without hesitation, Sanguine started licking and lapping my hole, Drake still busy working my front.

This... this was something else. My body was on fire, my chest loosening up by the second but I was so lightheaded I was afraid I was going to pass out. I felt like I was going to fall; I wanted to lie down but I couldn't move. Sanguine was like a devil, licking and teasing my hole, and as his tongue roved deeper, I felt it start to penetrate me.

"Fuck..." My hands dug into the chair to steady me, my other hand resting on Drake's head. This was too much, it was too much... I didn't think I was going to last long but I didn't want it to end. Only in my wildest dreams did I ever think I'd be worked over like this, it was almost too much to take in.

Finally, when my mind felt like it was going to boil over, Sanguine removed his tongue, though Drake had no desire to stop licking my dick. I shifted to pull myself away from the cicaro's mouth when Sanguine's hand planted itself on my shoulder, then he put another hand on the small of my back and put pressure on it.

No, no, he wasn't done. I made no move to resist, the sengil had done a good job not just prepping me, but making me want it. I leaned back and grabbed onto the chair. I took a deep breath, and as I inhaled, I felt pressure against my hole.

I grunted and tightened my grip on Drake as I felt the head of Sanguine's cock penetrate me. I immediately started urging Drake to move his head back and forth, my hips rocking just slightly as the sengil pushed his full length into me.

A moan broke Sanguine's lips and a small grunt so close to my ear I could feel his hot breath. With Garrett and Silas forgotten by my horny, sex-driven mind, I started moving my hips into Drake, and after a few good pushes, I felt Sanguine start to thrust into me.

"Oh... shit, yes," I groaned. There was a tight suction below me as Drake locked his lips together, behind me Sanguine found his rhythm and started fucking me. Both of us still standing, me with one foot resting on the chair, the other on the ground, Drake on his knees tasting and sucking every inch of my cock.

Sanguine put his own foot beside mine and grabbed onto my shoulders. He started picking up his speed, roughly pounding into me like he seemed to know I liked. Garrett did me the same way. God damn, I loved how chimeras fucked.

And the chimera knew how to fuck, but, of course, he did he was like seventy years old or something. No doubt he had been fucking chimeras since he was fifteen. Like all of them they seemed to know the right spots to hit, when to slow down, when to speed up. I felt like a virgin in front of these guys, some untrained peasant who'd only known what sex was through porn movies and the oral fun I'd had with Reaver.

It wasn't just Sanguine fucking me though. Drake and Sanguine were both working like a team. They worked on me like they were performing a play. When I felt like I was getting close Drake withdrew his mouth in favour for my balls, taking each one into his mouth and lightly sucking on them as Sanguine slowed down his thrusts to just a slow jolt of his hips. Once my threshold had gone back up, it was back to the rough fucking and hard licking that they had been doing before. For what seemed like forever, they both drew me to my peak, only to slowly let me back down.

Then it was time, finally. The burning in my chest was roasting me alive as my body started to reach its threshold for what seemed like the tenth time. When Sanguine's hips didn't slow and Drake's mouth didn't withdraw, I gave out what could only be a cry of relief. I braced myself on the chair and closed my eyes as Sanguine's thrusts became quicker, hard stabs into my sensitive and filled ass. One after another, each hammer blow pushing me closer and closer to the edge.

I let out a loud cry, holding onto the chair for dear life as I came hard. Sanguine stayed behind me, jamming that fucking cock of his in and out of me, and as he grunted and moaned, I realized he was cumming too. I held onto the chair and the pet's head and squeezed my eyes tight, unable to stem the moaning cries spilling from my lips.

I came, a lot, it wouldn't end. Every time I thought I'd left the last wave of intense pleasure, another one was right behind it. When my long and exhausting orgasm was done, I was on my hands and knees on the floor, Sanguine still thrusting his stiff cock inside of me.

He withdrew and I thought they were going to leave me, but Sanguine pulled on my arm and the next thing I knew he was pushing me onto the bed. Drake was standing beside him, his cock long and thick, the head of it pink with lust and shining with precum. The cicaro had some of my cum on his face, a bit of it dripping down his mouth which he was licking up with his tongue.

I leaned against the headboard panting; my cock was soft from the long ordeal. I wasn't a fucking chimera like them who could go a thousand times, one after the other. I was just a normal human who got exhausted. Though they didn't give a damn about that, obviously.

Without giving me a moments rest, Drake leaned down and separated my legs, no words escaped his lips, no comments, he just leaned down, and like Sanguine, started licking my hole, devouring the cum that Sanguine had left behind.

Sanguine put a hand on my knee and pushed it back. He looked at me and smirked before we started making out on the bed.

"I always enjoyed that fire he had inside of him, that unsatiatable lust," Silas said quietly, a glass of rum in his hand which he swirled. The king looked over at Garrett, taking in and treasuring the anxiety radiating off of him. "He fucked me into the ground in Aras. I loved how he never held back a single moan. Tell me, love. Have you made him moan that loudly? Sanguine and Drake make quite the team."

Garrett stared at the scene happening in front of him, the small table lamp in his bedroom illuminating Reno, Sanguine, and Drake but shrouding the two of them standing in the doorway.

Garrett looked ill, to the point where Silas wondered if he was going to throw up.

"Y-yes," Garrett stammered. "We're still getting to know each other's bodies but we're very s-s-sexually compatible. He's such a giving lover. I... I do love that about him."

The king smiled thinly and put a hand on Garrett's shoulder, there was a light *clink* as he set the glass of rum down.

"You're so tense, Garrett." Silas's voice suddenly dropped, and with it Silas could hear Garrett's pulse speed up even more. "It just goes to show how unlike Elish you are, more like Nero when it comes to your emotions. Nero begged me, Garrett, begged me as the concrete was creeping up to his mouth. He was pale and sweaty; his entire body was trembling as he begged my forgiveness."

Garrett was shaking, even his chin was quivering as he watched Reno lying on the bed with Sanguine. He was making out with Sanguine like he hadn't a care in the world, Drake between his legs doing what he does best.

"I... I am s-saddened to hear that, but Nero did... did deserve it."

There was silence between the two.

"Garrett – do you think I'm an idiot?"

Garrett stiffened, only his left hand moving up to his face. He clasped his hand over his mouth, his eyes wide and his heart thrashing inside of his chest. Without wanting to, he looked over to his king and slowly shook his head.

"N-n-no," he stammered.

King Silas glanced over to the activity taking place at the other end of the room, before fixing his emerald eyes back on his second born. "I look past a lot of things, Garrett. You all just don't think I do because I am not some boastful ego-maniac who has to shove it in my creation's faces every time I do something nice for them. I have been forgiving, Garrett, because I preferred to have Reaver on the run because *it just amuses me so much.*"

Silas's tone dropped. "Garrett Sebastian Dekker..."

Garrett swallowed; his own green eyes fixed forward, staring unblinking at Reno. Drake was riding him now, Reno's deep, lustful moans filling the room.

"I saw the video. I saw the three masked men enter the hanger while my beautiful Reaver was being brutally raped by Nero. I saw the limp on the third one, the same limp Reno still has. Reno and two others helped Reaver escape. All of this during the time you two broke up."

Like a rubber band snapping, Garrett's vision shot to Silas. Not able to handle the stress, Garrett turned to walk out of the doorway they were standing under, but Silas grabbed onto his arm. He clenched it hard and glared at Garrett.

"Now, Garrett. I'm willing to forgive you for not telling me about this sooner, and I'm also willing to forgive you for supplying the fucking Falconer which conveniently happened to have its tracker disabled for two days – Do you know why I am going to forgive you, lovely?" Silas dug his fingers into Garrett's arm; white shreds of skin could be seen coming off around his fingernails.

"I-I'm sorry," Garrett stammered. His shaking hand was still being held over his mouth like he couldn't believe what was happening. It was as if a nightmare had descended from the heavens. One that brought forth every fear Garrett had since he first fell in love with Reno. "I-I love him. I just – I didn't know what to do."

Silas shushed him, though his nails were still digging deep into Garrett's flesh. "Yes, yes love. I understand. You love Reno and when you love the men in your life, I know you love them with all your soul. That is why I myself love you, Garrett. Though you are a weak, pathetic coward, if there is one redeeming quality about you it is that, unlike so many of your brothers, you love with all of your heart, no holds barred."

The king pulled on Garrett's arm as the black-haired chimera avoided all eye contact.

"Garrett, look at me."

A wave of what looked like physical pain washed over Garrett's face. He stared at the floor, Reno's moans still sounding from the corner of the bedroom, getting deeper and closer together as Drake road him to his peak. All three of the men shrouded in darkness but for the single lamp on the side table.

"Garrett, don't make me ask you twice."

The hand that was still covering Garrett's mouth slowly lowered. And with eyes that held in them a pain that no mortal could know, the pain only someone who had lost boyfriend after boyfriend, fiancé after fiancé,

Garrett Dekker turned and looked at Silas.

His face dissolved as soon as he saw the anger on King Silas's face; his eyes filled and his hand once again covered his mouth, unable to hold back the agony threatening to burst from his body.

"Forgive me, please. Please, Silas… don't take him away from me." Garrett swayed, before sinking to his knees. His head shook back and forth. "I've been good. Out of all of your creations I have never given you trouble. You've said that to me."

Silas stared down at him; his face relaxed and calm but his eyes seared Garrett's flesh. He glared at Garrett as his second born grovelled in front of him, even going as far as to take his hand and grip it.

Silas and Garrett both looked towards the bedroom as Reno let out a gasping cry. They saw Reno, Sanguine on top of him now, grab onto the sengil's backside and grip it hard as Sanguine slammed himself down over and over on him. Below, three of Drake's fingers had disappeared into Reno's ass, the cicaro now licking and sucking on Reno's chest as he fingered him.

"Garrett, I have no time to play games with you. No time to take Reno into my custody and torture information out of him. My mind is elsewhere right now and not into tormenting and mutilating that stupid greywaster." Silas's tone dropped another octave. He put a hand on Garrett's cheek and petted it; it was now wet, soaked in Garrett's pleading tears.

"Reno has already cum twice and I have commanded Sanguine to keep riding him until he goes a third time." Garrett looked up at Silas confused; his face holding both horror and perplexity as the king spoke.

"The third time he orgasms, in the throes of it, I have already ordered Sanguine to slash his throat–"

"What!? Silas–" In a movement of pure stealth, Silas grabbed Garrett's mouth and held his hand over it. He kneeled onto the floor so he was face-to-face with Garrett.

Silas's face was aflame and his grip tight, not a shred of empathy and humanity to be found.

But there was never any to begin with, perhaps hundreds of years ago when he was still human, but now? But now… no, he was a monster and Garrett knew it.

Which is why Garrett's chest rocked, his brain jammed, and his stomach threatened to throw him over the edge. The chimera in that moment felt like he was going to have a nervous breakdown. He didn't know what to do. What could he do? There was no winning situation here, there was nothing to be done but try and salvage what he could.

And the most important thing to him in his world... was Reno Nevada.

"I will not play games with you, Garrett," Silas hissed at him. His grip tightened around Garrett's mouth. "I have no time for such idiocy. So I will make this simple: Tell me where Reaver is, or Sanguine will slash Reno's throat. The order is already there, Garrett, and only you can stop it. Tell me right now, or else Chally will be cleaning up the blood spray on the ceiling."

Sanguine? Garrett couldn't move. Like King Silas's words held a physical weight, he keeled over, his back bowed and his head hung low. It wasn't until Sanguine let out a sharp groan that he looked over to the intense acts that were still going on.

Would you do it, Sanguine? Even though – you know everything? As Garrett's eyes took in the heated sex between Reno and the other two, he knew that mercy was an impossibility. If Sanguine resisted, his loyalty would be questioned. No, Sanguine had no emotional attachments to Reno, and in his eyes Reno's job had been done; he had gotten the keycard.

Sanguine would kill Reno, that Garrett knew was true.

A wave of dizzy nausea crept up Garrett's throat like a bloated worm. He felt like he was leaving his body, flying up and through the ceiling far away from this situation, far away from Skyfall. *No, this couldn't be happening... dear god. Elish, what do I do? I... I can't lose him.*

Then a loud moan. Garrett's eyes shot back to Reno and he saw a flicker of silver in Sanguine's leather boot. The silver of one of his hollow daggers that he always kept on his person. Silas had never been one to lie, but seeing the reality right in front of him drew Garrett even closer to the edge.

Reno was thrusting into Sanguine. The sengil rising up and down with his hands brushing dangerously close to the top of his boot. Drake's face had changed in this time as well, and Garrett realized that the cicaro was in on it too. The orange-eyed, curly-haired chimera was watching Sanguine with a grisly smile on his face, his fingers thrusting in and out of Reno like he was trying to accelerate him to his peak.

"You're hesitating?" Silas withdrew his hands from Garrett's face, his eyes narrowing. He rose to standing, and when Garrett grabbed onto his shirt, the king wrenched it away.

"Sanguine… do it."

"NO!" Garrett suddenly screamed. As reality hit him like an arctic ice flow, he jumped to his feet and ran towards Sanguine, just as the sengil was reaching to his boot.

With no more hesitations, no more buying time, Garrett tackled Sanguine and together the two of them tumbled to the floor. Swiftly, the sengil pushed Garrett off of him with a snarl, but not a moment later, Garrett had Sanguine's knife in his hands.

"Plaguelands!" The words came out as a strangled cry, a desperate noise that carried on it a sadness no one but Garrett truly understood.

He fell to his knees, and with a cry, he slammed the knife down onto the carpet. "He's going to the plaguelands. Perish has Killian, they're going there and Reaver is chasing them."

"GARRETT!" Reno suddenly cried. He scrambled to his feet, looking around in confusion; the only man out of the five who didn't know what was happening.

But what happened next wasn't what Garrett was expecting at all.

Silas stared at Garrett like he had just uttered black magic. He stared at him in a way that made Garrett's heart palpitate; the mood around them quickly plunging into an even deeper darkness.

"P-plaguelands? Perish… Perish is taking Killian to the plaguelands? Up north? The highway near Melchai?" Silas's tone dropped to a harsh whisper, an uneasy anxiety-riddled rasp that made even Reno shut up.

Garrett nodded, and to everyone's shock, Silas stumbled back, almost falling until Sanguine helped steady him. The king looked stricken and pale, an uncharacteristic flow of anxiety radiating off of his body.

"That can't… he…" Silas took a step back, shaking his head. "We need to stop him. We need to stop him. Garrett, he's taking Killian to Sky's old lab. It has the…"

Garrett shook his head, tears streaming down his face. He rose to his feet. "What? What does it have there?"

Silas looked at him, his lips tightened. The king stalked up to Garrett and grabbed his shirt; his teeth clenched tight and his green eyes wide.

Garrett could only stare back, bewildered.

"It has the machine we used to condense our radiation, you fucking fool. He's taking Killian to that lab, ground zero of the Fallocaust. Sky's O.L.S is trying to make Perish re-enact the Fallocaust, YOU FUCKING

IDIOT!" Silas screamed. He raised his hand and smacked Garrett across the room, the chimera flying backwards and crashing into the side table.

"Sanguine, evacuate the family. Get Ellis on the phone. Immunity or not, take them to the Dead Islands. Get them as far away from ground zero as you can. NOW! Command them not to return until my signal. And get Elish, he won't argue. Tell him… tell him Jade's in danger and do not let him question me."

"But… the chimeras are immune…" Garrett said weakly.

"The sestic radiation can condense and explode, especially that much of it. I had entire cities melt hundreds of miles away from ground zero. It can happen anywhere it's gathering. I won't risk the family, not even Jade," Silas said.

There was a flurry of activity around Silas as Sanguine and Drake dressed, though the king was still staring forward in shock, like he was in a stunned stupor.

"We must hurry. We must hurry." Silas sunk to his knees, his face the colour of tallow.

"My love… my love is going to destroy the world… again."

CHAPTER 55

Kiki and Sanguine

"YOU CAN SPEND AS MUCH TIME WITH HIM AS YOU LIKE. I will tell the thiens you have free access to my lovely back room, Kincade. Come here at your will and visit him. You can even hold his hand, though I would watch his grip. He seems to be slipping already and with one squeeze, he would break those fragile little fingers."

"When... when will you let him out, Master Silas?"

"Oh, Kiki... you will be nothing but bones by the time I let him taste the outside air."

The concrete was cold underneath Kiki's cheek but he was the closest he could possibly be to Nero so that was okay. The young chimera closed his eyes and squeezed Nero's hand, and knowing that he could hear him, he started talking to him in a subdued voice.

"And I made sure to feed your cats... Ares and Siris came over just yesterday to check in on me. It looks like Silas has no intentions of taking over the skyscraper but I was thinking of asking Ares and Siris to stay with me for a while. It's lonely without you," Kiki said.

He looked down at Nero's pale hand. It was the only thing sticking out of the large square of concrete, everything else past his wrist was encased in a sealed tomb. Only a half of an inch of space between Nero's dying body and then seven inches of concrete.

Kiki looked behind him and felt a cold shudder go through him when he saw the other concrete prisoners. Five of them, all immortal chimeras whose names were not allowed to be mentioned. All chimeras who, at one point in time, had made King Silas angry enough to forbid their very immortal existence. They were now locked inside their mental dungeons, starving and dying only to resurrect in the same maddening darkness.

And now Nero, the man that Kiki loved and admired more than anything, was doomed to the same fate. He would slowly starve inside of his eternal midnight and die, then emerge in the same blackness only to die again several days later. With no eyes, no voice, and nothing but a tube for his nose and a hand for Kiki to squeeze.

But Kiki knew he could hear him; Nero squeezed his hand whenever he asked. Nero even twisted Kiki's raccoon ring on his finger as if Nero wanted to make sure it was really him.

He had given me this ring because I was his little raccoon. He gave it to me and I knew it meant he liked me more than the others.

Kiki had stayed with him every night since it happened, only leaving to make sure all of Nero's pets were fed and to get something to eat. He would come back and tell Nero all about his day, even though when Nero was free he had often told Kiki to shut up. But the sengil knew his master didn't care right now; he was the only thing that was keeping Nero on the fringes of sanity.

So I will be here... for as long as I can be.

The young chimera, only sixteen years old, leaned down and kissed Nero's hand slowly before resting his cheek against it. He looked up at the grey concrete, finding it hard to believe that his master, in his entirety, was inside it.

"I... I heard from Sanguine that... it helps them when you tell them what day and time it is. He says it helps them stay in reality and not get too lost in their own minds," Kiki said quietly. "It's Wednesday and it's 12:30 pm. I'll tell you that every day if you wish." Nero squeezed his hand at this. Kiki smiled and squeezed back.

Though his smile turned into a frown before his lips disappeared into his mouth. He knew it wasn't appropriate to say it but he did anyway.

Kiki took a deep breath and twisted his raccoon ring around on his middle finger. "Why did you do it, Master? You must've known Silas would eventually find out... I wish I'd had the authority to tell you no. I thought you would know better." His brow creased as he thought back to those weeks in the Cardinalhall Mansion. It had been fun doing those things to Reaver but in the end... look at where they were.

"They tell me you deserve this but I can't stand to see you like this. It seems to go against the very fabric of the universe. You're a powerful beast, a god, and now you're..." Kiki flinched as Nero clenched his hand hard but he continued on, "And now you've been removed from my life. Master... I didn't want to tell you this but..."

Kiki took a second breath and ran his face down his hands. He closed his eyes and sniffed. "King Silas is sending me into the greywastes; he says I am going to be given to Theo to be his servant and cicaro. Theo, of all people. Theo's a mad hatter and Grant lets him get away with everything. Silas even says he filed his own teeth down to points."

Nero clenched Kiki's hand tight. The young chimera set his teeth and tried to resist the pain, but a moment later, he gasped and cried out as the brute chimera's grip became molten steel.

"I'm sorry. What can I say? I have no rank, Master. What King Silas says I have to do. Do you think I want to be given to him?" Kiki cried. He tried to pull his hand away but Nero wouldn't let him go.

"What can I do? There is nothing I can do..." Kiki's eyes started to burn. "I wasn't created to be a hero, Master. I was created to be a cicaro and a sengil. What can I do?"

The rough concrete met his face again as he leaned his forehead against the cold tomb. He moved his head to the left and saw the five other tombs standing in the frozen darkness. They were silent right now but usually at least one of them could be heard moaning or gasping for air. They must be sleeping or perhaps resurrecting inside of their coffins.

What can I do? Nero's grip loosened and Kiki slowly pulled his hand away, never taking his eyes off of the only piece of his master he had now.

There must be something I can do.

"Kiki?"

Kiki looked over his shoulder, a tall shadowed silhouette was in the door.

"Come to visit the living dead?" Kiki sniffed and rubbed Nero's hand caringly.

Sanguine nodded and pattered into the room, wearing coat tails today and a white cummerbund below his red bowtie. He silently walked over to Kiki and kneeled down beside Nero's hand. The sengil of Silas Dekker grazed his fingers along Nero's hand before looking up at the concrete brick.

"Hello, Nuky... are you feeling madness yet?"

Sanguine and Kiki both looked down and watched Nero's hand move until he successfully gave Sanguine the middle finger. The sengil-chimera chuckled before taking Nero's hand into both of his.

"He still has his sanity, Kiki, but it will not be for long. Soon he will stop responding to your voice. Soon he will even stop squeezing your hand. Nero and I both know this. We know what happens..." At the mention of him, Sanguine looked behind his back at a concrete tomb that was oddly covered in pink heart stickers. He smiled sadly before brushing Kiki's hair back.

"Do you have the strength to endure what this will put you through? Do you know what it's like knowing a loved one is in there?" Sanguine asked. A flicker of sadness came to his eyes and Kiki was sure he almost saw wetness.

"Nero is all I have, Sanguine," Kiki responded. "I love him."

"All sengils love their masters."

"I *really* love him... one day I want to marry him." The look Kiki had was that of any teenager gazing upon their first love; though Sanguine had been a teenager himself and he knew not to discount or belittle the boy's feelings. Chimera teenagers were hard enough to reason with but they became worse when you tried to downplay the love they were so sure they were feeling.

Jade's devotion to Elish said a lot about teenage love. It can be intense, overpowering, and chaotic... especially when the man you love is a ninety-one-year-old immortal chimera with too much pride.

Though it had taught Sanguine one thing – a young chimera in love was an unstoppable force, but one that could be used and manipulated.

Sanguine smiled; his eyes squinting as they so often did. He put a hand on Kiki's black hair and brushed it back.

The young man's brilliant eyes looked up at Sanguine, and the demon-chimera smiled even more inside of his head when he saw the deep pools of sadness that lay in each one.

"Walk with me, little one." Sanguine rose to his feet. Though he glanced to the concrete tomb that was covered in stickers and, while Kiki was getting up, he walked to it and gave it a kiss.

"I wonder if he knows... how close he is to Nero," Sanguine said, more to himself than Kiki, before turning from the tomb.

They left the room and walked down the elegant hallway full of paintings and sculptures, but to Kiki's surprise, when they went to the elevator, Sanguine pushed the button for the roof.

"Silas will be leaving Alegria and Skyfall shortly," Sanguine commented. His red eyes flicked up to the ceiling before the corners of his lips rose.

Kiki was quiet, only staring at his hands, imagining Nero's burly strong fingers slipping into his. He missed him and Kiki's mind was with his master, not what Sanguine was saying to him.

The elevator doors opened to the roof of Alegria. Sanguine stepped out onto the roof, his leather boots with a high heel clacking against the asphalt ground. Kiki watched him warily as the demon-chimera casually sauntered up to Silas's personal Falconer, his fingers flexing and waving like he was singing a tune inside of his head.

Kiki followed, though his orange eyes continued to look behind him just to make sure the elevator doors were going to stay open. He felt apprehension at being up this high with only Sanguine. Though the sengil had never harmed Kiki, he had heard enough stories about Sanguine to be wary.

Sanguine traced a finger along the plane's shiny black metal before grabbing onto the outside handle and sliding the door open, then he jumped inside.

Kiki quietly walked over to the Falconer and saw Sanguine opening up the several wooden crates that were always inside of the plane. They were full of supplies mostly: parachutes, survival food, powdered water, and pills and liquid to stem the radiation for any non-chimeras who might be travelling along.

"Yes, that will do…" Sanguine mumbled.

Kiki froze when Sanguine's eyes shot to him, it always seemed like the sengil was grabbing him with those red eyes. Corrupting and tainting him with nothing more than a blood-filled stare. The demon-sengil had a look to him that matched the calmed madness inside of his head. A madness that no one knew but the demon himself.

"Yes, this will certainly do."

CHAPTER 56

Killian

THE GREY SUN HAD STARTED TO SHINE THROUGH THE haze that covered the plaguelands, beams of light that shone through the overcast sky with a half-hearted brilliance. Like an underpaid worker, its attempts to burn the smoke fell short of anything that could be called sunlight. But it did try, though whether it was because it was its duty, or because it could do nothing else... I didn't know.

And as was my own duty, I carried on behind Perish. My feet soaked in blood and my lips so chapped my rough skin was coated in a thin, crusted layer of red. I had no more facial hair. It had fallen out, the same with the slaves. The only man out of all of us who still looked like a human was gliding ahead, long and sure steps like he couldn't get to his location fast enough.

I stayed in his wake, the slaves behind me plotting the best way to eat me. I could hear their voices in my head when the silence got too loud. Each and every one of them and the hundred others I could hear inside of my damaged mind, telling me again and again that I would taste nice.

I bet you would taste nice.

I'm not going anywhere.

Whatever you say.

I turned around and saw crimson spots behind me. Though the grey ash had caked itself against my bloodied boots I was still leaving behind a trail. This was familiar to me, though I didn't know how it was. I think at one point in my life I had left a blood trail for someone. I didn't know who though, every time I tried to think of what my life was like before

Perish the voices got angry at me.

The best meat is in the ass, just wash it good and take off that thick layer of skin – it's sweet and juicy. The next bit would be the thigh, and don't discount those ribs. If you can find a pressure cooker you'll be living like a king.

Live like a king – I lived with a king.

My boots scraped and I pivoted. I turned around with my eyes wide when I saw Danny approaching us. I hadn't even noticed he had fallen behind. He stumbled up to Perish; his face peeling in thick white sheets, the bright pink showing through like his skin was old blistered paint.

"We need to rest. Edward's ready."

Edward's ready.

Edward – is – ready.

Behind me I could hear thin rasping breaths, deep inhales that sounded like a suction after it had cleared all the water away. It was the sounds you would hear in a horror movie, when they would run into a pitch-black room only to realize they had trapped themselves inside with the monster

I turned around and slowly drew my gaze up to the slave.

Edward was on his knees, his head bowed and his shoulders moving up and down to accommodate his deep, scratching breaths. His clothing was stained grey with outlines of yellow pus from the sores that had burst all over his body. These sores had rotted straight through his skin, all the way down to the bone which shone in a brilliant white unsuited for this slate terrain.

The slave drew his remaining hand up to his face, and even in the throes of my own madness I felt myself take a step back from him.

Edward had chewed the tips of his own fingers off, this fact displayed on showcase as he put his index and middle finger into his mouth and bit down on them, long huffs of air escaping from his nostrils as his mouth chewed his own flesh. He looked at us as if confused; his eyes holding a thin yellowed film.

Perish handed me his assault rifle and I held it. He walked to Edward and knelt down beside him before reaching into his bag and grabbing a penlight.

"We were fascinated as all hell when we saw what the radiation was doing to the survivors," Perish said in a casual tone. I saw Danny's face twist and Teejay look away. I knew they didn't appreciate Perish's nonchalant attitude.

"Some of them became these crazed beasts, like a zombie with rabies and a bit more intelligence. Some of them became dull-witted and dense, good for feeding the survivors but not much else. We decided to separate them and class them as subhumans, for eating or just hunting for sport." Perish put his pen back into the bag and Edward's face flopped back down. "They bred and continued to evolve into their traits... soon we had rats and ravers."

Perish got up and nodded to me. "Shoot him, Killian."

I stared at him for a second and looked down at the assault rifle. I held it in my hands and took a step towards Edward.

Danny and Teejay both cleared away, their dead, soulless eyes staring at me with weighted agony. But no one made a move to stop me and I made no move to stop myself. One less slave to try and eat me. Even though Edward hadn't spoken in days, he still spoke a lot in my head.

I wonder if he will still talk in my head when I shoot him. I shouldn't be too sad then. Though my head was an auditorium of many voices, I would recognize his. He had been the one to try and save us.

No, no... he had been trying to eat me, not save me.

Edward was making no move to run or plead for his life. He only stared at the ground, his hand in his mouth as he chewed on his own fingers, more blood speckling the grey, hitting the rocks with a light sound.

Like drip drip drop little April showers.

I think it was April now. No... it was May.

You died in April or May, Edward. I'll remember that.

I pulled the trigger and Edward's body snapped back. In a heap, he fell backwards, his milky eyes staring off into nothing as the pool of red grew underneath his head.

Goodbye, Edward.

Now you're... Deadward.

Danny swore and Teejay sniffed. I whirled around from fright as I saw a shadow beside me but it was only Perish. He rested a hand on my shoulder and patted it.

"Good little lunatic. Okay, let's go."

"Wait... we need to get some of his meat." Danny's boots crunched and I heard scraping as he turned Deadward onto his side, then with a final push, he rolled him onto his back.

"No, the lab isn't far, leave him for the radrats." Perish motioned me to follow him and I obediently shadowed his footsteps, still holding the assault rifle in my hands.

"Fuck that! Are you fucking joking?" Danny said in a hoarse voice. I turned around as I heard an odd noise and saw Danny twisting and pulling Deadward's fingers off, a rope of tendon following behind the now severed digit. He quickly stuffed it into his pocket, only giving Teejay a quick glance as the second slave kneeled down and started trying to cut Edward's remaining arm with a jagged rock.

I watched them as Perish's steps got further away. Danny pulled Deadward's pants down, his white pale ass exposed to the irradiated air. Desperately Teejay started trying to slice the flesh, exposing yellow pockets of fat with each slash, the entire time giving Perish fearful glances as the scientist walked further away from them.

Like animals the two of them gave up on the sharp rocks and started to bite down on Deadward's arm and the soft skin of his side. I watched, unable to look away, or just too sick in the head to, as they devoured him like ravers. Desperately trying to get as much flesh into their mouths as they could, though they didn't swallow it. With the sense that only a starving greywaster could have, they ripped off chunks of the dead slave and pocketed them in their shirt and jeans; red seeped through the cloth and denim.

"That will be you next." I jumped as Perish hissed this into my ear, before laying a kiss on my neck. I cringed and he chuckled before kissing me again. "What are you going to do to defend yourself? Nothing? They're going to eat you, Killian. They already have it all planned out. They're starving and desperate and you are such a delicious little thing."

"I know," I whispered dully back. Danny's face jerked up and in his mouth I saw Deadward's cheek. He picked it out of his mouth and stuffed it into his bulging pockets.

"I've seen it happen; I've seen ravers eat people, a lot of people…" I said. I turned and stared in the direction we were walking.

In front of me was a single road leading though mounds of hardened metal, some sticking out a storey into the air. They rose up from the ash like the living dead rose out of graves, no longer the thing they once were, just a monster unrecognizable under the weight of both time and the death.

This had been a city once, but just once. I looked past the wavy, creased metal and spotted a scorched concrete barrier, holding nothing back now but more dirt and metal.

"Where are we?" I whispered.

"Mica Creek," Perish replied beside me. "Further north is a place that was once called Jasper. If we kept walking in this direction, we would reach Edmonton. We never renamed it since, like the rest of the world, it is uninhabitable. One day the radiation will make it livable, in about four hundred years unless another Fallocaust happens and the slaves don't kill you."

I shifted around uncomfortably; I clutched the assault rifle to my chest and tried not to whimper. I might not have tears left, the air seemed to suck all the liquid from my body, but I felt no urge to cry anymore. I think I was done with the crying; I was done feeling weak and helpless.

"I won't let them hurt me," I said quietly just as Danny was removing Deadward's eyes, pinching each ocular between his fingers before he popped them into his mouth. Immediately Teejay went for the other one but Danny was quicker.

"Hey!" Teejay said loudly. "Leave it for me!"

Danny didn't answer; he put the eye in his mouth and I heard a pop as he bit down on it. Teejay swore at him and gave him a rough push. I looked to Perish to see if he was going to do anything, but he only watched. Firm in stance and poise, the scientist didn't move an inch.

Danny pushed Teejay back with an angry bellow before the two of them went tumbling to the ground, the dead, chewed-on body underneath them. Then they started hitting each other with weak punches.

Perish finally let out an annoyed breath and stalked over to them. He leaned down and picked up Teejay who was on top of Danny and yanked him back. Danny jumped to his feet.

Then something happened, something I didn't see coming. In an instant, Danny picked up a rock beside him and slammed it into the side of Perish's head. Teejay quickly grabbed Perish's arms and held them back.

"Killian, shoot him!" Teejay suddenly screamed. I stared at the two of them in shock, my mouth open and my body welded to the ground. I couldn't move.

Perish's eyes were glazed over, a strip of red running down the side of his head. He couldn't keep his weight; he couldn't move and made no effort to move.

"Killian, SHOOT HIM!" Danny yelled, his voice breaking under the desperation. "Fuck, kid, shoot him! SHOOT HIM!"

Shoot him? I looked down at the assault rifle Perish had given me then back to Danny. I was holding a gun in my hands. This meant something, this meant I could kill the people who've been hurting me.

The person who... who had been hurting me?

"KILLIAN!"

"I know you... you're sick, but trust me. Shoot him, Killian."

"Killian, SHOOT HIM!"

I had the gun. I had the power. I had a way of protecting myself. Finally I could be in control; I could make the rules... I had the gun, I had the gun.

A low thunder resonated through my brain. A roaring that took with it all the abilities I had inside of myself to sort through my own reasonings. It was like an earthquake, a concussion of energy that took no survivors and cared little for who was innocent and who wasn't. All this roaring wanted was for me to take that control back, to stop being someone else's victim.

To stop letting other men hurt me; I was so tired of being hurt, of being bullied, terrorized.

I was tired of being threatened with cannibalism, rape, and murder.

I-I think I was just tired.

Of everything.

That was the only way I could justify what I did next.

Danny, tired of my hesitation, or maybe he saw that Perish was starting to thrash, got up and started advancing on me. His arm was outstretched to take my gun away; outstretched to snatch away the only control I had.

I saw him and my mind jammed, immediately my instincts kicked in and I saw him as nothing but another man sent to hurt me, sent to manipulate and control me. I saw him as just like the others, another asshole to beat me down for his own amusement.

I pulled the trigger.

Danny got knocked backwards, a plume of ash bursting from his jacket. He was thrown off of his feet as the crack of the gun ripped through the irradiated air, and with a hard *thunk*, he landed on the ground.

Before he could finish his scream, I shot Teejay too, and like his friend he fell dead to the ground.

I stared at the now three dead and dying slaves. Perish on his knees with his hand on the side of his head. I didn't know what to do, or what I had just done. All that my damaged brain was letting me do was stare dumbfounded at the scene in front of me.

Pockets full of slave meat. Danny's chest sending a light fountain of blood up in the air as his heart started to die. I had shot him in the heart.

How had I shot Teejay?

I walked over and poked him with my gun. I saw I had gotten him in the chest right below his neck.

"You saved us," Perish said, before coughing into his hand. He looked up at me, his blue eyes looking like they could smile. "Good job, Killian. Okay, give me the gun now."

Thoughts passed through my mind, driven in a black car with tinted windows. They were nefarious and dark thoughts, thoughts that included everything from rape to torture, cannibalism and murder. I stared at Perish as he slowly rose to his feet, the gun still in my hands.

I could do a lot to him. I had the gun; I had the power.

Perish kept smiling and held out his hand. I took a small step back and in my mind I saw him dead. I saw my hand with the knife, cutting through his windpipe, sawing through his tendons and finally his spine, until his head came off of his body. The thick coppery smell of blood sunk into the room like the radiation sunk into my bones.

I had killed him before. I had overpowered him once.

"The lab isn't far... let's get warm, have some good food, and I'll read you *Cat Wings*. Remember *Cat Wings*, sweety? I saw you throw that book on the street so long ago." Perish's voice jumped an octave.

In a slow movement, he reached into his bag. I craned my head, remembering briefly that book from a time I could no longer recall.

Cat Wings... someone had read that to me but his image was lost. I knew he was important but my brain was destroyed. What had once been a tightly knitted organization of wires had been clipped and snipped by pliers. Everything was all frayed now.

"Want to see? The colours are so nice; I bet the colours match your eyes." I leaned forward some more to see the book. Maybe I would remember more things if –

Suddenly Perish grabbed me and yanked the assault rifle out of my hands. I screamed at him and tried to take it back.

"No, Killian!" Perish barked, putting the assault rifle on the holder behind his back. "You're too unstable; you'll hurt yourself. Sweety, calm down, it's okay. The slaves are dead and they won't hurt you anymore."

"No!" I cried. Perish grabbed my hands and held them as I struggled. I had no strength left in me so I stopped. "I need something. P-people, everyone, everyone wants to hurt me."

Perish stared at me and I saw sympathy on his face. He shook his head and squeezed my hands before letting them go. "We're almost at the lab, love. It's almost all over, and you'll never have to worry about anything ever again."

"No, no, no," I said, even though I made no move to get the gun back from him. "Everyone wants something from me, even if it's just to see me suffer."

Oddly, Perish paused for a moment. His icy blue eyes, still soft, looked at me, and a sad smile appeared on his face.

"I understand…" he said slowly, and he put a hand on my back. He started walking me in the direction we had been heading. "I do, sweety, and it's okay. It will all be over soon. I promise, I'm sorry this has been so hard on you but I had to do it. Sky… Sky and I had to do it."

"Why?" I croaked. I looked behind me, seeing the three dead slavers start to get enveloped in the haze of the plaguelands.

I heard a jingle of keys and a shifting of the collar I had around my neck. A moment later, I heard a *click* and the collar fall to the ground, something that had caused me so much anxiety now no longer a part of my life. Just like the slaves, they come out as quickly as they had come in.

"Because you saw how much I was suffering once, and you loved me enough to put me out of my misery. I'm going to show you the same love, Killian. I am going to make it so you never have to worry again, you never have to be scared of men mistreating you," Perish whispered. I felt his lips press against my cheek. "I will never hurt you again either. Sky isn't going to hurt you anymore. His memories got what they wanted."

Sky? He called me Silas at night…

There was no live wire in my brain sending off alarm signals; the alarms had been silenced. I had nothing left inside of me, just that fleeting moment of power I had tasted when I held that assault rifle. The taste felt bitter in my mouth now, like it had purposely come forth just to tease me.

I had always been the victim and it looked like I was always going to be the victim. That was who I was born to be. Though that fact rested awkwardly inside of me, and when I tried to swallow it down it got stuck like it was covered in barbs. Perhaps even though my mind had resolved itself to such, there was a piece of me that was still fighting.

I didn't know why I would bother fighting. Look at the world around us; look at the scorched terrain, the grey ash and the endless sea of blood and tears. The human race had stopped fighting a long time ago, like me they were just walking dead, waiting for the inevitable. The hard facts of living in the Fallocaust were that, chances are, the most useful you would ever be was giving someone else a good meal.

Or a good fuck.

Or maybe just a laugh.

In the end, we all wound up the same. Dead like the slaves behind me, free arian men who made the mistake of either breaking the law or being in the wrong place at the wrong time.

"Can I go home, Perry?" I whispered quietly. I wrapped my arms around my jacket and looked around. "I won't live long here, the radiation is going... is going to kill me."

Perish took my hand and held it, together we kept walking down the scorched road.

"I told you, love, you don't have to worry about that. See that hill?" I looked as Perish pointed towards a tall mount of grey ash, the remnants of melted beams sticking up out of it like ribs. All of these twisted sculptures were around us, each one making its own design that, in a clearer state of mind, I would have found beautiful.

They were... everywhere now. The metal made the grey ash rise like bulges. The only tell-tale sign that something bigger stirred underneath was when the ash blew away to show their distorted shapes. This must have been a big city or at least one with a lot of metal.

"We made a door in that hill," Perish said, his voice had an air of almost child-like excitement in it. It was an odd thing to hear given the heavy situation we had been in for what seemed like months now. "We're almost there."

My head shot towards the hill and I paused for a moment. "We're... here?" I looked behind me, the slaves now disappeared. They were just a memory now, one I might forget soon given my mental state.

He nodded and took a deep breath. "I'm... I'm not even nervous, but Sky, Sky's nervous and he's getting quieter. He got what he wanted and in exchange I was able to get into that laptop. Okay, Killian, let's go." Perish took my hand and started pulling me off of the road towards the bulge in the ground. Not a single blade of yellowed grass, or a black tree to be seen, it was all just charred earth and ash.

"Laptop?" I asked quietly.

Perish kept pulling me. "The research I needed, yes. He owned Elish's laptop before Elish did. Sky knew how to get through all of Elish's security; he had installed them himself. I found out how to make you immune to radiation but in exchange… his memories wanted their own things. It was worth it though. I know you don't think so but it was."

I nodded, though a lot of what he was telling me I didn't understand and I was too tired to search my memories for the answers.

So I followed him, tired and exhausted. Each step was painful and had been painful for days, but I found my feet easily taking me towards the grey hill. I didn't know what he was going to do to me in there but that was the last thought on my mind. He promised me comfort, food, a warm place to sleep. In my mind that was all that mattered and it was those promises alone that made me sprint to the door with my captor and friend.

Perish grinned and I saw a grey metal door in front of us, scorched black but still holding the same yellow sign we had seen when we were crossing the border. *Keep out, by order of Skytech.*

Perish brought out the same set of keys he used to unlatch my collar and slipped a key with a Sonic the Hedgehog cap on it into the lock. He turned it and laughed when it opened. "There we are… there we are, Killian. We're here. We made it."

Perish stepped in first and coughed into his hand. There was rustling before he clicked a flashlight on. He shined it down and I saw that this room was only the size of a closet, below my feet was a hatch with another lock on it. Spray painted on the hatch with pink paint were the letters *SPS*.

Perish closed the door until all that was lighting this musty underground room was the flashlight. I stepped away as he unlocked the hatch and started climbing down what looked like a ladder.

I hesitated but followed him; slowly I climbed down each cold rung, feeling the rust come off in my hands making me sneeze and cough.

My body jolted when my foot hit the floor. In the darkness I had had no idea if the floor was ten feet down or a hundred and ten. It appeared to be about twenty feet from the hill above us.

Perish took my hand and started walking with me through the darkness. I shone the flashlight around and saw we were in what I could only describe as an unfinished basement. Wall-to-wall concrete, dirty floors stained with oil and paint, and rows of dusty boxes and crates all stacked on top of each other.

There was another door. Perish dropped my hand and I stood beside it with the flashlight. He walked into the darkness and I heard the sound of rusty hinges and him murmuring to himself.

Then there was light. I squinted my eyes and swept the room as two long florescent lights flickered on above us. In the distance I heard the roar of a generator and the vents above us kicking in.

"Wow, everything still works, can you believe it?" Perish chuckled smacking the dirt and dust away from his hands. "I managed an email out to Mantis back in Kreig. I wanted to make sure this place was functional and look… it is. My old lab. I spent so much time here."

"Who's Mantis?" I coughed again into my jacket. Perish opened the door he had left me beside and laughed again as he looked inside. He looked… giddy. I don't think I had ever seen him so happy.

"He's a friend of mine, a dear friend of mine. Wow, come look… it's dusty, but it's mine."

I peeked my head in and was struck by just what I was seeing.

A hallway leading to a large living room, the furniture covered in sheets, further back I could see a clear glass separating the farthest wall. Behind that wall I saw lab equipment, machines I didn't recognize, white walls… an entire laboratory just behind the living room.

And a kitchen off to the left, and bathrooms and bedrooms. I walked in and tried to take it all in, feeling my nose burn and my heart jump just from the sheer relief that I was out of the greywastes.

Perish walked ahead of me, his boots leaving trails on the carpet underneath my feet. He opened up a glass door that led to the lab portion of the apartment and looked inside. "Everything is here. Mantis updated everything. Okay, well, we don't have much water just enough for drinking and one bath. We don't have a hot water tank either, it's tapped dry. There is next to no drinkable water in the plaguelands unless you filter it but, well, Mantis again."

I stayed in the living room and tried to pull on a sheet that was covering a couch but I didn't have the energy. Instead I just sat down on it and watched Perish as he disappeared into the lab, before coming back with several huge blue containers. I could hear water swishing in them. He then lit the stove and put some water into a metal pot before sliding it onto the hot element.

The couch was comfortable, even though I felt bad for the marks I was leaving on the sheets. I was filthy, but still it was a relief to have something soft under me, so I leaned against it and closed my eyes.

Without realizing it, I fell asleep. I think it was a combination of both exhaustion and just feeling safe for the first time in months. I was finally indoors, in a place that had electricity, water, and safety from the elements. The slaves were also gone, it was just me and Perish now and there was a familiarity in that which comforted me.

I woke up sometime later to Perish softly shaking me awake. Immediately my eyes snapped open, confused as to where I was with the usual nightmares still driving shotgun in my mind.

"Shh, it's okay, sweety. Wake up," Perish whispered.

I looked at him and my eyes widened when I saw how much he had changed. When I'd fallen asleep he had a thick beard, a dirty rugged face, and his duster and clothing were filthy and smelling of rot and sweat. He was a greywaster down to the gun on his back and the kill count under his belt.

But now… I recognized this man. I mean, I wasn't crazy enough to have forgotten him, but… seeing how he looked now just solidified the connection between Perish Fallon and Dr. Perish Dekker. The man I had met on the streets of Donnely, he looked like him.

To my surprise, I felt a smile come to my lips. He was a familiar face, a friendly face. It was like he had come here to rescue me. He was my tie to the life I had led before Mr. Fallon had taken me.

Dressed in a crisp lab coat, freshly shaven, clean, and smelling like fragrant soap, Perish smiled with me, though I couldn't understand the sadness in his eyes. He reached a hand up and traced my cheek before saying with the same smile. "Hey, lovely boy, you slept for quite a few hours. I got a lot done while you were resting. Want to take a nice bath? I only used a small amount of water; I saved the rest for you."

I let him help me to my feet but when I took a step I stumbled. My bloodied and blistered feet had taken a turn for the worse. Or maybe the survival instinct inside of me, the one that kept me going in the greywastes, was gone. I didn't need it anymore; I didn't need to push myself to make it another mile… I could relax.

Perish helped me into a large blue bathroom with blue-grey tile, his hands gentle, and his touch soothing and slow as if not to spook me. He walked me over to the bathtub with several inches of steamy water and started to undress me.

There was a small shred of me left to feel uneasy with him undressed me like this, but I was too worn-out and dazed to do more than just wish he wasn't. Honestly, I didn't care. He had seen me naked, he had sucked my dick and I had done the same to him, over and over again. If he was going to bend me over and fuck me, so be it, at least I was warm and in a nice environment. It would be a lot better than being raped in a burned-out building surrounded by slaves.

Perish removed all of my clothes. He swore when my boots came off and took in a sharp inhale of breath. "Fuck, look at those. Don't worry, Killian. I'll wrap them for you before we go to sleep tonight. I have medication here too, the kind you always liked to take. It's old but I remember Rea- I remember most of the pills you took were scavenged anyway."

I looked down at my feet, feeling a sick knot inside of my stomach when he put my leg on the top of the ceramic tub. The back of my foot was rubbed raw to the point where there was an obvious groove from my shin to my heel. My toenails had turned black too from the radiation, and as I glanced at the sock Perish was holding I saw two of my toenails crusted into the grey fabric.

"It… it will be over soon," Perish whispered to himself, and with that self-resolution he took a deep breath and put the smile back on his face. He reached up and grabbed a bottle. I perked up when I saw it was pink, I loved that colour.

Perish squeezed the bottle into the bath water and handed it to me. "Okay, have a long bath. I'm going to get dinner ready."

"Okay." I looked down at the bottle and saw it was Mr. Bubble. I didn't trust that big smile on Mr. Bubble's face though so I turned the bottle around. "Thank you."

Perish paused; he looked at me strangely before leaning down and kissing my cheek. "The fact that you're thanking me after everything we've done to you says a lot in itself. Please, Killian just – trust me. I know what's best for you; I know what's best for both of us now."

He turned to leave.

I looked up from the bottle and turned to him. "Are you going to kill me?"

Perish stopped in the doorway, he didn't turn around. "W-wash up, Killian. It'll be all over and done with soon. You did your part, you survived the journey here, leave the rest up to me and Sky."

CHAPTER 57

Jade

REAVER WALKED AHEAD OF US, ELISH WALKED beside me. It seemed my master knew sooner than I did when a cluster headache was about to come. He caught me as soon as the pain ripped away my reality and near him I stayed until the worst of the pain had subsided.

There was nothing but guilt inside of me for being a burden on my master and my travelling companions. I had been doing everything I could to numb the pain that seemed to have taken permanent residence in my brain.

Elish had control over my drugs but he had been liberal with them since he had come and gotten me. I was hopped up on morphine and Dilaudids with a bit of Xanax. The Xanax didn't help my headaches but it did help my mind calm down.

Reaver himself had been popping Xanax like they were candy, on Elish's urging as well. Everyone including Elish had been walking on eggshells with him now, not just because he blew up a house with his store of radiation, but because he was even more on edge since Garrett had called us.

Lycos's deception had gone deeper, deeper than Elish had known, and in the end that stupid chimera and his husband might have Killian's blood on their hands.

Because now we knew… Killian was in danger; Killian was with a bona fide psycho.

Reaver had been silent when he heard the news, but quickly he disappeared into the greywastes and didn't return until we made camp to have our four hours of rest. When he eventually slinked back into our camp he was stained with blood and holding a dead baby urson cub in his arms.

The mother urson was too much effort to carry apparently, but the babies were good roasting size. We put it on the spit after Big Shot skinned it and had a good meal while Reaver drugged himself into a deep sleep from a mixture of Xanax and Oxycontin. Drugs and murdering things, that was Reaver's way of coping with situations. Though that being said, what else could he do?

That evening I was sitting beside Elish. He was picking meat off of the shank of the urson cub and handing me pieces. Big Shot and Deek had collapsed beside the fire already asleep. Their preferred method of eating didn't require cooking so they didn't need to wait for it to be done.

"Remember potato fries?" I leaned my head on his shoulder and took a thick piece of meat from him. It tasted weird, it had an aftertaste that held the same stale, musty aroma that the irradiated bear seemed to carry with it, but it wasn't altogether bad.

Elish handed me another piece. "Yes, I also remember tea, hot showers every morning, and not having to worry about the world ending again. I wish I could throttle Lycos's neck right now for his stupid decisions."

I swallowed down my food and watched the fire crackle and snap. "He seemed really desperate to keep Reaver safe from Silas."

To my surprise, Elish shook his head. "No, not from Silas, from me. Lycos didn't want me to have him; he wanted to pretend Reaver wasn't the man I had engineered him to be. Lycos believed he could love the darkness out of him, while my approach was to train him to control that very darkness."

Elish's face hardened and I knew what he was thinking.

"You're doing a good job," I said supportively. "Sure he blew up a house but it could have been worse right? At least he hasn't killed all of us."

My master's expression didn't change, if anything the creases that appeared on his face whenever he was frowning, deepened. "Yes, however it still puts me in a difficult position. Though the dog and the half-raver are disposable, I would be rather annoyed if he killed you in an explosion. You might be immune to the radiation but once the radiation catches something on fire your skin will burn all the same."

The entire world might change, our lives might change, and hell, even we might change… but if there was one thing that would always be the same it was Elish having to downplay his feelings for me.

But I knew him and I loved him, even if he'd rather swallow a hot iron bar than admit he loved me in front of someone.

I shifted into him and shook my head when he offered me more urson meat. I was still hungry but I wanted him to have some first. "You would be more than annoyed. Who else would ever put up with you?"

"Mmhm."

Elish gave me a sideways glance, and when he saw I was smiling, he shook his head. "There's no reason to smile, Jade. We're in a bad situation right now." Though as he said that he put his arm around my waist and pulled a blanket over me.

"Yeah, but we are… not me, not you… *we*," I said quietly. "I missed you."

"Nonsense, you seemed to have been having the time of your life being a raver," Elish responded casually. "Don't tell me it hasn't been a dream of yours to tear out my throat?"

I pretended to mull this over. My heart sang when I saw just the slightest hint of a lightness come to his face.

I decided to be playful. I leaned over and nipped his neck. "Maybe we can try something new when we get home?"

"New?" Elish raised an eyebrow at me before brushing away my playful nip like he was swatting a fly. "Chimeras have been having death sex since the first of us became immortal. Never an interest to me though. I would give as good as I take and you are still very much mortal."

Elish put the now empty plate down onto the ground, and I got up and sat down on his lap with my blanket. He tucked it under my arms and tightened his grip on me.

This, all of this, was how I knew he'd missed me too.

"How's the seeds?" I asked quietly. "Are we okay?"

He was quiet for a moment; the sounds of the boys' snoring drowning out any crackling or popping the fire might be making.

"Right now nothing else matters but making sure Killian is still alive." Elish dropped his own voice, even though Reaver was snoring the loudest. It was obvious he was dead to the world right now. "I expected and calculated for none of this. All seeds I have carefully tended mean nothing if that boy dies. There will be no controlling Reaver and it will be years until I can get what I need from Perish once Sky's O.L.S is removed."

"I can still go into his mind... I know how to do it now," I whispered. "Perish used sex as a way to focus my abilities; I could do the same back to him with your permission. Really, master, I know I'm sick but I can still do it."

"Sex and pain," Elish murmured. "An outside stimulus to focus all of your energies into one place. We have been using that method for quite a while. I used sex with you to draw out your own thermal abilities. But no, Jade, you will be doing nothing outside of aura reading until you are immortal. These cluster headaches are nothing to ignore. As soon as we have Killian and Perish, I must take you back to Skyfall."

"Are you going to make me immortal?" I looked at him in awe, but Elish only shook his head.

"No, I always found it unfair when an immortal was made before their brain reached maturity. You're only eighteen and you still have a year of growing at minimum. If I had it my way I would wait until you were twenty-five or even twenty-seven... but I feel that will not be an option," Elish responded. "I wish we had developed that technology."

"What do you mean?" I asked.

"There was what Perish called a spiderwire, a piece of technology that, when implanted into the brain, would make the host still age," Elish began. "He developed it with Silas since Silas and the other two born immortals still aged until they were around twenty-four. Though it was never mastered or finished. Perish moved on to... create his abominations and fall further into his own mind."

"Was he a mad scientist?" I whispered.

Elish smirked at my choice of words. "Sure, we'll go with that. Perish has a lot of technology he never finished. It was unfortunate that Silas hated him so but I suppose it must've been hard for him to look at Perish. Silas would always see Sky in him and that would remind Silas of his permanent absence."

I looked up at him in admiration as he spoke, not just from the story, but because I just loved it when he told me stories. When he spoke to me in that tone, it reminded me of the night I met him, the night my entire life changed.

"Well, we won't have to worry about me for long. I'll be nineteen soon enough." I yawned and closed my eyes. "You missed my birthday you know. What a horrible master."

Elish gently tucked my bangs back into my wool hat. "Mmhm, yes, I realize I did, as Reaver missed Killian's. It seems we have bad luck when it comes to your birthdays, we always seem to be in the greywastes."

"And you never tell me when it's yours, aren't you ninety-one now?"

"I am."

"You look really good for your age."

I grinned as he chuckled. He patted my head and said softly, "Very funny, Cicaro. Sleep now. I'll keep watch until Reaver wakes."

He wasn't shifting to put me down on the ground so I closed my eyes and leaned my head against the crook of his arm. If there was any subtle way for Elish to show that he missed me too, it was the small acts such as this: holding me while I slept. I was eighteen years old now; I was a full-grown chimera adult with an ability no other chimera held – and yet I think even when I turned ninety-one I would still be a boy curled up in his master's arms.

I drifted off to sleep feeling comfortable and safe, the nightmares not ravaging my mind like they had been for the past few months. Elish's crystal aura seemed to chase away the darkness from my mind and coat me in a barrier of calm tranquility.

I was jostled awake sometime later though by a jump in his heartbeat. I opened my eyes to ask him what was wrong when suddenly he jumped to his feet.

"Reaver," Elish said lowly, but his tone was sharp.

I… I didn't like his tone.

My head turned and Reaver was already standing. He looked around the dark camp we had made and I saw his pupils retract. "A truck?"

A vehicle? I craned my ears and the first shudder of anxiety found me. On the lower registers I could hear the high tones of struggling engines, engines trying to make it over the bumpy greywaste ground.

Elish put me down. I grabbed the assault rifle Elish had laid down beside where he was sitting and handed it to him. Big Shot and Deek were now awake; all of us standing tense beside the flickering fire, our ears now picking up the low rumbling sound.

"It's a Charger plane and they have vehicles on the ground." Elish's tone dropped lower. I looked at him and felt a surge of fear rip through my muscles like they had just gotten electrically charged. The cold calm expression on his face was only a mask to hide the apprehension I could feel in his aura. "They already have seen us. I'm assuming your explosion in that abandoned house was noticed."

My master's eyes swept the dark terrain around us. "We're going to have to kill them. There is no places to hide and even if there was, they would see we're hiding and shower us with bullets. This has to be handled civilly at first, but the moment we have a chance…"

Reaver nodded grimly and his eyes travelled to me. Around us and above, the sounds of vehicles could be heard. "You need to hide the kid."

Elish was still for a moment before he nodded. "Come, Jade."

"I can stay and fight!" I hissed but he grabbed my arm and started pulling me towards a mound of rocks, his grip was hard and his mouth a thin line. Elish didn't answer me and I valued my consciousness enough to not argue any further. He found a split in the rocks and handed me his assault rifle.

"You… you'll need it," I whispered and tried to give it back but he shook his head.

Then Elish handed me our bag, the one with the laptop in it and said quietly, "This is an order and you will not disobey it. If Reaver shows any sign of releasing radiation, run. But for right now you'll use your thermal abilities and make your body as cold as you can. If the Legion takes us escape during the struggle and find shelter. Then you will go to Garnertown and locate a town called Mantis. Go there, and demand to know where Mantis is. Find him. Do you understand me, Jade?"

"Mantis?" I whispered. I hadn't heard of him.

Elish nodded, his eyes watching the camp. I could hear ammo and guns being exchanged and the engines in the distance starting to become louder. "Yes, he in the greywastes. He is an arian made immortal but not a chimera, appears as thirty-three, dark brown hair, and a serious face. He's an old friend and he will hide you."

"Okay," I whispered. Elish turned away from me but I grabbed his arm.

Like he knew what I wanted and needed, he leaned down and kissed me, the first real kiss we had shared in months. I took him in and as I felt his warm lips press against mine all of my fear washed away.

I was a chimera… and I was going to act like it. If there was anything I had learned about being a chimera and the cicaro of Elish Dekker, it was that I needed to follow orders even if I didn't like those orders. Hiding while the others went to face the Legion head-on filled me with frustration, it made the blood under my skin simmer – but this wasn't about me or what I wanted.

So I stayed put. Even though the atmosphere around me was tense and full of apprehension, I stayed still and watched Reaver, Elish, and Big Shot gather all the ammo and weapons from the bags and put it on their person.

Then the floodlights above us.

I shifted my body so I was tight up against the rock and stayed perfectly still, only a small sliver of the light was on my sleeve, the rest was still hidden in the shadows. I couldn't see much from this angle but I could make due enough to know what was going on.

Immediately I drew up my thermal abilities and started to spread the coldness to my body. I wasn't as good at it as Elish, I had no formal training especially since it had been deactivated last year, but I knew enough. I managed to cool my body down just as headlights appeared over a ridge in the distance.

They were coming; they had seen us but it would be okay… I was in the company of murderers. Of men who would kill whoever needed to be killed to keep their secrets safe and to continue our search for Killian.

We would be okay; we were chimeras.

Elish, Reaver, and Big Shot were standing in front of the fire, their hair blowing from the wind of the chopper blades. In a stroke of intelligence, I saw that they had only given Reaver a gun. Big Shot's gun and Elish's handgun were tucked behind their bags. I'm guessing in case the Legion demanded they surrender their weapons.

Dust was being kicked up everywhere from the landing plane, coating our camp in a cloak of dust and ashes. The fire was quickly extinguished and our world was now only illuminated by the vehicles, bright lights from the headlights in the northwest, and the floodlights of the Charger above us.

And the noise. I wanted to plug my ears as the deafening roar threatened to slay my other senses. I found that I had to concentrate hard to keep my body at a cold temperature with the mind-fucking noises it was being exposed to. Not just the Charger plane, now visible in the sky and starting to touch down on the surface, but the single headlights now breaking the dome of night that had surrounded the camp.

Elish crossed his arms. His body stance rigid but confident; his face the solid form of acid. Reaver wasn't any better, he looked like he was going to go Fallocaust on the legionary. I think I had him to watch out for. I just hoped Big Shot would have enough sense to run too.

The black plane touched down. I heard the engine give a shift before the motor waned and slowly died. The chopping of the air starting to become slower just as six legionary quads broke into our camp.

The twelve men on the quads got off, and immediately there was the sound of clicking as they all drew their guns.

"Hands away from your pockets, do not put them near your guns," a man on one of the quad commanded. "We are the Legion of Skyfall. You will comply with everything you are asked."

The quads all turned off but the air around us only seemed to become more tense as the tranquility of the greywastes started to seep back into the camp. It was a false calm, the eye of the storm, or perhaps the beginning of the storm.

"We have nothing to declare and nothing to hide," Elish spoke calmly. "What is your business here?"

Suddenly there was a thumping noise from the Charger plane, everyone including the soldiers turned towards the plane as the sliding door opened.

When I saw who it was a sickening heat flushed my body.

Kessler appeared with another five legionary behind him, his grey eyes wide with incomprehensible shock and his mouth open. He was staring at Elish in stark disbelief, seemingly not believing who he was seeing. My heart dropped down to my feet, my insides twisted to ice making my body shiver even more.

Elish… Elish… what now?

"E-Elish?" Kessler stammered. His eyes shot from Elish to Reaver and they widened once more. He stood there for a moment, struck dumb, and shook his head back and forth. "What- what is this?"

My master didn't even waver, it was impossible to read the emotions on his face. Reaver, on the other hand, I saw his eyes narrow and his stance change. His head lowered and his fingers flexed, and it was in that moment that I remembered – he had been taken by the Legion.

And not only that… he had killed Kessler's son and had been killing legionary since he was a teenager.

Shit, this wasn't going to end well; no way this was going to fucking end well. Do I leave now? One of my pointed teeth found the bottom of my lip and I bit down on it.

"It is what it is, Kessler." I looked up and saw Elish crossing his arms back over his chest. The legionary forming a half-circle around Kessler, their guns drawn and pointed at Elish, Reaver, and Big Shot. Deek was standing in front of Reaver, a low growl tickling the inside of my chest cavity.

Kessler looked at Reaver and their eyes locked. Kessler tensed his grip around his gun; I could see his knuckles start to turn white.

"So this is where you've been? Where is your pet? Y-you… fuck almighty, Elish. You snatched Reaver in Aras, didn't you? I knew he couldn't have vanished into thin air – it was you the entire time. Why?" To my surprise, Kessler lowered his gun; his unemotional face starting to show signs of wear.

"I have my reasons. You know them and you know why, brother," Elish responded, an acerbic taint edging his cold tones. "The most important question here… is how are you going to handle this? I suggest you take great thought in it, Kessler. Because how you handle this encounter right now is going to shape the rest of your immortal life."

Like they were two junkyard dogs, Kessler and Reaver continued to stare one another down. "I know how I'm going to handle this already, Elish. I need no prompting from you. You're going to give me Reaver and I won't say anything to Silas. I'll do that because you're not only my brother, you've been my friend."

"That's not going to fucking–" Reaver shut his mouth as soon as Elish raised a hand.

My master turned back to Kessler. "The boy will not be leaving with you; you can get that notion out of your head right now. We're on an important mission, a mission that, if we fail, can wipe out the entire north of the greywastes. I suggest you let me go, kill these legionary to keep their silence, and forget this ever happened, Kes-"

"HE KILLED MY SON, ELISH!" Kessler suddenly roared. At this outburst of emotion, the legionaries raised their guns again, and I saw Reaver's eyes quickly dart over to the guns stashed behind the bags.

Elish didn't bat an eye. "He wasn't your son. He was a chimera given to you, Kessler. If anything, he was Nero and Theo's son if you wish to get into genetics. Though I find this stance you have, and the glint in your eye, rather humorous." My master lowered his hands and took a step closer to Kessler, in response Kessler took one back. "For what reason do you think you have the right to give me orders? I know it was you who captured Reaver. I know it was you who handed him off to Nero to get raped and tortured for a month. Now tell me, *brother*, does Silas know of this yet? Because I know every last detail and it would please me greatly to tell King Silas what you let Nero do to Reaver."

The crack started to form, but it was only for a fleeting moment before Kessler's eyes hardened again. "Silas will soon forget what I've done once I hand-deliver Reaver to him. If not, I'll take the punishment. My loyalties are with my family and Silas. Threaten me all you want, traitor. I'm not leaving without Reaver; I suggest you cut your losses and come back to Skyfall. Stop embarrassing yourself by pretending to be a greywaster."

"Go fuck yourself." Reaver's low voice brought another wave of tension into the already tense scene. I saw Elish grab Reaver's shoulder as Reaver took a step towards Kessler and pull him back. My breath caught in my throat when I saw the legionary around them draw their guns up higher.

This wasn't going to end well.

Kessler glared at Reaver. "I'll be personally fucking you this time, boy. I will fuck you until *you* call me Daddy. I plan on fucking you all the way to Skyfall."

Nope, it wasn't.

Then hands on me.

I gasped from surprise as I was grabbed from behind. I swore and suddenly cried out, a surge of inner anger coursing through me. I had been too engrossed in what was going on in front of me, I had shut my ears and my senses off to what was happening behind me.

I snarled and swore as two legionary dragged me into the camp, both of them holding my arms and another one with a gun pointed to my head. I tried to drag my feet, tried to struggle until the tip of the gun roughly knocked my temple sending a shot of pain through my skull.

I heard Elish suck in a breath. I didn't want to look at him; I didn't want to see the disappointment on his face.

But my eyes found his anyway, and when I looked up, I didn't see disappointment – I only saw fear.

I stared back at Elish; I stared at my master with the floodlights still on him, making him look like an ethereal being, a demigod dropped down from the heavens. Fear was not suited for his face, fear was not suited for *him*. But oddly, I didn't feel scared to see him like this. It drew up something inside of me that I don't think even he knew I had.

Because as I watched his purple eyes widen and his lip tighten, something inside of me shifted, something I think broke away from me. The boy who clung to his master's cloak as he shielded him from everything bad, crumbled off of me like I was shedding dry mud.

I think I knew this was up to me now.

Kessler grabbed me roughly by the collar and pulled me close to him. I could smell Old Spice aftershave on him and the stench of gun powder.

"Interesting fucking find. Huh, Elish?" I heard Kessler laugh, knowing like we all knew that Elish was going with him. "So now I ask you… what now? Do you want to come with me like a traitor and present yourself in front of the king? Or do you want to hand Reaver over to me and I will give you your squalling infant back?"

Elish looked at me, Reaver fuming beside him, specks of black dripping from Reaver's clenched hands. I saw Big Shot behind the two of them too, holding onto Deek's collar, staring at me with his own green eyes wide.

"You are making grievous mistake after grievous mistake, Kessler," Elish replied coolly. "I'm giving you a single warning: hand my cicaro over to me. And if you dare threaten his life a second time, I will make you regret it."

"Making your own threats, huh?" Kessler said. I felt the cold tip of an assault rifle get pointed to my head; I hadn't realized it before but I had started to growl. The anger was rising like lava, coating my chest and shooting its white hot anger throughout my body.

No one talks to my master like this, not even the Imperial General.

"You're in no position to threaten me," Kessler went on. "You got ten seconds, Elish. Let me take the clone or I'm shooting your husband on the spot."

My master took one last look at me then to Reaver.

Reaver gave him a slight nod, and I lost it in that moment.

"Don't do it!" I suddenly yelled through a snarl. "Don't you dare, I'm fine! He's more important! Finding them is more important! GO! RUN!"

Suddenly a thunder clap of sound, and a wave of heat that seared my brain and blinded me of all my senses. I stumbled, my world spinning around me.

I heard the dog give off a vicious snarl and more gun blasts.

Elish screamed. Elish screamed? I fell to the ground, smelling the dense and musty earth, and put my hands to my head. I felt numb wet flesh where my scalp used to be.

I withdrew my hands and looked at them, they were slicked with blood. My head started to feel funny, colours were staring to appear where there had once just been grey.

"Jade? Jade?" The air broke with the sound of gunshots. Reaver ran past me, he had his gun in his hands and there were sparks of light erupting from it.

Some on it, some around it... my vision was starting to... to go glassy, hazy... bright...

"Jade. Maritus?" My head flopped back and everything was upside down, then his hand on my skull, trying to stem the blood. But what was wrong... did I get shot?

No.

I was a chimera, I... I needed to act like it...

"Come on, little husband, look at me."

"Jade?" his voice broke. I heard a shudder come from him, a choked cry, and a warmth start to come to my head, an energy I had never felt before. It seemed to gather around me, inside me and out, like I was slowly drawing the energy of the universe into my body.

"What have I done? – Maritus, don't leave me."

Elish held his hand out to Jade's head, his white skull visible from the piece of scalp that had gotten torn off from the gun blast. Elish wasn't sure how bad it was but he could see skull and the path of the bullet a strip of char on the exposed bone.

"Maritus?" The gun blasts and the shouting behind Elish meant nothing, their mission meant nothing. Every seed that Elish had ever planted, seeds he had been tending for over twenty years now meant little to him as he held his husband's head in his hands.

Jade's glassy eyes barely moved, and though there was only a small amount of blood seeping from the cicaro's skull Elish couldn't tell just how badly the gunshot was. All he knew was that he had to get Jade back to Skyfall as quickly as he could.

Then, like a dozen tentacles had burst from the night to drag him back to hell, Elish felt hands grab him. With a bellow of rage, Elish jumped to his feet and took a swing. His fist connecting with the face of one of the legionaries, and as he punched the soldier with all his strength, he could feel the soldier's jaw shatter underneath his fist.

More people grabbed him, then the feeling that something was thumping against his back. Elish whirled around and went to punch the person who shot him, but Kessler saw him coming. The Imperial Commander raised the butt of his gun and cracked it over Elish's head.

Around him the legionaries were holding Reaver, the dark chimera bleeding from the head, neck, and chest. He was riddled with crimson holes, Big Shot as well, and Deek was nothing but a mound of grey fur by the ash-covered fire pit, still and silent.

Elish was on his knees, his chest rising and falling as his energy got zapped from the bullets lodged in his back. He looked up at Kessler, dressed in his imperial black and blue combat armour and cape, holding a gun to his head.

"Don't fuck with my family, Elish." Kessler's face was stern and his grey eyes blazing with a fire only a man who had lost a son to torture and murder could wield. "You let him kill my son, I will take your fucking husband in return. It could have been different, but that ship has sailed." He nodded to one of the legionaries. "Finish off the dog and the ugly one."

So I have lost everything then? Elish glared at Kessler, trying even in this submissive position to keep his chin held high and his shoulders square. He'd had to face King Silas many times this way, and he knew even in the grievous of situations that he had to keep calm.

The man will pay, he might value his family but I have his heir under my own thumb. I need to get Jade out of this situation. I will pay Kessler back for this later, tenfold.

"And the traitor?" the legionary Kessler had addressed asked.

"Take Elish to the plane. And on second thought – put a bullet in the pet's head. Finish him off and make sure Elish sees it."

"Don't you touch him!" Elish roared, at the same time Reaver leapt to his feet, both injured chimeras gaining strength from Kessler's final words. Another gunshot went off behind them, landing in the grey ash beside Big Shot, a burst of dirt flying up into the air.

Elish pulled his arms free and attacked Kessler, taking the Imperial Commander down to the ground as more gunshots broke the night air.

Elish punched Kessler. The Imperial Commander's head snapped back, his nose now crushed against his face.

Kessler responded with a hard blow to the back of Elish's head. Elish braced himself but the bullets in his back continued to drain his energy; when Kessler hit him again, he started to see his vision get framed in a blurry haze.

Kessler got up and kicked Elish in the side. Elish gritted his teeth, all of his remaining energy stores now being used to keep himself conscious.

Kessler rose, and to further humiliate Elish, he spat on him.

"That's for Timothy, you fucking traitorous piece of shit. Don't fuck with my family."

Elish clenched his teeth; he opened his mouth to deliver what he knew would be his last scathing remark when he heard a small voice sound only a few feet away from him.

"Don't fuck… with mine."

Elish's head quickly turned towards the voice. His eyes widened as he saw Jade standing up, his yellow eyes vivid and glaring at Kessler.

All at once Kessler whirled around, seemingly crazed with anger. He opened his mouth, his arm rising towards Jade as he shouted at the remaining legionary to shoot him. Elish shouted at Kessler but a moment later he stopped, his tongue seemingly gluing itself to his mouth as he witnessed what happened next.

There was a surge of energy, a dark matter unseen to the naked eye but vivid in Jade's eyes. Like a smoke, this very energy coated the yellow in the boy's eyes, making them appear so black it seemed to confuse one's own senses. A black so condensed and dark, it was as if you were peering into the universe before the sun's creation.

Elish stared at the boy in awe as this energy drew into him, filling Jade's body with its invisible yet depthless black. This was no sestic radiation, no explosion of white energy, this was something else. An ability, a power that even Silas couldn't wield properly.

Then the release, a silent but deafening expulsion of energy that made no noise, made no concussions or earthquakes. It was invisible to the physical world, but on the mind it was fatal.

One by one Kessler and the legionaries dropped their arms, their faces becoming blank and void of expression. They stood like frozen sculptures for a single passing moment, before they fell to the ground dead, blood trickling down their ears.

Elish watched them fall, an expression of disbelief on his face, but quickly he turned to Jade as the boy let out an agonizing cry. Elish caught him just as the boy's legs gave out from under him, and swore as his cicaro's eyes started to roll to the back of his head.

Then the seizure, the grand mal seizure like Jade had suffered the previous winter.

"Can you stand?" Elish barked to Reaver. He held Jade tight to him as the boy twitched, feeling his muscles rapidly contract and stiffen under Elish's firm grip.

"Reaver?" Elish's usually firm unwavering voice was strained with desperation. He watched with grimness as he saw a small drop of blood fall down Jade's ear canal, landing on one of the violet-ruby studs in his ears.

"I'm dying... but I'm... I'm trying," Reaver rasped. He was being helped to his feet by Big Shot, who had two bullets lodged in his chest and shoulder.

Elish's arms almost gave out, the fabric against his skin now wet and cold from the blood leaking from his back. "I have to get him to Skyfall. Silas couldn't even kill one of us this way without it fatally destroying his... his brain. I need to get Jade to Skyfall."

"Go..." Reaver took a step before he stumbled. "Leave me... a quad. I'll go alone, I'll be faster. Big Shot... is the dog dead?" The dark chimera sunk to his knees again and Elish could see now that he had several bullet holes in his back. He was dying and quickly.

Elish turned from the scene, from the dark chimera surrounded by bodies, and jumped onto the plane. He put his dying husband into the co-pilot's chair and turned the key to start the engine.

Big Shot was in the door dragging the half-alive deacon dog. He looked at Elish, his own face flushed and pale, and then to the cockpit. "He goes, I go. You help dog?"

Elish stared at him for a second, the fate of the deacon dog far away from his cares in the world, but he nodded at the half-raver anyway. Elish owed the half-raver Jade's life and if he was left with those bullet wounds he would die right there with the dog.

So he quickly helped the half-raver push the giant dog into the plane.

Reaver was leaning against a quad, staring forward as if in a daze. Elish stumbled over to him and pulled something out of his pocket.

"This won't help for long but it will help," Elish said to him. "It's adrenaline and cocaine, with a bit of meth thrown in there. Take a token size amount through your nose and ride until you die. Get as far away from this scene as you can and die somewhere out of sight."

Reaver took the bag, blood streaming down his forehead, and nodded. Then, to Elish's confusion, he brought out his knife and sank to his knees in front of Kessler. With the plane roaring in the background and the scraping of Deek's dying body against the plane's floor, Elish watched Reaver saw off Kessler's head.

"Throw it down the first hole you see, or a canyon if you pass it," Elish replied when he realized what Reaver was doing. "He'll be resurrecting for at least five months and it will take him a month if not more to find a legionary base this far north." He got out his own knife and helped Reaver finish the job.

"As soon as the boy is stable I will find you," Elish said to him. He wedged the knife into Kessler's spine and pried it away from his skull. "Follow the highway I mentioned, look for yellow signs. Our meeting point will be the town Mantis. Will you remember this when you wake?"

Reaver nodded and rose, Kessler's head now under his arm. "I'll be fine once I come back. With a quad, I'll make fast time to the plaguelands. Don't worry about me, just go… go fucking save that husband of yours."

Elish steadied Reaver and helped him onto the quad, the dark chimera's face grey and his hands trembling from blood loss. There was blood everywhere, even dripping off of his boots.

There was little more to say. Elish turned on the quad and tied their bag of food and water to the back rungs.

"You're set." Elish paused. "Go to Mantis when you find Killian."

"I will…" Reaver put his hand on the throttle and turned the headlights off. He hesitated for a moment for he gave Elish one last glance. "Thank you… for everything."

Before Elish could respond, Reaver pressed down on the throttle, and sped off into the darkness.

CHAPTER 58

Killian

THE LAST TIME I HAD LOOKED IN THE MIRROR I hadn't recognized the man staring back at me. This strange man, not a boy, had a thin blond beard over his face, dirt incrusted in every crease and divot, and an expression that held nothing but a blank slate. He wasn't anyone who I had known, only his blue eyes were familiar to me, a blue that broke up the monotone landscape around me and the derelict houses I had once found myself walking through.

But now as I looked in the bathroom mirror I still didn't recognize myself. Who was this person? His head was scabbed and his blond hair patchy, with unhealthy strands that looked more like dried grass than actual human hair. His face was gaunt and sunken in, like a victim of famine and war. And his face… his face…

His face held no blank slate, instead there were wide staring eyes, the eyes of someone who had seen too much and had experienced worse.

I looked down at my clean clothes, a crisp lab coat and a pair of grey cloth pants with a black stripe up the side. I smelled of soap and what Perish had told me were dryer sheets. Pieces of fabricy paper that smelled like vanilla. He had stuffed them in our new clothes to make them not smell like must.

"Killian?" I turned towards his voice and my socked feet took me to him, the sound of a spoon hitting the edge of a cup could be heard.

Perish's face brightened when he saw me. He was holding two coffee cups in his hands, looking more than ever like the man I had met in Donnely. He motioned me over to the couch and I obediently sat down with my hands folded over my lap.

"Watch out... it's hot," Perish said lightly. "It's old... really old, but it had enough chemicals in it to preserve the chocolate flavour. This is hot chocolate. You probably had the Dek'ko kind, right?"

I nodded my head. "It was in a gift basket that was given to us before we left," I said quietly. It made me uncomfortable to think of anything that had happened in my previous life so I left it at that. I took the cup from Perish and blew on it. It smelled wonderful, this laboratory was full of good smells. Such a far cry away from the smell of rot and old buildings.

What an oasis...

But I felt like a wild animal being brought down here, an animal that was being forced into domestication. I knew even in my sore and weary mind that I didn't belong down here and I didn't belong with Perish. My place was at the surface with the people that I loved.

The person I loved... I knew if I even grazed over a part of my mind, the part I had closed off for my own protection, that I would remember him, but it was too painful to think about. It was like I had blocked him out of my day to day thoughts. My brain's last desperate act of self-preservation.

I knew I missed him though – I knew I had once hoped that he would rescue me.

Maybe deep down inside, my heart had realized that he wasn't coming for me.

I sipped the hot chocolate, this evening ending day three of being in this laboratory with Perish Fallon. He had spent a lot of time in the other end of the apartment, where the lab was and all of these large machines. He would come out every couple hours with a smile on his face, telling me that everything was going as planned and we would be ready to get to work soon.

Sometimes he came out sad though, still smiling but sad. When he had that expression on his face I'd give him a hug, even if it made the tears come to his eyes.

Perish had taken me to the safe place and even though I had mixed feelings over him and what had happened above us, it still hurt my heart to see him sad.

This evening he had come out for the last time with the same flickers of despair on his eyes. So I told him we could watch a movie together and sit on the couch with some good food. He loved this idea and that was what we were doing now.

He put on *Jurassic Park* and smiled when he asked if I remembered that that was his favourite; once I thought about it I did remember. I curled up next to him with the hot chocolate and a bowl of popcorn and we watched the movie. He was quiet almost the entire time. I think I remember that not being the case the first time.

Perish brushed my scabbed and unhealthy hair back. He had given me a pill he said would make it grow faster. He even apologized.

"My little sweety," he whispered. I looked at him and smiled before letting him peck my lips. "How do you feel?"

"Better," I said quietly. "It's warm down here and the rashes are disappearing like you said they would."

Perish nodded and gently touched the healing one on the side of my face. "They'll be gone soon. I feel badly for sacrificing Jade for access to that laptop but… without the research I was afraid I'd end up killing you."

The soothing energy between us halted as I pulled my face away. My brow knitted but before I could say anything Perish made a soothing noise and put his hand back on my cheek. "It's okay, sweet one. Elish could always create another one."

These names… I recognized all of them…

"Perish… why did you let Sky control you like that?" I whispered to him. "Why did you let him kill Jade?"

He gently pulled his chin up, a look of love in his eyes that I had seen many times.

"I don't want to talk about that tonight. I just want to sit here and love you," Perish whispered, the sadness came to his eyes again. "Let me kiss you, Killian."

I stared at him back, feeling perplexed that he was asking me permission. No one asked me permission; they just took what they wanted.

"Okay," I said, more to be polite than anything.

Perish cupped my cheek in his hand and drew me in, I felt his still slightly chapped lips against mine before his mouth opened. I opened mine, unable to ignore the pressure welling in my chest; it travelled up to my brain and started making me feel lightheaded. In response, I pressed back and felt his tongue slip into mine. Automatically I put a hand on his side, remembering this as something I often did, and stroked it.

We kissed deeply and when Perish pulled away I could see tears in his eyes. The sadness was back, so I wiped the tears away one by one.

"Don't do this," I suddenly whispered to him.

Perish froze, caught as much off-guard as I was by what I had just said.

"I have to, Killian." He smiled again and leaned his forehead against mine. "We might be happy now but we won't be for long. Please, sweety, just... enjoy the comfort and love we have now. Promise?"

"I promise," I said back to him. He nodded at this and leaned in, and we kissed again.

"You're strong enough now... it will be tomorrow. I have already put it off for as long as... as I can," Perish said. "But don't worry; it will all be over soon."

He keeps saying it will all be over soon. I wish I had the will inside of me to stop him from doing what he's doing... but I didn't.

I'm tired. I'm just... I'm just tired. Not a fatigue that a good night's sleep will cure, or a vacation to Skyland. There is a weariness inside of me, one imbedded in my bones that I don't think any amount of rest and relaxation could cure.

This other man I had once loved is gone; the life I had once led was gone. I feel like a husk, a shell of a person who had once been so full of life. Now through months of careful bloodletting that boy has died, leaving no phoenix to rise out of the greywastes ashes, just the charred bones of another sacrificed soul.

I took his hand into mine. "I'm not worried, Perry. I'm okay."

Perish didn't respond, he simply stared at me, seemingly taking me in with his pale eyes, two slabs of ice that once burned with hostility. That was all gone now, every bad thing about him seemed to have disappeared since we had left that abandoned shack.

Once he... no Danny, it was Danny. After Danny had hurt me and I got that last dose of radiation, Perish had started treating me nicer. And now that we were in the lab... it was like he loved me again.

It was like Sky was completely gone now.

"You will be okay, you're going to be amazing," Perish said. "Just do everything I say, do you promise?"

I nodded. What else could I do? There was nothing left for me to say. No argument on my lips, no will in my body. "I will."

"That's my baby. Good."

We watched the rest of the movie together, eating popcorn and drinking hot chocolate. Perish only watched some of the movie, most of the time I could see him watching me out of the corner of my eye. It felt like he was trying to get as much of me as he could. He was looking at me like I was going to go away soon.

Was I?

When it was late and the movie was over, I took off my shirt, leaving my cloth pants on and got into bed with him. A warm double bed with soft blankets and thick sheets that wrapped me in a cocoon of warmth. I had come to love this bed, I could spend days in here and not be bored in the least.

Perish left his table light on which he did sometimes. He liked to watch me sleep and I didn't mind that either. If something was going to happen tomorrow maybe this would be the last night he had with me.

I closed my eyes and got comfortable, hearing Perish's steady breathing beside me. I felt the bed shift underneath me, then to my surprise his hand on my side. I opened my eyes and let him run his hand up and down the curve of my side, a catch in his eye that made the drowsiness drain out of me.

Our eyes locked and I saw his chest quickly rise like his breath had caught. He rubbed my side gently before leaning in and kissing me. The hand then travelled to my cheek like it had on the couch and he drew me in deeper.

His minty-smelling breath was hot against my face; rapid breathing that brought a heat to my head. He kissed me again and this time his hand slipped to the small of my back.

I felt a burning inside of my throat that quickly made its way up to my head and down to my groin. I pulled away with a gasp only to have him pull his lips back to mine.

We kissed again and the hand slipped down my pants. My face flushed as he traced a finger down my backside before gently grabbing it, pulling me so close to him our bodies were now touching.

"Let me have you," Perish whispered as our lips broke, only to join once again. "One night, our last night together. Let me have you just once."

I pulled away, but all I could do as my mind turned over what he had just said, was stare at him. He kissed me again and lightly dragged his roaming fingers back over my side, down between my legs.

I pulled away and felt my body flinch and tense under his touch.

Perish let out a long, heavy sigh.

"I'm sorry for everything I had to do to you," he whispered, his voice tight as his eyes swept my broken and bruised chest. Red, rough patches of skin, huge black and purple bruises, and still hidden underneath the blankets, feet tightly bound with white gauze. "I wouldn't have hurt you unless it was necessary. Sky would only give me information if I let him take command... unfortunately he saw you as Silas and it confused him."

Then he smiled sadly. "I suppose it shows how lost I am to speak of Sky like his O.L.S was actually him. I know it was just his crazed memories, though those memories were still smart enough to use me as a puppet."

"You didn't need to listen to him," I whispered back, his body shifted until it pressed against mine. I was uncomfortable with him being so close but I didn't want to be rude.

"Yes, I do. I have to listen to everything he tells me to do... I have no choice but... it's okay," Perish said with another smile. He leaned down and started kissing my neck. I felt a hand trace the rim of my pants before slipping down. "It's... just perfect now."

I whimpered when I felt his hand stroke my penis. I closed my eyes, and just like when we were on the surface, I let him do what he wanted to do.

But he stopped.

After a few moments of silence, I opened my eyes and saw Perish looking at me. An odd look was on his face... one I hadn't seen before.

Then he removed his hand and instead he stroked my remaining hair back. "I would die happy if I could only have you once, Killian, but I would die miserable if I ever had to force myself inside of you. I won't go any further than light touch... will you let me?"

I hesitated. "You're not going to make me?"

Perish shook his head. "In your state... it would break my heart to do it. I think it would've broken me even more if you agreed now that I think of it. If I was ever to make love to you, I would want it to be with the Killian who cut off my head... not this poor boy on his last legs."

He drew me in and I heard him sniff. "Perhaps just let me hold you tonight. All night. I think... I think I would like that even more than... than that."

The hesitation dissipated as Perish said those words to me. Knowing that he wasn't going to force things to escalate, I shifted into his arms and let him hold me tight against him.

"Thank you for stopping me," Perish whispered in my ear. I felt his hands start to gently stroke my sides and his touch further relaxed me. "I love you."

I closed my eyes and further melted into his arms as he lightly stroked my skin.

"I love you too, Perry."

I woke up once, a night terror laying its claim on my damaged mind, but as soon as I let out my first whimper he was there to hold me and reassure me. I clung to him tightly.

But when day came Perish wasn't in bed, and I was happy to feel a little bit more on this planet.

With a yawn I walked into the living room to find him. The smell of breakfast was heavy in the air and my stomach was growling.

"Killian."

I turned towards the living room and saw him sitting on the couch. He was dressed in his lab coat and his eyes were red and swollen like he had been crying.

"What's wrong?" I whispered. I walked towards him as he motioned me over.

"Come here," he whispered back, patting his lap. I walked over to him and sat down on his lap. He shifted me until he was almost cradling me and kissed my head.

"You know I love you?" Perish whispered.

"What's wrong?" I said in alarm. I looked around and glanced up at the ceiling. "Is someone here? What's wrong, Perish?"

Perish shushed me and took a deep breath. "I need to say something to you. Please, listen and don't forget my words, okay?"

I looked at him in surprise before slowly nodding.

"Everything I have done to you... I did it to help you," he said to me. "The love that you showed me so long ago in Donnely. I never forgot that and I... never will forget it. You showed me patience and love, and in the end, you showed me mercy. Because you saw how much I was suffering and you didn't want me to hurt anymore."

I looked at Perish as if looking at him would explain why he was talking like this, but my mind only blanked under his words.

He continued, "Sky... Sky brought with him a lot of memories.

Memories of things that happened between him and Silas when they were in the throes of ending the world. I apologize that it had to be the way it was, but Sky told me I had no choice. I had to let him do what the O.L.S wanted to do and in return... I would be able to protect you. I would be able to give you a gift that... that will change your life."

"C-change my life?"

Perish nodded slowly, tracing a finger down one of the healing radiation rashes on my face. "I promised you, Killian. I promised you that I would make it so you'll never be hurt by another man again and I am going to keep that promise. I am going to give you the tools you need to conquer every single one of them if you so desire. Do you want to be strong, Killian?"

Do I want to be strong? Of course I did.

"Do you want to take your control back?"

"Yes," I whispered. Suddenly my throat started to burn, it was getting difficult to breathe. "I don't want to be a victim anymore."

He nodded again; his eyes fixed on me. All the desires in the world seemed to be encapsulated in those eyes. "Me too, Killian, me too."

I felt his arm move; I looked down and saw that he was holding two small smooth objects. The first was a small plastic device the size of a pebble, the second seemed to be just a pin-sized metal tube with dozens of long thin wires sticking out of it.

"What are those...?" I whispered.

"The first one is my O.L.S, it has my brain matter in it. The second is something I found for you in Kreig. I perfected it for you," Perish said quietly, turning the devices over in his fingers before putting them back into his pocket. He leaned in and kissed me. "Something special I had been working on for years. Having this lab... gave me the chance to complete it. It's yours." He held it up but when I tried to take it he smiled and pulled away with a shake of his head.

"No, not like that." He slipped them back into his pocket and put his arms around me. He held me tight to him though his free arm was rummaging through his lab coat again.

"Close your eyes for a moment, love."

I didn't think anything of it. I was still tired and sore from my journey here and my mind was only starting to come back to me. I closed my eyes until an odd noise filled my head, a snap of a cap or something.

I opened my eyes.

"No, Killian… close your eyes."

Suddenly I felt a sharp jab go into my arm. I jumped up from fright but as soon as I did he grabbed me and started shushing me. I let out an anxious cry as he dug the needle into my arm, and slowly started pushing on the plunger.

"Perish… no, no, please don't…" I stammered, anxiety ripping through me like a lightning storm. "Perish, I don't want to die. I don't want to die."

"I know, I know, sweety, shush." Perish tightened his hold on me, the entire needle now sticking into my arm. My body started filling with a sickening nausea; my mind started to fade. "It's okay, Killian."

"You're safe now."

"No one will ever hurt you again. You won't let them."

"I love you, Killian."

"I love you so much."

CHAPTER 59

Reaver

I'D RUN THE QUAD UNTIL I HAD DIED ON IT. I'D JUST been able to regain enough of my body to turn the vehicle off before I rolled off of it, dead.

The white fire came and slew the darkness trying to pull me to oblivion, and as it sewed my body back together my thoughts were only with Killian. I saw the boy's flawless face in those flames. So clearly I was sure if I came close enough, I could smell his fragrant soapy scent.

I was close, and I knew I was close.

Drawing up all remaining stores of energy, I had managed to ride the quad into the morning. The first slivers of grey sun had just started peeking out over the east when the blood loss had overwhelmed my body, blood loss and what I think was a shot up liver but I didn't know. In the end everything would come back as good as new, with the bullets laying forgotten on the greywastes floor. That was my gift, the gift of immortality.

A gift my boyfriend did not have.

I was back on the quad now, riding it as fast as I could down a stretch of broken pavement half-consumed by ash and dirt. The wind was blasting my face and the bits of dirt kept getting into my eyes. But that was the least of my worries, every hour I spent on this thing was half a morning of walking. I was going to use this quad until the gas ran out.

Elish would be in Skyfall by now with Jade, though whether the pet would make it or not I wasn't sure. I had bled out of the ears once, another time that I had died. Though instead of using my brain to kill people, I had gotten strangled by my dad.

Jade's brain was already overloaded. It looked like that even though the Dekker's could create talented chimeras, their technology had reached past the abilities of an organic human brain. The kid's mind was failing.

Elish was doing what had to be done for his cicaro and I was now doing what had to be done to find my boyfriend, though that was easier said than done.

I wasn't expecting a big sign announcing the plaguelands but I was hoping for some sort of signal when I crossed the borders. Elish had told me to watch out for yellow signs but so far I was just riding down an empty highway, dodging rusted out cars and medians stacked in preparation of the war long dead. The road was the one Elish had told me about though, so unless he had gotten it wrong this road was going to lead me into the plaguelands.

My mind refused me to acknowledge it, but as I sped down the highway my eyes kept checking behind all of the medians, and when a car was intact, inside of the car as well. Killian wasn't as strong as us, he was just a normal greywaster and it looked like he had travelled an incredibly long distance with Perish and those slaves. Killian wasn't used to travelling on foot this much, and I was worried that Perish wanting to go to the plaguelands might outweigh wanting Killian to come with him.

Or Sky. Whoever the fuck was controlling Perish's mind' I didn't know how the fuck it worked. I just knew it wasn't good. I just knew that this O.L.S was making Perish crazy and that meant I could no longer rely on his love for Killian to keep my boyfriend alive.

I spotted several structures in the distance and decided to take a risk and check them out. There weren't many buildings in this area of the greywastes and the ones that were here had collapsed. It was rare now for me to spot a standing structure and I knew if Killian had seen it, and he was alone, that was where I would find him.

Though in the same string of thought, it also pumped my heart with anxiety. It brought me back to the house with the dirty curtains and carpet, when I had found the blood and semen.

And I well… had exploded. Literally.

My mouth pulled down as I veered off of the road towards the three buildings, all three surrounded by telephone poles in various states of falling over.

The radiation was something new, something I had never felt close to doing before. It was also something I now had to control. Elish was supposed to teach me that but I guessed it all came down to just sheer will and discipline.

That I could do. Or at least that's what I told myself.

I jumped off of the quad and turned it off, giving the engine a much needed cool down. I looked around the first house for any signs of visitors but there were none. Without wasting time, I checked the second and finally the third.

I stopped like I had physically hit a wall when I saw the boot prints. Immediately my mind started locking itself down as my gaze swept the prints I now recognized as Killian and Perish's. I walked inside, ignoring the hammering thrums of my heart.

"Killian?" I shouted. I stopped and listened but I heard nothing back. I wasn't expecting to hear anything though, these prints looked days old.

Days old... possibly a week but the greywastes preserved prints as good as the moon during the dry seasons. We hadn't had any rain or anything since Elish and I had seen the snow on the Coquihalla. So it could've been longer, but still... I was heading the right way and he was still alive. That was enough to bring a small glare of light to my dark mind.

Then another sign. I walked over and picked up a tipped over can, smelling the corn before I saw it. I brought it up to my nose before taking the spoon and shovelling some of it into my mouth. It was still good, so it couldn't have been too long. The radiation might've preserved things but once it was open the bacteria would get to it, and if not that, the radrats or the bugs would. This can hadn't been found yet, it tasted fine.

I ate it, and with one last visual check of the house, I walked out and made a mental note that the boot prints were heading back towards the road. Then I got back on the quad and chucked the can behind an old and very charred camper van. Feeling better than I did before, I revved the throttle and carried on towards the highway.

Where were these signs? I knew they could be another day's ride away but I was anxious to get into these plaguelands. I wanted to fucking find him now, not tomorrow, not the next day. I needed that boy in my arms soon.

I tried to math out in my head how much time I was saving being on the quad, but my math had always been restricted to what I could count on my fingers. Leo had tried teaching me mutiplifractions or whatever they were fucking called but it never clicked in my head. You didn't need to do a math problem to blow someone's head off.

With my eyes peeled in every direction, I didn't even notice the gas gauge quickly going down under the full-throttle speed I was pushing the quad. I made it another four hours before the quad started to lose speed. I gave the gauges a glance, hoping it was just a small rise I was going up, and swore when I saw the orange ticker hovering on empty.

This made me grit my teeth but I was taking it over a hill. The terrain in front of me was more flat and with that flat area the gas chamber wouldn't be on an incline. It wouldn't be much but really any time on this quad was bonus time. I would be able to catch up to Killian and Perish hopefully before they got to their destination.

I'll use every last fucking drop of that gasoline. I leaned forward on the four-wheeler and sped down the road, still no yellow signs but at least I knew I was in the…

There are no words to explain the spasm of horror and anger that ripped through my body when I saw a figure perched on top of a concrete barrier off to the side of the road. A slender figure with shining, wavy blond hair, dressed in a leather jacket and a red shirt underneath. He was crouched down with his arms hanging off of his knees, watching me with a grim expression on his flawless face.

My first desperate reaction was that the corn had been spiked and I was hallucinating, but I knew better. I killed the engine on the quad as my eyes burrowed into his emotionless face and jumped off of it, immediately reaching for my gun.

"Put it away, we don't have time for that," Silas said as he rose to standing. He reached behind him and grabbed a red container. I could smell it from here, it was gasoline.

If I had killed this man's fathers, if I had raped his boyfriend after trying to rape him, I would have dropped the gas can and booked it back to Skyfall. But showing that he wasn't afraid of me and still the king that ended the world, he jumped down with the gas can, landing quietly only ten feet from me.

"What the fuck are you doing here?" I snarled, raising my gun and pointing it at him. "Get the fuck out of here and leave the fucking gas can while you're at it."

Why did he have it in the first place? He would never want to fucking help me save Killian.

"We – don't – have – time – for – that!" Silas spat. Though he stayed in place and didn't move another inch. The king I had once known as Asher brought an anger to my veins that made me feel like my blood was on fire. I was shaking with rage as I pointed the gun at him, and every inch of me wanted to pull the trigger, take the gas can, and run.

So I clicked the gun to automatic, fully prepared to shoot him in the head, when there was a different click behind my own head.

Silas looked past me and nodded to someone, someone that couldn't have existed because I hadn't heard him approach and no one ever got the drop on me.

I saw a flicker of black out of the corner of my eye and another one to my right. Feeling the hair start to prickle on the back of my neck, I decided to turn around to face who had gotten the jump on me.

I recognized them right away, there was no way in hell I couldn't recognize those two.

Sanguine was to my right and Jack to my left. Sanguine with the same smile I had seen in his photos and Jack with his hands clasped behind his back. Sanguine was pointing an assault rifle at me, and Jack was just staring at us.

"I'm not fucking going with you." I whirled around to face Silas. I felt a flushed heat come to my face as I looked past him down the road I was supposed to be driving on. "I don't have…"

Silas walked past me, seemingly feeling more confident now that Satan's lapdogs were behind me. To my absolute perplexity, he walked up to my quad and started taking the gas cap off.

"I'm not taking you anywhere. Get that out of your mind right now," Silas said. His voice was odd. It was tight which was something I hadn't seen in him before. For a moment I dropped the anger and confusion I was feeling, and to further shock myself, I lowered my gun. I don't know why, or if it was even a good idea, but I did it.

"This is what's happening." Silas looked past me and held out his hand. Jack handed him the gas can, already open. "I'm going with you to Sky's laboratory."

"Get the fuck out of here," I said lowly, though I let him pour the gas into the quad. Once I shot all three of them I would be needing it to take me to the plaguelands.

Silas didn't miss a beat, like a pit crew he handed the gas can back to Jack and took a soda bottle of oil from Sanguine. "Reaver, listen carefully.

I know you were raised a savage but you can listen, yes?" His emerald eyes flickered up to mine. He… he looked so much like Asher.

Of course he does; he was Asher, you idiot.

"Perish is implanted with Sky's O.L.S," Silas explained. I was about to tell him I already fucking knew that but I realized that would lead to the questions of how I knew it, so I caught myself and decided I had to play dumb.

"This has made him extremely unstable. This isn't about him hurting Killian. What is in that laboratory is a machine and a room that has the power to start another Fallocaust. To envelope the world in another strong dose of radiation. Not only will Killian die in that explosion, Skyfall will be in danger, and Aras. Everywhere, Reaver."

I stared at him, feeling a thousand ways of saying I didn't fucking care if the world died again crawl on my lips, but all I cared about was that Killian would be in the center of this explosion.

"I don't want this to happen and you don't want Killian to die." Silas screwed the lid back on the quad and took a rag from Sanguine. He started wiping his hands. "You have no idea where the laboratory is, do you?"

My teeth clenched. I wanted to say yes but my inner greywaster was being overshadowed by the reality of my new situation.

Two dogs were fighting inside of my brain in that moment, a moment that I never thought I would see. Face-to-face with my old friend Asher, the King of the World I now knew as Silas Dekker. A man to whom I hated more than anyone with the possible exception of Nero. A man that I was going to one day permanently kill.

I was in the company of enemies, with the born immortal I was cloned from standing directly in front of me.

Who knew where Killian was. Who had just told me that he was in immediate danger.

What choice did I have? My stomach seemed coated in brine, leaving a sour and unpleasant taste in my mouth. This was against my nature. Every fiber in my being was telling me to grab my gun and get as many bullets into Silas as I possibly could. But I knew I couldn't, I knew I had no choice.

I looked behind Silas, down the stretch of road, as if anticipating in that moment to see the explosion that would spread radiation over the entire world – again. Everyone else I didn't care about; it was that boy who made me swallow my pride and my anger.

It had always been about him.

So I *was* growing up.

"How do I know this isn't a trap?" I said to him. I was confused when I saw a fleeting hint of relief come to his face, though a moment later it was gone.

"You don't," Silas said. "You wouldn't believe any reassurances so why bother? I've laid my cards out on the table, Reaver. This goes above my games, above my desires for you…" He handed the rag back and I saw his eyes narrow. "I don't like this either, but he has Sky's O.L.S, he has a piece of… him. I am proposing nothing but your help in stopping Perish and retrieving Sky's O.L.S from his brain. You will get Killian and after that what you do is your issue."

"You'll take me after I have him," I said darkly, before shooting poisonous glances at the two demon-chimeras. "I can take you but these two need to piss off. Three against one and I'm fucked. Don't think I don't–"

"They're not coming," Silas cut me off. He jumped on the quad and shifted himself backwards to make room for me on the front. "They'll slow us down. They have orders to make it back to the Charger plane I have a day's walk from here. Just me and you. You can take me, you've demonstrated that. Get on the quad, Reaver, this has already taken too long."

He paused for a second, his face darkening even more. "We make a good team, we proved that when we outran those ravers. No matter what complications our relationship–"

"There is no relationship!" I snapped. I heard chuckling behind me and I whirled around wanting to punch the silver-haired one, fucking Mr. Chuckles over there, right in the mouth.

"No matter how complicated we are, we make a good team. Together, you and I, Perish and Sky don't stand a chance. You have little option, Reaver. You can walk and spend ten days at full chimera speed until you get to the lab and another two weeks before you actually find the entrance. Or you can get on the quad and we'll be there by tomorrow afternoon."

Tomorrow afternoon? My stomach felt full of butterflies, or wasps anyway. The anticipation of seeing him… of seeing Killian.

With Silas beside me.

Greyson, what would you do?

I sighed and shook my head. What choice did I have? I had never had a choice, even if this was a trap... I knew he had my balls in his hand once again. He was right, I didn't know the exact location of the lab and if it was still a week away...

"Alright," I said bitterly. I holstered my gun and got onto the quad, with a turn of the key the machine rumbled to life. "Let's go."

"Goodbye, loves, I'll be back soon... don't leave the Dead Islands until I page you. Keep safe." I heard Silas say over the quad. I didn't wait for the other two assholes to respond. I tightened my grip on the throttle and sped away.

I had nothing to say to him, and feeling his body so close to mine was making my skin crawl. I didn't want him behind me, where he could easily pull out a knife to kill me, but as I rode on I put those concerns to rest. If Silas was going to take me back to Skyfall, he would've done it while those goons were around.

Though when I saw his hand appear, two hours of silence down the highway, my entire body tensed in anticipation to whirl around and attack him. But as I looked I saw he was handing me goggles.

"Fuck off," I spat, but he only pushed them into my arm. I grabbed them with a grind of my teeth and steered the quad with one hand as I put them on my head and over my eyes. I could see better this way, those fine grains of greywaste ground were starting to irritate my eyes.

Silas was being quiet which was a credit to him, but I couldn't get my head on straight knowing he was behind me. Silas Dekker, Asher Fallon was behind me, inches away from my back, from my throat. I couldn't believe I was letting this happen; it went against all my natures both as a greywaster and a chimera.

In the early evening, after a long day riding the quad, I noticed the road to my left starting to dip. I watched the terrain and saw that a drop off was starting to form behind the medians. Sure enough, two miles ahead I saw a large dip in the road, almost half a mile down; it looked like a large crater.

I slowed the quad down, Silas was silent while I did. I got off of it, though I left it idling, and grabbed one of my knapsacks. The knapsack that held Kessler's severed head.

I took the bag and started walking towards the crater. Below my feet I could see broken medians and chunks of concrete that had fallen sometime after this bomb had hit the earth. It gathered at the bottom of the crater like water collects in a pool, all of it covered in snares of rusted wire, and from what I could make out, several cars.

Without a thought, I tossed the knapsack down the crater, watching with grim pleasure as the brown bag hit the bottom with a satisfying *thunk*. A moment later, my own spit joined it (that was for spitting on Elish) and I turned and got back on the quad.

"I won't even ask," Silas said from behind me. "Just like I won't ask why you're on a legion quad, *Raven*."

"Good, don't," I said acerbically back and continued down the highway. I actually got more out of Silas's little quip than he knew. It meant that once again Kessler had decided to leave out his knowledge of where I was. It also meant that Silas didn't know I was starting to tap into this sestic radiation thing.

Those were both cards I could use in the future. For Kessler it was obvious blackmail once he eventually did crawl himself out of that crater, and as for the radiation, it was something I could do if I needed to go kamikaze on the King of the World.

Nothing interesting happened for the rest of the day. It wasn't until late in the evening when I was fighting off fatigue that I felt Silas tap my shoulder.

He pointed to my right; I looked over and saw a row of yellow triangle signs, all of them reading 'Keep out by order of Skytech'. They were the signs that Elish had told me to watch out for. I was here. I was on the border between the uninhabitable plaguelands and the northeastern greywastes.

"I can feel you starting to get tired," Silas said. "Let's stop and sleep for a few hours."

"I'm not going to sleep with you around," I said back darkly. "I'll be fine."

"The quad needs rest anyway. You're already risking it overheating, look at the engine gauge," Silas said. "Just do it. I need to stretch my legs."

I gritted my teeth again but slowed the quad down to a stop. I turned it off and jumped off, feeling my own legs frozen and stiff. I grabbed the pack that Elish had filled with food and water and walked towards a median on the other side of the highway.

Silas walked around. I heard a few bones pop as he stretched. I took out a bottle of water but as I reached in to grab a Dek'ko energy bar I paused and debated the intelligence of that. But then again I had seen these same bars in the legionaries' pockets and I had a legion quad so I could explain it away easily.

I sat with my food and water my eyes never leaving the king.

There was definitely something off with him. Silas wasn't making smart comments or walking with that swagger he always had. He was tense, and his usually calm and smirking face was dark and lined.

I chewed on my energy bar, picking apart and analyzing every movement he made. He was pacing like a tiger in a zoo, his hands moving from being on his hips to crossed over his chest.

This was not like him, not at all.

I wonder if this was as hard for him as it was for me.

Silas wiped his face with his hands, giving a nervous look down the highway. The signs were long behind us and now we were surrounded by what looked like melted metal. I had seen structures similar to this in Gosselin where a lot of the bombs had dropped but nothing compared to this terrain. It was like the entire world had caught flame.

"Is this because of the Fallocaust?" I suddenly asked. When he looked at me I pointed towards a large hunk of metal. It was such a weird shape it was like it had been melted down to bubbling magma and hardened again.

Silas nodded. "Yes, this used to be a big city. I lived here with Sky and Perish."

"The radiation exploded it? How? Why did this place burn but everywhere else is preserved?" I realized that Silas had nothing on him. No bag of water and no food. I despised the thought, but the melted metal around us and the charred landscape were starting to make the reality of just what we had to stop Perish from doing become a bit more real.

So I threw him an energy bar and then a bottle of water. He caught both in his hands but said nothing about it. He knew if he thanked me I'd tell him to shove it up his ass.

I wanted to kill him. Dear fucking god, every instinct in my body wanted to kill him. To the point where my hands twitched for my knife, my mouth salivated with anticipation of tasting his blood again. It was such an insane notion that I was riding with him right now, but the circumstances outweighed my need for revenge.

I had to have control; I couldn't let Reaver win this time. I had to keep this uneasy truce between us and find Killian.

Then what?

I didn't know, but I'd take it as it came.

After Silas took a drink of water, he answered my question. "The machine Sky created was basically a special room. When Sky or I went into that room and released our radiation it contained it. The more we released the more condensed it got. Later, Sky added these magnetic-type strips, Mag-strips he called them, to the walls to also draw out our radiation at a quicker pace. After he dragged me to this location he pushed us both inside of this room and shut the door."

I realized I had stopped chewing as I listened. I didn't want to admit this fascinated me. Who else knew what caused the Fallocaust besides him?

He continued, "He took me in there, and when I refused to release the radiation he tapped and extorted every trigger I had, every weakness. Sky knew me and he knew he had to break me down mentally. Because he believed the pulse would destroy the electronics, and thus, stop the Governments from dropping bombs on all of us. I had helped him come up with the idea but as we continued on our journey... I had second thoughts. I didn't want to risk it."

Silas let out a long breath. "The radiation between the two of us condensed and condensed; it was so bright. I had never seen such a brilliant and deadly white light. It was so much pressure against my body, and yet, I stayed entirely intact. After it had condensed to his satisfaction, he pressed a little blue button on a remote he had."

Silas paused, the sound of the energy bar wrapper crinkling underneath his hand. "The pressure immediately left my body, only to be replaced by a roaring that almost deafened me. I fell to my knees with my clothing burning off of my body. The light was everywhere. He would tell me later I looked like an angel... but he just looked like the same devil to me."

He was silent again, then his tone dropped. "We ran out of the laboratory as fast as we could, the radiation thick around us. I knew we had precious little time before the lab exploded, before the city exploded, and sure enough, it did. We got far enough away that when the blast happened we were able to resurrect out of the flames. If we hadn't gotten far enough it would've taken twenty years for us to resurrect without immediately burning alive again. The fires of sestic radiation do not quell easily; they're hot as you can see."

He took a small bite and stared down at the bar. "When we got out of the city though, we realized – it had been a mistake. Just as I feared, not only did the electronics get fried... but the sestic radiation had... it had... killed the world. All we could do was run back to what would become Skyfall and clear it away, the survivors safe underground being minded by Perish."

Silas fell into silence.

"Both of you sound like batshit crazy assholes," I said, taking a drink of water before I lit a cigarette. "Especially Sky."

"I loved him all the same," Silas replied.

"He didn't love you though, eh? Nothing like hating you so bad he decided to learn how to kill an immortal," I said, making direct eye contact the entire fucking time I said it. Though as I did I realized this was also something I shouldn't know, so I added, "Perish told me all about what Sky did."

There was a thousand pounds on my shoulders and twice as many worries, but I felt satisfied as I saw the pull on his lips. I stored that away in my brain to use for fodder later. I liked knowing his weaknesses. A lot of his weaknesses, I realized, I had learned during our drinking nights back in Aras. I knew his sensitive areas were not only Sky, but rejection as well.

Poor miserable little king. I am a patient man, eventually I will kill you.

I have all the time in the world. I also have your first born and top councilman. Your second born and president of your scientific research company. And, hell, I even have Kessler's son, who I am sure will be more than happy to fill in as Imperial Commander once his dad is realized missing.

Silas gave me a hard look and shook his head slowly. "You can nip all you want, Reaver. I am holding off riling you up for the sole reason that we need to get to Sky's lab, not rip each other to bloodied pieces. I suggest you grow up, and put Killian ahead of your childish need to feel like you have the verbal upper hand with me."

"Killian is all that matters," I said coldly. I had forgotten how quick he was with his words. I had enjoyed Silas ripping Reno down when my friend had thought he had verbally topped him. He was a wordsmith that one and a manipulative fuck too.

"Then prove it and stop trying to give me reasons to attack you," Silas replied. "When this is over with we can go back to our games, until–"

"It's not a game!" I suddenly yelled, rising to my feet. To my own shock, I felt a flood of emotion go through me. I think I was more mentally at my limit than I realized.

Silas gave me a dismissive look before taking another drink.

I ground my teeth. "You don't get to pick and choose when you decide to take life seriously. Don't you see what this does to your family?"

Silas rose to his feet, dropping the energy bar wrapper onto the ground. He dusted off his hands. "Everything ends up being a game. When you're my age and you have seen everyone you love die, you will stop seeing people as people. They are nothing but ants in an ant hill, and you – nothing but a god among insects."

"I'm not talking about the shit fucks in the greywastes or your stupid Skyfallers, I am talking about your family," I said lowly. I started walking back towards the quad; I think we both realized no one was going to be sleeping. "You have like forty of those fucks, half of them are immortal, if not more. They aren't people who live and die and yet you treat them worse than an abusive boyfriend."

Silas paused and I realized I had said way too much. He had been out of my life for so long I had forgotten that I wasn't supposed to know anything about this. I steadied my heartbeat, it had sped up during my outburst, and forced it back into its normal rhythm.

"You don't understand anything," Silas mumbled to himself. He put a cigarette to his lips and lit it. "When you're mine and we rule the world together, you will. Until then… you will not intimidate me, and you won't take my aversion to your bait as weakness either. I merely have more pressing issues on my mind."

"We're not going to rule the world, Silas," I said to him.

To my confusion, he paused. He stared forward and I saw his Adam's apple move up and down as he swallowed whatever weight my words had put on him.

"You… you called me Silas. You've never called me by my name before," Silas said quietly, but a moment later he shook his head. "Let's go."

I put out my hand to stop him, feeling my patience and restraint starting to wear down. A nerve was becoming exposed and he was stabbing it. "I know I was cloned from strands of Sky, but you get it out of your fucking head that we will ever be together. Not now, not after Killian dies as an old man, not a thousand years after. It's not going to happen."

Silas's emerald-coloured eyes drew themselves up to mine.

And then Asher came back – I knew he was in there somewhere.

"Oh, it will happen, *bona mea*," Silas's voice dropped. I could see the darkness start to gather around him. I knew Nice Silas had just been shot in the head in front of me. Well, I had pushed him, it was my doing. "We have forever to rip each other to shreds, my love. Rest assured, you will be mine and you will love me more than any man has loved another man. This, yes, this, Reaver Dekker... I promise you. Even if it takes all of eternity, I will not give you up. I will have you, because I love you."

I stood my ground, a cigarette hanging out of my mouth. I smirked at him as he glared back at me.

I leaned over until I was right in his face, our cigarettes, a blue ember and a red one, touching to create deep violet. I glared him down and our eyes locked, a depthless black and deep forest green. The colour that the world is now and the colour that the world used to be.

Reaver Merrik and Silas Dekker, almost the exact same person and yet literally born a world apart. Two men who had led such vastly different lives and yet here we were face-to-face, locked in what I knew would be the fight for my freedom. What could have been star-crossed lovers in a different reality, had been reduced to two mad men with the power inside of them to end the world.

He didn't know what he had created in that lab, just like Leo didn't, just like Elish didn't. Silas would soon see just what he was dealing with, the entire world would see. Because I was only getting stronger and I was only going to get smarter. I was growing up, leaving my teenage attitude behind. I was learning control, I was learning patience, and I was learning quickly.

I was the Reaper and he was the Ghost, and his soul was long overdue for collection.

"We'll see, Silas," I whispered to him. "We'll see."

CHAPTER 60

Perish

IT HAD BEEN A LONG JOURNEY, A LONG AND PAINFUL journey… but it was almost over, it was almost done. Though it had been one of the hardest things Perish had ever done, he had endured; he had succeeded.

He had opened up the boy's brain; he had seen the physical organic object that held in its synapses and blood cells everything that made Killian, Killian. With gentle and steady hands, he had cut through the soft tissue and had implanted in the boy not only his own brain tissue, but the device he had shown Killian the previous day. A small device he had called a spiderwire.

What Sky had done to Killian had almost killed him, but this time the end did justify the means. Sky's memories got appeased with their pain and torture and Perish was able to do what he had wanted to do all along.

Perish had kept his promise. Though the promise didn't mean that no man would ever harm Killian again, it meant that the boy was now given the tools to fight back against his abusers.

Killian will now be in control; he will now take back his power.
You will be my beautiful personification of perfection.

Perish leaned his back up against the operating table. His eyes were closed and his breathing laboured, with the sounds of the beeping machines filling up the heavy air around him. It had been a long surgery and he was exhausted. Usually when he was performing this surgery he had Sid's help, but it was only him in this underground lab. He had to be the surgeon, the nurse, and the assistant.

But it had always been up to him and only him. Even before the Fallocaust it seemed that he was the sane one trying to keep everything together. What an act of irony that in the end it was he who had tasted insanity.

If only they could have seen him at his prime… if only Killian could have seen him.

Perish opened his eyes; his chest heavy and his face still flushed though he had wiped the sweat off of him. He turned to see Killian's pale fingers, his arm hanging off of the operating table just enough for him to see his black fingernails, now surrounded by grey, blotchy skin.

He reached up and brushed his hand over the fingers, soft and slender digits that could turn a devil into an angel with its caring touch. This boy had tamed the worst of them with these very fingers, fingers that Perish had held just the previous evening.

Is it strange that out of all of them… he is the only one I will miss? Over two hundred years and it all came down to this boy. Perish sighed and ran his hand down his face, ignoring the wetness gathering at the corner of his eyes.

I have fulfilled the end of our bargain – you got your torment but I got to save him and make him whole again.

'Yes, you did it, brother.'

He knew it wasn't really Sky. The voice that had been trying to control him for months now was only misfiring synapses and random brain cells but it still sounded like Sky. Even though his brother had become a monster he was still his twin; he was still a part of him.

When you died you took half of me with you, Sky.

Perish stayed sitting on the laboratory floor, catching his breath and trying to unwind his mind after the twenty hour surgery. Finally, when he could no longer stand his own thoughts tormenting him, he rose to his feet and turned to Killian.

The young man was laying naked on the operating table; his grey skin the colour of death. He still showed all the marks that Sky had made Perish put on him, disfiguring scars and large patches of radiation burns; ones that seeped into the skin leaving open craters in his flesh. He was hooked up to many different machines, all of them monitoring some aspect of his body, giving him fluids or filling him with as much morphine as his slender body could take.

Though that wasn't the most disturbing thing to be found on the boy. Killian's head now held a long and angry incision, one that started at his ears and wrapped around the back of his head, all held together with surgical staples. Underneath his head was dried blood and the remnants of gauze, dirty medical equipment, and the leftover wires that Perish had snipped off of the device he had implanted in him.

But Killian didn't die; he had survived the surgery… and that in itself deserved celebrating.

He needed the boy alive for what he was going to ask of him next.

'He'll understand one day.'

The scientist closed his eyes, those words seemed to haunt him more than it comforted him.

"I know," Perish said out loud. He drew a hand down and brushed Killian's remaining hair back with a sad smile. He was sad that he wouldn't be able to see him one more time with that golden, fragrant-smelling hair; the poor boy had pulled almost all of it out.

"Please never forget me, Killian."

Perish leaned down and kissed Killian's cheek, glancing up at the heart monitor to make sure his heartbeat was strong. He rested one more hand on his chest before turning and leaving the operating room.

As soon as he stepped into the main area of the laboratory he took in a deep breath of air, trying desperately to clear the melancholy weighing heavy on his emotions. Usually when he was feeling sad about what he was going to have to do, he looked at that boy's sapphire eyes. Or gave Killian a reason to talk to him just to hear his voice. But now there was no one to break up the anxious storm gathering in his chest and heart. He was alone now with not even his brother's sporadic and sometimes violent memories to keep him company.

I had always been alone. Even your voice is false, Sky. I know it's not really you. If it had been you, you would've never demanded Killian's blood in exchange for that information.

Perish crossed the white tile floors, walking past the rows of filled shelves, and found the small, narrow hallway that immediately sparked memories in Sky's O.L.S. One of his memories was taking Silas down this hallway, the two of them fuelled with their hatred and love for each other. They had destroyed each other many times over before they had finally reached this room, that destruction was evident on Silas most of all.

Perish took a right at the hallway and entered into a large room. The floor was white tile and the walls as well, except for a metal door embedded in the left hand side of the room. Beside the door was a small control panel with two rows of white buttons and several switches.

So this is where it all ends. I made it this far. I got Killian here alive even though Sky did a good job trying to stop that from happening

Perish flicked one of the switches on the control panel and opened the door. His eyes swept the small room, covered from floor to ceiling in shiny reflective metal. He ignored the smell of radiation and left it open to air out.

How silly. Well, I don't want to be locked in there with it smelling this way. Too bad all the air fresheners are long past giving off pleasant smells.

Time passed with the scientist quietly working inside the small laboratory room. There was too much to get done and the flow of time was still the same enemy it had always been. The more he looked around on his laptop the more things he realized he had to get in order. There were emails full of files and research to send off to Sid and Mantis, and an immortal's life full of memories he wanted to keep preserved before he stepped into that room.

Killian obviously has no email address. I will make one for him. There are so many things I want him to have.

And with that boy a constant image in his mind, Perish found himself wandering into the operating room.

As if to show himself just how his efforts hadn't been in vain, he reached out and put a hand on Killian's chest. Immediately he felt the sharp burning needle pricks come to his fingers. He clenched Killian's chest hard and forced a surge of sestic radiation into the boy's warm body.

The static needles jabbed at him like a thousand soldiers wielding spears, but he focused all of his energy into his hands and bit through the pain.

Then, when Perish was satisfied, he withdrew his hand and looked at the boy's chest.

If he was still a normal arian his chest would've had a half-inch deep imprint of Perish's hand. It would be red, swelling, and in an hour a fluid-filled blister would form... but the boy's body held nothing but sickly grey skin, and deep blue veins that coated his chest like a rat's nest of fishing line.

My solemn goodbye. Perish walked out of the surgery room and grabbed several boxes he had. He turned a left at the hallway that led to the white room he had previously been in and walked to a single metal door that opened to a flight of stairs. He walked down them two by two until he got to the bottom, another hallway in front of him, though this one was much like the tunnel sewers they had seen in Kreig.

Perish squinted as his eyes adjusted to night vision and sprinted down the sewers, taking twists and turns that only Sky's memories remembered, until he got to a second metal door.

This door was reinforced and seven inches thick, a fireproof door that could withstand the white flames of hell that rode behind the condensed radiation like a chariot. He threw the box in and left it propped open with an L-shaped rusted pipe. Then, without another glance, he ran back; the large cylinder tunnel filling with the sounds of his boots on the smooth brick.

He didn't like feeling rushed, but at any time–

"Perish?"

Perish stopped. A quiver of anticipation went through his chest and he felt himself stuck in limbo. A brief period in time that offered, in its fleeting moments, a chance to call all of this off.

"Perry?"

Perry...

Though the nickname had been Perish's for centuries now, just hearing Killian's weak and confused voice call it immediately made tears spring to his eyes. All of a sudden the reality of what he was doing, and what he was going to do, came crashing down on him.

With a stifled sob, he leaned a hand against the metal door frame for support and brought the sleeve of his lab coat up to his face. He cried into it briefly; his chest filled with pain and his throat dry and tight. His mind seemed to fill with fears, and in the dark corners he felt small fleeting surges of doubt. But he had already come this far, there was no turning back.

What would I go back to? Reaver will never trust me again. Silas will hunt me like a dog and then encase me in concrete for the next two hundred years. No, this had to be done, I made this decision long ago and

I told myself over and over that I would go through with it.

I am ready.

So Perish closed the metal door behind him and took in a deep breath. After taking another moment to gather himself and his nerves, he made his way into the operating room.

Killian was sitting up, his sapphire eyes glassy and staring forward. He turned to look at Perish and his face lightened.

"Perry… you've been crying."

Like a trigger being pressed, Perish's eyes started to well again. He put a hand to his face and nodded before trying his best to smile.

Always other people first. Oh, my sweet heart, promise me you will never change.

Please never change.

"I know, sweety, I have." Perish walked towards him, and still holding his weighted smile, he brushed back Killian's hair and removed the breathing tubes he had in the boy's nose.

"How do you feel?" He reached a hand out and stroked the thick red incision in the back of Killian's head, when the boy flinched he cooled his touch. "Can you walk?"

Killian started to shift off of the bed, and as he did, Perish gently extracted the tubes sticking into his arms. When he was free of medical equipment Perish took a step back, waiting for the boy to answer him.

Killian was very much in a daze. He looked around the surgery room as if he didn't know where he was and furrowed his brow. Perish took this moment of confusion to dress him in his cloth pants. He gently put them onto the boy and lifted him off of the hospital bed to tie the laces around his waist.

"What happened?" Killian murmured. Perish put a lab coat on him and held out his hand.

The boy took it and stepped off of the hospital bed.

"I made you better, love," Perish said with a smile. "That's what happened."

Though the boy saw right through the smile. The lines in his furrowed brow deepened, and he continued to look around the operating room, then his vision fell down to the bloody surgical tools.

"What did you do to me?" Killian's voice raised an octave. His face twisted in a nervous fear that Perish immediately tried to quell with a shush.

"It's okay, Killian. I… I won't tell you now, love. I don't want to upset you. But I wrote it down, alright? Can you listen carefully as we walk?"

Killian nodded, and started walking without Perish's help towards the long hallway.

He held Killian's hand as they slowly walked down the hallway towards the room. Perish squeezed it and gave him another smile. "When the time comes, I want you to go through that door. Go right, right, left, right, and you will reach a thick metal door. Inside it is a quad you can ride right out of here and a duffle bag that is green that has in it things I want you to take, okay?"

Killian stared at him blankly. "Right, right, left, right."

Perish nodded and kissed his cheek. "That's right, baby. Ride the quad straight and eventually it will lead you to the end of a large sewer, after that you'll be in the plaguelands. Keep riding straight, that will take you southwest, out of the radiation. I even put a map in the big pocket of the duffle bag. An easy one for you to read."

The boy, still looking half-dazed, nodded. "You'll meet me there, then?"

Perish's chest shuddered as he took another breath, months of steeling himself for this moment and he still couldn't grab proper hold of his emotions. Unlike Silas, Reaver, and so many others, he didn't have the strength in him to harden the churning feelings right now. Seeing the boy staring at him with such sad confusion, and knowing what he was about to ask him to do, was slowly tearing him apart.

"No, love, we're going to have to say goodbye now," Perish whispered. "I'm going to have to leave you."

Killian's face crumpled and immediately Perish put his arms around him and held the boy to his chest. Tears streaming down Perish's cheeks as he bit his lip to keep himself from breaking down.

He closed his eyes and took another deep breath. "There is a flare gun inside of that bag. Once it's dark I want you to shoot it up into the air. There is a man who's a friend… I mentioned him before. Do you remember Mantis?"

"Don't leave me. Why does everyone leave me? I… I don't want to stay with Mantis. Why can't I stay with you?" Killian's voice was broken, full of fear and made shaky by the tears Perish knew were running down his own face.

"Because you don't belong to me, sweety. You're not mine to keep," Perish whispered to him, clutching the boy to him tightly. "You belong to someone who loves you very much. I know your mind is a bit scrambly but you'll remember him as soon as you see him. Once you remember Re… him, you'll…" Perish chuckled. "You'll probably hate me for a while."

Killian pulled back; his eyes red and his cheeks streaked with tears. "I love you, why would I hate you? Why… why are you doing this?" He looked around and pursed his lips. "We have everything down here. Why can't we… stay. I'll stay with–"

Perish shook his head and Killian stopped mid-sentence. The weight of the boy's words wore heavy on the doubts he still had. The doubts that told him that he could stay down here with Killian, spend the rest of their lives making each other happy.

But that was a fool's dream. A dream that could never be realized.

You're not mine to keep, love, and I know eventually our happiness would pass. Even if I took you for myself, we would only be tormented and tortured, chased and hunted, until the ends of the earth. By both the man who loves you, and the man who wants nothing more than to see you dead.

And eventually you would get your mind back, and you would be nothing more than my prisoner.

You're Reaver's, not mine.

Over two hundred years, and that was the most painful thing for me to have to accept.

"You'll understand one day, Killian." Perish put his hand back up to Killian's cheek. He wiped away a large tear slipping down the boy's pale face. "And when you do understand… I want you to know: you made the last of my days the best ones I had ever experienced."

Killian stared at him confused. "You're… you're immortal, Perry. Where are you going to go?"

Perish withdrew his hand and turned to the control panel embedded in the wall beside the door. With his heart racing, he pressed a button and flicked a small switch.

His eyes flickered up as there was a low whirring sound. And though the metal panels inside of the room didn't move, Perish could feel the pull as they snared his energy in their field and urged him closer.

"I'm going to go be with my brother; he's been waiting quite a while for me," Perish whispered.

The scientist wiped his forehead with his sleeve, and for what seemed like the hundredth time today, he took a deep breath for courage. With Sky's memories reassuring his nervous brain, he tried to calm himself down.

I'm not even scared for what I am going to do; I'm not scared of the darkness I know is coming. I hurt inside because I have to leave Killian now. I have to leave him alone and know that once that door closes... I will never see his face again.

I love you, so much, Killian.

"Okay... it's time... this will help your pain," Perish whispered. He reached inside of his pocket and pulled out a small pill of morphine. He put it to Killian's lips and obediently the boy opened his mouth. Without even asking what it was, he swallowed it. His blue eyes, as blue as the summer skies of Perish's childhood, staring at him in fear and confusion.

"You're going to feel a lot of energy, and see a lot of light... but do not be scared it won't hurt you anymore." Perish reached behind his neck and took off his chimera necklace; he started to fasten it around Killian's neck.

"In about ten minutes it will all be over." Perish's voice caught in his throat again. "Now listen carefully, Killian; this is what you need to do after the light fades..."

Killian

I stared at him, blankly and confused, watching his mouth move as he told me what strange thing I was going to have to do after. I didn't understand it, but he was an immortal and it wasn't like he was going to be away for long.

He seemed so... sad, and every time I disagreed with what he was asking me to do he started to cry again, so I agreed. Whatever made him happy. He was all I had left in the world and the only man I could trust. I remember he had said that to me again and again on the surface.

Perish loved me and I trusted him, but why was he asking me to do this to him? What was going to happen in that room?

"I love you," I said to him, just because I wanted to make him happy, but once again I screwed up because he started crying again.

Don't cry, Perry…

He held me again in his arms, and though my body was tender and sore, I let him squeeze me tight. I squeezed him back and this time when he pulled away… he kissed me.

I pressed back and opened my mouth just slightly. He opened his and together we kissed, our arms wrapped around one another.

When he pulled away, he took a step back; his chest rising and falling with a deep breath. He looked at me and I looked back. We stayed with our eyes locked, neither one of us looking away.

There was a click behind us which drew both of our vision away from each other. He turned around and checked on a gauge of something on the control panel and nodded to himself.

"Are you ready, Killian?" Perish gave me a smile that I knew was fake. He swallowed hard and opened the door to the metal-plated room.

"No," I whimpered. I didn't want to be alone, and I didn't want to go out into the greywastes. I wasn't going to either, no matter what he said. Once I did what he asked, once I opened the door after he was finished, I was going to stay until he came back. I refused to leave him. You don't just leave someone you love.

"Come give me one last hug," Perish whispered. Immediately I ran over to him and dove into his arms. He squeezed me so hard I thought my ribs were going to break. I held him back and blinked away the tears still falling down my cheeks.

"I love you, Killian. You're going to be something amazing, I promise you," he whispered.

"I love you, Perry… I love you," I whispered back. I shut my eyes tight and buried my head into the crook of his arm. "Please, don't do this."

He pulled away, leaned down and gave me a kiss on the lips.

"Goodbye, sweety. Thank you for showing me mercy. Thank you for loving me through my madness, and thank you for showing me there is still good in this world."

Perish turned from me. He walked into the room and turned around, his hand on the metal door. He looked at me; his blue eyes heavy and full of what seemed like a thousand emotions at once.

Our eyes locked, dark blue and light blue, and as he slowly closed the door, he smiled at me and mouthed one last *I love you.*

Then the door closed.

CHAPTER 61

Reaver

I COULD FEEL THE QUAD START TO LOSE POWER AND I knew that this time the four-wheeler wouldn't be able to be resurrected. It had been pushed hard over rough terrain for a long time and if overheating wouldn't kill it, the fact that we were once again running out of gas would.

Silas was quiet when, with one last pathetic whir, the quad died underneath us. I jumped off with a slew of curse words shaking my head.

"We're not far now," Silas said jumping off too. He grabbed onto the quad and started rolling it off of the road beside a baked-black median. He clapped the dust off of his hands and looked around the deserted plaguelands.

"How long?" I asked. Not wasting any time, I started walking down the old road, now streaked with black char marks and holding a large amount of stray gravel. On either side of us were large mounds of hardened metal and spikes of rebar sticking up out of the ground. This entire place had been burned to a crisp, only the thickest of metal seemed to have escaped the white hot flames. This place was the plaguelands, though I had no idea how the radanimals they were supposed to have here actually survived, though Silas did say this charred terrain was limited to the city.

"A couple of hours now, I think." Silas's head shot to me and I knew he had heard the spike in my heartbeat. "It's behind one of these metal mounds. Our lab was underneath a large skyscraper."

"Why didn't it burn?" I kicked a scorched black rock with my foot and watched it bounce along the ground, eventually it stopped in a large pothole and settled on top of a chunk of median.

"It did, it burned to cinders," Silas replied. "The previous lab was completely gutted but somehow it didn't collapse. This one was re-built, though I didn't find out until much later."

Even hearing his voice made me unsettled and on edge, but when I was quiet my thoughts nagged at me like a splinter stuck in my eye. My worry for Killian was cannibalizing all of my emotions and in this present situation hearing Silas talk outweighed driving myself into insanity worrying about that boy.

I heard his soft boot steps behind me, quiet like the ghost he was. It wouldn't be soon enough that I stopped being in the presence of him. Though I wasn't sure what was going to happen after I got Killian. If he had it in his mind that he could kidnap me and take me back to Skyfall his head would be resting at the bottom of the pothole like Kessler's.

Faster boot steps sounded until he was walking side by side with me. I twitched my mouth to the side, though I didn't voice my displeasure.

All the screaming and ranting in the world over him being with me, and physically close to me, wouldn't change that I needed to find Killian.

But it continued to make my mind reel that he was unguarded right now. My tongue was sore and bleeding in some places from biting down on it; the pain helped focus me.

"Stop doing that," Silas said darkly.

I gave him a sideways glance; I hadn't done a fucking thing.

"Stop bleeding." He glanced back at me and his eyes narrowed as they locked on mine. "Stop tempting me. I can smell it in your mouth. Have some self-control."

"Or why don't you just go fuck yourself instead?" I replied in a cold tone. And just because I honestly couldn't help it, I bit my tongue harder, letting the coppery blood flow into my mouth.

Silas twitched at this and inhaled a deep long breath.

"Yes, words are all you have since you're such damaged and ravaged goods." My heart jumped a second time and I felt a cold heat start to creep up my neck, pooling in my ears and behind my eyes.

"I can only hope it was videotaped." His eyes shot to mine, though I was staring forward, trying to wipe my mind of all the emotions that were a wellspring inside of me.

"I will show it on one of my Skyfall channels. Reaver gets raped bloody by–"

I spat the blood right on his face. Silas recoiled back, shutting his eyes out of reflex. Then, just as he was opening them, I reached up and backhanded him right across the mouth.

He didn't fall, but he gasped and took a few steps back. I stopped and crossed my arms, daring him to attack me.

Silas glared at me; his own trickle of blood starting to drip down his nose.

"My apologies."

I unfolded my arms. I wanted to give him a confused look. I wanted to take him and wring his neck for this odd state he seemed to be in. Take him by his stupid blazer collar and shake him back and forth until he started acting like Asher again.

He was worried.

I had never seen Asher Fallon or Silas Dekker worried. Perhaps that was what was unsettling me about this. I could see times where it was like he was forcing himself to match me, but for the most part his mind seemed to be in outer space just like my own was.

All of this made me uncomfortable. I felt like I was walking on dozens of face-up glass bottles, all shaking underneath my feet. I didn't like it because I didn't know how to handle it. If we were anywhere else doing any other thing, I would have exploited it and used it to satiate my need for revenge; a need now baked and embedded in my bones.

But it wasn't about me; it was about getting to the lab where Perish was keeping Killian.

I didn't answer, I just kept walking.

"I punished him, you know," Silas said behind me. I could feel the heat on my neck from his eyes. "He will be gone for as long as you wish. I will let him out when you say it so."

I turned around, the heat on my neck quickly becoming a burn, an uncomfortable feeling that made my insides squirm. I wanted him to shut up; I needed him to shut up and just… act like Asher, not this… this whatever he was. Yeah, the Fallocaust could happen again and maybe the reality of that was lost on me, but I needed to find Killian, that was my only purpose here.

"What do you mean he's gone?" I asked slowly.

Silas's face was blank of expression; he had a stance of someone casual but his voice and his eyes gave him away. That was where the worry started and I knew those roots were deeply imbedded in him.

"It's how I punish my disobedient chimeras. The immortal ones," Silas explained, sliding his hands into his pockets. I was happy that his eyes flickered away from mine. He started scanning some of the bigger piles of melted debris. "I encase them in concrete tubes. I give them air holes and I leave them in there to resurrect, only to starve and die again days later. I have some who have been in punishment for decades."

That was twisted. I enjoyed hearing that and picturing Nero experiencing the same fate.

"I gave Nero a space so his hand can stick out. Just so his little pet Kiki can have something to hold. I didn't feel like giving him a voice."

"He deserves it," I mumbled. I turned away from Silas and started walking up some of the mounds of metal, I didn't know what I was looking for but I wanted to do something anyway.

"Nero is different... he's my third born. He can handle rape, pain, and physical torture so I didn't bother with that. Oddly though, he hates being alone. He gets lonely, which is why I always gave him a cicaro to dote on."

"You like giving finely crafted punishments, don't you?" I asked. I skidded down off of the hill and landed back on the pavement with a *thunk*. "I'm looking forward to taking a page out of your book when I punish you."

Silas's face held not even the most fleeting of expressions; he remained calm and almost robotic. Still it was in his eyes though.

"Oh? And how will you punish me, Reaver?" he asked with a cool, almost casual, tone.

"Where would the fun be if I told you?" I gave him a passing glare before I disappeared behind another long, almost tree-like twist of metal.

"Yes, true," Silas murmured. "Tearing each other emotionally and physically limb from limb is much more important than just admitting you were created for me. That not even Lycos and Greyson could–"

"Don't even fucking say their names! And don't call him Lycos, he was Leo!" Red suddenly burst from behind my eyes. It was like his flaming words had unexpectedly found a spring of oil.

Just the mention of my dads...

My dads.

Their memories weighed painfully on my shoulders, on my heart. I turned from Silas with my teeth clenched, holding back the emotion I could feel rise in my throat. Every time I swallowed the inflammable liquid rose.

He had shot him.

Why are you walking with a man who killed your fathers right in front of you?

You fucking IDIOT!

No! No! I shut my eyes and stalked forward, knowing that if I even looked at him I would whirl around and attack him. I would rape him until he screamed for mercy; peel his skin from his body.

Reaver, Reaver, what are you doing? You're no Reaper. No Reaper would walk beside the man who had caused all of this.

No, I couldn't lose control; that side of me couldn't win. I had to find Killian and he was the only man who knew how to get to the lab and get inside.

Bury it inside of you, Reaver. Push it into the void.

"I let them share a cell."

I froze on the spot.

"Greyson sang to Leo, to soothe him. Leo cried, apologizing for getting found out. It was… so sweet. I remember the song too. I always enjoyed it. *Of all the money e'er I had, I spent it in good company–*"

I spun around. And as I lunged at Silas, I left the restraint behind. I left the mature chimera that I had tried so hard to be, behind.

I had tried. I had tried but I could only be pushed so far. The void was bursting, overflowing, and filling my body with a toxic adrenaline. The same burning fire that turned my blood into gasoline and my body into an atomic bomb.

Greyson had sung that song to me when I was small, and it was because of the realization that Silas was telling the truth that the last of my control had been consumed by flames.

Silas was expecting it, but even when he made his entire body boiling hot to the touch I had not a care to give. I fell with him to the ground, and with tears stinging my eyes, I started strangling him with all the strength in my hands.

My lips pursed, my hands became vices; his touch turned to an electric current but still it only strengthened my grip. I squeezed my hands around his throat as the tears dripped onto his face.

He killed them; he killed the two men who had loved me no matter how bad of a kid I was. He had killed them in front of me with cruel indifference. My own fathers.

I would find him on my own; I would find Killian on my own. I would…

I had to kill Silas. I had to kill all of them.

Blood vessels started to pop in his eyes; his body was gathering electricity and shooting it into my bare hands but still I squeezed the life out of him.

Tighter… tighter…

Suddenly everything became white.

Out of shock, my hands snapped away from Silas's neck. Or they felt like they were. I couldn't see anything, my entire world was white, like the signal had been lost on a television set the world had just ceased to produce colours and textures.

Then the sound. A low rumbling like a deacon's growl. Though instead of my chest vibrating, my entire body was shaking and thrumming like an earthquake. Only this quake was imbedded in the atmosphere around us. The very air was quaking, the electricity surrounding us was being scrambled; the light was being eaten alive and yet it was all around me.

We were too late.

The Fallocaust was happening again.

"Killian!" I screamed. I tried to run though I was blinded. I made it several leaping paces before I tripped over something and fell.

I struggled to get up and tried to shield my eyes with my arm.

My arm was almost see-through. The light easily penetrated my skin, making my flesh glow red. I could see every small vein and an outlined shadow of my bones.

I held my hands out in front of me, my fingers looking like a colour x-ray.

He couldn't survive this… he was gone. Even in the midst of the world ending around me, the roaring consuming all of my body in its noise, I dropped to my knees and stared forward.

I was too late.

I was too late.

Then, like a suction, I felt every part of my body start to pull. It was like someone had grabbed my skin and was slowly tugging it away from my bones.

I saw a flicker of my dark brown hair out of the corner of my eyes as this vacuum started pushing all of the energy it had released back to its source. I rose to standing and stumbled forward, ignoring a strange needle-like feeling that was starting to envelope my body.

Then the light left.

I stood there in shock as suddenly everything returned to normal. I looked around, my eyes dazzled, and my mind in a state of shock and confusion. I didn't know what was going on, as quickly as the strange blinding light came – it had disappeared.

Nothing was on fire. Nothing was melting or burning. What was going on?

"SKY!"

I whirled around and was taken aback as I saw a look of absolute agony on Silas's face. He was shaking; his green eyes a glaring beacon of fear and anxiety. He looked at me for a second and then behind me.

Without a word, he ran ahead. I followed him, keeping his speed.

Did this mean Killian wasn't dead? The questions painted their dark pictures on my mind, of finding the boy dead, of finding the laboratory in flames. It coated my faint hopes in black ink and extinguishing the light of the lamp Killian held.

The lighthouse, my candle in the darkness, you always were there. Please, no, don't take him away from me. I can't live without him... not even when he's a hundred years old can I let go of that little fifteen-year-old boy I had seen walk into Aras.

Don't do this to me. I know I am not a good person but, fuck, I can't handle it.

"SKY!" Silas screamed an agonizing scream of both desperation and horror. It knocked against the dark void and fell lifeless to the ground. I had no sympathies for the Mad King; he just needed to take me to Killian.

Though that sparked a new realization inside of my head; that Silas had never given a fuck if the north greywastes were wiped out. He just wanted to get Sky's O.L.S back into his possession.

I followed him; the strange needles all across my body, blanketing me in a hive of energy that trapped in every agonizing emotion I was feeling in that moment. In my own desperate madness I thought I would start another Fallocaust on my own. The energy trapped inside of me was starting to leak out, like water to a derelict building, it was searching for cracks and weaknesses for it to exploit and destroy from the inside out.

I will give up everything for you, Killian.

I will give up revenge.

I will give up hate.

I will take you and find a small town and I will live with you forever, letting you win every argument, letting you bring home as many fucking stray cats and stray boys as you want.

Killi Cat, just be alive.

I don't want to be the Reaper; I just want to be yours.

That was all I was ever wanted to be.

I followed Silas, my own thoughts slaying me a thousand times over. After an hour of running without rest Silas stopped abruptly. He turned left and disappeared behind a large mound of twisted metal almost entirely covered in dust and debris.

I turned too, ignoring the pain inside of my lungs, and saw an open door and Silas disappearing down a metal rung ladder.

His eyes were wide, staring forward with the same shell-shocked expression he had once permanently plastered on Killian's face. I followed him down the ladder, our panting breaths echoing in the cold room, and jumped down as soon as I heard his feet hit the floor.

Without acknowledging me, he covered the distance from the ladder to a metal door across the room. I followed him and realized I was now stepping on carpet.

My breath caught. I swallowed down my own fears but they nagged me like needles in my throat. I wedged apart my clenched teeth and managed to say his name.

"Killian?" I screamed it, unable to control my own voice. I ran into the living room and looked around.

They had been here; they were here... "Killian!?" I saw Silas run into what looked like a laboratory and quickly followed him. My heart was hammering, and my lungs twin fire pits from the exhaustion of getting here.

Both of our boots echoed and squeaked on the laminate; our breaths matched in their laboured rhythms. He was still several paces ahead of me, and as soon as I had thought I was gaining on him, he turned a hard right and disappeared.

I turned around the same corner and saw Silas standing beside a door. I quickly pushed him aside and I opened it

And there he was.

There he was.

There was my angel.

"Killi..." I whispered.

I walked up to him. He was staring at the floor, his eyes dazed and his mouth moving back and forth like he was chewing on something. Immediately I knew he wasn't in his right mind and immediately I knew how to approach him. Slow and without fast movements, like you would an injured animal cornered in a pen. I had learned that from our experience in Aras.

"Killi Cat?" I slowly raised a hand and rested it on his cheek. In response, his eyebrows twitched like he was confused, before a moment later he raised his hand and put in his mouth the last bit of what he was eating.

I watched as his mouth moved up and down with a small smile. I didn't care if he never spoke again, he was alive. I petted his cheek and shushed him, taking in this boy who looked half-dead, with the solemn knowledge inside of me that he had never looked more beautiful.

"Killi?"

Killian's face scowled. I patted his cheek. "It's Reaver."

My heart filled when I saw his eyes widen. He suddenly looked at me and I almost laughed as his face adopted an expression of pure shock.

"Reaver?" he croaked. His voice was so rasped and broken but it sounded like angels to me. "I... I remember you."

Killian tried to lift up his hands, but before he could I gently took him into my arms. I held him and closed my eyes for a brief moment. I knew that was the only moment I had before I had to deal with the rest of this situation.

Then my hand brushed the back of his head. My brow furrowed as my fingers traced something odd, bumps in his scalp, hot to the touch. I gently tilted his head to the side, and felt the heat of the room and of my body, drain away, leaving in its place frozen liquid.

Killian had red and inflamed staples behind his head, starting from behind his ear and not ending until his other ear.

"I'm okay," Killian said faintly, but his words did nothing to quell the horror washing through me. It brought a tremble to my lips that cared nothing for the emotionless man I once was.

He had operated on Killian.

What had Perish done to him?

PERISH!

I hadn't even realized I'd screamed that until I had jumped to my feet. In an instant, the heaviness of my emotions dissipated. All of the agony I felt over what had happened to Killian seemed banished with the sole realization that the scientist had to be near.

He wanted a robot, a slave. He did surgery on Killian to make him love him, or, or something. It was him… it was him. No.

No.

It was Sky.

It was that fucking O.L.S implanted in his brain. Perish would've never hurt Killian. It was him.

A dangerous pulse of anger licked my veins and flushed my brain with their violent thoughts.

Stacking savage thought after savage thought on an already taxed mind, I let each transgressive image rush through me, letting it fill me and take me. With the dozens of emotions that had laid claim to my body over the last several hours, this was the one my chimera mind embraced.

In the throes of my own rage, my head snapped towards the sound of crying, but it wasn't Killian. I narrowed my eyes, briefly confused as to why I was hearing such a sound, before my legs took me to a door embedded in the far wall.

I opened it wide and it held open. I looked inside.

Silas was on the floor holding Perish's head in his lap. The scientist was dead, and from the looks of it the back of his head had been bashed open.

Strangely the king was rocking back and forth, the same shell-shocked eyes staring forward. He was mumbling to himself; his head also shaking like he was trying to deny what was going on around him.

Silas reached down and petted Perish's black hair back, before his eyes clenched shut, tears spilling from them.

"No, no," Silas kept mumbling; his voice a desperate whine. "No, no, not him."

"Not forever; I can't handle forever."

I stared at him, not understanding why he was so upset. I could see Perish's head had been smashed but that was a plus for everyone but me. Because I wanted to torture this Sky fuck for the rest of our immortal lives.

Immortal lives…

I walked up to Silas and Perish. I kneeled down and picked up

Perish's hand.

It was stiff and cold to the touch; the shock of it made me retract my hand.

My eyes travelled up to Silas. The king, with his eyes red and his mouth trembling, made eye contact with me.

"He's dead, Reaver. He killed himself."

I stared back at him, not knowing how to feel about this. I was confused, I was fascinated – and I was drinking in the look of fucking agony on him.

I smirked, and at my smile, he dissolved into hysterical tears.

The next thing he did blew my mind, and dismissed all of the logic in the world I had gathered to help explain Silas.

Because, with his face twisted in agony, he put Perish's head down, crawled over him and put his arms around me. Bewildered and confused, King Silas crawled into my lap and sobbed like a fucking child.

"Hold me, please. Hate me later. Punish me later, just hold me," Silas cried. His entire body was trembling like he was having a seizure or an anxiety attack. Perplexed, I steadied him enough so he wouldn't roll off of me and awkwardly let him sob in my shoulder.

"You… you hated him," I said to him. "You despised Perish."

I could see his jaw twitching with how hard he was clenching his teeth. He let out a sob and shook his head. "I hated him because every time I looked at him I saw Sky. Every time I heard his lucid voice I heard Sky. Now my last tie to my old life is gone. My Perish is gone."

I glanced down at Perish's open skull, my brow furrowing as I realized that there was no brain inside that huge gaping crater. I nodded towards it. "Don't you have Sky's O.L.S? Too bad, if you didn't kill Leo you would have the formula to make another Sky. Serves you right, eh?"

Silas looked down at Perish's skull and I felt his heartbeat suddenly spike. "His O.L.S? I could… I could… Elish would have the research. He could make me a Sky. I know he could."

Silas slid off of me and I rose to standing, feeling disgusted even having Silas so close to me.

I brushed it off and turned to walk back towards Killian.

To my complete shock, Killian was in the doorway. He was holding something in his hand.

"It's gone," I heard Silas say, his voice thin but hoarse. "His O.L.S is gone."

My eyes found Killian's; he was staring right at me. Though, unlike when I had first seen him, his eyes were focused. They were fixed on my own, with a sanity in them that I hadn't even seen when he was at his best.

"His fucking O.L.S is gone!" Silas screamed.

Killian's eyes flickered down and so did mine. Then his hand drew up, and pinched between his fingers was a small plastic device the size of a pebble.

Killian smiled at me.

And I smiled back.

"YOU!" Silas suddenly screamed.

In a flash, Silas tried to push me aside, but instead of letting him through I grabbed onto him. Using the same move Greyson had mastered while restraining me, I wrenched Silas's hands behind his back and pinned them to my stomach. The king screamed at Killian, thrashing his body and contorting it like a scaver caught in a snare, hysterically shrieking at Killian when he saw just what my boy was holding.

"Give me Sky! GIVE ME SKY!" Silas was the embodiment of madness, a hysteria that brought a smile to my lips and warmed the dark pits of my heart.

I drank it in; I held it to me and cherished it as you would a prized possession.

Yes, this was the feeling. This was what I live for; this was what I have bled for, been raped for, and separated from Killian for.

This was the Reaper; this was the Reaper working side by side with his Angel of Death.

"PLEASE!" Silas sobbed. I saw the tears start to drop from his face, his entire body heaving and shaking back and forth. His legs kept weakening; I kept having to thrust his body to keep him standing. I had never tasted such agony and fear on a man, and like the sweetest ambrosia, I savoured every second of it.

Oh, this is certainly heaven in the greywastes. Nothing could compare to this.

Killian took a step closer to him. An eerie, cold smile that had once seemed unsuited for his face, now graced it like a well-fitting glove.

"I'll leave you alone, just let me have him. Let me clone Sky," Silas sobbed desperately. "Give him to me. I need him. I need him to help me get well. I'll be normal if I have him, I know I will. I was before."

I leaned in and couldn't help pressing my lips up against his neck.

"Oh, *bona mea,*" I whispered in the most taunting manner I could muster. "I love tasting this agony on you."

"Killian... Killian!" Silas begged as I continued to kiss him. "Give it to me. I'll let you live in peace. I will... I'll..."

Killian slowly shook his head before leaning in further. I tightened my grip on Silas and smiled as my boyfriend brought the O.L.S right up to Silas's face.

"Look at me," Killian whispered to him; his voice was sane, his tone level. "Don't take your eyes off of me."

Silas whimpered but looked at Killian, slowly shaking his head back and forth.

Killian smiled one last smile, a grin showing a row of white teeth...

Then he popped the O.L.S into his mouth.

Silas shrieked as Killian bit down, the sound of crunching drowned out by the frenzied, desperate screams spilling like a torrent through Silas's lips. In my own throes of cruel joy I laughed, making him watch as Killian swallowed the O.L.S with a satisfied smirk.

The king thrashed, and in his own delirium he seemed to draw out of him an insane strength. With a cry, he snapped his arms out of my vice-like grip and threw me against the wall.

But he didn't attack Killian like I thought he would. Instead he fell to his knees, took in a deep breath and screamed. A torturous scream that brought on its heels a sudden snap of electricity, followed by a low, body shaking vibration.

Oh shit...

I dashed to Killian and grabbed his shoulder. I picked him up, and as Silas's screams echoed inside of the metal room, I ran down the hallway towards the living room.

I didn't make it by a long shot.

A wave swept through my body, a weighed pressure that almost knocked me off of my feet. I swore and looked around, temporarily confused by my surroundings and where I could find the exit.

The timer was now ticking down, the sestic radiation quickly gathering around the laboratory, condensing in on itself until the inevitable explosion of white fire.

"Go back down the hall. Go right," Killian suddenly said, his voice full of haste. "The door, there's a metal door... there's shelter... right, right, left, right. Hurry!"

I turned and ran, my teeth grinding as Silas's hysteria-filled screams scraped against my brain like sandpaper. I raced down the hall, the boy in my arms, and to the door on the right side of the hallway.

Killian opened it and I kicked it the rest of the way with my foot. I took one step through it before I saw the light again, followed by a roar.

Then darkness, burning darkness.

I woke up in a painful daze, flames all around me. I saw the ghostly outline of my burnt hand, several fingers roasted to charcoal, one of them even holding a flame.

I was being dragged.

My eyes squinted; I opened them wider and shifted around. Then a hand on my forehead and his sweet sweet voice.

He was dragging me to safety. I was the immortal one, not him.

I stumbled as I tried to get up; I looked around as confusion temporarily reigned in my mind. Everything was on fire, it was so bright… so… brilliant…

I turned and looked at Killian.

"Killian!" I cried. All my confusion snapped out of me when I saw that his left arm was blackened. His forearm's skin was split in half by the pressure of his cooked flesh, and his side was devoured by a black char that leaked blood and clear fluid.

"NO!" I put my hand to my face and shook my head. His eyes were glassy, his good arm still grabbing my collar, desperately trying to pull me from the flames. He was saving me before he died.

He was going to die; he was going to die. "Killian? Oh no… no, no…"

"Reaver… I'm okay," Killian panted, but then he stumbled backwards, his back hitting the brick. We were in a sewer, some sort of cistern. "Reaver… Reaver, we need to get to… right, right, left…" Killian coughed. I realized smoke was pouring in from behind us.

"Killi…" I moaned. I walked towards him, my hands trembling and my heart dissolving to nothing. "Killi… I'm sorry."

He steadied himself and tried to take a step forward but stumbled again. I managed to catch him and picked him up.

Killian coughed from the smoke. He looked at me with his eyes glazed and a face hot and flushed. "Reaver… right, right, left, right. Please, Reaver… you need to… to take me there."

All I could do was stare at him in horror, my mind numb, refusing to process what I was seeing.

I was seeing him die.

"Killi..." My voice came out a raspy, broken cry. I felt my eyes start to sting as I looked down at him. He looked so weak... he looked so...

Killian's face tightened and he glanced down at his charred arm. I looked down too, my body seemingly frozen in time.

Then a loud crack sounding from the top of the stairs. Temporarily snapped out of my shock, I looked behind me and saw the white flames shooting out of the doorway, the opal inferno burning the railing and making the metal a dusty white from the intense heat.

I needed to get him out of here... I... I needed to get him some place cold.

I needed water... something... something to cool down his body. I could save him, there was still hope. I could escape and find Silas and go with him to Skyfall. They had technology there for burns, didn't they?

My mind raced with delusional hope after delusional hope. Unable to stay where I was with the fire and heat blasting our burning bodies, I ran down the cistern with my boyfriend in my arms.

"Stay awake, Killi," I said to him, my voice tight. I looked down and felt my face twist when I saw the skin on his neck start to lift away from his body. It was peeling off in chunks with every step of my boots. He tried to hide the pain from me but I could feel it in his heart. Fuck, his heart was racing like he was going to have a heart attack.

Right, right, left, right – Fuck, Perish, you fucking asshole.

No, it was us.

We had did this. We had taunted Silas.

This was all my fault.

Killian was going to die and it was all my fault. Because I had to let Killian get his revenge, because I wanted to taste the agony radiating off of Silas.

The cistern was a maze to me, but in my mind I constantly went over Killian's instructions, and soon I rounded the last bend and saw where he was trying to lead me.

It was a door being held ajar by a rusted pipe. It was a thick door that looked not only blast proof but fire proof. So quickly I ran into the room and kicked the door stopper out of the way.

I heard it shut behind me but I was already eyeing up the quad I saw parked in the middle of a room full of supplies and boxes. The quad itself had bags tied to it and guns but…

"Reaver?" Killian's weak voice sunk my heart and made my mind halt its desperate delusions that I could get him out of this alive.

"Don't worry… we'll… we'll be out of this soon," I said hastily. "Just, hang on, Killi… just hang on…"

"Stay still."

I looked down at him and when I saw those blue eyes staring at me, glassy but alert, my composure dissolved into nothing. I gave a strangled sob and shook my head.

"No, Killi… we can escape… we have a quad," I choked. "I can take you to… to Skyfall."

The boy gazed up at me and I saw his face had turned grey; his lips were tinged blue and peeling off of his face. I could smell the burning; I could smell charred flesh and I could feel the wetness from the blood leaking out of his fatal wounds.

And his heart…

I could hear his once rapid beating heart start to slow.

"Stay still," he whimpered. "Hold me."

I sunk down to my knees, not because I wanted to fulfill his request but because I could no longer stand. I sat on the warm concrete and shifted until I was tucked into the corner of the room with him. Then I held that boy tight to my chest and rested my forehead against his.

The sounds of the building burning above us were drowned out by his quickened breaths and the small whimpers he let escape from his lips. I could feel those shallow but rapid puffs of air hit my cheek.

I looked at him, every part of me wanted to close my eyes to try and force us away from this place but I couldn't.

I couldn't stop looking at him; I couldn't stop analyzing every part of his face. That beautiful face like he had been carved from marble, with eyes so blue it was like he had stolen the stars from the sky.

Eyes that had once held laughter, love, hope…

Now they were wide and staring… they were…

They were scared.

My teeth clenched and I tried to tighten my grip on him, only to feel his small frame writhe under my hold. His body was a ruin, his arm charcoal and blood; his thigh and side open and exposed. He was so burned, fuck, he was so burned.

I was going to lose him.

Oh my god, I'm going to lose him.

"It's okay..." Killian whispered. His voice was getting weaker.

His voice was getting weaker.

"Promise me something..."

"No!" I cried. My eyes started to become blurry. My face burned, everything burned. "Don't... I'm not promising you anything. I... I'm not. I can't – Killi, I can't."

Killian's lips pursed before they twisted in a grimace as he tried to raise his good hand. I looked down and saw it was balled in a tight fist. He raised it but before he could reach out to touch me I took his hand and held it. It was burning hot and I could feel his rough skin shift around in my light touch.

He opened his mouth to try and talk but I shushed him. I didn't know why I did. I wanted him to keep talking... didn't I?

Or maybe I just didn't want him to cause more pain.

"Promise me..." Killian rasped. "You'll leave me when I'm gone. Please."

"Shut up!" I cried. I pressed my forehead against his and let out a sob, tears falling onto him. "Please... shut up."

"I love you, and... and I remember you now," Killian whispered, then his eyes shut tight and I felt his chest shudder. "Just... hold me, then... leave. Baby, you'll be stuck here for twenty years. You'll..." Another pause and I watched in horror as he took a shaky, congested breath. I looked down and groaned. Underneath his shredded clothes I could see crimson red skin and black.

"Reaver?" he suddenly cried. His face twisted in pain and I held him close to me.

"Shh... it's okay," I whispered. "It's okay... I'm here. I'm here. I'm not going anywhere. I'm here."

I'll be here forever.

I will never leave you. I don't care if I burn. I deserve worse.

Another loud snap rang out above us, one that I could feel vibrate the walls. I glanced up and saw the ceiling shift and move as the lab above us continued to burn. I ignored it and fixed my eyes back on my boyfriend, only to see his once alert and vivid eyes start to fade.

"Killi!" I screamed. The force behind my scream woke him up, but as he jumped from surprise he also cried out from pain. I drew him back into me, feeling my mouth fill with copper from biting down on my cheek and lips.

What do I do? What do I do?

I tried to shift myself to standing. The only solution my mind gave me was to take him out of the cistern, but at my movement Killian whimpered and his pulse jumped. I swore and shut my eyes tight and looked around the small room.

"Talk to me..." Killian whispered.

"I don't know what to say!" I cried. "I... I have to get you out of here. Killi. I know it hurts but–"

"Tell me about..." Killian paused. He took in another sharp breath and coughed; I saw blood sprinkle on my hand. "Tell me the story about... about when we first met."

My face crumpled and I shook my head, but as I did I felt his pulse start to slow and I knew it would be soon.

"Oh, Killi..." I whimpered. "Don't leave me here. You can't... I've barely had you. We've been apart for months. You can't, Killi Cat... you can't."

I saw him close those beautiful blue eyes. And as the silence descended on us, the fire raging upstairs and for all I knew right outside the door, I think I realized that was the last time I would ever see them.

I closed my eyes too, as tight as I could. I held him to me and started to slowly rock him back and forth.

"I remember when I brought you with me to sentry... on top of the east watch building. I was so nervous to have you near me, so... uncomfortable, because I didn't quite understand what I was feeling. Your hair was soft and blond, your face perfect in the moonlight. You were so... inquisitive, and it helped us talk because I didn't know what to say. I was so worried about scaring you away," I whispered, feeling his shallow breath on my lips. "I was this... bad guy and here you were wanting to be beside me. I didn't understand why such a beautiful boy would look twice at this... antisocial idiot that was me."

"But you did. And the prospect that you might like me the way I liked you scared the fuck out of me but... it also changed me. It drove me to do things I wouldn't normally do, like... like when I asked you to be my boyfriend," I sniffed and a sob broke my lips. "How about it? That's how I asked you, but you said yes. You said yes, and after that... we shared our first kiss."

I leaned down and kissed his peeling lips and felt his small frail body give the smallest shudder. "I will remember our time in Aras together, those couple of months before… this. I'll remember late nights watching movies. I'll remember drug nights with Reno, and dinner at Leo and Greyson's. I'll remember the first time you crawled over to me in the middle of the night and I didn't plan on pushing you away as soon as you fell back asleep. I remember when I realized… I was in love with you."

I took in a deep breath. "I love you… and I will do everything I can… to be with you soon… Killi Cat."

The silence fell onto the room like the world had disappeared around us. The only explanation I could give as to why it suddenly got quiet was that time had ceased to go forward. That the fabric of the universe had frozen, halted in its continuous rhythm, in response to what had just happened.

For as I spoke those last words to him I realized there was no longer any breath on my face. No longer a weak pulse sounding in the depths of my hearing. There were no more blue eyes, a colour unseen in this world. No more laughing, smiling boy, too naive for his own good.

The world had frozen, and time had frozen.

Because Killian Massey was dead.

I rocked him back and forth, even though I knew he couldn't feel it. I talked to him, even though I knew he couldn't hear me – but mostly I cried. I cried until his grey face was soaking wet with my tears and my mind was nothing but a useless snare of disconnected cords.

He was so light in my arms, light because what had made him my Killian was now gone. He was now just a physical body… but still I knew I would never leave him.

Killian was dead.

Killian was dead.

How could he be dead?

I sat with him in my arms, backed into the corner of the room. I didn't even care when I heard the metal snap around me, and I cared even less when the room started to get warmer. The flames of death would be a welcome reprieve from this agony I was in. With open arms I would take my twenty years of flames, because the pain of fire would be nothing compared to the eternity I would now spend without the love of my life.

And when I one day emerged, I would make it my mission to find out how to kill immortals. Because there was no part of me that wished to join the outside world. I was Killian's guardian; I was his protector, and I had failed. I had no will to live without him. I didn't even want to know what life would be like without my Killian.

I looked down at his still face and blinked away the tears stinging my eyes. My soul crushed inside of me when I saw his balled little fist on his chest. I had been holding it but I must've stopped while I was crying into him. It was clenched so tight; he must've been in a lot of pain.

I don't know how much of my mind remained; I felt shocked into a half-sane stupor. A part of me knew that I was in shock. I could only hope the shock didn't wear off before the flames consumed me. If I could die while I was still stunned, I would take it.

"My little Killibee," I whispered to him. I shifted him around so I could have a free hand and stroked back the remaining blond strands of hair he had on his head. My poor boy had lost a lot of his hair but he was still beautiful, maybe even more so now.

I ran a finger down his cheek and traced his jawline to his ears, half-expecting him to open his eyes.

And when he opens his eyes, I'll tell him… I filled up the loader tub with hot water for us to bathe in, because we were covered in blood, dirt, and C4 residue. I would see him take off his shirt and I would stare like an idiot because I was a fool in love. Though I hadn't realized it yet.

My eyes closed again and I let out a long breath, feeling the heat start to fill the room. The flames were closing in around us, ready to consume us both. He would be ashes in my arms and so would I… but it also meant beautiful… beautiful silence.

I will go wherever you go. I just hoped you were some place quiet.

Where you could be happy, without pain and without fear.

Where you weren't feeling this heat I could feel around me.

I opened my eyes and furrowed my brow. I looked down at the dead body of my boyfriend and stared.

I slowly realized it wasn't the room getting hot…

It was Killian.

I raised my hand and lightly pressed it against Killian's cheek. One of the few areas not burned.

Oh my fucking god.

His body was…

No… no, Reaver. Don't… don't torment yourself with… those thoughts.

He didn't.

Perish couldn't have...

Quickly I pulled my hand away and lifted Killian up off of me. I gently put him on the floor and rolled him onto his stomach. I shifted onto my knees and exposed the back of his head. The area where I had felt...

Where I had felt staples, before Silas had told me Perish had killed himself.

And there were... over a dozen of them stapled from one ear to the other.

I stared at the back of his head in shock as the pieces slowly started to come together, gathering like magnets to form a picture that, even in my most insane thoughts, I hadn't even thought was possible.

Perish... Perish...

You fucking... beautiful, brilliant man.

In my own shock, I found myself smiling, and as I lay my hand on the back of Killian's head and felt the searing heat start to radiate off of him... I started to laugh. I started to laugh hard.

And time started to flow forward once again.

Immediately I jumped up and ran to the quad. I turned it on and quickly opened the metal door leading to the outside.

A blast of heat hit my face like I had just opened the gates of hell, but there was no fire licking and tasting the thick metal doors. Though as I glanced to my right, I saw the heat waves radiate off of the cistern bricks and I knew then I had to hurry.

Still laughing. Oh my god, I was still laughing.

I was laughing like my mind had finally shattered as I lifted this immortal boy onto the quad and held him to me with one arm. I don't know what I was feeling in that moment and I think that was why the laughter rolled from my lips. Because like they had always said: laughing Reaver is a Reaver whose mind has just broke.

I don't fucking care! I have him. I have him.

I'll have him forever.

I clutched the boy to me and pressed on the throttle. The quad moved with ease, and without wasting any time, I turned it to the left and started riding as far away from the flames as I could. Killian was a ball of fire underneath my skin but the pain was the most beautiful pain I had ever felt. It was the pain of his body resurrecting, to make him brand-new and better than he had ever been as a mortal.

I would be there when his heart started beating. I would watch as the white flames inside of every immortal knitted his body back together.

I would be there when he woke, and I would be the one to tell him – we never had to worry about being away from each other again.

We may have spent a lot of time apart but now… but now…

He was mine for all eternity.

And with that thought, and a smile on my lips, Killian and I rode deeper into the plaguelands, leaving the greywastes far behind us.

I didn't look back.

But I did say goodbye.

CHAPTER 62

Jack

ELISH WAS SITTING BESIDE THE CICARO'S HOSPITAL bed, never leaving the sickly boy's side even though Lyle had already told him he was stable. Apparently though the boy's brain was in ruins and his recovery would be quite long.

This is just needless suffering, Jack thought to himself, his eyes absentmindedly flickering to the shadows of the room where Sanguine was standing in silence. *There is nothing wrong with being made an immortal at a younger age. I made Juni immortal as a teenager and he is no worse for wear.*

At the mention of his sengil, Jack looked to his side where Juni was standing. The boy was fifty-nine though his age had framed him as an eighteen-year-old. He had been one of the first non-chimeras to be given the gift of immortality.

Silas had made my loyal Juni immortal… and here is Sanguine trying to make me turn a cloak towards our king? The thought made the Grim's mouth down turn. He decided to turn his attention back to Elish. If only to appreciate the fact that he was not him, and he never had to fear for his cicaro-sengil's health again.

Jack's cold brother's eyes were hard; his lips showing a tinge of white from them being pursed. He had said little the entire time Jack had been here but Jack had expected nothing else. He was here to offer his silent support. Quiet company was the best company.

What a love-sick fool this one is. It's a pity he's fallen for such a fragile chimera.

"Do you remember when you were made immortal?" Jack said to Juni. The sengil was standing beside the sitting Jack, holding in his hand Jack's cape. A solemn expression on his face though that was his natural expression; he had always been a more gothic-looking sengil. The short black hair, tall stature, and square face never helped. The other sengils used to tease him and call him Little Frankenstein.

They were all dead now.

Juni gave a slight nod. "Yes, I would never forget, Master."

"And you do not mind being eighteen forever?"

"No." He was quiet for a moment. "I do not think I suffer mentally by not having my brain fully developed. And if there were any side effects I am sure one day the technology will be there that I can be aged. Either way, I am quite content, Master Jack."

Jack smiled at him, though he saw a flicker of blond out of the corner of his eye. He looked over, and sure enough, Elish was giving him a searing look.

The elegant chimera, with his hair now cut short and his clothing more casual than he usually wore outside his apartment, continued to glare at him. "Do not have veiled conversations in front of me, Jack. If you have something to say, say it."

"You love him and yet you risk him dying because you want him to be a full adult," Jack said airily. "I just don't understand; if you love him so why would you risk it? I almost lost my Juni and…"

"Juni is just a sengil."

"And Jade is *just* a cicaro, as you have said on many occasions. Or did that change in the greywastes? Are you calling him husband now?"

"Jade is many things," Elish replied and was quiet after.

Jack narrowed his eyes at this; he had expected more of a tongue lashing but, then again, it was Elish's little maritus in danger.

Parvulus Maritus, little husband, and that yellow-eyed cicaro probably didn't even know what Elish's nickname for him actually meant; though that was usually the entire point.

There was a knock on the door. Everyone looked to the other side of the room and saw Garrett poke his head in. His eyes swept the room and fell on Jade and Elish.

"Can we come in? How is he?" Garrett stepped inside at Elish's nod. The greywaster boy, with his hair half silver and half black, stepping in behind him.

"Lyle says he will live," Elish replied. "But he'll need intense therapy. We won't know until he wakes up just what he can do, whether he will still be able to walk, or talk... but he breathes and..."

Garrett finished Elish's sentence with a heavy smile. "And all we need is for them to breathe. He will mend himself during his first resurrection."

Elish nodded and turned back to his cicaro. The boy was covered in wires and surrounded by whirring machines; each one doing its job to sustain the cicaro's life.

"I need Silas back in Skyfall as soon as possible..." Elish's chest rose as he stifled a sigh. "With Reaver and Perish in the greywastes, he's the only one who can make Jade immortal if something happens to him. Sanguine... you don't know where he is?"

Jack was intrigued to see a look pass between Garrett and Reno, a fleeting exchange of glances but one that did not go unnoticed by the Grim.

Sanguine's face though, held no emotion.

"No, not yet, brother."

Elish nodded but said nothing else.

Suddenly Garrett's remote phone rang. Everyone's eyes shot to him as he dug it out of his pocket, his tongue sticking out of the side of his mouth.

He brought it to his ear.

"Hello?" Garrett gave everyone who was looking at him a smile but it quickly faded.

Jack frowned at this; Elish's jaw tightened. Reno was looking at his fiancé, confused.

Then Garrett's eyes widened and his mouth dropped open. He put a hand over his mouth. "Yes, we will... be right there. We... we'll be on the roof of Olympus."

Elish stood and so did Jack. The tranquility of the room gone as Garrett handed the phone to Reno.

"There... there was a very... very big sestic radiation pulse in the plaguelands, Elish." Garrett's knees buckled; Reno held him up though his face was the picture of terror. "Silas, Elish... Silas... it was Silas. The legion chimeras are heading there now. We must hurry. Sanguine, does Silas have his Falconer? Caligula and Nico are on their way here right now."

Sanguine shook his head. "I have his Falconer. If Caligula and Nico are heading our way they are flying a Fisherking most likely. We'll switch planes and get on the Falconer; it is faster."

"Prepare the plane then, Sanguine. Hurry." Garrett nodded, his face desperate.

Without another word, Sanguine disappeared out the door.

Jack grabbed his cloak from Juni, giving Elish a wide berth as the chimera swept past all of them, Garrett and Reno following behind. Before he left, Jack turned to Juni and gave him a quick kiss on the cheek. "Stay here with Jade and send for the half-raver to guard him."

Juni nodded. "I will not move until you return. Please, be safe."

Jack gave him a pat on the hand before he turned and ran to catch up with the others.

The mood was so thick that Jack could feel it weigh on his shoulders. Though thankfully as soon as they reached the roof the Fisherking plane was landing with the Falconer. The Falconer ready for takeoff.

Caligula greeted them with his boyfriend Nico, both of them stern in face and solid in stance.

Elish nodded at them before taking a step, but no sooner than his boot touched the metal did Sanguine say behind him, "Elish, I'd like to stay behind and be with Jade."

Elish paused and turned around. He nodded at Sanguine. "That would be appreciated. It will be your job to hold down Skyfall until our return, though we will not be long."

Sanguine bowed and walked back to the stairs.

Everyone boarded the Falconer with Nico taking the controls and soon, with barely a word spoken, they were flying towards the plaguelands.

I'm going back to the northeastern greywastes? I just left. I hadn't even had time to sketch out all my painting ideas. Well, I suppose it's always a treat to be outside of Skyfall, even if this trip is looking to be far from pleasant.

The Grim glanced around the plane, everyone looking angry and stressed out. Jack felt like striking up a conversation but his brothers and the mortals seemed to be in too foul of a mood to talk to him. It was their faults anyway; chimeras and their games.

And they seem to be keen on trying to suck me in.

Or Sanguine at least. At this thought Jack's heart gave a flutter. *Did he really want to re-kindle what he had destroyed so long ago?*

At the thought Jack felt nauseas; he hadn't decided how he felt about it. At one point in his life he was madly in love with his demon brother, but over the years he had taken every one of his feelings and had shot them execution style.

That chimera masochism – as predictable as our sexual orientation.

Jack looked towards the sudden sound of a muffled sob. It was Garrett; his hand was over his mouth and he was staring at the window of the plane. His eyes wide and his face twisted in pain. Reno was beside him, a statue of support though his pulse was a mess.

They know it has something to do with Reaver, but do I care? I don't know; I don't want to go against my king. Silas never showed hostility over me and Sanguine's paring. What do I possibly have to gain by siding with Elish? Juni is already an immortal, what is he going to do? Make my cat immortal? Sure he is a decent creature but after a year of sulking I get over my cats' deaths.

Jack watched Garrett and Reno embrace; Elish standing on the other side of the plane, his face carved granite. Everyone was a mess, everyone was worried… though not about the king.

When they were approaching the plaguelands Jack watched Garrett get out a blue bag from underneath a bench that doubled for storage. Jack watched, confused as to what Garrett was doing, until Garrett started handing Reno pills and throwing more to Caligula in the cockpit.

When it finally dawned on him, he chuckled in spite of the heavy mood.

Everyone glared at him.

Jack raised a dismissive hand. "I would have completely forgotten he isn't immune to the radiation; I suppose that is why my sengil is immortal. He would be covered in rashes and bleeding from the eyes before I even remembered to load him up with Iodine pills and radiation juice."

No one answered him and Jack was just fine with that.

Then they reached their destination, and even Jack's own face fell.

The charcoal grey smoke, the trademark wispy billows of sestic-ash that blocked out the very sun. In several days it would start to snow that ash onto the plaguelands and the outskirts of the greywastes. Beautiful to behold… but lethal to the touch, even if the unfortunate soul had a Geigerchip. Though with where they were it shouldn't hit any towns. Only radanimals and any rogue greywaster who strayed too close to the border would die from this.

Nico flew the plane low, but eventually after much arguing with Caligula, they decided to touch down a half-mile away from where the spike had occurred. Not only was it too dangerous to go any closer because of the visibility issue, it was now equally dangerous because of the heat.

"We won't be able to go far..." Caligula said. "Uncle Elish... what if Silas is trapped in there?"

"Then we're the luckiest men in the entire dead world," Elish said in a voice that could freeze even the white flames outside.

"What if it's Reaver?"

"I do not know," Elish replied in the same tone.

The plane touched down, and when Elish opened the sliding door they were all assaulted by an overpowering heat. They all stepped out, Reno, Caligula, and Nico, the three mortals, staying behind the group.

It was hell on earth, though in all respects it had been hell on earth for over two hundred and thirty-six years now. This was a different hell however; a three mile radius seemed to be engulfed in white flames. Dangerous still, unlike the usual orange and yellow flames of fire, these ones seemed to need little to thrive off of. They burned metal, concrete, even the greywastes ash was consumed for fuel. It ate all, and sent the remains into the sky to continue to cloak the sun and coat the world.

Jack looked around in awe, the black smoke was blocking out that very sun. No more did it hold a cloak of grey ashes, it had turned as black as Jack's own eyes. Black above, thick and encompassing, and white below, an almost transparent fire that seared and devoured everything.

A lethal radiation that, when in concentrated doses, could bring the opal flames of hell. With King Silas on chariot and Perish and Sky behind him, they road on dead horses and cast the earth into permanent grey.

The Fallocaust, the Apocalypse, the End Times.

They showed the world their hurt.

And it looks like someone was trying to show it again.

Though this time – where was the audience?

They all stuck near each other and headed towards the inferno. Jack noticed right away that his boots were sticking. He looked down and saw a trail of black streaks behind him.

The rubber on their boots was melting, each step was like trying to pull two pieces of glued paper apart. The black desperately trying to cling to the bottoms of the boots, leaving sticky strings in between.

Jack wiped his face, feeling like he was inside of an oven. The fire held nothing back; he could practically feel it baking his flesh.

"Garrett... it's too hot," Elish finally said, sweat beading down his forehead and his face flushed from the heat. None of them were any better. "We need to turn back."

Garrett's face was redder than all of theirs; he was in agony. Jack himself was concerned about Silas's fate but his brother could never hide his emotions well.

"Elish... I can't leave him there to burn. What if... what if Reaver is in there too?" His hand rose to his mouth, but any tears he might have would be sacrificed to the heat before they ever showed moisture. "Killian?"

In a rare display of emotion, Elish's face creased with a deep frown. He turned from the scene. "I'm afraid if Killian was with Perish, and if they are here... there is no way the boy could survive."

Reno beside Garrett let out a choke; he shook his head back and forth.

Elish put a hand on his shoulder.

"It would have been a quick death, Reno. The boy wouldn't have suffered."

Reno ripped his shoulder away from Elish, and to everyone's shock, he pushed him.

"He fucking suffered! Ever since you put us on that fucking plane, he suffered!" Reno suddenly screamed, the timber of his voice booming from intensity. "This is your fucking fault! This was your selfish plan; this was your doing! Was it fucking worth it, Elish? Was it? Jade is going to be a fucking vegetable. YOUR HUSBAND! Killian could be dead. Reaver might be burning alive for the next twenty-fucking-years! For what? FOR WHAT? Leo and Greyson died for this. You're the fucking monster! It's YOU! YOU ARE THE MONSTER, NOT SILAS!" Garrett grabbed Reno as he stumbled. The greywaster turned away.

Elish was still, his eyes staring. He didn't move or even make an attempt to defend himself.

Reno turned around, his face twisted in agony. "Was it worth it?"

Elish was silent.

"WAS IT WORTH IT?" Reno screamed.

Elish still wasn't looking at him, instead, with the roar of the fires ahead of them drowning out a lot of his voice, he said to Garrett, "Take Reno back to the plane."

Garrett put a hand on Reno's shoulder, but to Jack's shock, Reno whirled around and tried to hit him. "And you! You fucking told Silas he was here. I don't give two shits you should've let Sanguine kill me before you gave that information to Silas."

Now Elish did look at him, before his eyes shot to Garrett.

"I would... would never–" Garrett stammered. He took one look at Elish and visibly shrunk down. "Elish... I'm... I'm sorry. He was going to... to kill, Reno."

"You should've let him!" Reno sobbed. "You should have let him."

Suddenly in front of them there was a small cry of Elish's name. Everyone whirled around and stared in shock at a figure stumbling down the street.

"Killian?" Reno's voice caught in his throat.

Elish sprinted over to the figure. They watched as the chimera picked him up carefully and ran back with him.

It was the king. Jack ran to meet him but slowed his pace when he saw the state he was in.

Silas had been roasted alive, his skin was charred black in most places, carbonized and still smoking. His hair was charred off and his left eye a leaking piece of coal in its socket. He was so seared and blackened that when he opened his mouth to talk, his teeth seemed unworldly white and glaring.

"Elish... Elish, they destroyed my Sky," Silas cried as Elish lowered him onto the ground. "Killian and Reaver destroyed my Sky. They killed him. Perish is dead. Perish killed himself. Perish is dead."

Reno took a step back and turned towards the street Silas was stumbling down. With a cry of pain, he started running down the street towards the heart of the flames. Garrett chased him.

"Perish is dead?" Elish's eyes widened. He looked towards the road. Garrett was forcefully trying to restrain Reno as the greywaster tried to run towards the flames. Caligula and Nico appeared behind Elish to try and help hold Reno back.

"He's dead, I saw it with my own eyes," Silas said faintly. "I never wanted him to die; I never wanted him to be gone forever."

Reno screamed so loudly even Silas looked towards him.

His eyes narrowed.

"Help me stand," Silas suddenly said, his voice switching from weak to stone-cold.

Elish helped him to his feet and the king started limping towards Reno.

"Killian is dead." The tone was one born in darkness; Jack had never heard such a cruel sound even from Silas. "Reaver will burn beside his corpse. He will burn for twenty years in agony and in the fleeting moments of lucidity he experiences, he will get to gaze upon Killian's scorched bones."

Reno stared at him for a moment, seemingly stunned into a catatonic state by Silas's cold admission.

"The radiation would have killed him, ripping his body apart with invisible razors. Reaver would've seen it happen. Killian is dead and Reaver is dead. What a pity you didn't tell me where he was sooner. I would have had them."

"Y-you're lying..." Reno managed to say before the weight of Silas's words sunk him to his knees. "No... they're not in there."

Silas's eyes shot to Jack. Jack withered under his intense gaze. Even with only one eye he had lost none of his intimidation. "Jack was with me when I came to the plaguelands. He knows I was with Reaver, who was in pursuit of Killian and Perish."

All eyes turned to Jack. The Grim could only swallow hard before he nodded.

"Reaver was...yes, Silas met up with Reaver. I was there."

The world heard Reno's screaming. And if the man was a born immortal like Silas... the world would have seen another Fallocaust.

Jack turned, feeling a grip take his heart into its hands. Oddly, the space on the bridge of his nose burned, and he realized on top of that, his hands were trembling.

Reno was in agony, the flames baking their skin a cool ocean compared to the gut-wrenching screams falling from the greywaster's lips. Jack closed his eyes and tried to take a deep breath, but the sound of this boy in utter agony seemed too much to bear – even for the Grim.

There was a shadow in the corner of his vision; he glanced to his side and saw Elish walking with him. The immoveable chimera's eyes were staring purple stones and his jaw was locked tight.

"As such is the fate of any man who challenges Silas Dekker," Jack said coldly to him. Elish's lips pursed under his words. "I do hope you learned your lesson, *brother*."

Jack turned from his brother and started walking back to the plane, the sound of heartbroken screaming behind him.

Elish was silent and Jack knew it was because Elish had no words to say to him. His oldest brother, one he respected and loved dearly, had screwed up. And like always, the person who would punish him the most for his foolish dream – would be Elish himself.

"Let's just get to the plane then," Jack said. They both rounded a corner, stepping over twisted metal barriers, and headed towards the awaiting Falconer idling behind a large hardened mound of metal.

Wait.

Why is it idling.

Nico had turned it off.

The realization hit Jack and Elish at the same time. They both broke into a run, rounding the corner and pouring on the speed as they saw the black Falconer in the distance. Its motor was a high-pitched rev as it got ready to take off.

Someone was in there? Someone had the plane?

"Wait!" Jack yelled. His heart suddenly thrashing inside of his chest like he had just gotten an electrical shock. "Who's in there? WAIT!"

Elish got ahead of him, his scorched cloak smoking from the heat of the white fire they had left behind. Jack trailed. His eyes were fixed on the plane, trying to will it with his mind to not take off before they could reach it.

Someone is stealing our plane... how? HOW!? We'll be stuck here, stuck in the fucking plaguelands on the other end of the greywastes!

And if we are... if we are... all the chimeras who could come and get us have been evacuated to the Dead Islands on Silas's orders. All that is left in Skyfall are sengils and cicaros.

My god, we have no way of reaching them. Silas told them to wait for his order and his order only.

No, no, the plane won't take off. It must just be a greywaster. Oh you idiot, no greywaster could survive here.

"Elish... that has to be a chimera. Who the fuck – What's going on? Is it Reaver? Check!" Jack couldn't control his own voice. The reality of being stranded here was hitting him like a freight train and taking with it all the calmed resolve the Grim chimera had prided himself on having.

"No, it... it's impossible. Reaver can't fly a plane, fool!" Elish snapped.

"Then what!? Then what, genius!?" Jack snarled back.

"You are about to steal Skyfall property!" Elish suddenly bellowed to the mystery thief. "By order of King Silas…"

There was a slam and Jack knew that slam was the Falconer's sliding door on the other side of the plane. He looked desperately at the pilot's window and saw with his own eyes a dark figure sit in the pilot's seat.

The small side window opened just as the plane's motor switched to a different octave. As the greywaste dust blew up around them, the plane started to rise. Too far away to do anything, Elish and Jack both stopped and watched, dumbfounded, as it rose vertically up into the air.

And because they were watching so intently, they saw a pale hand slip through the small opening in the plane's side window…

A hand that promptly flip them off.

Elish bellowed with rage before drawing his gun and shooting several shots at the plane. But Jack was still looking at that middle finger. He could see a small silver band. A silver band engraved with a little raccoon that Jack knew had sapphires for eyes.

Kiki.

The End of Book 2 of The Fallocaust Series: The Ghost and the Darkness.

A NOTE FROM QUIL

You did WHAT to Killian?

Yes, yes, I did. Why did I do it? A lot of the books have been about Reaver saving/finding Killian and that is awesome and all… but I think it's time those two take it to the next level. It's time for Killian to come into his own, and it's time for Reaver to let him! Which has really made me excited to start Book 3. I have a lot of plans for that book already, and it will definitely be something else. Not only will we see Reaver and Killian have some much needed 'couples time' (though, of course, it won't be boring, they *are* in the plaguelands after all), we'll also see just how King Silas, Elish, Reno, and the others fair stranded in the northern greywastes.

And of course just what Kiki has planned…

Right now the next book I have coming up is the companion book to Book 2. A book focused around the early life and upbringing of Sanguine. It's called Severing Sanguine and will be out sometime in early 2015.

Another book I'm working on is from a different series. I started Book 1 of this series when I was fourteen, and rewrote it when I was twenty-two. After Severing Sanguine I'm going to do one last polish/partial rewrite and publish it. It's a fantasy book (with gay characters, of course) called The Gods' Games and it's my pride and joy. I'm hoping to release it Spring of 2015. Please look to my facebook and twitter for updates on that.

I would also like to thank my beta readers, and my facebook family. You guys have no idea how much your friendship has motivated me to

QUIL CARTER

continue my dream of being an author. Thank you for your support.

And as usual for updates on book releases, to view excerpts, or to watch me continue to go crazy, follow me on Twitter @Fallocaust and also find me on Facebook /quil.carter.
And thank you for continuing this journey with me.
Sincerely,

Quil Carter

Printed in Great Britain
by Amazon